THE NORTHERN STAR
-THE BEGINNING-

MIKE GULLICKSON

Disclaimer: This is a work of fiction. Any resemblance of characters to actual persons, living or dead, is purely coincidental. The Author holds exclusive rights to this work. Unauthorized duplication is prohibited.

ACKNOWLEDGEMENTS

The Northern Star novel series, in one semblance or another, has been in my head for nearly a decade. Time has helped bring it out, but so has the effort and encouragement of many friends and family. In no particular order (except for my wife, I live with her):

Melissa Gullickson
Put up with an absentee & moody husband.

My Parents
Listened to me lament over the phone when they just wanted to talk to their grandson.

Eric Tilton
An amazing artist & graphic designer.

Neal Tabachnick
Lawyer & Motivator.

Drea Clark/Justin McWilliams
Copy Editors.

Ruth Ratny
First person outside of friends & family to say "hey, you can write!"

James Aiden, Josh Newell, John Bruno, Brenden Clark, Brooks McLaren, Dan Snow, Wes Ryle, Nick Bobetsky
Read the book when it wasn't that good and gave me notes. If it's still not good, it's their fault.

For Melissa.

Your Support Means Everything.

PROLOGUE
CHICAGO. FEBRUARY 21ˢᵀ 2048. 4:00 A.M.

Cynthia Revo hadn't slept in three days. She and her team were close, very close. She'd imagined this day a thousand times over and the reality didn't match the ideal. She had pictured herself awake, no bags under her eyes, her short red hair neatly combed. Fresh clothes without a wrinkle. Champagne. Smiles. Maybe a celebratory lay. That's where her daydreams took her. But like all dreams, they were more fantasy than truth.

Her team of researchers had forced her to take a break. She dragged herself down the hall to her office and collapsed at her desk. Twenty foam coffee cups littered its surface, each with different levels of the fuel that had kept her upright. Five large computer monitors were mounted on the wall. The keyboard and mouse were lost somewhere in the maze of cups. A lab rat could find them, but it would take Cynthia a second or so. She was out in an instant.

The door crashed open and she shot her hands out, clearing the desk. Days old coffee splattered against the monitors and spilled onto the carpet. It took her a moment to realize where she was.

Harold Renki, one of her top programmers, looked like he'd seen a ghost.

"It's working! It's working!"

She looked at him like he was speaking another language. Not until he yanked her out of her chair did she understand completely. He dragged her toward the door until she got her legs moving to match his.

"When?!" she asked. She was still bleary and nauseous from the abrupt wakening.

"Just now, a minute, maybe. Tom's burning through the test. It was what you thought."

"Thousands?" she asked.

"Five thousand at this point."

Five thousand micro-frequencies, to penetrate the brain and read the synapses as they fired. They had started with two, now they were up to five thousand. They had started with four meager servers. Now six hundred of the best supercomputers money could buy were in a machine room cooled to -50 degrees Celsius.

They rushed down the dull white hallway with its fluorescent lights and cheap decorations. An unremarkable place for the greatest invention the world had ever seen.

They slammed through the doors onto a landing above the testing floor. Thirty other scientists were below them—some biologists, some programmers, some physicists, some doctors—and they all turned with smiles that said it was worth it. That the five years were not in vain, not a dead end like some pundits opined. For visionaries, showing the *rightness* of their vision was always the most difficult, because the vast majority of people look in front of their feet, but rarely ahead. When the visionary was right, then the masses nod and line up, happy to be a part of it. Happy to think that they would have thought of it too—it was so obvious, after all.

Cynthia pushed past Harold and ran down the stairs. The crowd parted like the Red Sea and she saw the twenty by twenty Plexiglas cage where they kept Tom & Jerry.

Tom saw the short redheaded person press herself up against the clear wall. He was eating a banana and he understood that if he kept doing this thing the hairless monkeys wanted, he would keep getting bananas.

Jerry was bummed. Tom was eating bananas and he wasn't. Jerry held a keypad. On it were four buttons: one green, one red, one yellow, one purple. In front of him was a computer monitor and at the bottom was a mirrored image of each button. When a picture appeared above one of them, he was supposed to press the corresponding button. Easy. He could do six per minute.

Tom didn't have a keyboard. He wore a metal helmet on his head. Attached to it was a wire that ran outside the clear cage to another place and then back. Tom wanted more bananas and with the red headed pale ape watching, he knew this was his chance. He looked at the screen and played the game. His images flashed by at one per second.

Cynthia's mouth was wide open. She watched Tom, the test chimp, tear through the image choices on screen using nothing but his mind. Jerry, the control, slapped at the keyboard every ten seconds or so.

The mind was finally free from its prison. Cynthia Revo closed her mouth and watched as Tom the chimp performed a miracle. This would change the world forever.

CHAPTER 1
IRAN, 2058

"Man, you're lucky to be black," Eric Janis said to the hulking soldier in front of him. They were off duty and in line to Mindlink with their families. It was summer in Iran. Sweat poured down the soldiers' faces. They used every ounce of shade they could find, even each other. They had long since torn down the analog thermometer outside their barracks, but the soldiers stationed there could guess the afternoon temperature within a degree. Eric guessed right on the money: 125 degrees.

"I don't think I've ever heard that," John Raimey said. He was dark skinned, with gray eyes that stuck out like a wolf's. A hooked scar curled around his right eye from a shrapnel blast. He and Eric had met in basic training almost twenty years before. Like most soldiers, they came from one of two places: Raimey, the ghetto. Janis, a microscopic town in the middle of Nebraska. The military is the true melting pot and despite their disparate backgrounds, they bonded immediately. In Chicago, their homes were within walking distance. Together they had served in various special operations units. First as Green Berets, then Detachment Delta, and now small clandestine units without official designations.

"I just mean *here*. I don't mean, like, anywhere else," Janis joked. "You don't burn, right? Because I'm fucking getting fried."

"Your Irish skin isn't meant for this." Raimey looked up into the sky and wagged his head as if he were soaking it in.

"How much longer d'you guess?" Janis asked.

"Two weeks, maybe more. We need to get the rest of the family out."

The Imperial Royal family. There were a lot of them. Second cousins, third cousins twice removed. It had been their only task while the rest of the Coalition Forces cordoned off the population for "oil sanctions." It was a group effort in the Middle East. China's camp was ocean side and the EU was north to the U.S.'s west, but in other oil-rich lands, sometimes it was one, two, or all of them that occupied. The oil was almost gone.

Off in the distances tendrils of black smoke rose into the air. The terrorists had lit an oil field.

Not terrorists. Locals, Raimey reminded himself.

"Raimey, you're up. Five minutes," a soldier called, referencing a tablet.

"Tell Tiffany and Vanessa hi," Janis said.

Inside the tent were what looked like ten dentist chairs. Eight were already occupied and the soldiers in them looked asleep. A thick wire ran from the head of each to a terminal outside the tent that had a satellite dish pointing to the sky. Two large fans uselessly blew hot air, turning the tent into a convection oven.

"You're on the number two Mindlink," a woman inside said. Raimey walked over, sat down and the woman handed him a machined aluminum headpiece that had glowing LED's on the inside where it touched the head. He leaned back in the chair and put the Mindlink on.

As he did, the smell of burnt shit and sweat, and the scorching heat, vanished from top to bottom. He was in his living room. Some soldiers chose outlandish backdrops when they connected in, he knew a guy who always met his family on Mars for some reason. Janis—who didn't have family—had bribed the head tech with booze to go to virtual Filipino hooker dens. "It's not real, but *damn*, it feels real," he nudged while detailing his exploits at the mess hall. But Raimey preferred seeing his home. It gave him an anchor to what was truly important. It reminded him why he had to make it back.

His wife Tiffany sat across from him on the couch. Caramel skin, long wavy black hair. She looked ten years younger than forty. Raimey appeared across from her and he immediately jumped over to the couch and they kissed.

"How are you holding up?" Tiffany asked.

"It's fine. Janis says 'hi.'"

"Are you safe?"

"As safe as I can be. It's pretty bad over here. It's the worst at the refineries and the wells." A red light appeared in the air and flashed slowly. It reminded Raimey that the military was listening. No mission details. "We're . . . off mission." The light vanished from the air like a mirage.

Concern washed over Tiffany's dark brown eyes.

"Hon, it's fine. We only have a few more missions and I'll be back."

"Vanessa!" Tiffany yelled. She looked around; there was no sign of their daughter. Tiffany's body vanished down-to-up and then almost immediately popped back into existence. "She's in the bathroom."

"When you gotta go, you gotta go," Raimey smiled.

"There was another terrorist attack in Chicago," Tiffany said.

"I heard. We may be re-assigned there. I might actually be home for once."

"New York had three last week. Just yesterday, a train blew up over one of MindCorp's Data Nodes right in the center of the city."

"That's why I moved us out to the suburbs," Raimey said. "It's going to get worse before it gets better. Just Mindlink, don't go into the city."

A ten-year-old girl appeared near the fireplace. Other than having her father's dark skin, she was a mirror of her mother's beauty. She wore pink pajamas.

"Daddy!" she hugged Raimey. He hugged her back, pressing his cheek against hers.

"Hey love," Raimey said. He held her at arm's length and looked her up and down.

"What time is it there?"

"Two."

"And you're still wearing pajamas?"

Vanessa shrugged. "I'm just online."

"Alright, but when I get home, pajamas are for nights and mornings, that's it. Tell me about school."

Vanessa did and Raimey listened intently. A few minutes later, a soft ping like a wind chime filled the air signaling his time was almost up. He kissed Tiffany on the lips and snuggled with Vanessa one more time.

"All right my lovely ladies. I'll see you next week."

He disappeared from the room, as did they, soon after.

—NEW YORK—

The founder of MindCorp, Cynthia Revo, followed her bodyguard through the surface debris of the New York Data Node. Sabot could have been a linebacker; he was half black and Samoan, six-five and thick. His dreaded hair hung past his shoulders. Cynthia was tiny, five foot, and thin boned. Her bobbed red hair had become her trademark. A 'Cynthia' was in vogue now. Behind them trailed an army man in his 60's, wide and fit with a plate of medals on his jacket and a small, soft man with square rimmed glasses and a weak chin hidden behind goatee fuzz.

"This is why we need to work together Cynthia," Secretary of Defense, Donald "WarDon" Richards said as they picked their path through the office wreckage. Ahead of them, a tank revved up and dragged away a subway car. It was apparent that no one in it had survived. Construction workers and firemen cleared the wreckage. Above them two cranes raised new rail to replace what had fallen down.

"They didn't take us off-line. We routed to the other Data Nodes in the region out of protocol. This is cosmetic. The Data Core was unharmed," Cynthia said.

She had come a long way from the day that Tom beat Jerry choosing images with his mind. The Mindlink arrived when the last of the accessible oil disappeared. There were articles and books (digital anyway) that stated she had saved the modern world. They were wrong. She had made the modern world obsolete. She had erased national borders. She had turned the earth into an apartment by creating a better one online. She had kept the company private and her personal worth was well into one trillion dollars. Ninety-five percent of the civilized world, including government, including military, used her technology to function. "We've had this happen before, Donald."

"But not this successfully," the pudgy man said. "Their weapons are the same, but they're getting more strategic. They used C4 and long range detonators."

Cynthia stopped and Sabot was immediately her shadow, scanning all entry points. There was a military perimeter around the wreckage, but bullets could thread the needle. He had recommended against her coming here.

"Who is he?" Cynthia asked WarDon.

"This is Dr. Lindo," WarDon said. "I should have introduced you.

Sorry. He's my advisor."

"I've heard of you. You developed the analytics program for the military," Cynthia said.

"Yes." Evan had come out of nowhere at the age of twenty-two when he created an artificial intelligence software that recognized trends in seemingly unrelated data and predicted future patterns based on this data with incredible accuracy. At its root, "Nostradamus" was a bit-torrent application, but instead of taking known bits of a file from registered locations to create a replica, it took pieces of data that had no recognizable relation and formed a hypothesis of action. Technology had always been the U.S. military's greatest weapon and Nostradamus was considered revolutionary for strategic warfare. At its best, it put them in the mind of their enemy. At its worst, it stacked the deck in their favor. It had won battles, saved lives, and predicted seeds of unrest. Evan was thirty-one now and the army's prodigal son.

"Why didn't your software predict this?" Cynthia teased. Lindo bristled but remained quiet. While he was soft shouldered and round, his eyes burnt with intelligence. She thought it was odd that he wore glasses given how cheap corrective eye surgery was. An affectation of some kind.

"That's why we're here," WarDon said. They made it to a construction elevator that had been quickly installed to replace the crushed one. The elevator shaft was undamaged.

"I've given the U.S. its own network," Cynthia said. "How much cooperation do I need to provide?"

They stepped into the elevator.

"Any more dead?" WarDon asked.

Cynthia sighed, but it felt forced. Her mind was racing.

"They found one. Our receptionist," Cynthia said. "Sabot, be sure to compensate the family."

"Yes."

They went down. For one hundred feet they stared at solid concrete and then it opened up into a cavernous space. It reminded Evan of an airplane hanger. The MindCorp technology was client-server. The Mindlink that a customer used at home was an interface, a glorified keyboard. All of the computer processing was done offsite at the Data Nodes. This was one of Cynthia's brilliant maneuvers. The technology was proprietary and extremely well-protected. Even the government didn't know exactly how it worked.

The style of the space was industrial: exposed beams around the perimeter, metal walkways throughout, snaked with ventilation. At the center was a giant black tube over twenty stories tall. WarDon whistled.

"You've never seen one?" Cynthia asked.

"No, just pictures."

"This is a Colossal Core, there are five of them in the U.S. It can handle over forty million users."

"And all of that got offloaded to the other Cores?" Evan asked. Cynthia nodded with pride.

"We keep headroom on all of our Data Cores. The re-routing was completely transparent to the user."

As they descended, the ants turned into hundreds of workers. There were metal beds surrounding the Core like petals of a flower. Evan counted fifty. Men and women sat on the beds and waited for technicians in lab coats to go through a checklist with them. Afterwards, the person put on a Mindlink and laid down. Other techs manned controls near the base of the Core.

"Are those the Sleepers?" WarDon asked, pointing to the people in the beds. Cynthia nodded.

"They program and maintain the system," she said. Evan and WarDon exchanged glances.

"I've heard they can do more. Quite a lot more," WarDon said.

"The theoretical is different than the practical, General," Cynthia said. "We've capped their bandwidth to 300 megabytes-per-second, only spiking it for specific projects."

At the ground floor, a man so obese he couldn't walk rode a scooter over to them. The tires on his Rascal screamed for mercy as he approached.

"Dr. Marin," Cynthia said.

"Great timing, Cynthia. We're about to fire it back up."

"Any issues?"

"A fiber line was damaged, but we've routed around it. We should be 100% in another twenty-four hours."

They followed Dr. Marin to the control deck right at the Core. It was an immense structure, more so because the giant tube was so dark. It was like a black hole caught in a bottle. Dr. Marin nodded to a group of technicians and two pulled down levers while the others typed quickly on keyboards. A sound erupted from the Core like a cold engine turning.

The entire tube crackled blue . . . then black . . . the engine turning . . . electric blue . . . black . . . the engine turning . . . BOOM! The entire tube filled with a coursing, electric blue, as if lightning had been trapped in a bottle. Everyone's hair stood on end and arcs of static electricity danced between the Core and the electronics at its base. Dr. Marin saw the concern on WarDon's face.

"It's completely safe. Everything's grounded."

WarDon nodded but he was unconvinced. He took a few steps back. Evan did the opposite: he walked around the Core as if it were an alien artifact. He immediately recognized its components. A huge bundle of fiber lines—tens of millions—ran the length of the Core. At its center was a thin metal plate that separated the two segments. That thin plate was the Data Crusher and how Sleepers could do what Evan had told WarDon they could. That benign piece of metal blotted out in the sea of pulsing blue was the key to Nostradamus and beyond.

= = =

"It's all very impressive," WarDon said. They were now at a conference table adjunct from the Core. Sabot poured water for them. Evan noticed that his forearm was as big as his own thigh.

Cynthia pulled out a joint. "Do you mind? I'm losing focus."

It was the opposite. Cynthia was, in fact, *gaining* focus. Without medication, she had almost uncontrollable obsessive-compulsive disorder. For programming and research, it was an incredible strength. She would get off the pills, get off the weed, and her genius would be paired with laser-like focus. But day-to-day it was crippling and without medication she had extreme difficulty communicating effectively. Sometimes she would speak in English and computer code, as if they were one.

WarDon put on his best, I'm-fine-with-it, smile. "Of course."

She sparked up.

"Why are you really here, General?" Cynthia asked.

"I guess we can cut to it. The U.S. is losing on two fronts right now, Cynthia, and both have major consequences that exacerbate the other," WarDon stood up and paced the room. "I was going to come to Chicago before this happened but it emphasizes our failure at home."

"The Terror War is getting worse and the Coalition is falling apart. We thought one of the few benefits with the oil shortage would be that our enemies couldn't get over here. But we were wrong. As soon as we invaded, many of them traveled to Canada and down. We have no proof, but we think some of our national enemies may have funded this emigration. There were also cells already planted in the U.S. that we didn't know about."

"I know these things. What does it have to do with me?"

"Nostradamus," Evan said. "Because we have no access to your software, we can't implement it effectively."

"The software is mine," Cynthia said flatly. "As is the technology behind it."

WarDon put his hands up.

"We're not saying it's not, quite the contrary. It's yours, Cynthia. MindCorp saved the modern world. Who knows where we'd be without you. Worse, for sure. But if we had access, *true* access, this software could follow trends. It could save lives."

"It's an invasion of privacy," Cynthia said.

"So are your Sleepers," Evan replied coolly.

"Sleepers are programmers, simple as that. They maintain the system," Cynthia said.

"Evan seems to think otherwise," WarDon said. It was clear they had pulled their trump card.

"Theoretically, yes. Early on we tested quite a few theories, many *with* government involvement. You should know that, Don. But they were deemed unethical, unnecessary, and dangerous. We cap the bandwidth on the Mindlinks to limit any . . . transgressions."

Evan interrupted. "There are five Sleepers in Chicago you don't restrict and they are gathering information that is privy only to you."

Cynthia turned to WarDon. "Are you spying on me?"

WarDon shrugged.

"You haven't been forthright, Cynthia, and the world relies way too much on your technology without understanding how it works. You're a privately held corporation and you are doing espionage. I have the list, I can show you." WarDon pulled it out of his coat; Cynthia waved it away. "This information would not be good going public. We are in dire times."

WarDon sat down. He continued. "I'm not asking you to stop. In fact, we are providing you a tool to do more. We're *asking* you to do more."

The room was quiet. Cynthia finally spoke up.

"I understand how granting access to Nostradamus on our network could help with the Terror War, but what does this have to do with the Coalition?"

"There's never been a true oil shortage before, Cynthia. As much as we've hemmed and hawed in the past, we've always found more. But those days are gone. If there's only enough food for two people, and three people are eating, sooner or later, two of 'em are going to realize that it can't go on . . . and every one of them wants to survive. Contrary to popular belief, I like peace. I *want* peace. But my job's to prepare for the worst. No one acts rationally when they're hungry and scared. Not people, sure as hell not nations. That's where your untethered Sleepers come into play. I need to know what our Coalition partners are thinking."

"If they found out, it could destroy my business."

"So would World War III."

"You can't be serious," Cynthia replied.

WarDon raised his eyebrow, but the rest of his face remained like stone. He was.

"Let me think about it."

WarDon stood up and Evan followed.

"Of course."

= = =

That night on their private train back to Chicago, Cynthia lay naked next to Sabot, pondering the meeting with WarDon. Sabot had been her bodyguard for five years and her lover for six months. He was the anchor that kept her reasonable in a sea that bent to her every whim, around people that would 'yes' her off a cliff and follow after her, just to be in her good stead.

As her influence overshadowed governments and changed the global culture, death threats would surface in the bowels of extremist blogs. A stalker was arrested and sentenced. Abduction attempts thwarted. And Cynthia knew she had high level enemies around her—

both government and corporate—that sought her opinion and joked with her, that complimented her. But when she turned away their smiles vanished and they glared at her with emotionless, chestnut eyes: the eyes of the hungry and jealous and wanting.

She lit a joint and pulled. She held the smoke until it burned and let it go. The smoke rolled over itself in the moonlight.

"What's up?" Sabot asked. He had woken. He pushed himself up on his elbows.

"My mind's racing. How dangerous is WarDon?" Cynthia asked. While Sabot never said it straight out, he had hinted they had crossed paths during his service.

"Politically?"

"Everything. Political, military, any way he could hurt me."

Sabot didn't hesitate. "If things get dire, they'll do to MindCorp what they did to the Middle East and Venezuela."

"No. They couldn't."

Sabot let out a short laugh.

"So you think they'll invade countries but not take over a corporation?" he said.

"Without me, it would fail."

Sabot raised an eyebrow. Cynthia realized that Sabot thought they would abduct her.

"No, they wouldn't. I'm too high profile!"

"Who would know anymore, Cynthia? MindCorp controls all the information. If they controlled it and you, they could say you moved to Antarctica to study penguins. They would rationalize it for the greater good. Things are easy for governments to justify."

"*Really*," she said, less surprised than she should be and not nearly scared enough. This was good weed.

"I'm glad you're taking it well," Sabot said. He rolled over and fell back asleep.

Cynthia almost turned in, thought 'fuck it' and smoked the rest of the joint. Sabot was right. WarDon was dangerous. He and the other politicians and officers put up brave fronts, but they were scared, fanatical in their fear of unimportance. Cynthia's invention had helped solve a global crisis among the developed nations with the dwindling oil reserves. But it didn't solve the *national* crisis. It, in fact, accelerated what policy had begun one hundred years before. Free trade. Global conglomerates. U.S. companies with their factories in China. German companies with their manufacturing in Mexico. Shoes made in sweatshops across Asia. Countries bailing out other countries, because each relied so much on the other. Nations had become states. And each of these states was governed by the global economy. The Mindlink caused further withering of nation relevance because in the digital space, location meant nothing. MindCorp had created a better world with less pollution, that offered limitless choices, and that they controlled completely.

Cynthia put out her joint and pulled the blankets up. She watched Sabot sleep until her eyes grew heavy. She knew she came with baggage and she loved him for carrying it.

The governments had become landlords and nothing more. But they still had guns. And they still had bombs. And they still had soldiers. They would not go quietly into the night. She decided to play along. If they were to become enemies, it would be better that they were close.

—VENEZUELA—

Hugo was being hunted. They all were. When the Coalition had invaded Venezuela five years before, the military aristocracy and the politicians surrendered for amnesty. They handed over Venezuela to save their hides. But Hugo—a General—and a few hundred other soldiers did not. They took to the mountains near the oil fields. That was what it was about, after all, the oil. In the years that followed they had grown in number. The Coalition had cordoned off cities and didn't allow travel. But Hugo and his renegades broke out many, and their numbers climbed to almost five hundred.

The refineries were heavily guarded, but the rebels knocked one out for a month. Battleships surrounded the oil pipeline to the sea, but they still blew it up. And the mountains were theirs. The U.S. had its fill of guerilla warfare and wanted none of it. The intruders kept their crosshairs on the mountains from the comfort of their citadels, but they didn't come hunt. It was not their land.

Except for him. Twelve Coalition soldiers had been dropped at the top of the mountain to find and assassinate Hugo. In a two-week span, Hugo and his patriots had killed all but one. They were high in the mountains, too high for the Coalition to send reinforcements and he knew the soldier was on his own. So Hugo spread his army out like a net in search of the final soldier.

That was one month ago and that lone soldier still haunted them. Camps would wake up to ten dead. Scout parties would never come back. And then he'd pick one off, two off—be quiet for days—and then strike again. He avoided the mines. He avoided the snares. He avoided feints to lure him out. They called him 'el fantasma.' *The ghost.* And it had begun to feel like he was a part of the forest and not a man.

Within the last two weeks, three hundred of Hugo's men had defected. They didn't ask, they just disappeared in the night. And while Hugo knew they had left on their own volition, others attributed it to the ghost. The ghost (*quit calling him that*, Hugo said to himself), the MAN— he was a MAN—had killed fifty men since they had chased him up into the mountains.

Hugo was down to twenty men under his command. As quickly as his power had risen, Hugo saw it fall. The Coalition had won. They would think it was their battleships and tanks and helicopters, but for

Hugo, it was this one man that had done it.

"Carlos has been gone too long," a lieutenant whispered. It was night and they sat around a small campfire at the mouth of a cave.

"Go find him," Hugo said, absently.

"No," the lieutenant replied. Hugo looked into his eyes and he saw the fear. The ghost.

"He's just a man, hermano."

"Maybe we *did* kill him . . ." the lieutenant said. A few pair of wide eyes nodded in agreement.

So this is what happens. Hugo thought. *We lose our country, we lose our dignity, and then we lose our minds.*

Hugo rose to his feet.

"Where are you going?"

"To find Carlos."

The lieutenant stood up. "I'll go with you."

"And what, have you shoot me in the back when you hear an owl?" The men around the fire laughed uncomfortably.

"I'll go alone, thank you. It's late, he may just be asleep."

Hugo walked out of the cave and made his way up the mountain. The view from here was spectacular. At night, nothing was wrong. The city lights twinkled, the shadows hid the sins. But in daylight, the land was carved into boroughs, the dust trail of the tanks easily spotted. Ahead, he saw Carlos asleep against a tree. He could hear him snoring. Hugo took a stick and threw it at him.

"Carlos!" he hissed.

Carlos shifted around in his sleep. Hugo rolled his eyes. Carlos was the laziest of his soldiers, but also his bravest. He was drunk much of the time. Hugo stood over him.

"Carlos!" Carlos rose up and then slunk back to the ground. It took Hugo a second to see that the tree behind Carlos was looking at him. Mike Glass, in full ghillie suit, separated from the pine. He aimed a silenced .22 Ruger at Hugo's head. The subsonic rounds were as quiet as a BB gun.

"El Fantasma," Hugo said. And then the bullet entered his eye.

CHAPTER 2

Justin McWilliams finally had enough money. He looked online at his bank account "like poor people do," typing in his username and password, seeing the balance on a flat screen monitor. He lived in DeKalb, Illinois. When he was born, the population was over thirty thousand people. Now it was two hundred. The other thirty thousand had left during the Great Migration when the government offered to move and place them in homes in Chicago. All that remained were farmers. His father farmed corn and soy and he was paid directly by the government. Not a lot, but like his father said: "In these times, at least we're paid."

Justin closed the browser and gathered himself. He heard the television downstairs and he could picture his father stretched out on his recliner, absently itching his junk. His mom would always say "Frank!" and his father would reply, "I can't help it the dang thing is so big," and throw a wink at Justin. It always made Justin laugh.

He heard the clanging of pots and dishes as his mom washed up after dinner. Justin took a big breath. It was time. He walked downstairs, his heart racing. He turned into the living room and caught the tail end of another one of his father's nut grabs.

Frank McWilliams saw Justin out of the corner of his eye and turned his head back.

"Hey J, are you done with your homework?"

Justin nodded that he was, but it was assumed. Justin's IQ was 190. He formed sentences at eighteen months, and he could solve advanced calculus problems by age four. Soon after, he was diagnosed with Asperger's Syndrome. He had difficulties in crowds and relating to people. Even at home, he connected with his dad but only communicated basics with his mom. He was twelve now.

"I have three hundred and fifty dollars," Justin stated.

His father smiled. "That's a lot of prairie dogs."

Four hundred and sixty-seven rounded up, Justin quickly calculated. Justin got seventy-five cents a prairie dog on the neighboring farms. He used a bolt-action, 22 magnum with a 4x Tasco scope. "You said if I saved up, I could buy a Mindlink."

"It costs three fifty?"

"Three hundred and ten with tax."

His father chuckled. "Mom can buy it online for you. Charlene!"

"I want to go into the city," Justin said.

Frank turned off the television. Charlene quit doing the dishes and leaned in.

"Justin, you don't have to," Frank said. "We get shipments every week."

"But if we go in, then I can get it tomorrow." Justin looked pained. When he was frustrated he'd pat his right hand on his thigh like he was keeping a beat.

"The city is very crowded, and noisy," Frank said slowly. He looked to his wife. He wanted his son to go, he wanted it to be his decision. But he had to know the facts. In the last year, they had seen Justin begin to open up. It was a fraction of what other children would, but it was enough to see the sweet boy inside. Before he would act out with tears or rage, but now he would try to explain himself. One of the reasons Frank sat in the chair and watched TV was that it was easier for Justin to communicate without direct eye contact.

"I want to go. That's why it's three hundred and fifty dollars."

"I don't understand."

"Two round trip train tickets are twenty dollars apiece."

Frank roared with laughter.

"I want to see MindCorp," Justin said. "I read that Cynthia Revo is like me."

= = =

Mohammed Jawal was sixty-three years old, broad shouldered and lean. Younger, he had been a striking man. Clean-shaven, he had the hard lines of a sheik. But his welcoming brown eyes played against his otherwise intimidating appearance. He had no problems meeting women.

That was twenty years ago. *Before.* He now had hair down to his shoulders, the black streaked with gray. His beard ended mid-chest. He had turned over his life to Allah and in doing so, he had turned his back on Western conventions, ones that he, much to his dismay, had once embraced.

It helped you know your enemy.

True. But at one time, that had made him his own. And they had used it for their purposes.

He was alone in a New York safe house. His soldiers were

preparing for their next attack. It was time for prayer.

"Allahu Akbar," he said. *God is great.* God *is* great. Their attack in New York had gone perfectly. Other cells were vicious and immoral, but when Mohammed formed the Western Curse, he and his clerics vowed to attack the problem, not just what was convenient. Those actions, hijacking a school bus, killing innocent people in the streets, were terrorism. They were evil actions justified under vague pretenses of Jihad. They were a blot on Islam. He and his clerics, back when they were scholars and politicos and industrialists and entrepreneurs, had clearly defined who they would attack: the heads. Always the heads. *We aren't terrorists,* he thought, *we are freedom fighters. They are on our soil, so we are on theirs.*

He folded his arms across his chest and recited the first chapter of the Qur'an:

"I start by the name of Allah, the Rehman, and the Raheem. All praise is for Allah who is the maker of everything, the Rehman, the Raheem, the final Master. (O Allah) we worship you and we ask help from you. Show us the right way. The way of those who got good things, not the way of those who were punished and not the way of those who believed in wrong things."

Like his other clerics, Mohammed Jawal was highly educated. His master's degree in political science came from Oxford and his doctorate from Yale. He was a published expert on middle-eastern policy and he had been invited to the White House as an advisor. They didn't ignore him. Far from it. They used him. He explained each culture and how it functioned. How they could gain favor. He thought it was to improve foreign relations. He found out soon it was prep for invasion. He laughed sadly when he thought about it. How naïve of him to think good of politicians. The President was there. The Secretary of Defense. The heads of government. Even representatives from China and the EU. All the heads. It's always the heads.

He had walked away flattered. And then six months later, they had invaded. They had taken his advice; they had contacted the royal families months before and offered not only amnesty, but gifts and futures.

Mohammed continued his prayer. He spoke in Arabic verses that moved him, that made him feel taller, closer to heaven, but at the same time meek in his God's presence.

"Allahu Akbar." Mohammed bowed. "Subhana rabbiyal adheem, subhanna rabbiyal adheem, subhana rabbiyal adhemm." *Glory be to my Lord Almighty.*

The Western Curse was growing. It was never about religion; they were not Jihadists. It was about what was right. He did this because the West had beaten and abused his country like a slave. The West only believed in slaves, from the beginning when the cotton crop had to be harvested, to the pawn dictator that did the West's wishes in a language they wouldn't even take the time to understand. Slavery was all the West knew and it was time to break those bonds. It was time to pull the slave master off his horse and beat him down until he lay dead.

Damn the West for making me do this. Damn them for treating their privilege like it was their right.

= = =

It had been a month since Cynthia had agreed to help the United States. In that time, Nostradamus had been integrated into the global MindCorp network and Cynthia had recruited and implemented Sleepers to spy on the United States' allies.

Nostradamus was interesting to Cynthia, and that made Evan interesting to Cynthia. The AI program was set up at a base in West Virginia and she tethered it to the closest Data Node. All Cores were connected, so Nostradamus could now "scrub" for data (as Lindo called it) to mine patterns from what appeared to be random information. It accessed all e-mail, all IP telephony, all virtual chats, anything financial that was purchased with credit. Anything that left a trail. It even mined news feeds.

"Scrubbing will take months, but once all the data is collected, the program will begin to see patterns the army can use," Evan explained.

"It's quite brilliant," Cynthia had said.

"Thank you. It works two ways. It treats all information bit torrent and it treats the entire landscape of information as a codec. That's what the scrubbing's for. It lays a foundation of data that the AI can then reference for anomalies. From there, it sees a pattern," he continued. "Your network is billions of times more vast, we've only used Nostradamus on battlefields and with specific reconnaissance where it behaves more like a chess computer. But the same patterns will hold in cyberspace. I designed it to work micro and macro, it just comes down to processing power and storage."

"You think ahead," Cynthia said.

"Always."

Peering into the EU's and China's backyard had fallen solely on Cynthia. When she introduced the Sleepers to WarDon and he explained to them the terms of their jail sentence if they committed treason, the mood dampened. It perked back up when they were told their salaries were doubled. In three more weeks, Cynthia had promised WarDon a dossier so thorough on the leaders of the EU and China that they could write that person's biography in such detail and cadence that the subjects themselves would think they had written it.

"If a person's thoughts are a bag, the Sleepers are pulling that bag inside out. There's nothing they can hide," Cynthia had said when she had outlined the process to WarDon.

"How don't they know?" WarDon asked.

"Think of it this way: we're currently in my office and you can see and interpret everything around you clearly. The desk, the seat cushion, me, Sabot, the streaked window behind me. You think you see it all, because you rely on your senses, but there is more data in this room you *don't* sense. There are terabits of broadcast waves and cellular waves coursing through and around us, but we don't even think about them because their spectrum is outside our perspective. But if I turn on a TV or radio, boom! There it is. It's the same online. We're working behind the scenes, on a level they can't register because even online they rely on their base senses."

"Couldn't another Sleeper?" Evan asked.

"If it was a non-MindCorp Sleeper doing espionage, yes. But we are sifting through their actual data stream. We aren't hacking into it. We own it."

= = =

Now, she and Sabot had been summoned to a new military research center being constructed north of Chicago. It was called the Derik Building. It was five stories tall, dark and wide. At the front, it seemed hospital-like. But as Cynthia walked through, she could read signs directing staff up and down and to different wings. "Testing Range." "Prosthetics." "Server Field." "Surgical Center." "Lab Hanger 1." "Lab Hanger 2." "Lab Hanger 3." Cynthia saw the Lab count reach eighteen before their escort directed them down a hall that consisted of conference rooms. Around them, construction workers and painters worked feverishly. The escort opened a door to one of the unfinished conference rooms. Evan and WarDon stood up as they entered.

WarDon and Evan had been mum on why they brought her here. WarDon was quiet, but in a good mood. He had a dazed, strip club smile on his face.

"How flexible is the Mindlink with applications?" Evan asked.

"Outside of cyberspace?"

"Yes."

"Assuming the subject has the proper aptitude, with the right software driver it can do anything, really. You've seen what we've done with manufacturing. Why?"

"What do you know about prosthetic limbs?" Lindo asked.

"Haven't had any use for them—what is this about?" Cynthia was tired of the build up, she felt like she was being pitched by a carnie. Show the chick with the beard, already.

"The Terror War," WarDon said.

"That's what Nostradamus is for, isn't it?" Cynthia asked.

"It's a start," WarDon said. "We think what we're about to show you will finish it."

"What?"

"A soldier that's virtually indestructible," Evan chimed in. "Our war isn't with nations anymore, never mind the issues with our partners in the Coalition. It's terrorism, plain and simple. Always needling us, picking at us, three months of calm followed by a bombing. War is easy compared to this. It's predictable. Vetted. There's a defined finish to it. We can't go into New York with tanks and attack choppers and level a building they're entrenched in. We can't kill one hundred of them by cutting down a thousand of our own."

"This soldier would somehow stop this?" Cynthia asked. "The technology to do that . . ."

"I've developed over the last six years, ever since the Mindlink could process 2-way information," Lindo said.

Next to Evan was a table stacked with lead aprons. He handed them out.

"Come with me," he said.

21

They put them on and followed him through a door into another room. A dozen engineers in similar aprons stood around a huge block of an object that was ten feet wide and taller. It was covered in a tarp. Evan nodded at one of the engineers and he hit a switch. The tarp rose up and Cynthia gasped at what was revealed. A colossal metal man sat in a chair like a king. She walked up to it, miniscule compared to it. She looked at the armored feet. They were the size of a snow sled, but remarkably articulated.

The legs were protected with thick armored plates, but between the slits and at the joints, she saw shock absorbers. Their pistons and springs were gray and green like the rest of the body, and glistening with oil.

There was a ladder.

"May I?" Cynthia asked Evan.

Evan beamed at his invention. "Yes, you may."

She climbed up the ladder to see the bionic more closely.

It would take two men to get their arms around each square thigh. The thighs had a different suspension system from the rest of the leg. Ten rubber coated slats were sandwiched together. She didn't understand how it worked, but it was clearly for shock absorption. She would inquire later.

The pelvis and thighs were separated from the upper body by a pair of huge drive chains, each link the size of a human head. Gear teeth stuck through them.

The upper body was gigantic, but still human in form, like a bodybuilder dipped in metal.

The metal hands curled over the end of the armrests. A person could sit in their palm and the knuckles were bulbous with armor. But the joints and seams along the fingers and creased into the top of the hands showed a level of articulation that was astounding. It was the most beautiful feat of mechanical engineering Cynthia had ever seen.

Cynthia saw that there was no head. In its place was a void, and she understood why they needed the Mindlink.

"A person goes in this?" she asked, disbelieving. She leaned over the dark pit. The compartment was small. "No person could fit in this."

"A soldier would have to make a physical concession," Lindo said.

"Fuel?" Cynthia asked.

"It's powered with electrical cells. It can recharge off any electrical line. I also have a hydrogen generator attachment I'm working on."

Radiation symbols were painted on its chest and back.

"What makes it radioactive then?" she asked. She climbed back down to the floor.

"The armor. This particular example is made out of depleted uranium. It's more toxic than radioactive."

"That would kill the person in it," Cynthia said.

Lindo shrugged.

"Eventually. The interior is lead lined, we have RAD treatments devised."

"And it works?" Cynthia couldn't take her eyes off it. It sat over them like an ancient god.

WarDon spoke up.

"We need a custom Mindlink interface in order to bring this to life. We modified some of your online software to test it, but this needs to be a fully contained Mindlink interface. We can't do it without you."

"This is the prototype, there is more to it than this," Lindo said. "But we can't get there without your help."

Her enthusiasm vanished. "You're asking a lot. Access to my network is one thing, it's on my terms. I can cut Nostradamus, I can pull the Sleeper program if there's a conflict, or I think it's being abused. But you want secrets."

Evan started to say something. Cynthia held up her hand to stop him.

"You're too smart to play me for dumb," she said.

"With the Terr—" WarDon began.

"The Coalition started the Terror War, Donald!" Cynthia said. "I don't see the problem, outside of the problem. Transportation is limited and incredibly expensive now. They can't be shipping more terrorists over which means there are a finite supply. Find them and root them out."

"We're putting our best and brightest on that as we speak," WarDon said. "But we still don't have the armor we need to protect those lives. The cities are horrible places for war, Cynthia. It's all high ground. We can't bring in heavy armor. We bring in a small team that must—on the fly—decide who is a terrorist, who is a civilian, all while bullets fly past them that can go through our best body armor.

"You're worried about your secrets? What about American lives? Would your secrets stop MindCorp from being the largest corporation in the history of man? Would it help a competitor get out of court if they stole your proprietary technology?"

Cynthia was quiet. WarDon had made a point.

"MindCorp is a monopoly in the truest sense," WarDon emphasized. "And the U.S. understands how important it is to our way of life. But Goddammit Cynthia, have you seen a dead body? I've seen thousands. I've talked to the parents."

"A self-contained Mindlink can be reverse engineered," Cynthia said through gritted teeth.

"A dead kid can't," WarDon spat. He left the room.

Evan sat across for a moment, quietly flipping a pencil end-over-end on the table.

"I'd be very respectful of the technology, Cynthia. I would keep you abreast of everything," he finally said.

Cynthia shook her head no.

= = =

After Cynthia and Sabot left, Evan walked to his office. Along the way soldiers and researchers said hello and he said it back. He had designed his office to be among the thousands of research servers in cold storage. The core of the core, he liked to think. He thought his CPU was the most important of them all. He liked to think of his brain as a machine.

He walked through the field of servers and into his office. After he closed the door, he stood with his back against it for a moment, breathing deeply. And then he screamed. He screamed until his throat shredded and the veins on his neck stood out like worms. He gathered himself.

"It's fine. All in due time. All in due time," he said aloud. "*Patience*," he emphasized. *I hate patience*, a voice in his head shot back.

He needed the self-contained Mindlink and he had thought with Captain Happy—that was what he called the bionic soldier—he would have tricked it out of Cynthia. She was right. A self-contained Mindlink could be reverse engineered. He had hoped to do that for an army of Captain Happy's and more: he was constructing a new weapon underground in Virginia.

24

She's too smart to trick, Evan thought. She was the smartest person in the world.

The computer terminal at his desk pinged. He walked over to it and put the Mindlink on. This terminal had a direct tie line to Nostradamus and the AI had picked up a pattern.

Already.

He was impressed with himself. There was an increase in Muslim named passengers on two 'L' trains in Chicago. While normally it would be one in two hundred, on these cars there were five to two hundred. In addition, four graduates from Berkeley who had belonged to extremist political groups were also on these trains, separated in pairs. Nostradamus had tracked their purchase history. One had used his parents' credit at an online sporting goods store to buy four balaclava masks. Half of the Muslims on the train had moved to Chicago within a week apart five months before. One of the Berkeley students with an electrical engineering degree was a janitor at MindCorp Headquarters. One of the Muslims was an off duty train operator. Another of the Muslims had recently watched video related to the occupation in the Middle East. One of the Berkeley students had read a book about a bank robbery in 1997 at a North Hollywood bank perpetrated by two heavily armed men. A shipment of fertilizer to a farmer with a liberal dissident past outpaced his land size and yield. A city garbage truck had gone missing seven months before.

Sixty-five percent of all passengers taking these trains took the next train north. Nostradamus crunched other mundane information. E-mails. Travel patterns of the general populace that had moved here within the last five months, past travel logs for the names listed, chats and e-mails associated with the Berkeley students. Once it latched on to a pattern, it could raise it above the noise floor of the zeros and ones that made up our digital lives. With 66.7% accuracy Nostradamus predicted that both the MindCorp Data Node north of the city and MindCorp Headquarters would be attacked today.

The protocol for Evan was to report this immediately to WarDon, who would then galvanize the proper military division into action. But Evan saw the long view. Cynthia was too smart to trick, but she had emotions. He smiled and then he instructed Nostradamus to ignore these patterns, backup to a local drive, and erase the information from its shared log.

He'd let this play out.

= = =

Frank felt that today was a turning point in Justin's short life. That morning, he and Charlene had woken to Justin standing next to their bed.

"Morning, bud," Frank said, stretching. Justin had a huge grin on his face and his eyes were alight. Frank had never seen that before.

"Can we go?" Justin asked. Frank looked at the clock. It was 5:00 am.

"The earliest train is at 7:00 am," Frank said. Instead of throwing a tantrum or not processing this basic reality, Justin nodded.

"I'll go downstairs and wait."

Frank got out of bed and got ready. When he came down, Justin had packed their lunch and coffee was brewing. Charlene choked up. Frank put his arm around her.

"What?" Justin said. His voice was back to flat, a tell of Asperger's.

"Nothing, Justin. Are you excited?" Frank asked.

The flatness vanished. He looked directly at them. "Did you know that MindCorp is not only the tallest skyscraper in Chicago, but it is over *three times* as large, in cubic volume, as the Sears Tower? Cynthia started MindCorp ten years ago, she said the Mindlink was like a photographic negative in her mind that never let her . . ."

He rattled off facts and Frank and his wife bathed in them.

The sky was clear and Frank watched Justin as he stared out the window and the landscape changed from field after field, to abandoned suburbs, to the dermis of the city—the ghettos—to the gigantic cement and steel tentacles that reached up into the sky. Before the Great Migration, DeKalb had been sixty miles outside of Chicago. Now it was just forty. From the silo on the farm, the wall of skyscrapers looked like a tsunami coming to shore. And now they were there.

It was dark in the city, something Frank hadn't expected. It didn't register right away. The hour trip in and the rapid change of the landscape, made him feel like he had traveled further and longer than he actually had. The thousands of skyscrapers acted like ivy encroaching a window, choking out the light.

"How're you doing?" Frank asked Justin. His son smiled up at him.

The train slowed down on its way to O'Hare National Train Station. From that hub they would go into the city. Frank furrowed his brow looking at the train schedule monitor on the wall of the car. With the Great Migration, Chicago had bloated to four times its previous size. There were hundreds of train and 'L' schedules.

"The 7:00 a.m. train gets in at 8:30 a.m." Justin looked at a clock on the wall. "We're arriving on time."

He scanned the schedule, it flickered different routes like a stock ticker. "The 8:50 a.m. train on Ramp 14 arrives at Ogilvy Transportation Center at 9:25. From there we take the Blue to the Red to the M, which will take us directly to MindCorp."

"You're sure?"

"Yes."

"Okay, then you're in charge. You can handle it, right?"

Justin squeezed his dad's hand.

They left O'Hare National and the ground dropped below Justin as the train track rose and they entered the city. They glided twenty stories above the streets. Above and below them, dozens of tracks and trains crisscrossed, servicing different parts of the city, now no longer downtown centric. During the day they were gliding caskets, homes for bums, derelicts, and drunks who never left them as they spun around their tracks like perpetual motion machines. During mealtimes and at night, the trains would be flooded with the bed-headed masses taking a break from their online jobs, networked interests and social clubs. Taking a break to breathe air that didn't smell like them, walking in the park to get the tingling out of their feet.

The Mindlink had turned the city into a dorm. There were stores and restaurants, centers to congregate, but most services provided home delivery. The roads were empty except for government subsidized service vehicles, police, and electric delivery trucks. It was walk or rail. Bike tires were too expensive.

The Mindlink (and Mindlink accessories!) were sold throughout the city, but the only place that could fill a child with wonder was located at the building where Cynthia sat at that very moment, one hundred and fifty stories up. Justin and Frank got on the M rail and it quickly separated from the tangle of tracks around it. It had one stop on its monitor and they were just a mile away.

The train slowed like a rollercoaster at the end of its ride as they approached MindCorp. Frank looked around. There were no other trains. There were few paths to MindCorp and this was one of them. The negative space between MindCorp and the other buildings made it feel surreal, as if it was a portal into another dimension. And then Frank realized that this was true, and probably intentional. This *was* science fiction. MindCorp *did* create another world.

The building occupied four city blocks and it looked like a gun pointed at God. It was black and clean without a hint of rust or neglect. In fact, it was one of the few buildings in the city that still maintained the air of prosperity.

"Is it as big as you pictured?" Frank asked Justin. Justin didn't respond. His face was pressed against the window taking it all in. The building looked magical, it looked powerful. It looked like it ruled the world. They entered a tunnel halfway up MindCorp and in that momentary darkness, Frank blinked his eyes, turned around, and realized they were the only two people on the train.

Of course. Everyone else already owns a Mindlink.

But it made him shiver. It didn't feel right. Surely in a city of fifteen million, someone else would have to stop by.

The train came to a halt and the door whooshed open. They stepped out to no one. On the far end, a line of twenty unmanned kiosks had countless Mindlinks (and Mindlink accessories!) queued up behind glass on mechanical arms. They heard a clatter from far below, followed by another, but it was nearly drowned out from the automated monitors that welcomed them to MindCorp.

"No one's here," Justin said.

He looked up and down the two hundred yard hallway. There were a couple of trashcans, but no janitor. At the kiosk there was a help button, but no one that smiled and said 'hello.' At the far end was a store with its security gate rolled down. The lights were out. It felt deserted.

"I think we're late to the party," Frank said. "Let's go ahead and buy one and get some lunch before we head home."

Unceremoniously, Frank and Justin walked over. They looked at the machine, shrugged, and then Frank swiped his credit card. A box big enough to hold a bicycle helmet slid off its rack and fell to the bottom of the kiosk. The door opened, Justin picked it up, and that was that.

"Hey!" someone hissed. It came from the store. Frank searched the darkness for the voice. A young, round, black woman appeared at the gate fumbling with her keys. "Don't you know?"

"Know what?" Frank said. They walked toward her.

"We're under attack!"

Just then a flashing light spun and a siren bellowed. Chatter echoed up from below. Gunfire.

= = =

Raimey had been back in Chicago for two days and already the shit was heating up. Nostradamus had pinged the potential attack just minutes before. The team was so caught off guard, they had to change into their gear on the way. They were en route to a Data Node north of the city to intercept a potential terrorist threat.

"I thought we were on leave," Janis said as he stripped down to nothing and put on his black Kevlar suit.

"Dammit, Janis. You don't wear underwear?" one of the soldiers barked after getting an eyeful of his undercarriage.

"Not when I'm just walking around," Janis said, like it was obvious. He slapped a cup on and punched it. "But I protect them when it counts."

Raimey viewed the information that Nostradamus had sent his HUD comm, a transparent monitor just off his line of sight that showed real-time information. A mile out from the Data Node, they heard the explosion. The aftershock ricocheted through the close-cropped high rises, raining glass on the dazed citizens below. They heard it clang against the truck's armored roof.

"Sounds big," a soldier said.

"Call fire," Raimey said into the comm; it was linked to Headquarters.

"Already did, they will wait for your word," an operator replied. The operator flew a drone ahead of them, circling the scene. It flashed from infrared to HD, searching for hostiles. "We see no action at the Node. The bomb has gone off, but no action."

They got to the Data Node. Just like the one in New York, the office building was destroyed and there was damage to surrounding buildings, but the terrorists had made no attempt to enter the Data Core where the bulk of the operation occurred.

Strange. Raimey thought. They set up a perimeter and searched through the surrounding buildings.

"What was the delivery device?" Raimey asked.

"Hold," the operator said. She reviewed the footage frame-by-frame. "It looks like a truck, maybe a garbage truck. The drone was too far away when the bomb detonated to have a 100% ID."

He had seen this. He had done this in battle. This was a diversion.

"Check other Cores and transportation centers," Raimey said. He mirrored the channel frequency to his team. "Everyone pull in. Let SWAT handle this. This doesn't feel right."

"Diversion?" Janis said. Raimey could hear that he was jogging back.

"Yep."

"It's a good one."

"Yeah. We're the only anti-terrorist team here."

Just then the operator wired them into a police band. Shots had been fired at MindCorp Headquarters.

"I have another drone flying that way," the operator said. "It'll be less than five minutes."

The team converged from various alleys and buildings and they headed to MindCorp.

= = =

Sabot didn't bother with an explanation. Cynthia was online in a sea of data, building the final report for WarDon on China and the EU, and then in a flash she was over his shoulder. For a split second, she thought he wanted to fuck, until he ignored her playful banter.

"You're not going to believe what China has!"

"No talking," Sabot said.

She knew there was trouble. Sabot kept a 10mm Glock on him, but he went to a hidden compartment in her office and pulled out a massive, 10 gauge shotgun that had a twenty round drum magazine.

"Stay behind me."

"What about the cameras?"

"They shut them down."

"The elevators?"

"They're gone too. But one stopped at the 145th floor. Be quiet."

The 145th floor and higher were executive offices and also Cynthia's home. Immediately she understood the ramification: they knew her home was on these floors, they just didn't know which one. They were searching floor-by-floor.

Muted automatic fire came from below. Sabot turned back to Cynthia and put his hand to her mouth. She started to cry. He stared directly into her eyes. "This is why I'm here." He put his hand to her face. "We're going up top."

She knew to say no more. He opened the door to the stairway and another burst of machine gun chatter was louder, but still a floor or two down. They heard people screaming.

Sabot saw movement a flight up from him and he didn't hesitate. Sabot blocked Cynthia from view and fired his shotgun. The ten gauge buckshot ripped through the shadow and a man riddled with wounds tumbled down to their feet.

"Don't look," Sabot said as he pulled Cynthia past the man. His chest and face were ruined. Sabot quickly checked: the radio they used was open. His team would have heard the gunfire. Below, a stairwell door slammed open and a herd of footsteps made their way toward them.

He grabbed Cynthia and took her up to the roof. The frigid, whipping wind greeted them. Sabot flanked the door and pointed out a huge air conditioner twenty yards away.

"Get behind that. Don't come out no matter what."

She didn't object. She ran.

Sabot lay prone, off center from the door, and waited with three pounds of pull on a four-pound trigger. No one was going to take his girl.

= = =

Raimey counted four bodies as they entered MindCorp headquarters. A woman without a face and three sprawled security guards. The terrorists weren't taking hostages. When they arrived, employees were fleeing from the building. Raimey kept ten of the team back to watch everyone go, just in case the terrorists used the outrush as cover. They had already proven clever.

The elevators were shut down.

"We got to go up the stairs," Raimey said.

"This place is like a mile tall," Janis complained. They jogged to the stairwell and quickly entered, sweeping the immediate area. Police followed behind them to maintain the cleared floors.

"You always pride yourself on your body," Raimey said as they ascended.

"My body, not my cardio. You ever see me on a treadmill?" Janis replied. Both had their submachine guns tucked to their cheek, its red dot sight a part of their vision.

"We have action on the roof," the operator said in their comm. "Early report from the employees is that the terrorists went directly to the elevator."

"They're going for Cynthia Revo," Raimey said.

"Yes, that's what we believe," the operator said. "No employees—aside from those on the ground floor—said they saw the terrorists."

"Ok. Keep the cops coming, filling in behind us."

"Yes. Sending schematic of top floors."

In their HUD comm a map popped up, pinging their location in the building.

It took them thirty minutes to run up the entire flight of stairs. The main stairwell ended in a vault-like door to the executive suites. It had been blown open and the door hung like a hangnail.

"Careful."

They got in and found bodies, quickly clearing the space, calling out to the comm operator.

They found a body in the stairwell that had been shot at close range with a shotgun. The face looked like it had been fed through a meat grinder. They continued up the stairs and a smell they were all familiar with, the smell of open wounds, filled the air. When they got to the roof entrance, a pile of bodies greeted them. Quickly they checked. They were terrorists. Some with dark skin, others as white as can be. All walks of life together, with guns and bad intentions.

"U.S. special forces!" Raimey called out through the door. They'd have to drag bodies aside to get out.

"This is Jeremiah Sabot, Cynthia Revo's bodyguard. Come out slow with your guns down."

"Could be a trap," Janis said.

"Could be."

"You go out first."

= = =

Frank carried Justin out of MindCorp like an infant. In one hand Justin held the Mindlink. He sucked his thumb with the other. After two hours of hiding in a store, the cops had come out to the 'L' landing. In those two hours they heard gun fire above them and at one point a window crashed outward and a flailing body zipped past, hitting the rail and tumbling away.

One of the cops tried to help with Justin.

"I got him," Frank said. The look in his eye caused the cop to retreat.

The elevators were turned back on and they and others left the building in an orderly fashion.

Walking out, they saw a large black soldier with a hooked scar around his right eye. He was searching the crowd. His gray eyes found them.

"Is your son alright?" Raimey asked.

"No," Frank said. Raimey looked at the boy, he was shaking, nearly catatonic.

"He has Asperger's. He can't handle these kind of things."

Raimey gave a warm smile. "No one can handle these kind of things. Do you need a paramedic?"

"No, we just need to get home."

Raimey called over a cop. "Can you drive these two home?"

The young cop nodded and led them to his car. When he found out where they lived, he dropped them off at the most outward train station to O'Hare.

"I need special approval to drive out that far," the cop had said.

Frank nodded, exhausted. Whatever.

They got back to DeKalb at midnight. Charlene greeted them at the door with concern on her face. Justin had not spoken since the incident. His thumb was chapped from sucking it. He gripped the Mindlink like it was a teddy bear.

"What happened?" Charlene asked. Frank handed Justin to Charlene and he quietly wrapped himself around her.

"We're never going back to the city," Frank said. "Ever."

= = =

Cynthia was in similar duress. Her hands shook so violently she couldn't light her joint. She reached for pills and Sabot stopped her. He was eerily calm.

She had not seen the shootout, but she had heard everything. The sounds and cries were almost worse in her mind. Men pleaded for mercy and her lover gave them none. One sounded like a kid. Sabot used the shotgun to maim and if that didn't do the entire work, the pistol to finish. It was twenty minutes of hell and afterwards Sabot carried her past the bodies so she wouldn't see.

"It's not worth it," he had said.

They were back in her home. After special forces—and then the police—took their statements and they were all alone, Sabot took off his vest, put away the guns, and poured a tall glass of whiskey, ignoring the ice.

He lit the joint for her and held it for her to puff. On a whim he sucked on it too. She couldn't help but laugh.

"Life's short," he said.

He took her to the bath and got the water running. He took off her clothes and put her in, massaging her shoulders, the heat and his hands combining to bleed away her tension.

"How do you do it?" Cynthia asked. His hands felt like steel bars breaking away the knots.

"I won't let anyone hurt you," Sabot said. His voice was hitched. She turned and saw two tear lines down his cheeks. She pulled against him and felt protected. He could do it because he had to.

= = =

About the time the hijacked garbage truck pulled in front of the northern Data Node, Evan called WarDon and told him that Nostradamus had picked up a pattern. He watched the rest of the night unfold via Mindlink: news feeds, police scanners, military comms he had access to because of his position. He waited for the call and it came at 3:00 a.m.

He faked groggy. "Hello?"

"The bionic would stop them?" Cynthia asked.

Evan smiled and quickly pulled it back. A person could hear smile over the phone. "Are you ok?"

"I'm fine, but it was close. Nostradamus and the bionic, that would stop them?" Cynthia asked again. "Could you protect MindCorp?"

"Nostradamus can be tailored for any search criteria," Evan offered. "We plan on having the bionics on ready in every city like SWAT."

"Twenty five people died tonight," Cynthia said.

"I heard. I'm sorry."

"Let's meet tomorrow. I need to understand the software function and parameters for the . . . what do you call it?"

"Captai—" he stopped himself. That was his inside joke. "Tank Major. It's a Tank Major battle chassis."

"See you tomorrow."

CHAPTER 3

It took two days for Justin to re-acclimate to his normal. The night they got home from Chicago he had been almost catatonic. Charlene tried to put Justin down in his own bed and he clung to her like a monkey and whimpered deep in his throat. For the last two nights, he had slept with them. During the day Frank took him on long walks in the fields and pointed out birds and deer beds. That always seemed to calm him. *The city is too dangerous*, Frank thought. *Out here in the fresh air, out here where everyone grew up together and knows each other's history. It may be the only safe place left.*

They got back from their walk and were greeted by two familiar faces. Fernando and Margarito were migratory workers that went farm to farm during the harvest seasons, literally jumping rail throughout the country. They had worked on the McWilliams' farm since Frank was Justin's age.

Fernando was tall and handsome. The years in the sun had baked his skin dark and the deep lines from a lifetime of hard, outdoor labor enhanced his already good looks.

Margarito was short and fat. He had a loopy mustache and curly black hair that fanned out from a perpetually worn baseball cap. Justin liked both of them and when they met at the front of the house, Justin threw a quick wave and pressed into his dad, almost hiding.

"Hola, Justin. Como esta?" Margarito asked.

"Esta bien," Justin replied. "Y tu?"

"Soy MUY Bien!" He put his fist out and Justin bumped it.

"How have you been?" Frank asked.

"Good. Good harvest this year," Fernando said with a thick accent. "Clara sends her best." He turned to the fields. "The crops came in."

"We've had the perfect amount of rain this year," Frank said. They walked inside and Charlene brought them beer and Justin lemonade. They caught up. Frank noticed that Justin had grown restless.

Margarito was setting up a joke.

"A three legged dog walked into the sal—"

"I want to go upstairs!" Justin interrupted.

"Sorry, Margo," Frank said. "Are you okay?"

"I want to go upstairs. I want to try the Mindlink."

"We have guests."

36

Justin got flustered. He rocked back and forth. Charlene pleaded to Frank with her eyes. He acquiesced.

"Okay. Say goodnight to everyone."

Justin said goodnight to Fernando and Margarito and quickly hugged his mom and dad. He took the Mindlink box with him.

In his bedroom, Justin inspected the device. From the top, it looked like the skeleton of a bicycle helmet. It was machined from one piece of aluminum. The interior had LED-like red sensors that ran around the interior and two larger green sensors that pressed onto the top of the head. He unrolled a separate fiber line that connected the Mindlink to his home's data terminal. The brochure was a slip of paper:

Thank you for purchasing the Mindlink!

The Mindlink will provide you access to cyberspace and all of the programs and functions in it. These include:

–Work

–Social

–Games

–Misc.

To start your journey, unpack the Mindlink, plug it into your data terminal (50 megabyte up/down minimum required) and wait for the sensors to self-check (30 seconds). A reclined position is recommended. Put the Mindlink on, following the prompts to set up your account and access cyberspace!

Warning: 0.3% of the population is susceptible to seizures.

With reverence, Justin plugged the fiber line from the Mindlink into the data terminal near his desk. The sensors of the Mindlink playfully pulsed and danced while it booted up.

Justin went to the bathroom and peed. He didn't want to be mid-game or chat and have to get off. He came back, plopped into his dad's old recliner and gently put the Mindlink on his head.

As he did, his bedroom disappeared from top to bottom. In its place was a GUI screen that asked his name, his social security number, and a few more questions to confirm his identity.

He thought his name and it appeared. While he thought his name, his social security number filled in, because his brain—unconsciously to him—had answered that question on another level. The other questions he didn't even know he answered.

The first interface felt like he was in front of a gigantic touch screen. The next interface did not. He floated in a room. The room itself had no physical characteristic to it, no physics such as gravity or the faint movement of air we all take for granted. It was yellow and calming. He heard far off wind chimes. A question hung in the air:

—*What would you like to do?*—

It bobbed up and down in a friendly way. The Mindlink was a two-way highway and while the options weren't listed, suddenly he knew all of them.

Find Jared Stachowitz, he thought. He had never met Jared, but they shared a common interest in mathematics and software programming. Justin had won a speed math contest hosted by MIT's online university the year prior. Jared had come in second and when it was revealed that Justin was only eleven *and* he won without a Mindlink, he had become a micro-celebrity. Jared and he had corresponded over the year.

—*Hey JM! You finally made it! (Jared has accepted your invitation)*—

The words appeared in his head. The yellow room faded over to an auditorium with the longest chalkboard he had every seen. It was as tall and wide as a football field. Jared was heavy, balding and in his twenties. His eyes sparkled with humor. He was at the giant chalkboard. About one hundred people sat in rows of seats behind him. Some looked like models, some looked like superheroes, some looked as plain as they were in real life. Including Jared.

JM! Jared said/thought. *I didn't know if I'd see the day!*

"I finally got a Mindlink," Justin said aloud.

You don't have to talk out loud, you look like a noob. Just think it to us, Jared said back. Justin heard other voices too, but he realized none of their mouths were moving. Online telepathy.

Ok, Justin projected. *Is that what you look like?*

Yep. Young, fat, and bald. God gave me everything (LOL).

What do I look like?

Frankly, spooge.

Everyone laughed.

What's spooge?

(Frown) I forgot, you're twelve. Nothing. Don't worry about it. I'm teaching

these snickering assholes Sleeper software programming. A lot of them are my students, if you can believe that. I'll be done in an hour. Do you want to come back then? I can show you what I do.

That'd be great! Justin said. *Where should I go?*

When I first got on, I went to a racing simulator.

This flight simulator is cool, another voice interjected. Jared and Justin turned to a zombie named AAARGH4237.

I like planes, Justin said.

Send him the link, Jared allowed AAARGH4237.

—AAARGH4237 *has bookmarked a flight simulator he recommends. Would you like to go?*—

Yes, Justin thought.

See you in an hour, Jared said.

The classroom faded as Jared went back into his lesson, and an airfield materialized. Justin stood on an airstrip. Planes he was familiar with were already on the tarmac, but the one he really wanted to fly wasn't. He saw a shimmer to the left of the vision. He turned and instead of a Harrier, a Blackbird SR-71 sat there. His favorite plane.

In his head, he was asked if he'd like a tutorial. He said he would. A man appeared next to him. Justin understood it was a simulation, not a real person. Already, easily, it was clear who was real and who was fake. He wasn't sure how he knew, but he did. Like it was built in.

"Good morning," a young Chuck Yeager said to Justin. Justin immediately knew all of Chuck Yeager's accomplishments, as if he had known for years.

Chuck walked Justin toward the Blackbird.

"You're about to fly an SR-71 Blackbird, one of America's finest aeronautical marvels. A plane so advanced, that at one point it was thought that it couldn't be done."

Chuck went on about the Blackbird as they climbed up into it.

I want to fly, Justin thought. He had been given the option to either fly or ride.

Chuck helped him taxi the plane toward the runway. When they got to the long tarmac and the tower gave them clearance, they roared down the asphalt and into the air.

"You're doing good, son," Chuck said. Justin could tell he was impressed.

"We're gonna get'er up to eighty thousand feet and let her stretch'r legs," the legend said with a smile.

The SR-71 sliced through the air and pushed Justin and his virtual friend toward the heavens. The deep blue of the sky began to turn pale and then at sixty-five thousand feet, a sheet of star speckled black poked through.

Space! Justin thought.

"Alright, we're easing up to seventy thousand feet, we can now make a gradual ascent to eighty," Chuck said in the calm voice of a man who had tested the limits and come back to talk about it. "We are flying at Mach 3, that's two thousand one hundred and twenty-four miles per hour. We have fifty percent fuel reserve."

Justin suddenly had a thought. This was a video game, nothing more. There were no real world consequences. You could drive a funny car into a tanker full of fuel and nothing would happen.

"I want to fly into space," Justin said.

"That's a negative, the SR-71's peak altitude is eighty-five thousand, five hundred feet. We're on the wire."

"This isn't real. I want to go to the moon."

"Son, we all do and with American ingenuity someday we will."

Justin pulled up on the flight stick. The nose of the Blackbird tilted up and then, without his input, the nose dropped back down. The altitude meter said eight-five thousand, five hundred feet.

"That's all she's got," Yeager said.

A switch went off in Justin's mind and the hull of the plane flickered beneath him.

This is a program.

It seemed real, but it wasn't. The back of his mind felt like a muscle on the verge of cramping. It was uncomfortable, but at the same time, the strangeness wasn't unwelcome. It almost felt good.

I can go anywhere, the back of his mind whispered, and when it did, the plane shuddered and once again the hull went clear. But this time, all the way. He was riding on air. He still held the yoke, but beneath him was just earth. He didn't like it. The hull reformed beneath his feet like a piece of plastic that had melted in reverse.

"Son—"

Quiet, Chuck.

Chuck fell silent. Justin looked at his partner and Yeager was frozen like an animatronic doll shut down mid-movement.

Justin was too young to equate it, but his mind burned pleasantly like the beginning build of an orgasm. When he first put on the Mindlink, he became aware of the user options and search categories as if it was an old memory. It was the same for this program. He felt its processing, he sensed the root files that held the high resolution textures, the voice recognition software, the programming that weaved it all together. With that pleasant burning, his mind raced past the computational cycle of the server it resided on and subconsciously, he began to reconstruct it to his desires.

I don't want the plane.

The plane vanished, and with it, Chuck. It was now just him in the quiet void between earth and space. He rolled onto his back to look at the stars and the moon. They were bright and welcoming. They beckoned him.

I miss Duke. One of Justin's dogs passed away that year.

And Justin knew that against all odds, when he got to the moon, Duke would be there waiting for him. *Maybe in a doggie space suit with jets.* They could play fetch. Justin didn't have much of an arm, but he knew in space he could throw a baseball a hundred miles.

He rocketed toward the moon like Superman. Surrounding his periphery, gelatinous floating tubes nipped into his vision like a ball of parasitic worms. But they didn't bother him. They felt like they were a part of him. Like a jet's contrail, he left an oily mist in his wake. But it wasn't exhaust. This world had no pollutants. It was the mindscape of the most powerful Sleeper that had ever connected into cyberspace. It was the mindscape of a boy that was excited to see his dog on the moon.

He landed on the moon. He didn't know that the simulator didn't have this programmed. In it, the moon was a high-resolution texture, nothing more. But he landed on it anyway. Dust swirled up from his feet like snowflakes from a snow globe.

He saw the moon lander from Apollo 11. He saw the American flag, wavered and unmoving. Both were in the wrong location because he didn't know the particulars of the moon. He subconsciously filled in the blanks from his experiences and conjectures. For him, the surface felt like his sand box at home because it was what he knew. It wasn't a talcum powder-like dust, because those facts had never entered his mind.

He heard Duke before he saw him. And then Duke crested a gray hill and ran down wagging his tail in a custom made doggy space suit!

Awesome!

"Ruff!" he heard Duke say. How did he hear that? He knew that space didn't have oxygen.

Then, Justin caught a slight reflection of himself in the clear glass of his space suit helmet.

Ah, intercom.

The next bark was in crackling, low fidelity as Justin imagined it'd be.

Justin had a tennis ball in his hand. Duke jumped around him, wagging his tail furiously. Justin wound up and threw the ball. With no arc, it launched like a cannon shot over the hill that Duke had just come over, *waaaay* too far to run after. But Duke had a few tricks. His jet pack fired up and with another bark he shot after it.

Within seconds he was back with the green ball somehow in his mouth, beneath the doggy shaped glass helmet.

Justin looked down and the ball was in his hand again. The dog was just as excited for another go.

This is awesome, the King Sleeper thought as he watched his long dead dog fly after another low gravity pitch.

= = =

Justin played with Duke for the hour and he was sad to go. But Duke wagged his spacesuit-lined tail and Justin bookmarked the simulator for another visit before vanishing back to the classroom.

Jared was seated in the first row. A knight Justin had seen earlier was in the process of building a noble steed. The legs and the head were completely formed, but the rest was wireframe and code.

Remember the intrinsic order of Revo, Jared reminded. The knight nodded. Behind him on the giant chalkboard, some lines of code vanished and with it part of the wireframe of the horse. New code appeared on the board like a typed sentence and the wireframe of the horse's back appeared.

Good, Gegard, Jared said. *Sit down Justin. It'll be just a minute.*

Justin could tell that message was just for him. Justin sat down and watched while Jared taught the knight to build a horse for his role playing game.

After thirty minutes the horse was complete, if a bit wonky. For some reason it kicked with its front legs and one eyeball was bigger than the other.

Save it and we'll work on it tomorrow, Jared said.

Gegard stepped away from the chalkboard and as he did, the chalkboard flexed out and snapped back when he walked to the first row of seats.

Justin is the one who won the speed math contest last year, Jared announced to the dozen or so students.

Still looks like spooge.

Trent, I'll mute you.

A jock-type avatar threw his hands in frustration. *I'm just observing my surroundings.*

Jared turned to Justin. *How was the simulator?*

I went to space! Justin said.

You can't go to space, the zombie said knowingly.

I did.

Ok, you did. For being slack jawed and rotting, the zombie was surprisingly sarcastic.

Justin. Go up to the whiteboard.

Justin hesitated. He didn't like people watching him.

It's ok. This is a beginner's class. This is where we can trip and get back up, Jared reassured. Normally Justin would have shied away. In the real world he always felt like he was at the bottom of a crushing sea waiting to drown. But here he felt airy. Exceptionally aware. He wondered if this was what it was like to be normal.

Walking up, Justin hadn't noticed all the strange things in the room. Some objects were three dimensional like the horse. A race car sat to the left. When Justin focused, the object shimmied and he could see the flat screen of all the code that went into its design. Other creations looked like small floating mirrors. Some of the people held them in their hands. When Justin focused on them, he could see their application. Some were shareware programs, others plug-ins to some software application that Justin had never seen.

When you approach the chalkboard it gives you access to the programming software. It's Revo based.

MindCorp had its own programming language derived from Linux. It was the universal language of cyberspace. Justin walked up to the interface. He felt the giant chalkboard lock onto him and in the upper left-hand corner, a cursor blinked. *They'll watch me build the code?*

That way we can offer suggestions. This is for practice and fun, Jared said.

What should I program?

Revo is very flexible. You can code anything you want to.

I'll create a Duke. My dog. He was in space with me.

Okay, good challenge. The dog must behave like a dog, it can't be static, and it must obey commands. Tough first test.

Justin closed his eyes. He could still feel the program. He saw the string of code in his head to build Duke. Black and brown. Lean and strong. Always wagging his tail.

Holy shit, Jared said. The students murmured.

What? Justin said.

A dog barked in the room.

Justin opened his eyes and Duke was running around sniffing everybody out. He went to the horse and raised his leg.

I didn't begin building it! Justin said. Everyone was silent.

Dude. You did.

A timer was overhead to keep each student to thirty minutes. It had taken Justin 0.02 seconds. Two one-hundredths of a second. More people popped into the room. Within seconds, all the seats were filled.

Gotta be a hack.

Never seen that.

Why the fuck did you call me here?

Dude sweated the program, the whole place vibrated.

Jared stood up and gestured for everyone to quiet down.

Do something else, Jared said.

What?

Atomically perfect gold.

Without thinking about it, a plate of gold appeared six inches above the workspace and slammed down: 0.0001 seconds.

NO WAY! everyone howled.

Have him hack into something, a ninja said.

Shut up. We don't do that, Jared said. He sounded distant, thinking.

It was a fluke.

He couldn't.

If he can't then what's the big deal? They push away Sleepers all the time.

Have him hack into MindCorp; that'd be hilarious.

Yeah, hack into that.

I got through two portals before they booted me.

I got through your mom's portholes before she blew me.

The ninja and an alien with suckers for hands came to blows at the top of the seats.

Come on, Jared. Let him.

Jared, don't be a pussy.

*-Jared- -Jared- -Jared- -Jared—*a thousand 'Jareds.'

Fine, fuck! Shut up everyone. Justin, do you want to try and hack into MindCorp?

I don't know how, Justin said.

You didn't know how to make a dog but it's pissing on everything anyway. It isn't a big deal, just bragging rights. MindCorp doesn't take the hacks seriously. Hell, they used to hold contests to test their security.

Okay.

The room rebooted. The ninja and the alien warrior weren't allowed back in.

The whiteboard had vanished. In its place, like the rings of Saturn, were a billion tiny reflections that orbited around a dark, iron orb

All those glitters are programs, Justin, Jared said. *That orb at the center? MindCorp.*

This is cyberspace?

Yes, sir. Cool, eh? She built it like space, three-dimensional and all. But here, MindCorp IS the center of the universe.

Justin closed his eyes again. He saw: MINDCORP LOGIN V112.43. ADMIN.US.DN.1Col.IP72.243.993.42.42:7908

Holy shit. He's going at a Colossal, someone murmured. Then Justin heard no more. He felt the code wash over him, he could feel the firewalls try to misdirect him and his mind turned blacker than the night, blacker than the deepest void in space. And he could feel the program. The numbers became atoms. The code, living cells. As he barreled through security protocol after security protocol, hammering them with passwords, multi-threading, contacting employees as a peer to coerce information, multi-threading, discovering the root of the program and tearing it apart from the foundation up. Through these things that had never been done before, he finally felt alive. His mind unfurled like a solar flare and in this world, he finally felt complete.

= = =

Cynthia was in a meeting with Helene Rossia, the President of their Israeli Division, when the lights flickered and the room trembled. They steadied themselves.

"Whoa, what was that?" Helene asked.

"I'm not sure," Cynthia replied. She'd check after the meeting. They were discussing new security protocols and network redundancies MindCorp was implementing globally. They looked at a large map of the Middle East on a projector.

"If we spider-web the network . . ." Cynthia began. Suddenly the room jumped. Helene and Cynthia flew from their seats. The entire space slammed up and down like it was on a pogo stick. A seam formed across one of the walls and bright, purple light bleached through.

"What the hell is going on?" Helene yelled. They were getting tossed around like dice, slamming into chairs and walls, hitting the ceiling and then—as if the room was spinning—catapulting into the opposite wall. The seam opened wider and on a bad bounce, Helene vanished into the purple light, screaming as she went.

Cynthia ripped the Mindlink off her head. An emergency light flashed above her. *The Core.* In her ten years, she had never seen that light turn on. Sabot burst into the room. He didn't say anything. Cynthia jumped up and they ran to the elevator.

MindCorp was one hundred and fifty stories tall. They rode two hundred stories down. Beneath MindCorp Headquarters was one of two Colossal Cores in the region. Because of the support structure needed for the huge glass Data Core cylinders, it was much easier to build down than up.

It was immediately clear that something was wrong. A properly operating Data Core looked like a giant blue fluorescent tube. A thick blue arc of data light connected the fiber lines at the top with those at the bottom. But now the Core flickered and popped, booming with thunder.

"What the hell!" Cynthia said.

They got to the ground and as they did, the Data Core began to spin and pulse. The blue went to black and then snapped back to blue, like a kid was flicking a light switch off and on.

The ground floor was chaos. Spinning red lights flashed around the perimeter of the Core. A shrill alarm filled the air. The Sleepers that surrounded the Core were still out, but they rocked back-and-forth in seizures. A dozen technicians scrambled between them like medics on a battlefield, checking vital signs, throwing Mindlinks on to see what was causing the Sleepers to frenzy in their slumber. Cynthia grabbed Jim Schmidt, the scientist in charge.

"What's going on?" she yelled over the alarm. She saw two Sleepers shake themselves loose of their harness and belly flop to the ground.

"Something huge is altering the data path of the Core," he said. He had a Mindlink on.

"What do you mean?"

"Something online is out cycling our processors, it's dragging portals out of their orbits." Jim handed the Mindlink over to Cynthia.

"We're being hacked?"

"No . . . yes . . ." he shook his head, he couldn't grasp it. "I don't know. Whatever it is, it's ignoring the operating system of the Core. It just hit."

"Limit bandwidth to fifty megabytes," she said. She didn't want to have a seizure because of whatever was out there. Jim hit the keyboard and gave thumbs up.

She put on the utility Mindlink. Consumer Mindlinks were designed to allow access to the various programs in cyberspace. Sleepers used utility Mindlinks to maintenance the network, portals and programs, and the space in between.

While Cynthia had built the cyberspace construct to behave like space, in her universe even the voids held data. This allowed a Sleeper to move from portal to portal effortlessly (as well as through the portal's subset of programs) and to know their position in relation to any portal or program in the system. It also allowed them to see the data paths of the users online. There was no anonymity in cyberspace. Every user had a digital 'tail,' a distinct path that anchored them to their true physical location. Sleepers could trace this tail and find the user's origin. They could, if given permission, go in and read that user's thoughts.

What Cynthia saw staggered her mind. Jim had placed her just outside the anomaly's effect. The millions of portals normally spun in harmony on a three plane axis—x, y and z—orbiting the gravity core. While the majority of the portals—they looked like mirrors floating in space—were operational and followed their orbital path, one quadrant did not. In it, thousands of portals ignored the gravity core and churned on an entirely different axis like dirt circling a drain. They spun haphazardly, smashing into each and spinning off. As Cynthia drew closer, she couldn't believe what she saw.

A mist surrounded the rogue portals and Cynthia new what that mist was, even if she had never seen it on that scale. It was a mindscape—a visual manifestation of a person's influence in cyberspace. Sleepers had mindscapes; that was how they programmed. There was no physical connectedness in cyberspace. Hands and feet were programmed assimilations. It was the mind versus code all the time. The mindscape was how the two related.

But this . . . this . . . it was like God decided to try his hand at it.

"What could do this?" Cynthia whispered. *"Jim, can you trace this? It's not native, it's coming from somewhere."*

"I'll get Sleepers from a different Core to trace it. I need to pull ours offline."

"Do it."

Could it be terrorists? she wondered. *Impossible.* What she saw before her shouldn't be. The freedom afforded to MindCorp Sleepers was an illusion. Her online universe had been created with exacting, unbreakable rules. Yet those rules were being broken right in front of her. Someone had introduced chaos into a binary system of order. How? *How?*

Cynthia bumped her bandwidth up to two hundred megabytes, enough to move around, and her sense of the physical world vanished. She was now in the void, looking down on the mirror-riddled cyclone. She flew toward it.

Cynthia, we have Sleepers from surrounding Cores zeroing in on the anomaly, she heard Jim say. She could see them. For some reason, a Sleeper in cyberspace resembled a sperm with dozens of long tails that waggled and moved in all directions. It wasn't disgusting. It was almost angelic. She saw thousands of them drifting toward the turbine mess.

There is a gravitational center, Cynthia, Jim said. *The portals that look in disarray are not, they are breaking the laws of cyberspace, but they are breaking them with order.*

A giant mindscape, Cynthia projected. In the control room where

Sabot, Jim, and now a vacant-eyed Cynthia sat, her voice came over a loudspeaker.

Correct, Jim replied.

What is happening to the portals? Can any Sleeper go in? Are they being manipulated? Cynthia asked.

Hold . . . Jim said. *They are shut down. No occupants are in them at all.*

An odd thing to envision, Cynthia thought. A portal could house programs that held tens of millions of people in them. It could be New York City; it could be a sports arena or a re-enactment of the Battle of Gettysburg. It could be a corporation's virtual location. But in the anomaly they were all empty. Not one soul was in them. So whatever had caused this had intentionally or unintentionally booted people out.

I want to see what the fuss is about, Cynthia said.

Cynthia moved at the equivalent of light speed. The velocity combined with the sheer silence still amazed her. The gravitational center grew in her field of view.

A portal is the gravitational center.

She was in the mindscape and she didn't know if that would have any effect on her. It hung in space like a green poisonous cloud, covering all the portals in a mini milky way.

Are you getting this? Cynthia said to Jim. She watched as the mindscape poured out of the portal.

It's a shareware program. A flight simulator, Jim said in disbelief.

Do you have the tail?

We have the region, not the tail. We can't get inside the program.

Suddenly the mindscape vanished. The portals that had been pulled out of orbit fell back toward the beltway, slowly re-orientating to their programmed location in the construct.

It's gone, Cynthia said. *You got the region? China?*

Giant mirrors the size of states flew past her, finding their place.

DeKalb, Illinois.

That can't be. That's a farm com-

The universe started to pull apart. Cynthia's body stretched wide. Her round form thinned to a sheet of paper. Her face contorted in excruciating pain. The Sleepers around her became sunspots in her vision before vanishing. She turned her gaze and from another portal a million miles away, a mindscape had connected to the MindCorp gravity core like a parasite. Its tentacled reach vibrated and shook with energy.

We're shutting down the Core! Jim said.

One more second.

It's hacking through our firewalls.

We have to find it.

It is at the root program.

That's impossible.

She went dark.

= = =

Cynthia called WarDon. He was in Washington and directed her to Evan. Ten minutes later, she and Sabot were in his office. After Cynthia's recap of the events at the Colossal Core, Evan's own thoughts drowned out her babbling. The possibilities that this 'anomaly' presented were astounding to his future plans.

"But not terrorist?" Lindo asked absently.

"I don't know. Our data shows that both tails came from DeKalb, Illinois, a farm town. The population is in the hundreds and their data feed is three hundred megabytes up/down per home."

Lindo waited. He liked seeing Cynthia unraveled. He could use that.

She continued. "It doesn't sound like much, but to take over that section of cyberspace—roughly 0.0025%—would take a million terabytes of constant data programming and pushing, maybe more. I don't know. We're still crunching numbers."

"So it's impossible that it came from DeKalb," Lindo said.

"Improbable, not impossible," Cynthia corrected.

"Why do you say that? You just told me that it couldn't be done." Lindo was intrigued.

"If it was AI or some kind of software, it could push more bandwidth by first planting a codec in cyberspace and then compressing data at the tail. It's theoretical, but there's no reason that it couldn't be done. But if that were the case it would be a simple program, more of a cancer: no purpose, just growing," Cynthia said.

"Which doesn't explain the hack."

"Exactly." Cynthia confused was more rare than moon rock. "We're trying to piece it together. We know the hack came from an education portal."

"That had the login address to your Colossal," Evan baited.

"That was public information," she replied.

"Might want to pull that off-line now."

Cynthia gave a short, frustrated laugh.

"So what do you need, Cynthia?" Evan liked those words. They tasted better than steak.

"This could be the first attempt at cyber-terrorism. That's your jurisdiction isn't it?"

"Yes."

Evan and Cynthia looked at one another for a moment. Evan broke the gaze and shuffled papers around his desk.

"I assume we'll have full access to the data reports on this, full access to anyone we need to interview?" he asked.

"Per my approval, but yes."

"I'll speak to Donald and we'll investigate ASAP."

Cynthia got up and she and Sabot headed toward the door.

"Question," Lindo said. Cynthia turned. "This compression algorithm, this 'push' as you call it, that amplifies a mindscape. Do you know exactly how they did it?"

"Not yet, but we will."

"I'd like to know when you do," Lindo said.

Cynthia smiled and walked out the door.

= = =

Later that day, Evan briefed WarDon on his meeting with Cynthia.

"I'm glad they came to us," WarDon said.

"They really had no choice. It's not like they can go investigate on their own."

"They'll keep it discreet?" WarDon asked.

"Yes, definitely."

"Good, this is the last thing we need to freak out the public. Cyberspace is supposed to be safe. It'd fuck everything up, even for us." WarDon thought about their collusion with MindCorp against their Coalition allies. "We're going to keep this off the books. You're in charge and report to me as you see fit, but keep it analog. I'm assigning you the best soldier I've ever seen. He'll report at 0600 tomorrow. I'll brief him on the need for total discretion. He's young. A lot like you, actually. A prodigy. Don't let the accent fool you or the lazy way he looks around the room. He's a pit bull."

"Thank you, sir."

Evan hung up the phone and reclined in his chair. The hum of the server bays soothed him and while the lack of windows would make anyone else claustrophobic, they allowed Evan to forget about a world that he felt no longer mattered.

"Dim," he said, and the overhead lights dimmed to flickering candles. He closed his eyes and built his future in his head.

His favorite quote was by Louis Pasteur, "Luck Favors the Prepared." To Evan, life was preparation. It was the most important thing. It took chance and made it your ally. Preparation allowed him to direct conversations and manipulate other people's will.

He crumpled up the note he referenced while talking to WarDon. It had nothing to do with the anomaly at MindCorp. It had to do with pushing WarDon's buttons to get what Evan desired. In his cryptic scrawl the note read:

> Goal: Autonomy. Go-ahead to investigate on my terms.
> Key Points (WarDon)
> -Focus on national security. Focus on our current investigation of Coalition. This jeopardizes it.
> -Cynthia's concern. Out of their hands. Need us.
> -Discretion. No one should know.

At the bottom of the note:
> -Doesn't know the implications of the anomaly!! Play on fear, NOT benefit.

With his eyes still closed, he stood up and walked out of his office and into the field of servers. He held his hands out like antennae. He felt their vibrations. Even though he wasn't connected, he could feel cyberspace. He could feel the nations interconnected by fiber veins that pulsed light instead of blood. If the anomaly was what he thought it was, his plans could come together quickly. If not, well, it was just another bump in the road. Quitters never win.

Mike Glass reported to Evan the next morning right at 6:00 a.m. He was twenty-three, Kentucky born and bred. Six foot, a buck ninety, unshaven, he had long, sandy blonde hair, a bit greasy, that made him look like a front man to a bad rock group. But Evan saw what WarDon had warned: his eyes held no emotion in them. He watched Evan like a crocodile watched a baby gazelle drinking from the shore.

CHAPTER 4

"You seen anyone that doesn't look like you?"

"No sir, I have not," Tommy Spade—that was his stage name—said to the man who was blatantly ignoring the 'No Smoking' sign at his establishment. His real name was Seth Johnson, but he hadn't gone by that for a long time. Tommy Spade was his gambling name *and* his stripper name, not that it mattered much anymore. He was older, pudgier, and DeKalb had about five chicks *tops* who'd want his junk tick tocking over their nose like a clock's pendulum. Nope, those days were done.

He was the proprietor of the Paperback Grotto, an old style porno shop that had been in his family for seventy years. People laughed, but porn was his family's business. Tommy never understood why it was viewed as a dirty trade. He thought it was a necessity, just like food and water. Sex was a part of who we were, why be so damn uptight about it?

The Grotto had everything a customer needed for an old school spank or to liven up the bedroom with the better half.

Business had been shit, of course. No one was around anymore. The only clients he had were farmers who, in general, didn't use the Mindlink. As that technology had proliferated, the farmers had retreated from it almost out of principle. They were like the Amish now.

But it didn't matter. The Grotto was paid for and Tommy figured a few more years and that'd be it. The last porno shop on the planet. Tommy pictured himself like an old gunslinger, except he had dildos in his holster and tubes of lube on his bandolier. Maybe a disc of *Horny Housewives 300* as a throwing star.

That's a ninja.

Whatever.

The young man waited patiently. He had pulled up in a car, which meant he was either police or military.

"And you know everyone in town?" the man asked.

"There isn't anyone to know anymore." Tommy had already given the names of the twenty or so farmers.

"No one dark complected, different accent, that kind of thing?" Glass asked. He was thinking Middle Eastern.

"Well, we got migrant workers that help with the harvest, of course," Tommy said. "They come in a bit, like the traditional stuff, the arcades . . . "

"Arcades?" Glass raised an eyebrow: he was too young to get the reference.

Tommy hitched a finger toward the back of the store. "The wank boxes. Put in some money, watch a movie."

The young man nodded.

"How long have the migrant workers been here?" Glass asked.

"A few weeks now. They move from farm to farm across the country."

"Who uses them?"

"Everyone. We have no young population anymore and they're cheap and reliable. A lot of them have been coming here for twenty years."

Glass pulled on his cigarette. His eyes bugged Tommy, they were a dark green, but they conveyed nothing, like they had been whittled into his head with a pocketknife.

Glass took the list off the table.

"I appreciate you giving me the lay of the land."

"Are you an officer?"

The man gave a nod goodbye and left. Tommy Spade immediately regretted the names he gave this man. Those eyes showed no quarter. What was the military doing out here?

= = =

At the same time, Raimey and his team were dressed plain clothes in the alleys surrounding a dilapidated high-rise on the south side of Chicago. Cynthia's Sleepers had cracked the program that originated the hack. The tail of the programmer who built the software led here.

"It doesn't look terroristy," Janis said. The high rise was old and unkempt except for a garden that some elderly men and women were tending. Old people shuffled in and out. "It looks like an old folks home."

"Check on 176 Elk Street," Raimey said into his comm. "We're seeing a lot of . . . uh . . ."

An ancient woman eked out of the door using a walker.

"Geezers knocking on death's door," Janis finished.

". . . old people."

"It *is* a retirement home," the operator confirmed. She sent the data to their comm. The home was called Adventurous Gardens. Two elderly people held each other on the front page. The guy was hugging the woman from behind.

"Dude, are you reading this?" Janis's eye scrolled up and down as he went through the site.

"No."

"It's a retirement home for elderly singles! Married couples aren't allowed. Gross! The elderly are riddled with disease, you know. You read about that how gonorrhea gets passed around faster than their meds. So much loose skin . . ."

"You have a weird thing with old people."

"They smell like graveyards."

Raimey to the comm, "Should we just go in? I don't think this is what we think it is."

"It's your call," the operator said.

Raimey ushered Janis out of the alley. A centenarian smiled at Eric showing one brown tooth and a lot of gum.

"Seriously, man. Get me back to Iran," Janis whispered.

They went to the front desk. A kind looking women dressed in whites was there. Raimey showed her his ID. "We're looking for Jared Stachowitz."

Eric scanned a nearby TV room and spotted a punchbowl of condoms that looked worked. "Ahmygod. I'm going to puke."

"It's perfectly natural," Raimey teased.

"This way," the nurse directed. She took them up to the second floor. It was filled with state-of-the-art Mindlink terminals.

"Wow, I didn't expect this," Raimey said. "Are you seeing this?"

"Yep," the operator said.

"Most of the seniors prefer to be online," the nurse said. "It's given them a much fuller life, especially for our residents who are ill or weak."

She pointed out a skinny bald man in a worn out robe two chairs down. An oxygen tank was by his side. His chest rose and fell in bursts. He was linked in.

"That's Mr. Stachowitz."

"We don't want to kill the guy, waking him," Janis said. The nurse gave him an ugly look. "Seriously."

She went up to the man and shook him gently awake. His eyes

opened blearily and he blinked into awareness. He looked over and saw Raimey and Janis.

"I thought you'd come," he said in a weak voice.

= = =

Mike Glass enjoyed this assignment. The open land and sparse population reminded him of the backwoods of Kentucky where he was raised. He never knew his mother and Thomas Glass never explained what had happened. Mike had asked twice, got hit twice, and that had knocked the curiosity out of him. Thomas was a Marine ex-sniper, an avid hunter and a consummate drunk. Since he could walk, Mike and his father carpeted the hills and gullies hunting and trapping. Twice a year they would go in town to re-stock the cabin.

Glass could read, but not especially well. He learned in bits and pieces until he was fourteen when Ms. Kragley, a retired teacher, cornered Thomas when they had come into town for their bi-annual supply trip.

"Thomas, don't you walk away. Your son has never been to school. What are you doing?" she said. Thomas had that southern characteristic where, even though he was hillbilly white trash, he was as polite as a politician to women. If a man had said that to him he would have curb stomped his face, but because it was Ms. Kragley—who at one point had taught *him*—his eyes were cast down like a kittens.

"I'm teachin' him at home," Thomas replied.

"You are!" Ms. Kragley said. The book section was near them. She pulled out a children's book, flipped it open, and put it in Mike's face.

"Read this," she said. Thomas stared at his boots.

Mike knew some of the words, but not many. He didn't utter a word. She snapped the book shut and put it on the shelf.

"What's your name?" she asked.

"Mike."

"Would you like to go to school?"

"He ain't going to school, I need him around the farm," Thomas said. The politeness had started to melt away.

She studied Thomas. "I'm retired. Tutored then. Will that work for you?"

Thomas grunted, "okay."

"You're still up off 80?"

Another grunt.

"I'll be there at nine a.m. tomorrow morning."

On the way home Thomas didn't say anything about their encounter with Ms. Kragley. When they pulled up and Thomas threw the truck into park, he cracked the door open, paused, then said, "learning's good. It's a good thing for you." And then he went to the back shed where he distilled bourbon. Mike didn't see him for the rest of the day.

Mike never had an imagination. He didn't dream. He wasn't inherently curious and he didn't think about people's emotions or motives. He was either all process: "to get to here, do A, B, and C," or he was instinctually reactive like a venus flytrap clamping down on a bug.

When he turned eighteen, Ms. Kragley—not his father—suggested he enlist. In Mike's mind, the recommendation brought up two paths: 'Yes' and that would involve enrolling and going off to boot camp. 'No' and he would continue his study and his normal life.

He chose 'Yes' because he had never been out of Kentucky and he knew he could only go so far where he was. He wasn't educated and if his dad was any indication, nothing justified *not* enrolling.

He excelled and he was recruited into Seal training. He was a gifted athlete and his calm under duress—not yet diagnosed as sociopathic—gave him a 100% success record in training. During his psych profile they administered a Rorschach test. He described the ink pattern. The psychologist corrected him.

"You're supposed to tell us what you see *in* the ink."

"All I see is ink, doctor."

The instructors had never seen someone so calm under live fire, interrogation technique, and combat training. As a curiosity, they put a heart monitor on him before a live exercise. The average heart rate of the other elite soldiers, the best of the best, rose well into the hundreds, even at rest. Mike's hovered around fifty. One time sprinting for cover it rose to ninety-five. He was completely unaffected by the stresses of the real world.

And now he was in DeKalb, Illinois on a cool day that hinted at autumn. He liked his job, he supposed. The migrant worker angle was interesting. Off the grid, nomadic, and most likely undocumented. If terrorists were using these channels, it was an innovative way to go about it.

The owner of the porno shop said that two, Fernando and Margarito, had been in earlier, using the arcades. The owner had made a joke about Glass taking a DNA sample, but at that point the man's voice had already been pushed into the background. He would start with them. There wasn't a lot of ground to cover. Twenty farms and some dilapidated neighborhoods, most of which would not have any active data connection so they could be ruled out quickly. But you had to start somewhere and these two leads were as good as any.

Mike saw the tall, rusty trellis the porno shop owner described. "McWilliams" was at the top in a calligraphy style font. He turned underneath it to a mile long driveway. On each side, tall crops bent and swayed in the wind. The sound of the breeze slipped through the corn like a million whispers.

The house could have come from a painting. It was a white two-story set in a small yard bordered with a white fence. Smoke puffed out of the chimney. A barn was set back to the right and a small pack of dogs ran figure eights around the two buildings, playing.

He saw a man watching him from the window as he pulled up. He got out and walked to the house. The man opened the door before he had a chance to knock.

"A car, huh?" the man said. He had a smile on his face. Nothing to hide.

"Yes, sir. My name is Mike Glass, I'm with the President's office." Glass showed him his ID. The man glanced at it.

"Are you lost?"

"No sir, I don't believe so. Is this the McWilliams's farm?"

"I'm Frank McWilliams."

He reached out and Glass shook his hand.

"What's this about?" Frank asked. It was clear he still wasn't concerned.

"I'm looking for Fernando and Margarito. Are they here?"

Frank looked surprised. He stepped out to the porch and spoke quietly.

"They're at the dinner table. Is there a problem?"

"You've worked with them a long time?" Glass asked.

"Since I was a kid. They worked for my father."

"Then I doubt it. But I would like to speak with them."

Frank stepped aside.

"After you," Glass said. He never gave his back.

When Glass walked into the dining room, Fernando and Margarito were at the table with a woman—Glass assumed Frank McWilliams's wife—and a young boy. Margarito was using his hands to reenact a story. The woman was laughing. The boy had a thin smile on his face. He seemed off.

". . . and THEN I took the drug lord's head in my hands and," Margarito made a quick motion with his hands. "SNAP! Dead!"

"That's a horrible story, Margarito," Fernando said, but he was laughing too.

Margarito took a slow slip from a glass of wine.

"Well . . . most of it was true except the last part. I *was* in the Mexican army."

"You were a nurse," Fernando said. This got the woman laughing again.

"A medic," Margarito corrected.

They noticed the young man with Frank and quieted down.

"Fernando, Margarito, this is Mike Glass, he would like to ask you a few questions."

Fernando and Margarito looked at each other confused. Fernando spoke up. "You are police?"

"Military. I'm on special assignment with the President's office," Glass said. He turned to everyone else in the room. "This should be quick, just a couple of questions."

He asked if they had traveled with anyone. If they had seen or heard of any migrant workers that weren't the norm. They answered both in the negative.

"What happened?" the boy asked.

"Justin, shh," the woman said.

"No, it's alright. You heard about the Terror War?"

The boy seemed to retreat.

"First hand, unfortunately," Frank said. He ruffled Justin's hair. "We were stuck at MindCorp during the attack. The world's turning to shit." Charlene gave him a look. "Sorry, but it is."

"Well, it looks like they are trying to go online now," Glass said.

"Is that why the Internet went down yesterday?" Justin asked.

Glass smiled. "Top secret."

"I told you it was peligroso," Margarito said to Justin. "That two way stuff can't be good for you."

Frank turned to Glass.

"Justin just got on the Mindlink and then ka-put," Frank made a face. "The damn thing broke."

"I was in a flight simul—" Justin started. Glass's heartbeat rose to its max of ninety-five. No one knew. "-ator."

"I heard those are fun," Glass said.

"I didn't need the plane," Justin said.

"Really?"

"I program fast too," the boy said proudly. He didn't know what he was implying. "My friend Jared said I was the fastest he'd ever seen."

"Maybe someday you'll work for MindCorp," Glass said. Justin beamed at the thought. Glass couldn't believe it. Was it possible? He had to speak to Evan. "Well, it should be up soon. We're working directly with MindCorp to get things back on track."

Glass turned to Frank. "We're done." Back to the table. "Thanks everyone. Justin, keep it up."

The boy gave a weird, quick wave and the others nodded. Glass thanked Frank at the door and asked if there were any other workers currently on-premise he should speak with.

"Nope, it's just us," Frank said. They shook hands and parted ways.

Glass got in the car and headed down the dirt driveway. When he was out of sight, Glass pulled over, turned off his headlights and called Evan. This was not in the contingency plan. Evan told him what another unit had learned at an elderly rest home.

Fernando and Margarito slept in a lofted room in the barn. A long time ago the barn had been used to store hay, but the farm only handled crops now, so the barn had become a garage and living quarters for the workers that came to help.

Both men were buzzing from the wine. Not drunk, but another glass would have sent them into that territory. They shambled toward the barn after saying goodnight.

"I need some agua," Fernando said and slapped his buddy on the back. "My head is already starting to hurt."

"Wine does that to me, too. We just had two glasses or so, no?"

Margarito said. "Tequila doesn't."

"That's because you wake up two days later, Margo," Fernando said. They laughed.

The barn was one hundred yards away from the house, nestled up against a cornfield. One large spotlight hung over the double door entrance. The loft had two large beds, a bathroom and a kitchenette. On the ground floor were alcohol fueled ATV's they used to go to the main barn a half-mile away which housed the combines and large equipment used for the farm. On the walls were various antiquated farm tools: sickles and scythes, shovels and spades, heirlooms of the McWilliams's past.

"Tomorrow's going to be an early one, hermano," Fernando said. Margo grunted acknowledgement.

They slid one side of the door open and the rattling of the gate masked the already muted sound of a bullet leaving Glass's silenced Heckler and Koch Mark 23. Glass was crouched inside the barn, kneeling against an ATV. The .45 caliber round hit beneath Margarito's nose and lodged into the back of his brain. He slumped down to the ground.

Fernando saw the muzzle flash, saw his friend collapse, but didn't make the connection before another round hit him in the left temple and exited out the right side of his head, leaving a crater the size of a bloody orange. Glass moved like a cat and pulled them into the barn. He shut the door and went to the farmhouse.

He approached the back, indistinct from the shadows. He glanced across the kitchen window and saw the top of the wife's head. She was washing dishes. He moved against the house to the porch.

The door was unlocked. Out here, no one locked them. He quietly slid the door open, just enough to squeeze through. Glass was low, knees bent, hunched over with the slide of the gun near his head like he used it for prayer.

He moved through the dining room. He saw the top of the woman's head over the countertop he crouched behind. She was perpendicular to him. She stopped washing a pan and put it down. She looked out the window, thinking about something. Glass shot her in the head and swept around the countertop into the kitchen and broke her fall. He put her into the cupboard and listened for footsteps. Muted conversations. Nothing. He continued through the living room into the main hall. He paused to listen. He heard . . . water. Water pipes. Someone was in the shower. He moved up the creaky stairs and they made no noise.

To the right was the master bedroom. Glass could see the entrance to the bathroom and he heard the shower. To his left was the boy's room. There were posters tacked all over the door.

Glass drifted into the master bedroom. The man—Frank—was in the shower, washing away a tough day's labor. Glass leaned in and saw his outline through the shower curtain. Glass raised his pistol and shot the silhouette in the head. The shadow of a man washing his armpit collapsed into a heap beneath the bathtub.

No need to clean up now. All adults accounted for. He moved toward the boy.

He entered the room. The boy was on his Mindlink, seemingly unaware of his surroundings. Glass pulled a syringe filled with Sodium Pentothal out of his jacket. The boy turned, done with his session. Before the boy could react, Glass grabbed him by his shirt and threw him on the bed.

"Dad!" Justin cried. Glass didn't bother to cover his screams, there was no one for miles.

Glass popped the syringe into the boy's shoulder and pressed the plunger. The boy's struggle stopped. He stared glassy-eyed at the ceiling, unconscious.

Glass took two long zip ties and bound the boy's hands and feet. He carried Justin like a bride through the doorway. He hopped down the steps and exited the house.

He put the boy down in the front yard and went to the barn. He found large alcohol-based fuel canisters near the ATVs. He coated the base of the barn with one canister and lit it up. The fire bit into the fuel and the dry barn erupted into flames.

Glass trotted over to the farmhouse. He went inside and doused the lower level with the fuel and dropped a match. He came out through the front door and picked up Justin. The inside of the house was already engulfed—and through the windows—deep flickering orange danced on the lawn.

Outside the dogs howled and hissed at Glass. But they kept their distance. He was the predator, not they.

Ten minutes later, while he dreamt of a vacation he took fifteen years earlier with a stripper he had known (and adored), Tommy Spade's dreams ended forever when Glass cut his throat.

The Grotto went up in flames too.

= = =

It was night when Glass got to the Derik Building. Glass brought the boy to Evan's office and Evan directed him to a pair of Mindlink chairs next to each other. Glass put Justin down in one. Evan checked the boy's vitals.

"Was it difficult?" Lindo asked. Glass shrugged. Lindo checked the boy's pulse. He opened his eyes and shined a light into them.

"I sedated him with Sodium Pentothal. It should wear off soon," Glass said. Lindo nodded.

"You did well Mike," Lindo said. Glass showed no reaction.

Evan put a rubber tube around Justin's right arm as if he were drawing blood. He rolled a stand next to the chair that held a bag of IV fluid. With precision, he inserted an IV needle into Justin's vein and attached it to the bag. He taped the needle down on the arm.

"What's that for?" Glass asked.

"I don't want him to wake," Evan replied. He tapped the IV and watched the fluid drip from the bag. "You can go."

Without another word, Mike left.

He makes no noise when he moves, Evan noticed. *Not even his boots.*

Evan walked over to a server as tall as the room. It was new, backwards engineered from the self-contained Mindlink blueprint that Cynthia had given him for the Tank Major program. Two Mindlinks were attached to it with fiber. He turned it on and a hum filled the air.

He looked at the boy and marveled at what was in front of him. Lindo's eyes teared up. He rubbed them away. *No reason to celebrate.* Not yet.

Cynthia had thought they would find some kind of supercomputer designed to disrupt cyberspace by flooding a targeted section with data. A classic hack on a massive scale. "That would explain the chaos," she had said when she had briefed him just a few days ago on what they had learned so far. "During the anomaly, no program or portal functioned *differently,* like they were being manipulated—that would indicate intent—

they just weren't functioning, as if they had been short circuited. All signs point to a software program designed to overload our systems."

Evan had listened intently and didn't object to her hypothesis. But he knew she was wrong. She was too close, too shaken by what had happened to see her grade school error.

A mindscape is a human attribute. They would find a man. Evan didn't think it would be in DeKalb, he thought they would end up in China, or somewhere else after they unwound some kind of routing algorithm. He didn't expect a boy. But Evan knew at the end of the rainbow, they would find a human because that's the only thing it could be.

What seemed so complicated because of the preposterous nature of its scale, was actually simple. The boy didn't mean to cause the chaos. He just *did* it. He willed his reality into existence. The portals and programs that went dark were just caught in the wash of his jet stream.

The implications were enormous. The boy could manipulate and control cyberspace—at least theoretically—on a level that a thousand Sleepers could not. And it should have taken at least sixty terabytes per second to cause that kind of disruption, and the boy had done it on a three hundred megabyte line.

It had been theorized for decades that the human memory compressed data. It had to be true, because humans only used ten percent or so of their brain, yet they never ran out of space. An eighty-year-old woman could vividly remember her first kiss like it was yesterday. Using all the senses, the brain took memories and broke them down like Legos, only to rebuild again. That was why a perfume could trigger the memory of an old flame, or the morning sun on a calm lake would transport a person to a vacation they took when they were three. The raw data was parceled and shared to build different things. But that compression and decompression was all in our head, in one space.

As preposterous (*once again*, Evan thought) as it sounded, the boy's brain was compressing data and decompressing it in *cyberspace*. He was capable of transferring this ability outside of himself. No person or system has ever done this without a codec on the other side to decompress the data stream.

So . . . how?

Lindo put a Mindlink connected to the giant server onto the boy.

Lindo took the other and put it on himself. He lay down in a reclined chair and felt his consciousness get pulled outside his body.

Lindo hovered. Not above the boy, but inside the Mindlink the boy wore. He was analyzing the boy's brain by using the micro frequencies that made a Mindlink function as sonar. The boy's brain worked differently with a device that worked in the same predictable manner for ninety-nine percent of the population. Lindo thought he knew why.

After Albert Einstein's death, his brain was removed and preserved for research. Great minds of the twentieth century wanted to find out how the *greatest* mind of the twentieth century worked. Would they find that Einstein's brain was no different than their own?

No. They found it was quite different. Einstein was missing the parietal operculum (used for speech and language) on both hemispheres of his brain, but the inferior parietal lobe—which was responsible for mathematical thought, visual cognition, and imagery—was fifteen percent larger than a normal brain.

He thought differently and saw things differently not because of education, but because of evolution.

Evan gasped.

Justin's inferior parietal lobe was thirty percent larger than normal. And like Einstein, parts of his brain were completely different than anything Evan could have imagined.

Had Lindo seen this boy's brain without knowing its capabilities, he would have said either the person was dead at birth or a genius.

= = =

Justin woke up floating in a white space. There were no visual cues to call it a room. It could have been the size of a closet or as vast as the universe. There were no shadows or bends, no hint of distance. He sensed someone in the room with him.

"You're up," the man said.

Justin rotated to his right and sat up on the bed of air. The man wore all white. Justin did too. Suddenly Justin remembered.

"My parents!" Justin yelled.

"What do you mean?" the man asked calmly. He walked over to Justin.

"A man took me. He may have hurt them!" Justin said. He shook from the thought.

"Shh. They know you're here. Everything's alright," the man said. He was short and stubby and wore glasses. "My name is Dr. Evan Lindo. They asked that I help you."

"Help me? No. The man. He threw me down. He had long hair. He—" Justin started. He was confused. He didn't trust this, it felt wrong.

"This man?" Lindo asked. In the nothingness a picture appeared of Mike Glass.

"Yes! That man!" Justin said.

"He's not real, Justin. We've seen the dream you had of this man coming to your home. He came at dinner and asked questions and then left. Then he came back and took you. You've had a serious accident, Justin. You're in a coma. We're at a hospital right now."

"I don't believe you," Justin said. The room vibrated. Evan felt it, but Justin seemed unaware.

"You fell off your four wheeler while following Margarito and Fernando back from the utility barn. You hit your head and broke your neck."

"How am I here?" Justin asked.

"This is how we test coma patient's true brain activity. Your father Frank said you had just been on a Mindlink, which was a blessing. If you hadn't, it would have been much harder to connect to you, to even get here." Lindo looked around at the white space they were standing in.

"Can I see Dad?" Justin asked.

"Yes, very soon. Your father is going to help you recover," Lindo said. "Because you're here, we can now develop a proper rehab program to pull you out."

"What about my neck?" Justin asked. He was scared.

"Your hands and feet are reacting to us poking and prodding. Not perfectly, but that's fine. You'll recover once we beat this," Lindo said. "I need to go now, but have faith and know that your parents are right next to you. In fact, your mother is holding your hand."

"I feel nothing," Justin said.

"You will. In time. We'll begin the rehab very soon. In this space, it will feel like a couple of hours. Your father will tell you what to do and I'll be connected too, but only in voice. I know this is strange, and difficult to comprehend, but you're doing great. What would you like this room to be?"

"What can it be?" Justin replied. He was so confused.

"Anything. A beach with an ocean and jet skis. A house. A toy store. Whatever makes you the most comfortable."

"I want my Dad," Justin cried. He curled up into a ball.

"I know, son. And they want to be with you too. Soon," Lindo replied.

Justin didn't respond. He was curled in like an armadillo. The room shook again.

"I'm trapped here," Justin said. The voice came from all around. Evan could feel Justin's pain as if it were his own. The boy vanished from view.

"Why am I trapped here?"

"It's for your safety, Justin." Evan had to stay calm. However powerful, Justin was still a boy. "Don't disappear. Come back. We can't get you well if you aren't here."

Evan could feel Justin poking and prodding at his avatar. Suddenly he could feel Justin's mind encroach on his own.

"Justin! This isn't a game!" Evan yelled.

The boy re-appeared in front of him. "I want to go home!"

Evan got down on one knee. He saw that Justin's eyes were onyx black and the interior of his mouth glowed neon purple. "Then listen to me, Justin. If you follow my instructions and work really hard, you will see your home. You will see your mom and dad, okay?"

The black eyes and glowing mouth disappeared. Now a small, scared boy stood in front of him.

"I'll make this a beach," Evan offered.

"I like books."

"With books," Evan said. "Be brave."

Evan disappeared and a cabana on a Caribbean shore appeared around Justin.

Evan pulled off the Mindlink. Sweat drenched his body. The kid didn't realize it but for a moment he had hijacked the program, he had even crept into the interior of Evan's mind. If Evan had had any doubts about his actions to this point, he didn't now. The boy was extremely dangerous.

The false construct was necessary. You couldn't reason with a child. You couldn't kill their parents and then expect them to give you their mind. The boy wouldn't wake the entire time he was being used. Instead he would think he was doing exercises to improve his mind at the encouragement of his father. But the whole time, he would be dismantling infrastructure, hacking into secret files, influencing, and yes—even killing—foreign leaders.

Evan marveled at his own genius.

CHAPTER 5
ONE MONTH LATER.

WarDon hadn't been feeling well. His wife had thought it was the flu, but it had never quite reached the boiling point of either fever, puking, or pooing—or the hat trick of all three—that guaranteed a solid ten pounds off the waistline.

It had been going on for two weeks. His days always started off fine. He'd wake up at 4:30 a.m. for his five mile jog, then he'd hit the weights. He'd shower up and get dressed, his wife would have breakfast waiting for him, and he'd eat up and head to the Pentagon.

His life had become a series of meetings, and most of these were now virtual. Every morning he'd debrief the President and the Cabinet on local and global military matters and then meet virtually with every military branch for an update for the *next* morning's meeting.

He enjoyed his job; it was important. But he missed the front lines. He missed waking up on the other side of the world. The smell of diesel. The chop of helicopters. The echo of live fire. All of it. He felt like a woman whose best years were in high school: fond of the memories but tinged with bitterness. He didn't like getting old. He was sixty-two and still strong. His knees were good. He could bench three-fifteen. But dammit, he was starting to look like his old man. When he got a good night's sleep, the bags under his eyes still stuck around. He was pretty sure every morning his spine was fused solid for the first few hours. And the wrinkles . . . he had wrinkles on areas of his face he was certain didn't bend.

And for a few weeks now, sudden waves of nausea would overtake him randomly throughout the day. It wasn't the flu, that bug would have hit. He was worried. He looked like his old man, maybe he'd die like his old man. The Big C.

"We're confirmed for MindCorp tomorrow at ten a.m.," Evan said.

WarDon didn't reply. He stared off into space.

"Are you alright?" Evan asked. They were in a virtual room waiting on the General of U.S. Forces for Iran.

"I'm fine. Been under the weather lately," WarDon replied. Even in cyberspace, he took the handkerchief out of his pocket and dabbed his forehead. *Man, I feel like shit.*

"Flu? It's going around," Evan said.

"No. I've had this for a few weeks. Pink Flamingo," he said. "I don't know what it is, but I'm going to see a doctor. My wife's insisting."

"Pink," Evan said.

"Flamingo," WarDon replied absently.

"You have nothing if you don't have your health," Evan said.

The General for USFOR-IRAN appeared in front of them and they got to their meeting.

= = =

"THEY HAVE OIL?" WarDon's face looked like a blood blister. He was having a bad week.

Cynthia wore a Mindlink. A computer screen the size of a movie theatre made up a wall. "Yes. As you can see,"—on the screen a satellite image of a mountain range deep in China appeared and zoomed in— "the well is located deep in this mountain range. To get to it, they had to drill over fourteen miles. They are finding more pockets of oil in this region weekly," Cynthia continued. "The EU is a mess. Britain and France trust each other less than you trust all of them. The rest of them are bit players. China, on the other hand, has been busy. We found allusions to this information in a Presidential Advisor's personal folder, but other than that, nothing."

"If it's such a big deal—" WarDon started.

"They are keeping it out of the digital space," Evan interrupted. He turned to WarDon. "They are concerned with exactly what we're doing. Cyber-hacking."

Cynthia smiled. She loved information. "Exactly. This discovery is so big they were smart enough to keep it off servers, out of e-mails, conferences, all those things. They know the holes in the levee." Pictures of an Asian man in his 50's wearing a hardhat and sunglasses filled the screen. "This information came from the CEO of the drilling company working on the project."

"You found files?" WarDon asked. Cynthia shook her head. "Cut with the mysterious shit, what?"

"We went in," she responded. "No one else has been online. Not the President, his advisors, not oil workers. We used the void as our guide. It was the abnormality. So we waited until someone popped on. The CEO went online to discuss a completely separate project."

"You got in his head?" WarDon asked.

"Exactly."

"That can be done?"

Cynthia's silence was confirmation.

"How much oil?"

A graph popped up mirroring Cynthia's words. "Ten years of consumption for the entire population. Eighty years or more if they follow today's standard practice of government and subsidized use."

WarDon leaned back in his chair, which groaned under his weight. He shook his head and laughed. "Those sonsofbitches. Smart sonsofbitches."

"Can I ask a possibly idiotic question?" Cynthia said. "Why do you care? They can't jump start their economy with it, we're already adapting to life without it."

"Cynthia, don't take this the wrong way. You're smarter than hell, but you have too much trust in mankind," WarDon said. "They aren't thinking about bringing back cars or making Tupperware. They won't refine this for public consumption. What they have, by having these wells, is a perpetual war machine. Our military is nothing without oil and we have a limited supply of it. We got a lot stockpiled, maybe even decades, but if they got this, it doesn't mean shit."

"But why would that matter now? Everything's digital, the economies are intertwined and we rely on each other for consumption of goods and services."

"You're saying the countries don't matter anymore?" WarDon replied slowly.

"For economy, yes," Cynthia insisted.

"In an academic bubble you may be right, but the folks at the top, the Presidents, Dictators, Prime Ministers, all got there because they wanted to rule something. They aren't there out of civic duty; a *type* of person wants this. And if countries don't matter, why have so many of them? If you got the means, why not rule it all?"

"Not everyone thinks that way."

WarDon let out a huge belly laugh. "You Ivy Leaguers! Cynthia, come on! You've been in cyberspace too long. Where are your competitors? Why isn't your software open source?"

"It wouldn't work if there were competitors," Cynthia bristled.

"You guard your advantages so there *are* no competitors. You paid lobbyists to bribe politicians for favorable policies and you sued the hell out of any would-be competitors if they got within a hair of your patents. And God bless you! It's the American way. But why do you think a country would behave differently?"

Cynthia turned to Sabot.

"He's right," Sabot said. Evan couldn't remember another time where Sabot had spoken during a meeting.

"You told me five minutes ago that China has found an oil reserve and I immediately told you what that meant for the U.S., and Sabot," WarDon pointed to him, "thought it right away too. So either he and I are geniuses or we understand the underbelly of man." WarDon leaned back. "I know which one it is."

There was a moment of silence.

"So what now?" Cynthia asked.

"I don't know. I need to take this report to the President and we need to assess our options." WarDon turned to Evan who nodded in agreement. "As much as I'm ribbing you, I can't express how important your contribution has been."

"Thank you," Cynthia said. She underestimated WarDon. She understood why a lot of people thought of him as a bully, but she dismissed that now as just appearances. She had fallen for it too. He may not be a genius, but he knew his business.

= = =

WarDon and Evan rode from MindCorp to the Derik Building. Evan thumbed through the report.

"Bad?" WarDon asked. He was distracted. He still felt ill.

"I think Cynthia was being conservative. With just this vein, assuming a hoarder's mentality, they have one hundred years of oil," Evan replied. He licked his index finger and continued to flip through the pages.

"How much do we have?" WarDon asked. He was told awhile back, but dammit if he could remember. Meeting after meeting, he had become a bureaucrat.

"Two decades of aggressive use. We have native oil shale that can be refined, but the supply can't keep up with demand if there was a major war. We'd hit a choke point."

"Do you think I'm being paranoid?" WarDon asked.

73

"We're paid to be paranoid. But I don't think they're going to be actively aggressive. To that point, I agree with Cynthia. They've been our economic partners, hell, they *surpassed* us, a long time ago. Look at the history. They discreetly absolved our debt in 2021. That wasn't charity. They did that so our default wouldn't affect the global economy. That is more important to them than land. But their prudence is harder to gauge than a reactive government. I think they're keeping the oil secret 'just in case.' If something happened to cyberspace that made it uninhabitable, if a computer virus was created that could actually affect people—and there *will* be, Don, mark my words—that would be catastrophic and everything would topple. Very few things consumed—other than food and basic life necessities—are goods anymore. The global economy relies almost entirely on digital services. And technology hasn't given us more options, it's dithered us down to *no* options. Everyone, rich or poor, uses a Mindlink, and in that way, there's no diversity. If that interface gets compromised, there's no back up plan. We can't regress to an oil-based economy. There's nothing over the horizon than can replace the MindCorp-based economy. But if I'm China and I just found a vein of oil, I hang on to it like a food ration. It's not my first choice, but it's there if I need it. That can help them delay what, for everyone else, would be inevitable: total economic collapse, rioting, looting and government overthrows."

"Society would crumble."

"No question."

"What should we do?" WarDon asked.

"Expose them publicly. Humiliate them. Announce to the world that they have no problem letting the rest of us rot."

"What will that do?"

"They're as concerned with the economy as we are. They understand it's balancing on a needle. They don't want to use the oil; they want the digital economy to prosper. Their politicians will backtrack out of fear. They'll share it."

"Evan, they're not going to share the oil."

"There's something I should show you that will convince you otherwise."

Evan hadn't expected those words to come out of his mouth, but he was excited. He was riffing like jazz.

= = =

WarDon and Evan traversed the field of server bays to Evan's office. They found Mike Glass seated at the door, his feet kicked up like a mall cop. He quickly stood and saluted WarDon. Neither chair slid or made a sound.

"At ease, Mike."

"Anyone swing by?" Evan asked.

"A tech saw some bandwidth spikes on a quarter of the servers. I told him to come back when you're here."

"Good."

They went into the office. The "office" was the size of a basketball court. In a corner was a desk, a bed, a kitchenette, and a bathroom with a shower. The rest of it was used for Evan to experiment and design. The room was dark except at the center where overhead lights revealed a massive computer and two Sleeper chairs. When they got closer, WarDon saw a young boy asleep on one with a Mindlink on his head.

"You have a son?" he asked.

"This is the anomaly," Evan said, ignoring the stupid question. WarDon's face slid. He turned from the boy to Evan and back again. He noticed the IV drip. A screen the size of a van flickered on and Evan sat down in the other Sleeper chair.

"*The* anomaly?" WarDon asked.

"Yes. What caused MindCorp, for the first time in its history, to shut down a Core."

"Impossible."

Evan put up his index finger. "*Improbable.* But it's true."

Evan hesitated before he put on the Mindlink. "Before I demonstrate what the King Sleeper can do, to save our country I need about two hundred billion dollars and a forum to expose China."

"I'll check my couch cushions," WarDon said sarcastically. He still didn't know what to make about the boy. *This kid's abducted*, he thought. He glanced over to Glass who stood coolly looking in their direction and his heart sank a little. *No, he's an orphan.*

= = =

Pete couldn't help what he felt. He was the victim. His parents never believed him about his uncle. He was just a kid and he came to them crying and told them, but they didn't do a damn thing. He remembered his mom standing up and going to the bathroom like she had had a case of the squirts, and his dad moving his head around Pete's slumped, sobbing silhouette to get a clear view of the TV.

"You tell anyone about what we done, and I'll come back and cut it off," his uncle had said a week later, before he left. Shocking that Pete grew up into a piece of shit. He knew it, he accepted it. A lot of people had a monkey on their back, but Pete had a devil, and the little fucker was hot as fire and his talons dug deep.

He didn't need a shrink to know what had happened: his uncle broke him. Whatever circuits normal kids had in their head, his uncle pulled them out and swapped them around in his.

Pete had seen photos of Uncle Josh as a kid. The first photo, in the programmed series he watched as a ritual before he went out, *was* a photo of Uncle Josh as a boy. That was his type. Strawberry blonde hair, eight to twelve, freckles were a plus. He had found a boy a week before that matched perfectly. And just two train stops over.

His virtual server was a theater. It didn't have seating. He floated near the center of the screen. He was naked and the light of the photos bathed over him. Most of the thousands of photos he had taken himself. He had time to build his library. His craving had developed by the time he was eighteen, and he was forty-five now. He was nearing climax—the start of his night when he would disconnect and go out for real—when the images slowed down. He noticed this immediately because he liked them to flash by in a synaptic overload. It condensed his memories into one pleasure string that looped over and over him. Now it stopped. A photo of a young stomach (James Taggert, back when I was twenty) was frozen on the screen.

His Uncle Josh, as a boy, appeared in front of him.

"Peter," the boy said. It wasn't Josh's voice. It wasn't even a boy's voice. And it wasn't Josh—his obsession had made it so. It was a skinny, pale boy, around twelve, with dark hair. The boy turned and looked at the screen. The images shuttled back and forth.

"My, my. You are a sick fuck," the boy said. But it was a man's voice. "These are Peter Roach originals!"

The boy rotated back to Pete. They both floated mid-air, awash in the pedophile's sexual depravity. Pete tried to shut down the program.

"Not gonna happen," the boy with the man's voice said. Pete's head suddenly felt like a dozen fingers were prying into his skull.

"You have done some bad things, Peter Roach. I can feel them. I can *see* them. You are a vile thing. Barely human."

Josh made me into this! Pete wanted to yell but he couldn't. His mouth was frozen shut.

"Yes, he did. And you had no support. Your mom was a spineless enabler and your dad was an angry drunk." The boy floated closer to Pete. He could see his facial features. His eyes were all black. When he spoke glowing purple plasma filled his mouth. It was as if the skin of the boy was a costume for something more powerful. "But that doesn't matter because what you have done—however you got here—is worse. You have littered the world with the gravestones of boys who now share your same fate."

What are you going to do! Pedophile Pete asked.

End your torment once and for all, the boy said, and his mouth opened wide and the plasma ball rolled out and snapped to Pete's head like frog snagging a fly. And then Pedophile Pete felt nothing. His synapses coursed with data, his mind cycled at forty times its normal rate. It was his life flashing before his eyes, than it was light flashing before his eyes. And then . . .

= = =

WarDon couldn't believe what he had witnessed. He sat down on the floor and unbuttoned his collar. On the screen he had watched two things: Evan Lindo as Justin's father, guiding him through an exercise to 'heal the boy's brain.' And another where Justin's actions in that exercise killed a sexual predator. Lost in his thoughts, he heard Evan (*as Justin's father—what the fuck is going on?*) tell the boy he did great and that he should rest now. The boy asked when he'd see him again. Evan/Justin's father said soon, he would have more exercises tomorrow.

WarDon stared at the floor. He heard the leather creak when Evan sat up in the chair.

"Is it real?" WarDon asked. He didn't look up.

"It's very real," Evan replied. "Pedophile Pete is dead."

"I don't believe it," WarDon said.

Evan laughed. "Oh, believe it. We can head over to his disgusting perv palace and peek in. He's in his chair, eyes rolled back, tongue out, and probably nursing one hell of a nosebleed. It's called a Reverse Data

Push. The boy does it subconsciously. That's one of the reasons he's so powerful. He can put a codec inside a person's head and trigger it to take a stream of data and expand it logarithmically. It's like injecting the brain with a pound of heroin. It's too much, the synapses burn out, the cell walls rupture from the electrical impulses."

"And the boy doesn't know."

"No. I've created a construct that gives him the impression he is doing mental exercises to get out of a coma. He has no idea that those exercises are connected to real people or events."

WarDon finally looked up. He looked like a giant boy playing Army. "How not?"

"Cyberspace works differently, Don. In the real world if you want someone to shoot a gun they have to pull the trigger. But in cyberspace, if you want someone to shoot a gun you can have them turn a door knob and program it to be so." Evan walked over to the boy. "This kid is the answer to our prayers. You *must* get me the proper finances to see this through and then we can set up a strategy to humiliate China. Pink . . ."

"Flamingo. What does that have to do with it?" WarDon felt his head buzz. He felt . . . odd.

"You get me the funding and I'll make it so we can influence the world. I showed you that the King Sleeper can kill online but he can do something much more powerful. He can coerce. But the seed needs to be planted. China needs to be embarrassed and uncertain. It's like hypnotism. The person has to be susceptible. Pink . . ."

"Flamingo," WarDon said. He sounded distant. He felt a migraine coming on.

"I want funding and full control, answering to you only when I see fit."

"No problem," WarDon said. Suddenly he felt better.

= = =

The next day Evan met with WarDon to discuss the suggestion construct he would need to use the King Sleeper. They met in a conference room. WarDon didn't want to see the King Sleeper again. He hadn't slept all night.

"Don, you have contacts at the UN, correct?"

"Quite a few."

"Enough to call in some favors?"

"I'd imagine so."

"Good. I need them to host an energy summit."

"For the King Sleeper?"

"Exactly. We'll use the summit to 'out' the Chinese. The chaos of this assertion will make all participating countries—even those who aren't present—susceptible to the King Sleeper."

"I thought we were just going after China," WarDon said. Evan shook his head.

"We want them all. If China doesn't bend on its own, we can use the other nations to force them. This is a rare opportunity we're creating."

= = =

Twelve years as Secretary of Defense through three sitting Presidents, WarDon knew the secrets on Capitol Hill. He called in his IOU's. He skimmed off defense contracts and depleted slush funds. He blackmailed politicians who had closets full of bones. Within two weeks WarDon had secured the funding. To keep the plans out of the digital space, WarDon and Evan met in person. The President was away on some pointless fundraiser and Evan came down from Virginia—where the King Sleeper now resided—to DC. He and WarDon met in the Oval Office. Evan walked in to WarDon admiring a portrait of Abraham Lincoln.

"He hit every branch of the ugly tree, but he was a great President," WarDon said.

Lindo let out clipped laugh.

WarDon continued. "Back then it was about your ideas. You could be an ugly sonofabitch, you could have knotted up legs not worth a damn, because you weren't getting your photo snapped a thousand times a day, doing a video blog, or on late night TV. Citizens either saw change or they didn't and if they didn't you hit the bricks."

WarDon turned and gestured for the two of them to sit. "Now you gotta look like a movie star, and you got to grow another set of hands for all the dicks you have to hold to get here." WarDon kept his eyes on the painting. His tongue moved under his lips like something was stuck in his teeth. "I wanted to be President for a long time, Evan. I never told you that, did I?"

Evan shook his head.

"It wasn't for the vanity. I got enough power, maybe more power than the President. But he gets to make the final call. I've been through three administrations and while I've liked most of the Presidents personally—except McHale of course, he was a moron—they were better off doing Broadway than running a superpower. The word 'Politician' used to be despised. It was like calling an Asian a "gook' or a black—" WarDon waved his hand. "You get the idea."

Evan found WarDon's exposition interesting. He was more insightful than Evan had given him credit.

"Back in the day, it was a duty. It didn't end in a book tour and a TV show."

Evan realized that WarDon had tobacco chew in his mouth. WarDon spit into a trashcan that had been there since Andrew Jackson took office.

"I just wanted one that really had an opinion that was theirs. That wasn't driven by polls or a backroom deal. I don't even think about it much anymore . . . and that makes me sick a bit. They got no convictions. They're polished like a brass banister on a stairway. They got no grit."

WarDon shot another loogie into the trashcan. "I feel like my hand's been forced because of their ineptitude. President Michaels will be included, I assume?"

"Yes," Evan said. "Less so, but we'll need him to agree on policy. He's already malleable because he innately believes what we believe. Upsetting the applecart will open the leaders' minds to new possibilities. We need them to be open to new concepts in order for the King Sleeper to successfully coerce their policy."

"How does the boy do it?" WarDon asked. "I saw what I saw, but I still can't fathom."

"It's simpler than you think. It's just subliminal suggestion on a massive scale. It's very similar to what was done in 1950's when they'd flash "drink Coke" during a movie. Except this barrage is ongoing, day in, day out. It'll seep into their minds like it was their own idea. But they have to be accepting of the message first."

"You couldn't say "Kill the Prime Minister," WarDon replied.

"Exactly. That wouldn't work unless they really *wanted* to kill the Prime Minister or they weren't adverse to the act of murder itself. We'll see policy shifts of ten percent if we're lucky. But in voting governments that's enough and it'll be a huge edge."

"It's amazing isn't it? Frightening," WarDon replied. "We're taking away free will."

"Not really. We're becoming their First Lady. Gentle whispers in the night. We can't make someone change a view they strongly agree with. That's why we need turmoil to begin the process."

"I bent some arms. The UN will host the energy summit. They just need to know the date. This will work?" WarDon asked.

"History favors this approach," Evan replied. Evan relished history, it was a costless case study, mistakes and victories that could be cut and pasted in any era if you were acute enough to adjust for the times. "Pink . . ."

". . . Flamingo. History's important." WarDon replenished his tobacco and offered some to Evan, who declined. That night Evan headed back to the base in Virginia to get everything in order. He told WarDon he needed three months.

CHAPTER 6
THREE MONTHS LATER.

Xan Shin sat across the airplane aisle from President Jintau and watched out of the corner of his eye with a bit of befuddlement.

Why was he coming?

The President had been acting strangely. Not overtly. He wasn't coming into the office wearing his pants on his head. But Jintau was a confident leader, and lately he was . . . softer. Xan would walk into his office and the President would be staring off into space. He would not eat because of nausea.

That President Jintau had accompanied him on a plane to the United States only added to Xan's growing concern. Jintau had agreed to attend a Coalition meeting sponsored by the UN to discuss future energy 'resource' policies. Oil. They mentioned it last in the document "wind, solar, thermal, nuclear, natural gas, and oil." But the conversation will be about oil. It made no sense to go. Xan had expressed that to the President, but he and his advisors all agreed that regardless of the tenuous relationship of the Coalition, Jintau believed: "Like parents to a child, we need to project a united front."

Xan's surprise continued when every other countries' leaders agreed to attend. All leaders from the European Union. All non-voting leaders of the United Nations. All of them except a few African warlords. With all of the dissent in the Coalition, the importance of this meeting was the one thing they agreed on. Xan's purpose for going was clear; he didn't understand what possessed his President to follow his.

They were on a small plane, but Xan pictured the fuel injectors taking that precious liquid, spraying it into microscopic drops and igniting it with a spark, gone forever. He could see the jet fan spinning out the window and he watched it, because each spin was closer to the last he would ever see. He felt a headache push in on his temples and he closed his eyes. Maybe some rest would help.

Xan was forty-nine and he had served many roles for China. He was a polymath. At twenty-two, he joined the Chinese aeronautical division as an engineer and test pilot. He flew into space and landed on the moon in 2036, the first space mission to have done so since the U.S. Apollo Missions. But while his fascination was with aeronautics and space travel, those days were dead. He might as well have been a blacksmith. So he transitioned his skills and imagination to another division far less interesting, but one that he still excelled in because excelling is what he did: weapons and online infrastructure.

Xan was unexceptional in physical appearance. He wasn't short or tall, five-foot eight and one hundred and sixty pounds. While many Chinese had very distinct, almost sharp characteristics, Xan's features were like antique glass that had begun to sink toward its base. His eyes turned down, his nose was flat and long, and his mouth was too large for his face. It revealed a toothy smile that made him suddenly interesting, but that smile rarely came out. Deep frown lines hyphenated the corner of his lips.

Xan had always been a serious person. Even as a child his mom would tell him time and time again "don't forget your joy."

Well, mom—what was there to have joy about?

Be respectful of your elders!, his long dead mom demanded.

Sorry, he said back. She was still around after all these years.

"Headache?" the President inquired.

Xan opened his eyes. "I'm fine, sir. Thank you."

The President was a thoughtful man who had historically shown good judgment. But this wasn't a good idea. The energy summit was masturbation. The oil was gone. Xan could care less about the oil. As the old generations died out, the new ones would grow up without it. The world would survive. It would prosper and evolve. The 'how' is what Xan feared. The new frontier was cyberspace. And it wasn't a new piece of discovered land—or even a world—it was infinite. And while MindCorp had given it structural order, it was still a derelict society trying to find its way. There were positive aspects, but the majority of what it allowed was for people to wallow in their filth and desires. It had become a drug. Who would guide this new era? To Xan, that was all the mattered.

They know we have oil, Xan thought. While most of the world's satellites had died and burnt up on re-entry, there were still a few up there ticking, and a couple of loops over a certain mountain region in China would show a lot more activity than what someone would expect. It would even show what looked like a pipeline. What could, actually, not be confused for anything else.

They'll bring up the oil vein. That's what this is about. The President shouldn't have come. We should have shored up the ports and cut off diplomatic ties and waited for the other nations to shed their old skin and its nagging, itchy expectations. And afterwards, when the world was sober, come back.

Xan closed his eyes and drifted off to sleep. He woke up upon landing and the headache was still a houseguest he couldn't get to leave.

= = =

John Raimey was held hostage and worse, running late.

"Babe," he said, somehow managing to frown and smile at once. "I got to go!"

Tiffany looked down at his penis. It had another idea. Raimey's eyes followed hers.

"Damn this thing!" he grabbed his wife and pulled her into the shower. She squealed as he pushed her back against the shower wall and kissed her deep, their tongues dancing together, firm and soft, in a motion they had learned over the ten years they'd been together.

Instead of dropping down to suck on her nipples, he picked her up like she was a feather.

She pulled her own hair and moaned as he attacked her with the same passion as he had the first time they lay together.

Ten minutes later, Tiffany moved from the shower to the bed and crashed on the comforter not caring that she was wet. She watched her husband get ready. He was applying deodorant and brushing his teeth double time.

She admired his physique. His chocolate skin stretched across his muscular back. His triceps hung from his arms. Even just after sex, it made her blood warm.

Raimey disappeared into the closet and reappeared dressed in his fatigues. He quickly moved to Tiffany and planted a big kiss on her mouth and then ducked down to her belly and gave her a zerbert.

"You are a bad woman," he said. She smacked him on the ass as he left.

"You like it."

"Yes . . . I . . . Do."

Tiffany watched her soldier leave and for the first time her stomach didn't sour. This was one of the few missions he had been cleared to tell her about. He and his team were supporting the Secret Service at the UN Energy Summit.

"We're just glorified security guards," Raimey had said the day before at dinner. "That place has been locked tight and cleared for two weeks now."

= = =

"My balls itch," Janis said while he rubbed the butt of another soldier's rifle against them over his fatigues.

The rifle's owner snatched it away. He put the butt of his rifle up to his nose and faked a whiff. "It smells like your sister."

Janis's eyes softened and he slowly pulled his equipment out of the locker. "My sister's dead, dude. Not cool."

"Oh, man. I'm sorry. I was just fuck—"

Janis jumped on him. "HA. You Mexican motherfucker! I got you Carlos. I'm in your head, bitch!"

The other soldiers laughed. This team had been together for over five years and they had bonded into a family. Since the early twenty-first century, The Terror War had never ended. There were breaks. There were different faces and organizations, but their tenet was the same: destroy the U.S. Kill the infidels. When the Coalition invaded the Middle East the mess just splattered. They had been overseas for two years organizing the occupation and handling specific missions against high value targets or hostages. But the Middle East was flooded with soldiers, and the general populace had been moved around and stripped of technologies that would allow them to coordinate. In the U.S., Raimey and his team lacked the luxury of support or the benefit of superior technology. In the last four months eight of their men had died. Two years in Iran had produced one casualty.

The twenty soldiers remaining laughed and joked like high school jocks because they had no choice. This was what they trained for. They understood their worth and they understood the absolute cost.

Raimey walked in and while they continued smile, they lined up on each side of the locker room and saluted.

"At ease, sorry for being late."

Raimey went to his locker and started packing his armor and gear.

"Are we taking a plane?" a soldier asked.

"I think we're on a cleared track," Raimey said. The military would clear train tracks so they could use high-speed rail. "You all ready?"

"Oorah," they said.

"Oorah," Raimey replied. They marched out to their transport. It was a nine-hour train ride from O'Hare to New York City.

= = =

There are two types of genius. Imaginative genius is found in people who can, from out of the blue, come up with a previously unheard of or unrecognized concept or solve a formerly unsolvable problem. They stare at the sky, watch the clouds roll past, and then *poof*, they understand how to inhibit the HIV virus so it doesn't attack white blood cells. There is no pattern, there is no focus on research. The knowledge comes to them like God itself whispered the answer into their ear.

Intellectual genius involves research, patterns, and adaptation. This genius takes information and existing ideas or inventions and gleans new solutions and knowledge from them.

Cynthia Revo was an imaginative genius. The Mindlink had been in her head since she was thirteen. Evan Lindo was an intellectual genius. He lacked imagination, but when pieces of a problem were laid before him, the solution—the bridge to span the chasm—assembled in his mind.

Evan was in a military bunker one mile below Wilmington, Virginia at the heart of an army base. WarDon knew where he was, the President knew too, but other than that and his hand selected staff— which now numbered in the hundreds—they were completely off the grid. The engineers and scientists moved around him like worker bees. A quarter mile up and all around, blowtorched metal fell, disappearing mid-flight in waterfalls of fire.

There were technical aspects of MindCorp's operation that were known to the outside scientist or computer engineer. The client system of the Mindlink, the two-way data feed and the multi-aliased frequency modulation that allowed the brain to be read and fed by the Mindlink, those could be discussed and duplicated.

Where it got complicated wasn't in *one* user connecting in, it was how MindCorp could keep track of six billion users connected in. How they organized the data into threads that could be easily tracked and properly maintained. MindCorp had had a one hundred percent up rate until Justin decided to fly to the moon. Before that, for the last ten years, their servers had never crashed. Ever.

The Data Nodes, Data Crushers, and how the Sleepers interacted with them was the mystery that had kept Evan sleepless for the last five years.

Data Nodes were local, regional, and national hubs where all the data of the world coursed through with astounding order. In each was a Data Core—the blue fuses all the data streamed through—and those were integrated with Data Crushers, the interface that MindCorp Sleepers used to connect into cyberspace and maintenance the system.

The Sleepers were the key, they were what kept the system constantly functioning, and their interaction with the system was the big "HowdTheyDoThat?!" But Cynthia had given him the cypher when she had provided a self-contained Mindlink for the Tank Major program. Five years of pain, suffering, and a growing inferiority complex was wiped out in one week of backward engineering.

He hated Cynthia, he supposed, but he hated her like one company hates its rival. It wasn't personal. It was professional. She was smarter than he was and he couldn't stand that. She knew something that he didn't and it gnawed on him like flesh eating bacteria. It was like none of his accomplishments mattered in the giant shadow of that little redhead.

"Banging her bodyguard," he mumbled while he worked on a circuit board near the gigantic black tube of an unpowered Data Core. *It was so obvious.* He wondered about the voice in the back of all people's heads that said mean things for no real reason. His seemed to do that a lot.

He smiled a bit and the very act made him feel better. He heard whistling and he realized it was him. She was an imaginative genius: the upper crust of genius-dom, the ones that are always put on a pedestal. He was an intellectual genius: the grunts, the blue-collar union guys that ground and ground to get an inch.

He was okay with that. *I'll be the turtle, she can be the hare.* The Data Core was on schedule, the King Sleeper rested comfortably in a room a few hundred feet from where he worked. And because of that boy, he had leapfrogged her. He understood facts of cyberspace that she could only consider as theories. And by the time she found out, it would be too late.

Justin clearly proved that innate aptitude played a much higher role in Sleeper efficiency than their education or experience level. There was a swimming aspect to cyberspace, a liquidity in the medium that didn't treat everyone fairly. It was fascinating. Even in cyberspace where the mind was free, there were Darwinian principles that separated the weak from the strong.

Why aptitude over education? That was the question he had asked himself time and time again. It was the way the mind interacted with the Mindlink. Brains were just gooey processors, in the end. But they behaved in ways that no microchip or supercomputer could. It was the inferential leaps. It was the lack of rules. That was the key. This was clearly proven in 1997 when an IBM computer called Deep Blue took on the chess master of the day, Gary Kasparov. Computationally, Deep Blue should have never lost. But it did. Since then, computing power had grown by a billion and yet the same outcome still occurred as it did in 1997. The man could win. Not always, maybe not as often, but much more than he should. It wasn't cold hard processing power—humans lacked that—it was our imagination that allowed it. A computer tried to get there another way, pure math and analytics. And sometimes it would succeed.

Both had their weaknesses. But what happened if a high aptitude Sleeper was combined with a supercomputer? What happened when you gave one exceptional human mind as much computational power as ten million Deep Blues? That was the question. Evan whistled while he worked because the King Sleeper had showed him the answer: Engineered evolution.

Days now. Just days. And the world would tremble in the wake of his invention. It would kneel before the United States—before *him*—cowering and awaiting sentence.

"Yo," a slow, southern voice said above him. Glass.

Lindo was so focused he didn't see the black military boots and blue jeans two feet away from where he knelt. Lindo didn't look up, he was almost finished wiring the Data Crusher interface, a Mindlink on steroids.

"No problems?" Lindo asked.

"No problems. We're all set."

Lindo closed his eyes and ran down the checklist. It was all done. Everything was in place. Tomorrow will be an interesting day for the world.

The chess game begins.

CHAPTER 7

It was a crisp fifty-eight degrees in New York City. Thin clouds hung like kites in the blue sky, and the sun snuck through the rows of skyscrapers and bathed the streets in its golden warmth.

Raimey couldn't enjoy it. He was surrounded by chaos. The Great Migration—when suburban families had migrated back to the cities after the oil ran out—had taken place over the last ten years and it had caused the already massive infrastructure of these cities to bloat like a tumor.

2020 population of New York City: 10,220,454. 2058: 55,873,200. 2020 footprint of New York City: three hundred and five square miles. 2058: six hundred square miles. Twice as large, five times the population. New York had become a sweatshop.

And they had come to complain. Five million frustrated souls surrounded the UN building. Even from his elevated position, Raimey could not see street. Down every avenue he scanned, the earth curved before the end of the protestors.

They carried empty gas canisters and signs: "Where's the oil?" "The Coalition IS Terrorism." "Cynthia should run it."

Raimey didn't know why they were here. The oil decline had been public for decades; did they choose not to see? They were shuttled into huge cities. They were given tax breaks for their useless cars.

When he and the team got to New York the night before, he had thought it would be a simple job. Babysit the perimeter. Watch the President. Look for anything suspicious. He was wrong.

Fifty-eight degrees was the temperature but it wasn't the heat. The energy off the crowd made Raimey sweat. The noises coming from it didn't sound human, it sounded like a mass of howling dogs.

"This is fucked up," Janis said in Raimey's earpiece. His team was placed throughout the building. Over the comm a few soldiers echoed the sentiment.

"No time for commentary, guys. Stay focused. The package is arriving in five minutes," Raimey replied. The Chinese President and the EU Prime Minister had already entered the building.

He scanned the crowd. How could he possibly assess a threat? A platoon of soldiers in full camouflage could be ten people deep and he wouldn't be able to spot them.

He heard the thump-thump of the President's air convoy. Three

Apache helicopters descended amongst the skyscrapers and formed an air perimeter over the crowd. The crowd's hair blew back and their signs folded from the helicopter's thrust. The sight of such powerful weapons turned their wrought panic into momentary awe.

Raimey watched the President's helicopter hover down in between the Apaches.

"Secure the President," Raimey said to his forward team that included Janis. Six of his guys were at the helipad, support to the Secret Service.

"The Package is out and secure. We are heading toward the entrance," Janis said. Normally full of humor, he now sounded like a Speak-and-Spell. This was business.

Raimey turned back to the crowd. Their awe was over. The millions of voices built onto each other into a deafening crescendo.

"The Package is in the building. We're peeling off," Janis said.

"Okay. Let's get inside. Ramirez and Tate—get down to the parking garage and work your way up."

"That's been cleared, sir," Ramirez replied.

"By us?" Raimey responded.

"No sir, by the security detail."

The UN building was under lockdown for the last three weeks. It had been swept by dogs and specialists for any potential threat. Since then nothing had gone in or out. Raimey nearly acquiesced.

"Check it out anyway," Raimey said. "There's too much at risk to get sloppy."

"Yes, sir."

= = =

Xan was not at the UN summit. He wasn't even in New York. He was on the western fringe of Chicago on an unapproved tour of one of MindCorp's largest Data Nodes.

Harold Renki walked behind him. Sixty years old and very tall— almost seven feet—he peered down at people like an ostrich. Harold was one of the original scientists that had worked on the Mindlink prototype. He had witnessed the now legendary beginning with Tom and Jerry, the apes. One of his patents helped make it happen.

A brilliant computer programmer, he specialized in software that dealt with efficient multi-threading: the act of a multi-processor computer prioritizing and parceling data to each individual CPU for maximum efficiency.

Each MindCorp server had over two thousand 1-terahertz cores. A Colossal Node, as they called the big ones, had over one thousand servers attached to the Data Core—the big blue "fuse."

A bloated version of his patent made it possible for all this data to come through the Data Core reliably, efficiently, and—most importantly—with traceability.

The tour had gone longer than Harold had expected. For his information, he would get ten billion dollars—no small sum—but he had thought it was for consulting and sending schematics, not chaperoning. When he got the call that Xan was coming over, his heart had skipped a beat. Suddenly what he was doing felt illegal, a cheat against his benefactors. Harold had excused the conscious staff from the Data Node so that they could watch the UN summit. Xan and he had walked through the beds of Sleepers and none of them even fluttered an eyelid.

"What is this?" Xan asked. They were now beneath the Data Core, a place that few people ever got to see. Above them, the electrical aqua blue stormed and crashed in its huge glass tube. It felt like they were staring up at an aquarium caught in a hurricane.

One hundred feet beneath the catwalk were the servers. Heavy air—at negative 50 degrees Celsius—constantly sprayed onto them and while the heavy molecule fought condensation, a light fog hung over the field of processors like a haunted graveyard. It felt ominous, dark and powerful. A hum filled all frequencies, but aside from the Data Core's constant blue dance, Xan saw no moving parts.

"Those are the servers, memory, the man behind the curtain, so to speak," Harold said. "There are two million processors here but this is a Colossal. What you want to do is a heck of a lot easier than this. You're looking at two, three servers, tops. Six thousand processors total."

Harold rarely looked down at his work anymore. It was beautiful, in a gothic sort of way.

"And that will get us in?" Xan asked. Xan made Harold uneasy. The little Asian spoke quietly and concisely, but something about him seemed unpredictable like a dog with its tail tucked down.

"Along with what I gave you . . . if you do the treatment to the hacker."

"Forced Autism."

Harold winced. He didn't like the term. He had been there during the first experiments when they didn't know the consequences and people willfully volunteered. The results were so inhumane that even the military balked. Plans for further tests were scuttled quickly.

"Forced Autism, Forced Savant, whatever you want to call it. With the right candidate, yes, definitely. They overload the system. Most people are using less than one percent of their brain when they're connected. A Sleeper, like the ones we weaved between to get down here, they use four to five, and they can program real time. A Forced Savant uses 85% of their brain."

"But they need a guide."

"Yes, the procedure makes them erratic and distant. Most of them don't live long either."

"How long?" Xan asked. His voice made Harold sleepy.

"A month maybe. Except for the initial experiments it really hasn't been explored because of the ethical considerations."

Xan's laugh was sharp and loud, in complete contrast to his voice. Xan peered over the rail to the servers that stuck out like tombstones amidst the rolling fog. "Ethical considerations are always the battle cry against breakthroughs. Birth control, nuclear power, stem cells. All things we take for granted. Now this . . ."

Harold shifted around in his white coat uncomfortably. He really just wanted the money.

Xan continued. "Tens of millions have bled on battlefields. Tens of thousands now, every year, and no one bats an eye. But you try to evolve the human race and peer past the event horizon into God's will, and the mysteries that make us, and suddenly it's unethical. The edge of knowledge is always unethical. You can't merit ethics on a few deaths. It puts the individual above the common good."

Xan turned to Harold. "We're up-to-date on your schematics. This last pass and the information you've given me today will put us back on schedule."

"How long?" Harold asked. He really didn't care. Something nagged at the back of his mind. Maybe it was his conscience.

"Four weeks, maybe less."

Piggybacking the MindCorp servers, Harold thought. The stealth program he built for China that allowed this access was so discreet that it would take years or lottery luck for MindCorp to notice. It was possible that they would never know.

"Five up front, five on the back, per our arrangement," Xan said. He put his hand out. "It's been a pleasure."

Harold shook it. Xan gripped quickly, and using his left hand, flashed a blade across Harold's neck. It was so sharp, it took the neck a moment to realize it was time to bleed and then it poured out like the mouth of a river.

Harold passed out after two thoughts: *He cut me!* And, *I just started World War III.*

He died ten seconds later. Xan disappeared up the catwalk past the rows of a hundred Sleepers, up the elevator and out the door. No one saw him. The security cameras were off. All conscious staff were excused for the two hours. Per Harold Renki's demands, fueled by his greed.

= = =

The UN summit was another opportunity for a bunch of politicians without business credentials, doctorates, or scientific backgrounds to pontificate to their electoral bodies.

Raimey let the drone of the slicksters fold into background noise. He was at the top of the conference room. It was shaped like a giant bowl tiered with desks and divided into quadrants by stairs that ran up the sides. At the bottom was the podium where the politicians said their peace. He and Janis were the only two soldiers present. Janis was across the chasm, mirroring Raimey's movement. Everyone else had nice suits, perfect hair, and glowing white teeth.

"Can you believe these assholes?" Janis said in Raimey's ear. Raimey looked across the cavernous room to his friend and couldn't help but smile. They shouldn't talk like this over the comm.

"Lot of talking," Raimey replied.

The room was packed. Nearly the entire Coalition was present with the individual European Union countries taking up the bulk of the seating.

The Chinese representatives included President Jintau. He had about a dozen advisors and young, intense men that could only be his security.

The same went for the United States. President Michaels came with half his Cabinet and a security detail. He studied a sheet of talking points and occasionally glared at the Chinese President. Other countries sat in the cheap seats toward the top.

They were ten minutes into the Summit. The head of the UN thanked the first speaker, who had said nothing useful, and announced that President Michaels had something to say. This drew some murmurs, but Raimey had to do everything in his power to hold back a yawn.

= = =

President Joseph Michaels waited for his introduction. He was as disinterested in the other speakers' point of view as Raimey. His focus was on the Chinese President and the betrayal of trust that had occurred.

No one had expected President Michaels to speak. In fact, he was not known for being a great speaker. He was good one-on-one or in small groups. Town hall meetings, schools, any event that was intimate, where he could look a man or woman in the eye and tell them he cared. That was his wheelhouse. In front of a few hundred or more eager faces and his hands got a bit damp and a little shaky. His throat would tighten and his heart would double up like he was on his morning run.

It showed in debates, but the good thing—as his political advisor had pointed out—was that no one voted. The hardcore Republicans did, of course. The hardcore Democrats did, which was annoying. But no one else bothered. The hopeful and downtrodden had given up. They had heard the words without actions too many times. Unlike the politicians that wanted their votes, the masses understood history. They had seen the pattern. *Fool me once.* Nothing was going to change. There were too many lobbyists, too much big money, and jellyfish for leaders. Instead of a mass uprising, a revolution to take the country back, they acquiesced and anesthetized themselves online. Without the Mindlink, the earth would have been in cinders. It was medication against reality as much as a new way of life.

While three billion people were watching the conference live (and another two billion would watch it online in the next day or so), Joseph's heart pounded, not because he was nervous, but because he was angry. He was angry with China, he was angry with the EU. He was angry with the Senate and the House and the legacy of politicians before him who had failed. So many crises that could have been avoided, not in hindsight, not after the twenty-four hour news coverage, but clearly, crisply from day one.

For the last fifty years the United States had stumbled and tripped over the tenets that had defined its greatness. The Constitution was warped and manipulated to protect the rich. Corporations were given the same rights as citizens. Super PACS fed politicians with unaccountable outside influence, guaranteeing the decay of the political system's purpose to protect the people. Financial disasters and no one in Wall Street went to prison. Again and again, a cycle of corruption unaccounted, just entertainment on the tube while another fat fucking American gorged on mac and cheese.

He knew that he was at fault. He felt the guilt itch at his temples and the shame in his soul. But he inherited many of these problems. The previous administration, and the administration before that, and the one before that, left him holding the reins of a horse and buggy already barreling toward the cliff's edge.

He looked up at the Chinese President and his anger grew when the man he had called a friend smiled and nodded at him.

Why did I want to be President? President Michaels asked himself. He couldn't remember. He heard his name and he stood up and he gathered the papers that explained in great detail China's new oil reserve and the steps they have taken to keep it secret. A part of him wondered, why? Why bother outing them? Shouldn't the U.S. be accountable for its own problems? Is China the reason we are in this bind? We were terminal long before this.

But the politician took over and he stepped up to the podium. He thanked everyone that was in attendance and those at home watching. And then he cleared his throat and tore into China. WarDon had provided him with incredibly accurate data on the date of discovery, the location, production rate, and the expected life of the oil reserve. He listed dates and read detailed transcripts between President Jintau and his advisors on strategies to keep the oil reserve secret. The evidence was irrefutable and the delivery scathing. It was the best performance of President Michael's career. He pandered to become President. He waffled to get votes. But here he listed facts and conclusions based on the aggregate of those facts. His old friend's smile faded when his name was called out again and again as the betrayer of the civilized world. It turned out the civilized world was not so civil.

= = =

Ramirez and Tate were already moving when Raimey had given them orders to double check the parking garage. They bounded down the stairs, four steps at a time, hitting the landing and chugging down to the next floor. The UN auditorium was four floors above them. The garage had a total of eight levels, the vast majority of them unoccupied. Parking garages were a relic of another time.

They hit the P8 landing and threw the door open. It flung against the backstop and the sound echoed throughout the parking garage. Only a few LED bulbs lit this level.

"I can't see shit," Tate said. "You bring night vision?"

"Nope. But I got a torch."

Ramirez flicked on his flashlight and scanned the structure. They quickly cleared the area. They picked up the pace to a jog as they searched the walls and ceiling for anything suspicious.

"They cleared it earlier," Tate said.

"Yep," Ramirez said. He and Tate knew that didn't matter to Raimey.

Except for a few rat turds, P8 was clear. They jogged up the ramp. In the empty garage, their footsteps multiplied into a platoon.

"It's damp down here. More than you'd think," Ramirez said. He could see water damage in the concrete. This building had a while to go before it was unsafe, but entropy had taken hold.

"Stinks a bit too."

"Not as bad as your ass," Ramirez said. Some recessive gene in Tate's German/Norwegian heritage had created the perfect farting machine. Long hours in closed proximity to him amounted to chemical warfare.

"True." Tate was a little too proud of his digestive tract. He once ripped one so foul that his bulldog Jasper gave him a disappointed look and left the room.

P7 was clear. Ramirez, Tate, and their ghost platoon went up to P6. More water, same thing as P7. A few places had cones creating a perimeter around especially slippery areas.

"How much leave do we have after this?" Tate inquired.

Ramirez threw his beam around, covering the floors. "Week, I heard," Ramirez said. "Raimey?"

There was only fuzz from the comm.

"You see something?" Tate asked, instantly focused.

"No, just wondering if we had backup."

"Not with all of this concrete."

"Hmph."

P6 was clear. P5 was clear. The water was getting heavier. Maybe a pipe had ruptured. A green slime coated the center of the garage floor and water openly dripped down from above.

"R-mer-z, re-or," their comm sputtered. It was Raimey.

"Shit," Ramirez spoke slowly into the comm. "Nothing so far. I repeat, nothing so far."

Up the ramp to P4 and they saw the source of the slip 'n' slide. A center portion of the garage was cordoned off with temporary hunter orange fencing. They could hear water splattering behind it. Signs were posted about an ongoing repair to the water main and the expected finish date.

"Well, there you go," Ramirez said. P4 was lit much better than the other floors. This floor and up must be used to some extent.

"Clear all around," Tate said into the comm. To Ramirez—"At least we got a workout."

Ramirez turned off his flashlight and walked toward the orange perimeter. Tate followed behind.

"We should go fishing if we get a week off," Tate said.

"I don't think Trish wants you fishing for a week." Ramirez pushed the orange flap to the side like a shower curtain. Seven large blue drums were wired together. Ramirez saw the timer as it wound down to zero. He screamed into his comm.

"BOMB!! WE GOT A B—"

They felt no pain. They heard no noise. For Ramirez and Tate, one second they were there and the next they were nothing.

= = =

From the outside, it looked like the UN building jumped. The massive crowd, waving around like cilia, stopped when the building let out a groan and a shockwave rolled down the road, knocking people down and bursting fire hydrants.

All of the windows of the UN building blew out, showering the police force outside with glass, severing the head of one unlucky officer.

Already tense, the crowd turned to madness. The old and the young got trampled under foot as the millions in the street stampeded away from the explosion, their mouths bent open, spit flying, their eyes rolling like cattle on their way to slaughter.

Inside the UN building, President Michaels vanished in fire, metal and cement. The floor shot up like a champagne cork taking two thirds of the world's leaders with it. The spine of the Chinese President pushed up through the base of his skull when his seat instantly accelerated from zero to six hundred miles per hour.

Raimey heard an indecipherable scream in his comm before the explosion. *Bomb*, Raimey thought, before the shockwave ripped through his body and turned his world to black.

= = =

Darkness to light, like he's swimming to the surface from the depths of the sea.

I need air.

Raimey hears screams around him. They're distant, muffled. He hears sirens and opens his eyes. In front of him, a dead man stares directly at him, his eyes wide in surprise.

He's missing the top of his head.

Sure enough, Raimey's right. The top of his head looks like a bowl. No mouth-to-mouth for this guy.

He's got no body.

Another good observation. The head bowl is just that. A political advisor now better used to serve someone corn flakes.

Raimey breathes. It's hot and gritty. He coughs and hacks. He tries to raise his hands, but they aren't working. He feels them, but they won't go in front of his face. He tries to stand, but his legs aren't listening either.

Shock, he thinks. *I'm in shock.*

Screams and moans fill the air. The room is a giant sinkhole. Bodies are strewn about in weird places, pinned at odd angles. Across the chasm, one body hangs upside down, like it's auditioning to be a chandelier.

Fire and black smoke.

He tries to get up again, but no go. This is the worst he's gotten it. This is bad.

98

Tiffany.

Vanessa.

He sees them. They are hovering in the center of what is now a black hole, wavering back and forth from the heat and fire. Tiffany has her hand on Vanessa's shoulder, comforting her.

I got to stay alive.

Dark spots pepper his eyes.

I got to live.

Like an old friend, the darkness embraces John Raimey and pulls him down.

= = =

Tiffany and Vanessa sat on a bullet train to New York. Tiffany still hadn't wrapped her head around what had happened. Both she and Vanessa had been Mindlinked into the rally. They had watched the newscast, they had watched the Presidents and Prime Ministers show up. It almost felt like a pageant. At one point, Vanessa squealed when a camera swept past and they saw John looking out over the crowd.

Then the bomb went off. The cameras shuddered from the concussive blast. Some broke off their mounts and dangled over the crowd as the tops of heads stampeded past. Others turned to snow.

Five minutes later, they were out the door heading to the subway station that would get them to the interstate railway. Tiffany threw her and Vanessa's clothes into a bag. Vanessa wanted to bring a stuffed doll—her woobie—and Tiffany made damn sure it came along. Now they had nine hours of silence.

Please God let him be ok. Please let him be fine.

She saw the building explode. She understood that men who get thrown from a bomb blast, just to dust themselves off for another battle, only existed in movies. That's not the way it worked.

Her stomach was lead. There was no acid, no tightness, just a pit that squeezed like a hand around her heart.

John's dead.

She saw a reflection in the window. Vanessa was playing with her doll. They were "walking" down the street talking about what was going on in each store. Tiffany burst into tears.

"Is it ok for me to play?" her daughter asked. Vanessa, so insightful and mature, even at ten.

"Yes, dear. Of course."

"Dad's okay."

"You think?" Tiffany snorted back the tears.

"He's the strongest dad in the world, isn't he?"

Tiffany laughed and the tears came back. John never missed a chance to flex for them. He was such a knob. Such a beautiful, goofy, idiot.

"He's pretty strong."

"The strongest." Vanessa paused. "Do you want to play with us?"

Tiffany didn't. She was tired and she was sad and she was torn apart by her daughter's innocence. But she played anyway. Vanessa took Tiffany to a land where the doll was a princess and they were on their way to a castle. She watched her daughter play and couldn't help but see John.

I don't want to be a widow.

Another tear, but the last for now. She watched her daughter create a world around her that didn't exist. As she gave life to a piece of sewn cloth stuffed with foam. For a child, the world is what they make it. For an adult, the world becomes a lesson in contrition as each dream fails to pan out. John. Her family. Tiffany stared down the barrel of her new reality.

God, I miss him already.

= = =

WarDon was alone in the Oval Office. After the bomb, he had numbly made his way there past the sobbing advisors, screaming secretaries, and frantic Secret Service agents. He could still hear the chaos as the organization pitched and rolled in the aftershock of the bomb. But here it was almost peaceful. Except for his thoughts.

Pink Flamingo.

For over a decade now, WarDon recorded his meetings. For online meetings he used a simple program called "Mirror" that recorded the video and audio from his perspective. For in-person meetings he kept a digital recorder in his pocket that he used software to transcribe later. He had had the recorder in his pocket the day he and Evan were in the Oval Office three months prior.

Pink Flamingo.

He was afraid to say the words aloud. When he had listened back to the tape to make sure he understood exactly what Evan was saying, for a second he thought the memory card had corrupted.

But twice, Evan said 'Pink' and he—in a voice without inflection—responded 'Flamingo.' And he knew without any doubt, what had happened: the King Sleeper.

He used me.

Right after the bombing, Evan had answered the hard line in the Virginia based bunker.

"What the hell happened?! Is the President okay?" Evan had said. He was a bad actor.

"You brainwashed me," WarDon replied.

"What are you talking about?"

"Pink Fla-!" WarDon stopped himself.

A chill came over the line.

"You can say it," Evan said. "Now that you know the trigger, it won't work. It only can affect you if you're unaware and susceptible." His fake shock was gone.

"How could you?" WarDon growled.

"You wouldn't have gone through with it," Evan said.

"YOU'RE DAMN RIGHT I WOULDN'T HAVE!" WarDon roared. "This is done! You are done! You got it? You're going to be a prime candidate for butt fucking when you go to prison."

WarDon heard Evan breathing hard on the other line. "Do you know your mom uses the Mindlink? So does your wife, she's on right now. Your two sons average ten hours a day. Same with their wives and Billy."

Billy was Donald's grandson. WarDon's face bent in horror. "What are you saying?"

"The Core is up, the King Sleeper is online. I'm just letting you know what your family is up to."

"I'll stop you," WarDon said. "This is breach of national security, you have gone too far."

"How?"

"WHAT DO YOU MEAN HOW? I'M THE SECRETARY OF GODDAMN DEFENSE!"

"Who would you tell?" Evan said. His voice was eerily calm. He was unafraid. "You saw what I can do. Who can you reach that I cannot?

Who can you persuade that I can't dissuade when they and their family's lives are at stake? No one. There's no one." He let that sink in. "If you do anything that affects my operation, your family is gone. Do you believe that I can do that?"

The phone was barely on WarDon's ear. His eyes were glazed in disbelief. "Yes."

"Do you believe that I WOULD do that?"

"Yes."

"Good. I will kill everything you love to save the world, Donald. Don't test me."

Evan hung up. WarDon had stared at the phone, his mind devoid of any recourse. The line went dead and after a few minutes he set it down, missing the cradle, and headed to where he was now.

He had raided the President's liquor cabinet. *Wouldn't need it now.* He pulled out a very old bottle of scotch that the President brought out for special occasions, and filled a tumbler to the top.

A one-finger pour was to calm the nerves. Two fingers, you had a bad day. Three fingers, you got fucked over and you were stewing. Four fingers, you did the fucking and you wanted to forget.

This was his fifth four-finger pour. Five times four. *What does twenty fingers mean?* WarDon thought to himself. He swirled the glass and watched the caramel-colored viscous drug twirl around like a ball bearing. The ice had thinned, whitening the middle. For some reason it reminded him of a galaxy.

President Michaels is dead. Two thirds of the world's leaders are dead.

He thought about his wife. He pictured her leaned back in the family room with a Mindlink on her head. She loved the news.

The lights were off and the sun was setting. Most of the room was in shadows. Except Abe. A sliver of light rested on his face. Another rested on Don's, exposing one red, wet eye and casting the other in complete darkness.

WarDon raised the glass to the painting and then emptied its contents down his throat. He put the glass down gently on a side table that came with Harry S. Truman when he assumed office.

The atomic bomb. Who thought there'd be anything worse?

He went up to good 'ol' Abe. He put his left hand to the painting's lips like he was shushing him, like he was telling the sixteenth President to keep what was about to be said between the two of them.

"Would you have *guessed* that the sheep was really a wolf? And it . . ." WarDon searched for the right words. "That not only did it want to eat the sheep, it wanted to eat the shepherd too?

"I put him in charge of a top secret online weapon that no one knows about and he runs a bionic division that has now perfected the implant needed to create a giant, invincible army. And if I tell anyone, my family dies."

And Evan would do it, a scaly voice in the back of WarDon's head said. *He would do it.*

"He had the boy's parents killed without hesitation," WarDon muttered. WarDon reached for the glass and then remembered it was empty.

Abe didn't know what to say. He just stared at him. WarDon kept his left hand to Lincoln's lips. WarDon didn't need Abe's insight. Let's face it, just to get him up to speed on computers would take a year. WarDon saw the checkmate; he knew Evan's end goal.

"This will end with no nations," WarDon said quietly. WarDon took the pistol out of his right holster and pressed it to his temple.

When the gunshot went off, the chaos outside the Oval Office stopped and the Secret Service rushed in, guns drawn. They found WarDon slumped against the base of the Lincoln portrait. His knees buckled against the wall when the round went through his brain, but they kept him up like broken stilts. It wasn't a clean shot. Blood pumped out of his head wound. The right side of his face was a bloody socket. The first Secret Service man got to him and looked at his good eye. That eye rolled toward him and kept going to white.

"Ihm srry," the General said. "Ihm s srry."

WarDon fell to the ground dead.

= = =

A milky light swung back and forth across John's vision.

Where am I?

He heard a faraway voice. And then it was right in his ear. "John Raimey, can you hear me? Can you see me?"

The blurry man turned to people Raimey couldn't see.

"His pupils are reacting!"

Another man leaned in and it looked like he was holding two scrub brushes.

Defibrillator.

The man with the light pushed the paddle man away.

"He's up. His heart's beating."

Is this real? Raimey asked himself. He didn't know where he was. His memories were like still photographs piled together in a box. A static photo of a friend. Him, he thinks it's him, with two women, one his age, the other younger. Bloody anarchy in a building that had been blown apart.

The man above him, the man with the light, pulled his mask aside. Raimey saw worried eyes and a frown.

"John Raimey, can you hear me?"

"Yes," he said in his head, but it came out as a painful grunt.

"We are taking you into surgery right now. You have sustained heavy trauma to your limbs. We need to stop the bleeding. Do you understand?"

Raimey's eyes quivered. He nodded.

"I'm putting an oxygen mask over your face now. It will put you to sleep. Do you understand?"

Raimey nodded again. Anything to stop the pain. His arms and legs were on fire.

"It's good to have you alive, soldier." The doctor put the mask over Raimey's face and immediately he drifted away. The last thing Raimey thought before he went out was that the doctor's words did not match his expression.

= = =

They got to New York. Tiffany pulled Vanessa off the train and they went to a kiosk with a digital map of the subway system. She searched for the hospital and it printed out the trains she had to take to get there.

More trains. More fucking trains. They got on the first subway.

The subway train rose to the surface momentarily and Tiffany saw a few electric cars whizzing around silently on the street. She wished she had one now. Contrary to popular belief, it wasn't a lack of energy that killed the electric car. It was the lack of petroleum to make plastics.

The subway cars were choked with people. She and Vanessa squeezed through the passengers, adding to the frustration of going train-to-train to get to the hospital. Everyone smelled like they hadn't showered. It wasn't full on body odor, more like fruit that was about to turn, sweet and pungent, perfume wafting over an undercurrent of funk. It made Tiffany want to gag.

The hospital was an angry beehive of scrubbed-in doctors and nurses. Ten hours after the bombing and it still sounded like a trading floor. Outside, ambulances inched forward in gridlock.

Tiffany shielded Vanessa's eyes, but through the cracks in her fingers, she saw bodies without limbs and cuts in flesh that went well past the bone. They made it to the front desk.

"My husband, John Raimey, is he here?"

The receptionist wore a communication Mindlink—a phone—on her head. The young woman's eyes were wide and glassy from stress. Tiffany clapped her hands in front of the girl's face and the girl finally noticed her.

"I'm looking for my husband. This is where they're bringing the UN victims, right?"

"Yes. If you could just take a seat." The woman was on autopilot.

"I really need to know if he—" Tiffany said.

"If you'd sit down, we can . . ."

Tiffany slammed her fists on the desk. Vanessa was so startled that she dropped her doll. Doctors and nurses within twenty feet snapped out of their shell-shocked daze.

"I'M NOT SITTING AROUND WHILE HE DIES. WHERE IS MY HUSBAND?! WHERE IS HE?! JOHN RAIMEY. HE WAS GUARDING THE PRESIDENT! WHERE IS HE?!"

"Ma'am?" a male voice said to Tiffany's right. She turned to see a young doctor in blood-covered blue scrubs.

"I just got here from Chicago. I'm looking for—"

"John Raimey. I heard. I stabilized him when he came in. We stopped most of the bleeding. They took him up to surgery."

Hope bloomed in Tiffany.

"He's alive?"

"Yes, but he's badly hurt. But I think he'll make it."

The doctor turned to the receptionist. "Get them visitor badges and send them to the fifth floor waiting room."

The doctor looked at the war zone that was his floor. "I need to get back to this. He should still be in surgery but he'll be out soon."

"What's your name?" Tiffany asked.

"Dr. Marshall," he said and added a quick smile that contrasted with his exhausted eyes.

Tiffany hugged him, ignoring the meaty scrubs. "Thank you."

= = =

They sat in the fifth floor waiting room. It had been two hours since Dr. Marshall had directed them to the surgery wing. The receptionist here had been professionally polite but a dearth of information. John was in surgery, that's what the woman knew and that's all she knew. The cafeteria was open till 11:00 p.m. and the vending machine was near the bathrooms around the corner.

Tiffany was out of fight. She was so tired she could barely walk. She dragged herself over to where Vanessa sat and collapsed into a chair. Vanessa schooched over into Tiffany's arms and fell asleep instantly. Tiffany drifted off slowly, a mashup of the present and the past playing in her head.

= = =

Tiffany had met John in the cereal aisle of a Chicago supermarket fifteen years earlier. Tiffany was comparing Honey Nut Cheerios to Mueslix. It was late in the evening and the store was quiet. Not thinking, her cart was in the middle of the aisle while she weighed her decision. Her boyfriend at the time, a fuck buddy really, had bailed on her. So she had nothing to do and she was out of cereal, milk, and ice cream. Awesome Friday night.

"Excuse me, miss," a deep voice said. She turned to a large black man. He had a scar that curled down the right side of his face in a fishhook, just skirting his eye. Shrapnel from an improvised explosive device, she later learned, but the scar added mystery. He had sharp eyes that were downcast, not quite looking directly at her, like most people do out of fear of rejection. Her cart was blocking his.

"Oh, sorry," she said and pushed the cart over. He flashed a mouth full of braces and walked by.

"Thank you. Have a good night." He went to the end of the aisle and turned the corner.

She found her eyes following his projected path as if she had x-ray vision. She shook her head, the goofiness of it all, threw the box with the bee on it into the cart and went the opposite way.

He caught her next with a box of tampons in her hand.

"Miss?" he said. He was behind her. She froze, horrified that she had a box of thirty heavy flow tampons in her hand.

Suddenly he laughed. "I'm sorry, this is so embarrassing," he said. "I swear I'm not this awkward."

She put the tampons in the cart and turned to him. His face was alight with humor. She laughed too.

"Please let me try this again. What's next on your list?" he asked.

"Milk."

"Which way is it?"

She pointed toward the back of the store.

"Okay, meet you there." Raimey turned the cart and jogged the opposite way, leaving her to ponder what she had gotten herself into.

She could hear his cart chatter and squeal as he took the long route to the milk. She suddenly felt a youthful joy like the moment before a first kiss. She pushed toward the milk.

She could see that he was hiding out of view in the canned foods aisle. He playfully leaned over to see where she was. Finally, she picked up the milk. She heard his cart squeak toward her.

"Hi. John Raimey. Smooth operator," he joked. He reached out his hand.

"Clearly. Tiffany Thompson. It's a pleasure to meet you."

"I don't want to bother you, but the more I think about it the more I realize that we can't rely on fate. We have to go after what we want."

"You gotta just take it!" Tiffany said, snatching the air.

"Exactly!" Raimey smiled—she was flirting. He may not crash and burn. "I don't live here, I'm actually on leave for a few weeks, and I decided to visit some buddies. If I don't ask you out, I'll never see you again and I'll never get another opportunity to do so."

"You don't know me."

"We have so much to talk about, don't we?" he said. She laughed. "If you got a boyfriend, just take it as a compliment, but I'd like to at least take you out for coffee."

"John?"

"You can call me John or Raimey."

"You're awkward."

"I'm told that."

"A bit forward."

"It's a new approach."

"But all-in-all you did good."

"B, B+?"

They laughed. She gave him her number.

His smile lit up the dairy aisle and that memory lit up her mind. They went out for brunch that next day and the date lasted until midnight. They hung out the entire time he was on leave. When he went back, they e-mailed and spoke whenever they could. She thought of him as such a contradiction. He was loving and funny, he was fierce and unmoving. He was hers.

= = =

A surgeon walked into the room. He was covered in red.

"Mrs. Raimey?" the doctor asked. He pulled his mask off and it revealed a tired, pale man in his late fifties. Pale and tired seemed to be going around.

Tiffany pulled herself from Vanessa, who remained asleep, and walked over. She wrapped her arms around herself in defense of the news.

"Yes?"

"Your husband is going to make it," he said without a smile.

"What's wrong?" she asked. She could tell there was more.

"He has sustained grievous injuries to his limbs. Parts of his body have sustained second and third degree burns. He isn't paralyzed, his mind is fine from what we can tell, but his recovery is going to be long."

"What do you mean by "grievous?" she asked. "What does that mean?"

"His limbs are gone. A blast like that, just to be alive is a miracle, but we had to amputate."

Tiffany was quiet. Her ears beat with her pulse. She could hear a whistle in the doctor's breathing. "He has no arms or legs?"

"He'll need you more than he's ever needed you before, Mrs. Raimey. He's obviously very strong, but he'll need your help and support."

"Why do you think I'm here?" she said through clenched teeth.

The surgeon recommended that Vanessa stay in the waiting area and he took Tiffany to the recovery room. John was swaddled like a newborn baby. His face was bandaged and he had a breathing tube down his throat. There were cuts and burns on his face but they were superficial compared to the trauma the rest of his body experienced. It didn't look like her husband. It looked like a doctored photograph. His large body and his head, all by themselves.

He was semi-conscious, but his breathing was deep and strong.

"His vitals are very good," the surgeon said.

"John? Honey?" Vanessa said. She put her hand lightly on his chest.

His eyes fluttered open. The fear in them made her burst into tears.

"I'm here. We're going to get through this. We aren't going anywhere."

He blinked slowly to show he got it. One tear rolled down the side of his cheek and wet the pillow. He closed his eyes and went back to sleep.

CHAPTER 8

Evan sang in the shower. His day had gone from great to damn right fantastic. The world was already in the throes of post-traumatic stress disorder. In Greece, an extremist group had tried to stage a coup. The world financial markets announced they were closed indefinitely "in respect for this global tragedy." And the manufactured terrorist cell that claimed responsibility for the bombing had the military looking in all the wrong directions. "Allah's Will" was a phony, manufactured by the King Sleeper. The evidence trail to them was as subtle as spider webs. It would take time and a tremendous amount of resources to hunt them down. Some of the breadcrumbs led to abandoned caves in the Afghan mountains. Others led to existing cells that were insignificant to U.S. policy until now, but who would undoubtedly pull arms when the army came knocking on their door. The military's itchy trigger fingers would only make the Terror War worse. In a final stroke of genius (*speaking of stroke*, Evan thought, *why the hell not?* He squirted out some extra body wash) all the piecemeal data the King Sleeper had planted throughout cyberspace about "Allah's Will" would aggregate through Nostradamus, reconfirming the grift. *They're like weeds, those terrorists.* Evan beamed. His arm went to work. He had never felt so good.

AND—

WarDon ate his own bullet. Punched a one-way ticket to the great beyond. Evan hadn't predicted that would happen, he thought WarDon would just wisely step aside. For a guy who had "War" in his nickname, he sure wilted quickly. Maybe his war well had seeped dry a long time ago. Evan closed his eyes and worked faster.

For the weeks leading to the UN energy summit, the King Sleeper had sent soft suggestions to all potential incumbent leaders and high-ranking military officials to test for vulnerability and predispositions. Using that data, the King Sleeper began its coercion routine the second the bomb went off. Whatever brave masks these leaders wore to address their respective tribes, inside they were as scared as children. The King Sleeper took those fears and pushed them through doors they would normally not go. The influence rate, if the data was accurate (Evan had devised a program that seemed to work.) was upward of twenty-five percent. He had hoped for five percent to ten percent shifts. One in four of Justin's subjects were bending to the subliminal suggestions. Evan bit his lower lip.

And Lindo was the natural successor to the late Secretary of Defense. The Vice President was a pushover, thrown on the last ticket to appeal to the few female voters that voted anymore. He wasn't a drunk, but he *liked* to drink and he was a womanizer. His father ushered him through Harvard. Ward Williams, the Third.

"A fucking baby in a bear den," Lindo muttered. He was almost done. He could feel it building. He rocked with the motion thinking not about a woman, but all he had accomplished in such a short time. With his left hand he turned the hot water up until was painful. Perfect. His mind drifted to Cynthia Revo. Her tiny body. Her bright red hair. Being over her. OVER HER. He let the water wash over him, a baptism into the new world that he had just ushered in. The crescendo was about there. His right arm kneading like dough . . .

A rap against the steamed-out glass caused Evan to drop his dick. He turned away from the frosted glass door, covering like a woman caught topless in a changing room. Fear exploded in his belly and his mighty five-inch cock turtled up. *They found me. Despite the threat, WarDon told someone.*

"Who is it?" he demanded. His mind raced, how could he get out of this?

There was no response, but the knuckle mark on the glass door remained. It wasn't his imagination. He slid the door open and saw Mike Glass seated on the sink countertop. Lindo had known Glass for a total of four months now and what WarDon had said was true. This guy was ultra reliable, but dammit, the way he looked at Evan gave him the creeps. It was a shark's stare. A disconnected observation of his surroundings. He wasn't cocky. He barely spoke. But he regarded people like they were art exhibits.

"What are you doing here?" Evan looked for a towel near the shower. Glass took one from the counter and tossed it over. Evan retreated into the steam and came out wrapped. The difference in physique between the two was comical.

But I'm the brains.

Evan remembered an old movie called "Mad Max" where there was a character comprised of two people. One was an old, smart, a dwarf. The other was a giant retard. Together they were Master Blaster and they ruled . . . Bordertown. It was called Bordertown. Until the hero messed it up.

The point was, together they were whole. Lindo felt that way about Glass. Either by themselves was formidable, but together, they were unstoppable.

Glass hadn't given it any thought.

Glass hadn't responded to the question yet. He was just watching (or not watching, depending how you look at it). He was just there.

"So?" Lindo asked again.

"General Boen is coming up from Texas," Glass said in his backwoods drawl.

"He's retired, why?"

"He's an old friend of Ward's father. He's unretiring to take over WarDon's position."

"What! No. No fucking way."

"I'm just the messenger. I thought you'd want to know." Glass slid out.

Lindo looked at himself in the mirror and for a minute he didn't recognize the man looking back. He was only thirty-one but he could already see crow's feet and strands of gray. A vein running down his forehead bulged from the news. Another roadblock. He almost felt sorry for himself. *Motherfucker.* Earl Boen was a very respected General. Old as dirt but still razor sharp, he was the last of the old guard. Which would be a problem.

He would wonder why Evan was in charge of so many things with so little oversight. Evan guessed he couldn't say "because WarDon trusted me," after WarDon decided to re-interpret the Lincoln portrait with his thinker and the UN building was now a quarry. He would be skeptical and inquisitive. And he would have access to WarDon's files. Evan made a note to alter anything eyebrow raising on WarDon's personal data drives. But who knows what he could have on paper.

And the day was going so well.

= = =

Two days after the bombing, a janitor who had snuck away for a nap, found Harold Renki face down under the Colossal Core. Cynthia was so occupied assisting the military in the hunt for Allah's Will, she had suspended her normal work routine. She hadn't noticed Harold's missing daily reports.

When she first heard the news, Cynthia assumed it was an accident. When she was told that Harold's throat had been slit, that it was murder, she was beside herself. Who would have done such a thing? He was such a quiet and unassuming man.

She and Sabot were on their way to the Data Node to meet the police. She left a message for WarDon, unaware that he had decided to meet God and see what all the fuss was about.

"This has to be coincidence," Cynthia said to Sabot. The UN bombing and Harold's murder.

"Not enough information to know. Do you really know Harold?" Sabot asked.

"For twenty years."

"Let's check surveillance and go from there. I'd put money down that it has nothing to do with it. But not a lot."

There was no surveillance footage. In a closed system with one hundred and twenty security cameras, that monitored the outside and inside of the one hundred billion dollar Node, for two hours the system had malfunctioned. Smart men around Cynthia scratched their heads and worried about their jobs.

"How?" Cynthia said. Her voice was flat.

"It's impossible," one of the braver employees offered. He slouched like a dog waiting to be kicked.

"Obviously, it's very possible."

"There's no way it malfunctioned, that's what I'm saying. It's saying that in the programming, but there's no way," the man offered again.

Cynthia looked at him and then the others.

"What's your name?" she asked the man.

"Jeff."

"Everyone except Jeff is excused. NOW."

The others scurried out of the surveillance room.

"What do you think happened?"

"These just don't fail. They don't." He pointed to the monitor. "It's telling us it did but that's bullshit—pardon my French. It got hacked or something. There's no way."

"Hacked to shut down for two hours?" Cynthia said.

Jeff nodded. "AND to tell us that it malfunctioned. Dr. Renki had everyone take a long lunch break. Everyone except the Sleepers."

Cynthia and Sabot looked at one another.

"For two hours?" Sabot asked.

"To watch the UN address with our families."

Cynthia and Sabot were quiet for a moment.

"Jeff, that's all. Thank you for your candor."

"My pleasure. I'm sorry he died. He was a good boss."

Jeff left the room.

"So?" Cynthia asked Sabot.

"People get murdered for a reason or no reason at all. He was murdered in a high security environment. I'll pose the same question I did in the car: how well do you really know Harold Renki?"

"I've known him for twenty years! I've had dinner with him and his wife a dozen times," Cynthia said, defensively. She was unsure.

"I think you're confusing time with intimacy. I don't think you know this man at all."

"We'll see."

Cynthia put a Mindlink on her head and told a team of Sleepers to search for anything on Harold Renki.

"I want to see the body before the police get here," Sabot said.

"I'll come, too."

Sabot's official diagnosis was that Harold Renki was dead. They found him face planted on the grated catwalk and when Sabot rolled him over, his purple face looked like a waffle.

"This is professional," Sabot said. They were alone on the catwalk. Above them the Data Core did its aqua lightning dance. Below, the core graveyard curled with fog.

"How can you tell?" Cynthia asked.

Sabot looked at Harold's fingers. Nothing underneath the nails. He checked the back of his head. No sign of trauma, no muzzle bruise . . .

The guy couldn't reach his head. Harold was like a giraffe.

"He gave no fight. Look—his left hand is covered in blood, but his right isn't." Sabot put his left hand over his throat, reenacting what he thought had happened. "He reached up in surprise; I'm sure of it. I would."

Sabot examined the throat slash closer. Very clean, almost as thin as a paper cut.

"There's only one cut," he said. "He knew the man who killed him and he didn't see it coming."

Out of instinct, Cynthia put her hands to her neck.

"Was it a quick death?" she asked.

"Very."

CHAPTER 9

Tiffany sat next to John while they watched a movie in the hospital room. She and Vanessa had been in New York a month. They didn't have relatives or friends in the area, so Tiffany had rented a hotel room. The bills were piling up. Up until a week ago, she wasn't sure if she could stay, and it broke her heart. But then the military stepped in. A young man, Dr. Evan Lindo, had visited John and told him that WarDon was dead and that he was his temporary replacement. He took Tiffany aside and asked about their expenses. She told him and right there he transferred money into their account and a little extra for the next few weeks. His coming had been a true blessing. She could now focus on her husband. Dr. Lindo was coming back today and Tiffany was going to tell him how much his support meant to her and John.

Eric Janis and Raimey had asked to be in the same room. They suffered nearly identical injuries. Raimey's arms and legs were gone. His right leg still had about eight inches of thigh, and a remnant of his left arm went past his shoulder, but both were too small to attach any prosthetic. Raimey, so strong and capable, would now die if he wasn't fed, if he wasn't given water. Out in the elements he was as helpless as a newborn.

Not that Janis would let that get in the way of him making fun.

"Crip, pass the soda, please," Janis said to Raimey on cue.

Raimey turned to Janis. They were in beds about ten feet from another; swaddled in modified hospital gowns. Janis was divorced. His ex called but hadn't visited, so Vanessa helped them both and Tiffany would have them read to her to pass the time. The sad thing was that they didn't need physical therapy. There was nothing that could be done.

Janis started calling them "Crip and Crap," making up various adventures and personas that the "cripple twins" and their "cripple powers" would go on. It was hard to bring Janis down, and that helped, Tiffany thought. Because Raimey was not the same man.

Raimey grunted at Janis and turned back to the TV.

"I'm just messing around, John," Janis said. His voice was soft. He turned back to the TV, too.

"Honey, can I get you anything?" Vanessa asked John.

"A sense of humor," Janis muttered.

"It's not funny, Eric! This isn't funny!" Raimey growled. "Look at us for fuck's sake!"

"John, please," Tiffany pleaded. Vanessa had left to get a snack at the cafeteria.

"I'm sorry." John started to struggle like an inchworm, moving his body back and forth, trying to wiggle off the bed. Tiffany got up and went over.

"What are you trying to do?" Tiffany asked.

"I have an itch, Tiffany. I have an itch and I can't get to it."

"Well let me. Where is it?"

John held up his stump. "It's on the inside of my right forearm and it won't go away. Can you scratch it? Can you? Because it's driving me fucking insane!"

Tiffany deflated. Her husband was breaking in front of her.

"What do you want me to do, John?"

"Nothing. I want you to do nothing."

"Quit being a dick," Janis said. His humor was gone.

"Fuck you, Eric."

"No, man. FUCK YOU. You think I like being a potato head? Huh? Half my dick got blown off man, one of my balls is gone. You think I like that? What about our team? How are they doing? Not so good. Couldn't find some of them, you know. They just 'poofed' out of existence. Tell their wives your problems, their kids why you've been sulking like a BITCH for the last month. You got a wife and you got a kid and I don't have shit, except you, your wife, and your kid. So quit being a pussy."

Raimey's eyes had softened during Janis's thrashing. The room was quiet except for the heavy breathing from adrenaline between the men. Tiffany was frozen: was this how Eric and John's friendship would end?

Eric focused on the television.

"Eric," Raimey said. Eric didn't turn. "Eric."

Eric looked back. There were tears in his eyes.

"You're right, man. You're right. I'm sorry."

Eric nodded.

Raimey looked up at Tiffany. "I'll come back, I swear, okay? I know I've been feeling sorry for myself. I'm just scared. I'm really scared and I don't know what I can do. I've always been strong. That was what I was. I'm no scholar, I got no degree."

Tiffany got into bed with John and held him. His chest heaved.

"Eric?" Raimey said through his sobs.

"Yeah?"

"At least now your dick won't hurt women you know? It will be a normal size . . ."

Eric let out a hitched laugh that comes when crying. "Yeah, that's the bright side. Let's get in our wheelchairs and race around or something. I'm tired of sitting here."

Vanessa came in and looked at both men. Uncle Eric and Dad were both puffy and their eyes were red. She had missed something.

"What's wrong?" Vanessa asked.

"Nothing, hon," Raimey said. "Not anymore."

= = =

Evan was a busy bee. *Buzz, buzz, buzz.* He felt like he was always on a train. New York to Virginia to Washington, D.C.. Rinse and repeat. The King Sleeper was churning and burning a mile beneath Virginian soil swaying the world with his constant whisper. Evan had met with General Boen. He had expected a slouched old man. But Boen, who was in his seventies, looked like a fit early-sixties. Square shoulders, no pooch, his shock of white hair cut short just in case the Corps called. You could tell he ran five miles every day and did old school shit like a thousand push-ups and sit-ups before breakfast. He had unretired from his Texas ranch on the Brazos River and was getting up to speed.

Their first meeting lasted an hour. General Boen preferred to be outside, so they had walked to the Vietnam Memorial. Evan was panting. Boen apparently didn't sweat. They sat down and Evan provided him hand-picked files on the projects he was leading. He focused on the collusion between MindCorp and the U.S. against their Coalition allies and a dossier on the Tank Major program. Conveniently, he left out information on the King Sleeper. They discussed the Tank Major candidates and it turned out Boen knew one of them.

"It's a shame about John," Boen had said. He flipped through photos of Raimey laid out naked to assess the damage and gauge his general size for the Tank Major Battle Chassis. "Have you met his wife?"

"Tiffany? Yes. A strong woman." Evan tried respectful and solemn, but it was difficult. He was excited.

Boen let out a deep sigh. "I'll have to see Raimey one of these days.

It's been too long. One of the best soldiers I've ever worked with."

Boen handed back the docket.

"You can have it," Evan said. "It's to get you up to speed."

"giant soldier that's nearly invincible and has an artillery punch that can blow through armor and buildings," Boen said.

"That sums it up," Evan said.

"No reason to get into the minutiae, I got enough on my plate. You're the engineer, Don supported it, I'm sure it's an amazing piece of weaponry."

Boen suddenly probed Evan with his eyes. "Why do you think Don killed himself?" It felt like sunlight through a magnifying glass.

"I think he felt ashamed for what had happened. He took national security personally," Evan said. His gaze did not falter.

"You don't think it had anything to do with MindCorp and the U.S., a blackmail of some kind?"

"No, Cynthia is on the up and up as far as I know," Evan replied. No reason to feed Boen's suspicion.

"Anything else that could have caused it?"

The gaze was so intense Evan pictured his fat cheeks burning through to gum and teeth. But he didn't blink. "No. I don't know. The world just lost two thirds of their leaders on U.S. soil under his nose. Other than that . . ." Evan shrugged.

Boen broke his gaze and nodded to three soldiers that walked by. "Maybe you're right. Don just never seemed the type. I'd like to meet Cynthia soon. My daughter uses that damn thing all the time."

"It saved the world."

Boen rolled his eyes. "Ehh. Numbed it maybe. I can't get my daughter to the damn dinner table and she's thirty. One step forward for technology, two steps back for society. How much of it is used for porn?"

Evan couldn't help but smile. He intrinsically didn't trust the new General because he had a secret (and it was a doozy) but Boen was a tough SOB. Evan respected that.

"Most of it," Evan replied.

"Exactly," Boen said with finality. Case closed.

"I'll arrange for you to meet Cynthia."

= = =

Now Evan was back in New York for the last battery of tests. Both Janis and Raimey were extremely well trained and they had excellent psych reports (at least before they were turned into talking meat loafs). Janis dealt with stress by joking. Raimey was the quiet type. Either/or, flip a coin. But he was leaning toward Janis. He had no family ties. Evan rode the elevator up to their floor. Two burly men in suits accompanied him.

It was hard looking at either of them. They were so disfigured. Evan had always had a hard time with those things. Deformities, midgets, nerve or muscle disorders. It was all evidence to Evan that either there was no God, or God checked out of this roach motel a long time ago. You see a kid with spindly arms cocked like chicken wings, his head cast down because he can't control his neck and you know what? That God can go fuck himself. The alienness of disfigurement bothered Evan, but more so, it reminded him that life was too short and certainly not fair, and afterwards, best guess, we're just tasty food for the worms.

Developing the implant for the Tank Major platform had been more difficult then Evan had predicted. But it left no doubt that Cynthia was a coding genius. Even with the first iteration, there were only a few unforeseen bugs. They surfaced with his first test with Raimey and Janis. Evan reported them to Cynthia and a week later he had the new implant simulator in hand, officially: "Mindlink Spec Op TM V1.01." Evan was back at the hospital to make sure the implant still worked properly with the candidates.

The test for Tank Major implant compatibility seemed simple. Lindo put a modified, self-contained Mindlink on a prospective candidate that was wired to a tablet computer. On the tablet's screen was wireframe drawing of a man. Evan would ask the candidate to raise the man's right arm. If the candidate had the aptitude, he could do it without much thought. Evan would then go through the major muscle movements of the body. The motions that required fine dexterity were what tripped most candidates up. Move the pinky and thumb of the man's left hand, wiggle the toes, etc.

Both Janis and Raimey passed these series of tests easily. Next was an image of what amounted to a gun mechanism. A loading system that held ammunition rounds was attached to it. First, the candidate had to understand and then manipulate the loading system, then they had to load a round into the 'gun.' Then they had to fire that round and reload another.

Janis flew threw that. It took Raimey about five minutes. But after that, he could do it at a one hundred percent success rate. No sweat. His brain was like a mouse in a maze, a few dead ends meant nothing, because his mind was remembering, adapting, no different than a stroke victim who learns to speak again.

The last test was the hardest for the mind to resolve. The brain was designed to move arms, fingers, piston legs while running. But it was not designed to comprehend superhuman strength. When a person lifted weights and got stronger, the mind adapted easily. But to comprehend that it could lift four tons was an entirely different matter.

"Think of our ability to gauge effort and apply equal or extra force as a ten thousand step system," Cynthia had explained when they first began. "When a person lifts an egg there is a certain amount of effort required NO MATTER the person's strength. An eighty-year-old woman and a thirty-year-old power lifter need the same strength—and judgment of strength—to do it. Until our body cannot lift something due to strength limitations, our brain perfectly handles looking at an object, figuring out its mass—gathered from past experience—and picking up the item. And it does this without fail, within a fraction of an ounce, all the way up to the physical limitations of that person."

"That's why when you think an item weighs a certain amount and it's lighter it shoots up in your hand," Lindo said.

"Exactly," Cynthia replied. "We take it for granted. So the granny and the power lifter have the exact same mechanism until the granny runs out of strength. Then the power lifter can lift x amount more. His body is trained to do it and his mind—which has evolved over the last millions of years—has adapted to what the body is capable of *and* what the man has experienced in his lifetime: the same object and its weight, *similar* objects and their weight, you get the idea. It's logarithmic.

So the man can lift three hundred pounds and anything below it within a fraction of an ounce. That's nine thousand and six hundred steps of weight acknowledgement and processing."

Lindo could see where she was going. While Lindo could build Superman, could a person's mind handle being Superman?

"Now ask that same mind to lift four tons over its head," Cynthia said. "That's one hundred and twenty-eight thousand steps."

"Can it be done?" Lindo asked. He had dreams of a Tank Major army.

"Yes. Not with everyone and not without massive software manipulation and maintenance of the implant and the mind. The mind has to be tricked into believing it can lift eight thousand pounds. We've already dived into this and let me say, it's very complicated, the scope of this work is much more detail and resource intensive than I had originally thought."

"But you're still interested?" Lindo asked.

Cynthia smiled. This was the first smile she had sent Evan's way that was genuine.

"I'm more interested," she said. "The implant works, so that obstacle's out of the way. We are now building maintenance software that a candidate must use daily to manipulate the brain to use the implant and the Tank Major battle chassis to its full capability. They will have to do this daily for the rest of their lives as a Tank Major."

"What happens if they don't?" Lindo asked.

Cynthia shrugged. "Some will stroke out, we guess. The most likely thing is you'll have a Tank Major that can only lift two hundred pounds because the mind can't comprehend lifting any more."

= = =

Fascinating, Lindo thought. The whole thing was fascinating. He and his entourage were walking down the hall to Janis and Raimey's room. He heard a squeal down a perpendicular hallway and glanced over. His candidates were in powered wheelchairs using their mouths to move a joystick as they, apparently, raced each other down the hallway. The Cripple 200.

Lindo's jaw dropped, and for a moment, even he was having fun. A nurse darted out of the way as Janis and Raimey raced neck-and-neck toward Lindo and an invisible finish line. In Raimey's lap was his daughter, Vanessa. She cheered her dad on.

"Come on Daddy! Beat him!" she urged. Suddenly Janis darted his wheelchair toward Raimey. Raimey immediately corrected away.

"Hold on!" Raimey slurred to Vanessa between the joystick in his mouth. He slammed into Janis's wheelchair. Lindo could hear the electric engines of the wheelchairs grind from the sudden load. Their wheels rubbed against the other, a horrible sound, like a nail down a chalkboard, offset by Vanessa's laughter.

Janis's wheelchair rose up on two wheels and balanced on the fulcrum. Raimey's eyes narrowed—he smelled blood—and he snapped his head to the right a little more. Janis flew out of the wheelchair as it crashed over. Even as a stump, Janis squirmed his body so he landed squarely on his back, his chin tucked to his chest to avoid injury.

Raimey crossed the finish line—a janitor cart that was at the side of the hall. He stopped almost exactly in front of Lindo. Raimey took his mouth off the joystick.

"Good morning, Dr. Lindo," he said

"Good morning!" Janis echoed from behind them. Two nurses and Tiffany were righting his wheelchair and putting him back into it.

"You almost killed one of my candidates, John," Lindo said, smiling.

"It ain't racing if you're not trading paint," Raimey replied. Vanessa beamed up at Evan.

"So here's the deal," Lindo said when they were all back in their room. "I only need one of you right now for this project."

"You've been vague on what this project is, sir," Janis said.

"It has to be that way right now. But it's a very important project for our nation's security. Maybe the most important project in the last fifty years. We have a lot of pressure on our nation and it's coming from all quarters. The President's death, the Secretary of Defense taking his own life . . . these are things our enemies will prey on. They'll use this turmoil to their advantage. We can't let them."

"Still pretty vague," Janis replied.

Lindo smiled. "I know. Let's just say that this project eliminates any notion of our nation's weakness."

Lindo pulled out the Mindlink interface and put it on Janis. "I need to run a few more tests on you just to make sure everything is working properly."

Raimey cleared his throat. "What about me?" he asked. Lindo has already explained that Janis was the likely candidate because he had no family. It made sense, but still, during these tests Raimey had felt useful, relevant. He didn't want to go back to the abyss, where if he had hands, a bottle would most likely be in one.

"You're in queue, John," Lindo said. "I might need you in a month, a year, or tomorrow." Lindo turned back to Janis. "Let's get started. If all goes well, you'll be out of here tomorrow."

Lindo began the test with Janis and suddenly Raimey felt like the third person on a date meant for two. Tiffany and Vanessa appeared at the door and Raimey smiled sadly at them.

"Is it cool for them to come in?" Raimey asked.

Lindo glanced back and saw them in the doorway. "Sure."

They came in quietly. Vanessa climbed into the bed and rested her head in the crook of where Raimey's right arm used to be. Tiffany mouthed "are they going to use you?" and Raimey shook his head. She kissed him on the forehead and rested her hand on his shoulder.

"It'll be ok," Tiffany said quietly. Raimey nodded. It would. He felt better since Janis had put him in his place. He had it bad, but a lot of people had it worse. He needed to remember that.

Evan took the Mindlink off Janis and then did a routine physical, checking his vitals.

"Okay, we're good," Evan said. "Tonight's your last night in the hospital."

"What is that?" Vanessa asked Evan. She was pointing to the self-contained Mindlink interface.

"It's a computer I use to test Eric and your Dad for a really important project," he said in the tone spoken to children.

"What kind of test? I'm good at tests," she said.

Evan knelt down and smiled, glancing at Raimey and Tiffany who smiled back at his effort to engage the child.

"It's a test that shows how a mind works with different machines. This thing," Evan held the Mindlink in front of her. "Uses radio frequencies to read your mind or send stuff to it like pictures and movies. Cool, huh?"

"I know what a Mindlink is. Could I try it?"

"Vanessa, enough questions," Tiffany said.

"It's fine," Evan said. He looked to Tiffany. "It's harmless."

Evan put the Mindlink on Vanessa and adjusted it to fit her head. He brought up the test and before he explained what she was to do—

"There's a man on the other end," she said.

"Yes, there is," Evan said. On his tablet, the man started to dance.

Vanessa giggled.

"I'm making him dance!" she said, still not looking at the screen. The wireframe man's legs and arms were moving like a marionette doll. Evan turned off the program.

"Aww, he went away." Vanessa took off the Mindlink. "What happened?"

"The program went goofy," Evan said.

"Can I play again?" she asked.

Evan's head was spinning. Not like it was for the King Sleeper. That was the equivalent of aliens landing on earth, but still. The program was a one-way data feed. This girl should not have known what was on the screen without being shown. Yet, she did. Which meant she got into the program and understood what was going on. It didn't make sense, but this new world was still a mystery even with all the doctorates and technology and big words used to describe it.

"Of course," Evan said. He packed his things. "Soon."

He ruffled her hair. He would come back with a more relevant test. Maybe she was one in a hundred, maybe after testing some other subjects he would find out this was the norm. But he didn't think so. Raimey tested well . . . Evan looked at Tiffany. How would she test? He needed more subjects to understand what made someone unique before he could leap to conclusions.

Evan told Janis to pack his things and said goodbye. He didn't need to, but he would come back to test Raimey. If his daughter were there again, what the hell, maybe he'd test her too.

= = =

"How you doing?" Raimey asked Janis. It was midnight and neither could sleep. Tiffany and Vanessa had left hours before and Raimey and Janis had been quiet for the last hour, letting the television do the talking.

"I'm good, I'm curious to see what all this testing is about," Janis said.

"I'm happy for you, man. It sounds like it might be something very cool."

"Who knows? He couldn't have been more vague. Maybe I'm going to be the world's most efficient secretary," Janis said with a laugh.

"Whatever gets us out of here," Raimey said.

"It sounds like you'll be next," Janis said.

Raimey nodded and turned back to the TV. "Thanks for setting me straight, Eric."

"Ah, man. It was nothing."

"Not true, don't say that. It's too easy not to count my blessings. I'm not saying this isn't tough, I'm not saying I know what my next steps are, but you're right."

"It's either live or die."

"Yep, live or die, choose one," Raimey said. "I know I don't have to say it, but I always got your back. I hope we'll be working together soon, but if you ever need anything, I'm here for you."

"Same goes."

Raimey woke up the next morning when they wheeled Janis out of the room. They said goodbye, knowing that either they would talk soon or possibly never again. The project was top secret, the location unknown. There were a lot of people in Raimey's past that he wished he could see again. But they were elsewhere, some with different names, some with different faces. The constant Raimey had was his family. The rest of the world was slick like oil, slipping through his fingers, always flowing away. He had chosen this life, he had known what he signed up for, but watching his best friend get wheeled out, never knowing if the eye contact they now shared would ever be shared again, filled Raimey with melancholy.

Janis left, the door closed, and now Raimey had to face the world without his friend's bulletproof humor. He had to face the world with determination because his family deserved it—and more—they needed it. Raimey fell asleep and dreamed of a field of flowers, his daughter's voice just over a hill calling for him, and the sensation of being whole. Even asleep, he knew it was just a dream.

CHAPTER 10

Janis felt his hands. He didn't feel the air current, he didn't feel hot or cold, but he sensed the movement, the connection of his brain to a limb that he could move. That he knew, rationally, didn't exist. His eyes focused on the two shapes hovering over him: Evan Lindo and Cynthia Revo. They were grinning ear-to-ear.

"I take it I'm alive," Janis said with a thick tongue.

"Better than that," Evan said.

In the last eight weeks Janis had had two major surgeries. The first procedure culled him down to fit into the Tank Major battle chassis. They removed the majority of his large intestine, his stomach, two thirds of his liver and cut down his spine five inches from the bottom. They removed his shoulder joints and cut the lower two thirds of his pelvic bone, leaving the upper portion in the shape of a halo. They removed his penis.

Janis, who had been six feet tall and weighed two hundred and twenty-five pounds the day of the UN bombing, was now a head attached to a body the size of a sack of potatoes. He weighed eighty pounds.

He would never eat food again. He was fed intravenously with a high calorie/low waste nutrient solution. What left his colon and kidneys was cell waste, nothing more. With antibiotics and steroids, his body healed quickly. He was not allowed to look in a mirror; military psychologists forbade it. He was in their care two hours a day.

When his body had healed to where he could be put under again, Eric went back in for the spinal fusion surgery. The torque and power of the battle chassis was too much to strap him in like a kid riding a rollercoaster. The body would bludgeon and bruise from the g-forces of the suit in battle, both in what it would deliver to a target and what the suit would be targeted with. The only way to keep the human component alive was to mount it directly to a shock-absorbing platform that was then mounted into the chassis. In the platform the body was suspended in a shock absorbing gel, floating like a baby in a womb. The suspension platform was then hard mounted to the battle chassis with both vertical and horizontal suspension, guided by a computer that monitored the movement with gyroscopes that adapted the suspension platform for tilt and roll. The battle chassis moved around the suspension platform, not the other way around. For Eric, he would never feel the jarring reality of his body around him. It would feel to him like he was on a raft gliding over rolling waves.

Once the spine was fused to the suspension platform it would be a part of his body for the rest of his life. The fusion was painful. Not only were quarter inch pins put in each vertebra, they were then connected together by a rod that put Janis in perfect posture. He could no longer move his back.

It took Eric three weeks to recover from the spinal surgery. The pain was masked with drugs and a physician induced coma. If it weren't, if a dose was forgotten in the middle of the night, or the IV got crimped against the bed, his body would realize the trauma it had received and he would go into cardiac arrest. He was kept alive by the numbing properties of narcotics.

At three weeks they began to bring him out of the coma. When they saw he was coming to, they connected the implant into the back of the suspension platform. The modified Mindlink connected into the spine through the platform and hijacked the nerves that would normally be used to raise a leg, wiggle a toe, or give someone the finger.

He woke up with his brain already adapting to the implant. They had him connected to a computer and while his body was just a bag of blood, bone, and organs—on the screen—the fully limbed wire frame figure his mind was connected to moved like a man regaining consciousness: his arms raised and lowered, they went to brush his head. His legs rubbed together like they were starting a slow fire. His toes curled and straightened. As far as his mind was concerned, his body was whole.

Cynthia and Evan hardly left Eric's side. Cynthia hadn't been away from her home this long in ten years, but she couldn't tear herself away. She didn't understand the feeling of wonderment that had come over her through this process, but it was the same as a woman giving birth to a child. She was in awe of her own mind, her own will, her own ability to take this man who was nothing and turn him into a lord of war.

She and Evan had become, if not friends, respectful of the other's intellect. The Tank Major design was brilliant and Cynthia couldn't ignore the mind behind it. Sabot had seen this slow thaw and it made him uneasy—he didn't trust Evan—and jealous. For all Sabot had, he didn't have Cynthia's mind. He would always be a companion that Cynthia would have to dumb down to. Day-to-day it wasn't an issue. In their bedroom, the intellectual contrast never crept in. But after meetings with her scientists and engineers, she would explain what they had covered in metaphors, and that was enough for Sabot to understand that while she loved him, he was not a peer.

Lindo was, and in some areas, superior. The Tank Major program was an indication of that. And now they were working side-by-side, leaning over the bed of a man who had been reduced to a human bowling pin wrapped in gauze, with a web of wires shooting out from underneath. And they celebrated this monstrosity as if they had added and not taken away.

Sabot's face was as placid as a wax figurine. Lindo glanced at him from over the hospital bed and read nothing, par for the course for a soldier who could have been a professional poker player. But Sabot was in turmoil. He didn't like Evan. He saw the oily slick behind the eyes and he knew that Evan was a calculating personality, his comments and responses weighed and measured for the greatest affect. And those men were dangerous. They were manipulators.

He had told Cynthia as much weeks into the project and she had dismissed him.

"I can handle Evan," she replied. She was programming using the Mindlink. On a nearby screen, code scrolled upward faster than anyone could type. "He came to me, not the other way around."

He didn't understand Cynthia's obsession with this project. Either she didn't understand what she was building, or worse, she knew exactly what it was. And that meant that Sabot didn't know her as well as he thought.

Sabot had come from poverty. He had learned young that emotion was weakness and a gang would beat you up just to hear you cry. When Cynthia hired him, suddenly he was immersed in the company of the most powerful men and women in the world and their peculiar trait was one they shared with the masses that worshipped them: they forgot they were human. In the projects, strength and resolve were camouflage. Inside they all knew they were nothing. The wealthy were the opposite. They were so validated by their greatness that it never occurred to them that they could be wrong. Cynthia should have been too smart to fall into this trap. Yet here she was, evolving the art of war in a world that needed no more.

He waited for her to look up at him, throw a wink or a smile, or even take a few minute break so they could talk a bit. But she didn't. She was focused on her affront squirming in the hospital bed.

Sabot made a decision. He moved away from the window and felt the cold kiss of the outside world, the *real* world, retract its lips. He was tired of men playing God. Suddenly everything felt so pointless. The world was run by the insane, by the inane, that had everything but still wanted more—which showed they *shouldn't be there*. They weren't leaders, they were bottom feeders who learned to swim on their back, sucking all the light and hope from the world for the temporary feeling of levity. For the temporary feeling of relevance.

He looked at Cynthia and didn't know her. He looked at Evan Lindo and knew him perfectly. He looked at Eric Janis and a tear welled in his eye. He was a lab rat, convinced if he did right the cheese would be his.

He didn't know why the fuck he was here. Sabot walked out of the room, down the hall, and took the four flights of stairs to the main level. He left the Derik Building and walked five miles to a hotel. He had no home, but now he had a place to sleep.

He would talk to Cynthia tomorrow and she wouldn't understand, but that was fine. His mom was still alive, so was his sister. When was the last time he had seen them? Two months? No . . . it had been four.

He would see them tomorrow, stay for a week, listen. Listen to his mom. *Really* listen. Ask his sister what she's been up to. Follow up with more questions so he could hear her voice. The big stuff isn't important. We all turn to dust. The big stuff isn't big at all, in a galaxy of a billion stars, in a universe of a billion galaxies. With other worlds that have surpassed ours a million years before and would never know our failure. And other worlds awash in primordial ooze, sorting out the gift of life from the rubble and slime.

Line up the sight and pull the trigger, when the earth is gone, the universe won't tear. Smile. Be happy. Because the end is near.

= = =

Mohammed Jawal was in a New York safe house when the UN was bombed. He was connected into the news feeds and camera feeds just like everyone else. While others watched in horror when the UN collapsed into itself and the millions of privileged Americans crushed one another while fleeing, Mohammed cried. He thanked Allah. He blessed whoever had caused this beautiful wreckage.

The bombing invigorated his army and bold new plans came from it. While the media called their attacks on MindCorp "failed attempts," they were all successful. Mohammed wanted an air of dread. That was terrorism's greatest strength: perceived randomness. That no one was safe. He had infiltrated capitalism's most powerful institution and almost lopped the head off its queen. Now that queen would only focus on her well-being. She would focus on her kingdom. That left the government.

Dread. Had they ever felt it? They would know it now. The new plan was insidious but Mohammed's personal feelings had little to do with his objectives. They were days away from killing the extended families of military and political leaders. Grandchildren. Sons and daughters. Living grandparents. For some, close friends and neighbors.

Collateral damage. That's what the Coalition called it when they bombed the Middle Eastern towns, destroying whole residential blocks. Or when children, so frightened they peed themselves, were cut down by gunfire when they ran into the middle of a firefight. It was an accepted part of war. The military wrote reports on it. They discussed it in air-conditioned rooms while drinking coffee. But they had never felt it. They had never pulled aside rubble until their hands were raw searching for their only son. They had never been handed unrecognizable remains and told it was their mother. But now they would. They would finally feel the collateral damage of their war. The tangible agony of innocent lives lost. The question "WHY?" looping their brain in a harpy's scream, driving them insane.

Branches of the Western Curse communicated and coordinated through a shareware application that served no purpose but to send and receive imbedded messages. The shareware was 'lost' in that it had no portal. It could only be accessed for programming, as if it were still a work in progress not yet ready for public consumption. Functional code bookended the messages and leapfrogged over them. From the outside it was an incomplete, but properly coded piece of shareware. Internally, it was a way to discretely exchange messages that were untraceable to a source when it was not in use. Mohammed pictured it floating in space like a lone, dark asteroid.

But someone had broken in and requested Mohammed Jawal by name.

"It's a trap," one of Mohammed's officers had said.

But Mohammed didn't think so. The information in the message could be used against this person too easily. Even without verification, if it were anonymously sent to the media, the spotlight on this public officer would be so intense his hair would singe.

Mohammed didn't know how this man knew of him, but it appeared this individual had paid attention for some time. The man wanted to meet virtually, something that Mohammed and the rest of the officers forbade. But if this man were an ally, his resources could change everything. The UN bombing had thrown the world on an awkward axis, like a toy top wobbling as it lost its spin. If there was a time to be bold, it was now.

Nothing is free, Mohammed thought to himself. Mohammed could connect from anywhere; it didn't have to be at his safe house. In fact, he preferred it be somewhere public where an ambush would lead into a throng of civilians. He could have guards around the perimeter; that would make sense. The majority of the Western Curse did not look like Mohammed. They were clean-cut, dark skin, light skin, men and women. This, once again, was not about religion, but about equity. Cause and effect, an eye-for-an-eye.

After an hour of prayer and three hours of meditation, Mohammed went online and put a message into their unfinished shareware. He would meet this man who promised resources. He would meet him for five minutes and if that went well, they could plan accordingly. He'd send the location one minute before they were to meet via the shareware. Thirty seconds after it was posted, the time and place would be deleted.

What does 'Western' mean? Mohammed reflected. Almost the entire world was westernized. He had always equated it to a greedy, self-imposing ideology. He had given it an image and form, the U.S. occupying the majority of it. But was it an antiquated term, like 'terrorist'? What if people that were a part of "Western" society wanted it to burn as well? Was the enemy of my enemy my friend? *Or am I looking to not toil, to find the easy way . . . am I greeting the same monster in a different cloak?*

It took Mohammed time to find sleep.

= = =

Mohammed was in a Thai discothèque. It was modeled after discos from the 1970's. Barry White—Mohammed knew the name because the information came to him through the Mindlink—sang about love in his smooth baritone. On the dance floor, beautiful Asian women tranced. Men bobbed through the crowd, some with rhythm, most not. Everyone was dressed according to the time period. Bell-bottoms, afros, long hair, flowered shirts and hints of hippy. Cigarette smoke hung in the air.

The place was authentically filthy but Mohammed didn't worry about germs. It was a high-resolution texture, a design choice, nothing more. You could fuck anyone, you could take enough drugs to kill an elephant, you could even lick the toilet seat if you like, and nothing of consequence would ever come your way. Unless you wanted it to: there were programs that allowed a person to experience every disease known to man.

Mohammed didn't like how he felt as he moved through the crowd. He wanted to hate the decadence, the sexual casualness, but he caught himself looking at the women, he caught himself feeling the music. Not dancing, nothing silly, but the groove of it vibrating through him like a second heartbeat.

Woman watched him as he slid by, the path through the crowd tight and ever changing. He was looking for a tall black woman who would be toward the back of the club. He was a medium size white man with muttonchops, a mustache, a green sleeveless vest and bell-bottoms.

He saw the woman. She had a short afro and perfect dark skin. She leaned against a wall ignoring a very drunk white kid about six inches shorter than her. As he approached, it was clear to the woman who he was and he heard her tell the drunk kid to beat it.

"Hello," she said. Up close her eyes had a sad quality, almost like they were melting. Her voice was flat and lifeless. The woman gestured for them to sit at a nearby table.

"I'm breaking a lot of rules," Mohammed said after they were seated.

"Rules you created," she said with a smile, but it was cold. It was clear that this wasn't the "person."

"Rules nonetheless," Mohammed said. "You have five minutes."

"I only need one," the woman said. "I am obviously not a supermodel and you aren't a little white guy, let's just get that out of the way."

Mohammed nodded.

"Is your focus mostly on the United States?" the woman asked. "*The Western Curse* would seem to indicate that, but I understand that you are a patriot of your home country. Iran is occupied by many forces."

"Tell me what you want," Mohammed asked dismissively.

"I don't share your political view but I can empathize with it." She played with a discarded straw left on the table. "But a war is coming that's much more important than the one you are meddling in."

Mohammed started to interrupt and the woman's eyes shot up. They had changed. For a moment they were Asian and the fire in them caused Mohammed to back down.

"World War III is coming, Mohammed. It'll be a quiet little war—most of these people will never know—but it will decide the fate of humanity. Do you know what all of this is?"

The woman gestured to the bar, to the people dancing around them.

"It's a new universe. A place where truly anything is possible. A fresh start where all the mistakes we've made as a civilization can be righted. But it needs a steward and that day is fast upon us."

"This world is false. We can save the real one," Mohammed said.

The woman shook her head. "Not without this. You know where we were headed before the Mindlink. Society was going to eat itself. It's no secret. We've seen what we become when we're scared. But look at us now. In the last ten years, vehicle pollution has gone down to zero. We've diversified our power needs with clean or near clean energy. Physical possessions no longer matter so manufacturing has gone back to the essentials. Already, nature is reclaiming lands around the mega-cities. The Mindlink has turned earth into an apartment and that's *good*. You may empathize with your homeland, but you wouldn't live there. You're appalled by the Coalition, understandably so, but you are Western-educated, you've lived too long as Westerners do. You'd go back to caves? Maybe shepherd some sheep?"

The little white guy looked angry. The woman pointed her index finger to the table.

"This is *all* that matters. For the last one hundred years, scientists, philosophers and dreamers have looked to the stars. They saw man expanding outward. But the stars are *here*. The shared minds and the unlimited potential *inward* is our expansion. I don't think we'll ever leave earth. I don't think there's anything out there that justifies the cost. Why search God's universe when we can create our own?

"I don't deny the atrocities that have befallen the Middle East, but let's say you succeed. What next? You'll be hunted, that much is guaranteed. And you'll be found because someone around you will rat you out for money or amnesty. What about your country? You haven't been there in fifteen years and let me tell you, it's over. It's a wasteland, sucked dry and forgotten. Nothing will be re-built there by your enemies or otherwise. At this point, if you asked the Coalition nicely, they'd probably give it to you. Your cause is thirty years too late, Mohammed."

"What do you want?" Mohammed asked again.

The woman put the straw down. "Ten years ago, we, the Chinese, smuggled multiple caches of weapons and explosives into the United States. Not a shipping crates worth, I'm talking enough to start—and finish—wars."

"Why?"

"Because we could. Oil was running out and we had to plan for the future. Think of it as the inverse of a bomb shelter." The woman smiled and sat back. "I don't need you right now, but I may in the future. I'll be forthright: I want to compel you. I want to provide enough resources— weapons—so that you can't possibly turn my offer away. In exchange, you owe me. If I die, you owe my country or my successor."

"What kind of weapons?" Mohammed asked. Their own weapons were useful, but not sophisticated. He had a couple of Browning .50 caliber machine guns, a thousand assault rifles of various origin, and explosives; the most exotic was about one hundred pounds of C-4, the rest were created by his chemists, mostly fertilizer bombs and dynamite.

"Ahh, interested, right?" Xan/the black woman said. "Everything, barring vehicles. Any conventional weapon you can think of and their components. The most advanced body armor for your soldiers. Chemical agents, their delivery systems, AND . . ." Xan drummed the table for the build up, ". . . a few portable toys that have the habit of leaving mushroom clouds."

"How?" Mohammed was beside himself. Chemical? Nuclear?

The woman leaned toward him. Her eyes were Asian again. "The IOU isn't bringing in my mail while I'm away, Mohammed. Many of your soldiers will die. Maybe all. But those that live—I highly recommend you don't lead the charge by the way—will benefit greatly from this arrangement. This isn't a temporary partnership, but a beginning. I've read your books, I've watched your interviews and I understand your position. But when has an idealist won? When has 'right' ever had anything to do with it? You need me to make your cause relevant, I need you to secure my country and this world's future. But if you agree, there is no going back. I can promise one thing, we are dealing futures in life and death. Yours and mine are included. But is that such a large cost for the universe?"

Xan paused. He was done with his pitch.

Mohammed sat thoughtfully, regarding the beautiful black woman who had just offered him the world. "How can I trust you?" he finally asked.

"I will deposit five hundred million dollars into the account of your choosing as a show of goodwill. I will also provide a small cache of weapons so you can see how you'll be equipped. You have to lay low now. No more attacks on MindCorp. Nothing. The government's got their hands full searching for Allah's Will. This works with our plans. Be forgotten. They'll remember you soon enough."

= = =

Xan woke satisfied with his first encounter with Mohammed. He was at a military base located in northeast Beijing, a city bloated like all others in the world because of the oil crisis. The base was at the edge of the sprawling, smog-choked city that seemed to burn red regardless of the day. It was as if continental drift had broken China apart like a puzzle. From one window of his office he saw the city expanse dip over the horizon. From the other side of his office he saw farmers working land with their donkeys and plows.

Xan sat up from his reclined chair. It was a Sleeper chair and the more he was online, the more he appreciated it. It had electrodes built into the form fitted, reclined cushions to stimulate the muscles. A hole was cut out under the anus so that the bowels could evacuate without issue. When the chair sensed a finished bowel movement, a bidet shot up water. A funnel was attached to the penis and an IV was inserted to provide nutrients. He hadn't been under long enough to need these perks, but he would soon. This was the first time he had successfully used a Forced Autism candidate. He had done it from his office, but deeper in the base, in a section that once was an airplane hanger, was the Data Core that Dr. Renki had helped design and ultimately died for.

He stretched his arms to the ceiling and then walked across his large office to the kitchen. Coffee was brewing and he got himself a cup. Xan thought it was odd how Mohammed had changed his appearance so drastically. It was obvious that he didn't understand how the digital tail, which connected a person in cyberspace to their real world location, could be traced. He could be a talking giraffe and his physical location could be found in a millisecond.

But they could not find Xan or even know it was he who spoke. While Xan wasn't a powerful Sleeper without hijacking the mental horsepower of a Forced Autistic, he understood cyberspace and he knew the tricks. He looked like a black woman because he had paid a mercenary to wire a brain dead woman in the U.S. for him to connect through. The mind could be a CPU or a fuse, and for this poor woman whose life had all but ended—not at his own hand, she had attempted suicide—she was only a conduit.

If they traced Xan they would find the shriveled up husk of a former beauty queen, most likely deceased. She had been used, the identity now cracked. Her IV had given her two weeks to live. After that she would just fade.

Xan needed Mohammed because, while China had many operatives in the United States, they weren't an army. Mohammed had access to nearly a thousand individuals, some native to the U.S., some smuggled in, but all trained and willing to die for their cause. Xan needed their cause to be his. And now, after the meeting, he thought it was.

Instinct had saved many a bacon since man straightened their backs and Xan trusted his now. There was something in the shadows that Xan felt but couldn't see. He acted accordingly. He no longer kept staff in his office and he kept the door locked. He preferred the isolation and the silence, and over the last few months his trust in his peers, even his bosses, had grown thin. The death of President Jintau should have united the parties. They should have been relentless in their quest to find the culprit. But instead, nothing. Vacillating. Debating. And China wasn't alone. The EU—with their own cultural nuances—was behaving the same way. And so was the U.S. Countries prone to violent reactions against adversaries were acting like neutered dogs with a bitch bent over in front of them: curious, but for all the wrong reasons. Some of the more fringe politicians in the parties had even suggested that they offer the oil to their allies; that this unification would help solve the current predicament. Then, *then,* they could solve the terrorist problem.

On a whim, Xan spoke with the military doctors who treated the politicians and officers. Since President Jintau's death, complaints of migraines had jumped six hundred percent. Which meant, in real-world terms, that if ten officials used to get treated for migraines, now sixty do. It could just be stress from the upheaval and uncertainty, but it was not statistically insignificant, and that bothered Xan.

The Core was functioning at ten percent strength. Above twenty percent, Xan would have to be in the same physical location as the Forced Autistic.

Xan learned the hard way that Forced Autism was messy work. It took two days to complete the process, taking a conscious individual— who was most likely pleading for their life—and turning them into a CPU interface for cyberspace. What was left was a lobotomized, catatonic remnant of that former person. But their mindscape was up to eighty times larger than before the procedure.

Xan's team of technicians and surgeons had learned from the first three subjects' brains boiling out their ears. Today their fourth subject, designated S-04, did fine. Xan felt the expanse of his (its?) mind like it was his own. It was a strange feeling. It was like being able to see all around you at once and for a mile in either direction. Never having to focus, the information and decisions just rushing through your mind like an open dam. It immediately made Xan one of the most powerful Sleepers in the world.

Combined with the processing power of the Data Core, he could manipulate and hack the most difficult of security protocols. And because his ghost Core was parasitic and rode on the back of MindCorp's, it was virtually undetectable.

MindCorp thought they controlled cyberspace, and they did. They just weren't aware that an ear was against the door listening in to all of their plans and breaching the most top secret of files.

His phone rang. "Yes?" he said. He listened to the warble on the other line. They had saved him the trip. S-04 was fine, better than fine. It was time to move forward with the plans. "I'll be there tomorrow at 0600."

He hung up and walked to the northwest corner of his office. The contrast between the views felt like an optical illusion. To the north, rolling farmland, a distant mountain range and the gray ocean water. To the west, the jumbled heights of a thousand high rises, jagged and unplanned like broken teeth with the red, caustic atmosphere that hung over and around them like they were a city built on Mars.

He sighed. China's economy developed too late to include much of the population. Ninety percent of the people he now looked down upon, people he couldn't see, were living in poverty. The outskirts of the cities utilized the same technologies as they did one hundred and fifty years ago.

This economic and technological lopsidedness kept most of the population in the dark, unaware of the happenings of the world. *Maybe it was better that way . . .*

The peak of civilization was in 2005. That was the historic marker. Xan's mentor used to talk about that. Most discussions centered on Peak Oil, but what about Peak Civilization?

All countries and nations crumble, entropy was a law, like gravity. It took hold, spinning and spinning, like water against rock, the centrifugal damage unseen by one person's lifetime, but through generations deep canyons were carved and mountains turned to sand.

Our peak was in 2005. Now we're just hanging on, wondering what's next.

Xan looked out into the red haze. Coal. Abundant and deadly. How long until the earth gasped one last breath and died? Xan read a long time ago how a Chinese traffic cops life expectancy was in the early forties. Not from being hit by a car or violence but from the pollution. That had not changed.

Those rolling fields. Maybe regression was better. How many times has man achieved their dreams only to realize it wasn't enough? The human race pushes and pushes. We ignore our families, we half listen to our loved ones. We laugh so rarely. Always looking ahead and wanting what's next. But when we get it, it's just rot and disappointment.

S-04 was working which meant he was going to be online for one month straight. He had a hunch what was going on, why the world was so confused. And he knew where to start: with ones like himself, the shadow men. All governments had them. They were the ones that whispered into the public figure's ear. They were the third man back in the photograph. And they chose that, they wanted that anonymity, because that granted them power and the ethical leniency to do what was truly necessary for their country. To abduct eight Chinese Sleepers against their will. To kill an innocent scientist who knew their face. Xan knew to search three rows back; there he'd find the answers. Everyone closer were temporary fixtures. If they wanted their face seen, they weren't important. They were just pawns.

CHAPTER 11

"We'll be alright," Raimey said to Tiffany when she had put him to bed. It was his first full day back at home. The statement hung in the air like a question.

His physical wounds were healed, but earlier that day when she had changed his diaper and cleaned the caked shit from his ass, the sutures he had tried to place over his pride had stretched and torn. It was now night, time had moved on, but Raimey hadn't. He was humiliated.

Tiffany kissed him on the lips, slow. Unlike Janis, John's penis had been spared. She reached down and kneaded it with her hand. "You still have your most important part."

Tiffany bit down on John's lower lip, pulling it with her. John could hear the smile in her voice and the slight pain from her aggression got him hard.

She worked him, ignoring his input, riding him up and down, making him pay for all the nights he complained, all the nights she saw the reflection of his sad self-pitying eyes in the moonlight or dealt with his sharp remarks when she only meant to help. This was their catharsis. This was her absolving his sins.

After he came, he pleaded for her to get off him, but she wouldn't. She ground down hard, moving back-and-forth until his sensitivity got overwhelmed with lust and he rose again.

The second time he lasted longer and finally she collapsed next to him, her body vibrating, her legs jelly. She wrapped around him like he was a body pillow.

"I think we'll be okay. What do you think?" She was out of breath.

"Wow," he said. He gave her an eskimo kiss that turned into tongue. "Wow," he said again and laughed a real laugh for the first time in months. "I'm like your own personal dildo," he said, still in awe of what happened, still tasting her on his lips.

They snuggled, and for the moment, everything was fine. When they fell asleep, the future seemed like it would be all right.

= = =

It had been eight weeks since Janis was rolled out of their hospital room and Raimey hadn't heard a word from him. He had gone completely dark as was expected. Tiffany fed Raimey a bowl of cereal. It was dawn and the sun had just crept over the horizon.

Raimey was in an electric wheelchair he could maneuver with his mouth, just like the one he and Janis had raced a month before. General Boen was visiting today. He had called the day before.

Boen was the most thoughtful man Raimey had ever known, but like a true Texan, he was candy-coated steel. He was charming, honest, and caring, but underneath was a man who had seen blood and was willing to spill it.

Early in Raimey's career he was a mentor and later, a friend. When Boen had heard about the UN bombing and John's injuries, he had called regularly to check in. Now with his new position, he was in Chicago, "debriefing."

John thought it was odd that he was getting debriefed in Chicago instead of Washington. But since MindCorp, more and more of the country's power had shifted to the Windy City.

Boen apologized for the inconvenient hour but John and Tiffany shushed him: they would be up and ready at 6:00 a.m.

Tiffany dressed John in his military uniform, tailoring it to fit his new body. The arms were pinned to his back and his pants were cut and sewn to eliminate the pant leg. Tiffany stood back and admired her work. John moved around, self-conscious from the attention.

"What?" he asked. Even with his wife, he didn't like to be looked at anymore.

She kissed him on the cheek. "You look great honey."

He smiled, shocked. "Really?"

"Yes, you look strong and proud."

The doorbell rang and downstairs Vanessa yelled, "I'll get it."

General Boen had been around thousands of wounded soldiers. Some of the injuries were unseen: a soldier with tinnitus unable to hear. Others were horrific. Soldiers disfigured from fire or a bomb. Their limbs torn, their faces melted into a smear of skin. Boen did the best thing anyone could when he interacted with them: he treated them like people. He acknowledged their disability, but only up front. He'd ask what happened and how they were managing. But after that it was a one-to-one conversation, no pandering, no sympathy. Around General Boen, the crippled and the unfortunate forgot they were.

When General Boen came in, his warmth filled the home. He knelt down and spoke with Vanessa. He had even brought her a toy. He hugged Tiffany and told her how she was more beautiful each time he saw her. He turned to Raimey and said nothing, they just looked at one another. The moment was long enough to make the hallway go silent, just the sound of an antique clock ticking time away. And then General Boen saluted Raimey, recognizing his service and his sacrifice. No words, those were fleeting, and they never come out as intended. A salute. Well deserved from a man who would never pander or wilt. From a man who understood that Raimey's body was sacrificed for an ideal that was rarely met.

Raimey nodded and when Boen held the salute, he nodded some more, unable to speak. It wasn't long, but it felt like time had slowed. Finally, Boen put his hand on John's shoulder.

"I'm glad you made it, John."

Raimey cleared his throat. "Thank you, sir."

Boen caught up with the whole family over a quick breakfast of coffee and toast. He didn't have much time and he wanted to speak with John alone.

"Can we go for a walk?" Boen asked. Tiffany understood this was directed to John. She cleared the table and asked Vanessa to help her clean up. They went to the kitchen.

"Sure."

Boen followed Raimey out the door.

Two blocks away, talk of the weather turned to the tragic events from the last few months.

"Why do you think WarDon killed himself?" Raimey asked. He was so drugged on painkillers that for the first two weeks, he didn't know what had happened. "He was a tough bird, that was unlike him."

Boen had known Don for over thirty years and the suicide surprised him, too. "We're not sure. But it was definitely a suicide. He wasn't at the UN and he killed himself right afterwards. Maybe he blamed himself. He was in charge of the security."

"So they un-un-un-retired you," Raimey said. It was an old joke by now. Boen had been brought back three times since he officially got out of the game at sixty years old. Boen laughed.

"I was in a swimsuit when I got the call," he said and laughed some more. "You wouldn't recognize me in my retired life. I'm a whole different person."

Boen had retired to a small ranch on the Brazos River just west of Fort Worth. He rode horses, hung out with a pack of dogs that had adopted his land as their own, fished, canoed, drank Coors Light and listened to Mexicali. His wife, Deb, had died five years earlier. He missed her, but life was full of death and many of the ones he loved had gone back to the earth. Debra wouldn't have wanted him to stew. It was one of the reasons he had fallen in love with her.

"I never got to the ranch," Raimey said, shaking his head. He had forgotten about his injuries, he was just thinking about travel. It was so difficult now to go anywhere rural.

"Maybe someday, even still," Boen said.

"So what do they got you doing?" Raimey asked.

"Just helping with the transition, then getting back to drinking beer and catching some bass."

"Have you met Dr. Lindo?" Raimey asked.

Boen paused and Raimey registered that he was deciding what he could or couldn't say.

"You don't hav—" Raimey started.

"I am working with him right now," Boen said. "He's my primary advisor for new military efforts."

"I've met him."

"I know."

Of course he would, Raimey thought.

"What do you think?" Raimey asked. "I couldn't get a bead on him."

"He's very smart. Awkward. I wouldn't say he has a sense of humor but he has an energy about him like he's in on his own private joke. The really smart ones are usually socially retarded. Comes with the territory."

"You know he tested me and Janis?"

Boen's pause was longer. "I've seen Eric since he left the hospital," he said.

"Is he good?" Raimey asked.

"Yeah." But Boen's tone was uncertain.

It was apparent that he couldn't say more. Since Boen's original meeting with Evan, with each Tank Major progress report, Boen's initial casualness to the concept had turned into astonishment. Boen liked weapons and he believed that the best way to avoid war was to carry the biggest stick. But this stick was a hammer. The Tank Major was vertically scalable on all levels: for peace keeping, for urban warfare, and for (*heaven forbid*) a war between nations.

Boen was in Chicago to see the finished project. The first Tank Major was going to be demonstrated for the new President and the top brass of the military today at 11:00 a.m. That was why he had to meet the Raimeys so early.

He had seen the preparation, video of the surgery, how they fused Janis's spine to the inside of the battle chassis. It was permanent, there was no going back when a soldier gave a nod and signed the paper. You were a Tank Major for life.

Beyond his original disfigurement, they had cut Eric down further. He was a torso with a head. But Eric was fine with it. He understood what they were doing and he likened himself to the first astronauts. Someone had to do it and they had asked him. It was worth the sacrifice.

"John, I can't get into it too much but I may be coming back some day in a professional capacity. They're doing some amazing things right now and I could see you being a part of it."

"Does it have to do with what they're using Janis for?"

"Yes," Boen said, almost dreamily. Like Evan, Boen could see a platoon of giants walking into a battlefield immune to the bullets ricocheting off their armored skin. Tank Majors would save so many lives.

Raimey looked across a small pond and watched a few of the geese shuffle around each other on the opposite side. "I need to find a purpose again, Earl. I've been through some tough shit but this takes it, hands down. Just tell me when and where and I'm there."

"I know you feel that way, John," Boen said. He knelt down. "I can't imagine what you've gone through and I'm not going to pretend I can. But be careful and count your blessings. A lot of mistakes are compounded by further ones."

"You told me that a lot back in the day," Raimey said. "But what does that have to do with helping you?"

"I don't know." Boen got up with a crack of his knees. "Things aren't what they used to be, including you, including me."

"They sure as hell aren't. I knew who I was before. I had goals. Do my duty. Get my pension. Hopefully have another kid. Get old with

Tiff."

"Most of that you can still do, John," Boen said softly.

John turned like he had been slapped. "NO, I can't. Not like this. I'd rather be dead. I tell Tiffany I'm fine, but I'm not. If the bomb had worked a little harder or I was a few feet closer, everyone would be better off. This is unacceptable."

He looked into Boen's eyes. Boen had never seen them so pleading. "If you got anything I can help with, I want it. I need to move forward."

"Everyone needs that, John. But from where we stand, which way is it?"

John was silent. Boen stuffed his hands in his pockets and watched the gaggle quack and play. He looked at the dirty blanket of clouds overhead and felt the chill in the air. Seeing his friend so desperate for validation depressed him. He pondered how the true castration of a man was taking away their purpose.

= = =

Boen left Raimey at the front of the house and his chaperone drove him to the Derik Building. Boen learned it was a military research center that specialized in bionics and that MindCorp was now heavily involved. Apparently, the Tank Major project had piqued Cynthia's interest. Boen shook his head in disbelief. He had never liked government and private sector partnerships in the business of war. He felt it created looseness to a government service that needed to be monitored as gravely as life support.

He was old enough to remember when the military had outsourced manned operations during the Iraq and Afghanistan conflicts in the early twenty-first century. As a young soldier, he had run into these men. They may have had a corporate headquarters, even a business card, but they held guns with live ammo. They were mercenaries.

The U.S. military had justified the outsourcing because they were used as security detail for high-level local figures in the Middle East. But the U.S. learned that while they may have outsourced the responsibility, they didn't relinquish the culpability. Blood got spilled, accusations were made, and pointed fingers were stacked on fingers like Lincoln Logs. They hadn't outsourced people; they had outsourced the conditional right to kill. And the rules of engagement were different for a uniformed soldier trained and commanded under a rigid structure, than for a mercenary who made six figures, had a 401k, and was saving up for a boat.

Now the largest corporation in the history of mankind was partnered with the United States, designing a soldier that was the equivalent of one hundred soldiers. *Why?* Boen wondered. Everything he'd read about Cynthia would have caused him to predict otherwise. It wasn't that she was a hippy-dippy socialist, far from it. She was a true capitalist, providing a superior product, stomping out any competition, and reaping her just desserts without apology. But she sure as hell wasn't a loyalist. MindCorp made more money overseas than it did here. *Why do this?*

"You're caught up in the money. Money means nothing to me anymore. I have more than anyone could ever spend. It's knowledge, nothing more. It's the chill of learning something so new that I'm the only person in the world that knows it," is what Cynthia would have said to Boen if she had been seated next to him. But she wasn't. She was at the Derik Building, helping with the final diagnostic protocol of the first bionic soldier.

Boen suddenly felt old.

"We're about ten minutes out, sir," his driver announced.

"Help with the transition, get back to the ranch," he whispered to himself. But he was curious too, just like the rest of them: running toward the wail of sirens when it could only be gunshots or fire.

They pulled up. General Boen got out and loitered for a minute mentally rolodexing through the men he'd see inside, many of them associates he'd known for forty years.

The Gray Hairs, he thought with a smile. *When did I get so damn old?* Looking back was like time-lapse photography. Boen remembered his twenties and flinched at all the stupid stuff he had done. Wonder he was alive. He felt he could rule the world at thirty. He held Jenny, his daughter, for the first time at forty-two. At sixty-four he gave her away to a man who would be unfaithful and make her hate herself. Two years later Debra had cancer. A year after that, he put her in the ground. And now at seventy, back in the fold. *Strong for my age, but the knees can tell when a storm is coming, and the memory isn't quite as sharp.*

"What are you doing out here, Earl?" Jan Hedgegard, a Navy Admiral said from the window of his chauffeured car. "They didn't demote you to valet did they?" Jan opened the door and the first thing that set down on the salt blasted asphalt was the foot of a cane.

Jan just made my point, Boen thought. Jan used to do pull-ups with weights strapped to his waist. Jan bent his knees inward, and with help from the driver, got to his feet. He hobbled over to Boen and turned to see what Boen was looking at. Just another building across the street.

"Anything I'm supposed to notice?" Jan asked.

"Nope. Just thinking about how damn old we all got. How's Tom?"

"Still living at home, if you believe it," Jan said. Boen was asking about his forty-year-old son.

"They couldn't make it work, huh?" Boen said.

Jan shook his head. "Nope. Couldn't get past it. It was too much for both of them. I don't blame her though," Jan said.

Boen nodded.

"I always thought your girl and my boy could have been fine together. They used to be friends," Jan said.

"They were five, Jan. Hard to gauge the chemistry at that point," Boen said. They both laughed.

"Are you coming inside or are you trying to get hypothermia?" Jan said. "Help a fellow geezer out, I don't want these guys seeing me scuttling around."

Boen put his arm around Jan. They hadn't seen each other in years, but some friendships don't need daily watering. "I'll spot you."

Inside, they were seated on bleachers that had been rolled into a large space roughly the size of a gymnasium. The bleachers were encased in a Plexiglas box, three inches thick on all sides.

"I feel like a hamster," Jan said to Boen under his breath. They nodded at some of their peers.

Thirty yards to their left was an old tank. In front of them, about the same distance away, was a cement block twenty feet tall and fifteen feet wide. To its right was a decommissioned Humvee. There was also a shooting range. A .50 caliber machine gun was aimed at a hill of sand bags downrange.

"Are those RPGs?" Boen asked Jan. Next to the machine gun were a half a dozen tubes—hand held missile launchers, the same used by ninety-nine percent of the terrorists and fanatics they dealt with now.

"Looks like it," Jan said.

"Suddenly I want our hamster cage to be a little thicker."

"Or further away," Jan added.

Hearing protection was handed out as they came in and now Boen understood why—they were going to use live fire and explosives in front of them. That was highly unusual in a closed environment.

There were fifty VIPs present. The former Vice President Wade Williams was the last to arrive. He smiled his pearly whites and shook the hands of half the folks in the bleachers before he sat down. Boen knew that Wade didn't really know Joseph Michaels, the former President. They had been brought together to hit as many cross sections as possible. Wade's smile was a bit too genuine for Boen's taste so soon after the UN atrocity.

Evan Lindo walked into the hamster cage.

"Good morning," Evan said to them from a small podium in front of the bleachers. Boen saw a small, fit redhead sneak in after Evan and sit in the front row. No one else seemed to notice her.

"Is that Cynthia Revo?" Boen asked Jan.

"Ayup."

"It's been only three months since the UN terrorist attack. Three months since we lost President Michaels, the fifth time we've lost a President in our nation's history." Lindo waited as the words sunk in. "And we all miss Donald Richards. He was a mentor of mine, he taught me most of what I know."

Completely untrue, but oil them up.

"Don taught me a few phrases that he lived by. One, don't bring a knife to a nuke fight."

The crowd chuckled. Lindo had calculated it would.

"Two. Expect the best, prepare for the worst."

The group of military heads nodded.

"Globalization of our economies and cyberspace have blurred the lines between nations, but we are still a distinct culture. We still have borders we protect and citizens that rely on us. And we still have interests specific to the nation and our military. We cannot protect everyone, but we must protect our own. That's not callous. It's not insensitive. The United States is our family and sometimes you have to circle the wagons.

"Our President is dead. Our Secretary of Defense—regardless of how it happened—is no longer a pillar we can lean on."

Lindo made eye contact with many of the officers in the room.

"We have to lead. With our new President Ward Williams," Lindo put a hand out in his direction. *Turd.* Williams gave a wave that belonged in a parade. "And the men and women in this room. We are the ones in the watchtower."

Lindo put on a big smile. "This isn't a room of just military and political leaders. I'm proud and flattered to say that MindCorp and its founder, Cynthia Revo, has been integral to this project. While MindCorp is a global business, it's distinctly American. Thank you Cynthia for understanding our nation's needs."

The men in uniform clapped. Cynthia acknowledged the room but Boen thought she looked sad and unkempt. She quickly turned back to the ground.

"Let's acknowledge that our current military equipment doesn't address today's needs," Lindo said. "We have terrorists imbedded like ticks in our cities. We need fuel to run our vehicles and our supply is dwindling. We aren't fighting nations, but extremist groups. We need a military that is light and flexible. We need a military that *is* special forces.

"But we still need military might. We need a weapon—like the atomic bomb- that is a deterrent to both extremists and nations. I present to you the most devastating infantry weapon every built. The melding of man and machine into something better. I bring you the Tank Major."

On the far wall, a large garage door slowly opened. White light bled through creating a silhouette of a gigantic humanoid shape. Tank Major Janis walked into the room.

A gasp went through the crowd. He was eleven feet tall and almost as wide at the shoulders. He weighed eight thousand pounds. The room shook as he ran. His body groaned and hissed and a pair of gigantic drive chains around his waist—together two feet tall—spun furiously, counter to the other. His body was painted in green and brown camouflage and stenciled with radiation symbols on his front and back.

Tank Major Janis jogged around the room, passing the hamster cage. He then sprinted back and forth in a ladder drill, stopping and starting, showing the strength and impressive agility of the Tank Major platform.

His legs and feet were heavily armored, yet dextrous. As he created a mini-earthquake trundling around the room, his feet constantly adjusted to maintain full traction.

His legs were connected to the outside of his hips and this allowed the suspension built inside the thigh to move up and down, while keeping the leg a consistent length. Hung slightly back on each shoulder were gigantic metal boxes mounted on rails. It was clear they could be removed. His shoulders looked like what they were: an artillery chamber. His arms were long for his body and as thick as his legs. His hands were boulders. Each one could pick an engine out of a car. A massive anvil-like bridge of armor ran along his knuckles protecting the incredible architecture of his mechanized hands.

"Please put on your ear protection," Lindo said. The stunned crowd did as they were told. They could hear Evan through built-in speakers.

"Tank Major Janis can run at a sustained speed of twenty-five miles an hour. He weighs eight thousand pounds and is primarily built from depleted uranium armor. He can lift his body weight over his head and he can run through cement up to two feet thick."

"He is powered by a hydrogen fuel generator that charges a deep storage battery. This battery can last for two days at full operation. At normal operation, it lasts ten days. As long as the Tank Major has access to water and electricity, it can perform electrolysis and recharge itself indefinitely."

Janis walked downrange to the hill of sand bags. Two soldiers walked out to the machine gun and RPGs.

"He is essentially bullet proof," Lindo said. The machine gun erupted into chatter, spilling brass around the soldiers' feet as they fired. The armor sparked and some of the camouflage paint got mired, but the Tank Major stood unmoving, like he was being pelted with rain. They stopped firing and both of the men put an RPG to their shoulder.

"The Tank Major platform is blast proof both from direct projectiles and concussive blasts in its vicinity. While it can be blown apart or damaged, the current stock of weapons that our enemies have are unlikely to do so."

The men fired the RPG's at Janis. One hit flush and exploded, doing nothing. The other hit his chest and ricocheted off against the back wall, creating a five-foot crater.

"Oops," Lindo said. The crowd let out a dazed laugh. "You may have noticed that his fists are heavily armored. There is a reason."

On cue, Tank Major Janis ran up to the Humvee and scissored his hand down onto the hood. It was like a meteorite had struck it. The front of the Humvee crumpled like tin and the axles snapped, sending the wheels to the sides. Janis continued to pound his way through the Humvee, smashing it down into scrap.

"Each fist weighs five hundred pounds. This is his most basic strength. He is only using the high torque electric motors located throughout his body," Lindo said.

The entire audience was frozen in a scream. They couldn't believe what they were seeing. When Janis was done with the Humvee, he flipped it away from the hamster cage like it was made of foam.

"The large metal boxes on his shoulders are artillery magazines. In each are six artillery rounds that have no projectile. The artillery charge is used to fuel his most devastating attack: the hydraulshock."

Janis turned to Lindo and Lindo nodded. Janis ran up to the gigantic cement block and moved like his was going to punch it.

BAM!

The noise was indescribable. Even with the Plexiglas case and the hearing protection, Boen's ears rang. It was like a thunderbolt had gone off in the room. Boen didn't see what had happened. The Tank Major ran at the block and then cocked back its right arm like it was about to throw a straight, and then suddenly the room was filled with dust. The Plexiglas fractured into a spider web from the concussive blast and debris.

Boen heard gigantic exhaust fans spin up. The thick brown air thinned out into a light fog and Boen could see the outline of the Tank Major. When the air cleared out further he saw that aside for jagged leftovers at its base, the entire cement block was gone. With one punch the Tank Major had turned it into dust.

"The hydraulshock delivers three and a half million foot pounds of energy in a controlled delivery system, guaranteeing almost zero percent collateral damage, unlike traditional ordinance."

Lindo nodded again at Janis. He went to the tank with its foot thick armor. He reeled back.

BAM!

This time Boen saw (and didn't see) what happened. For a split second, the gigantic soldier vanished in a blur, moving as fast as a rocket. And then it was back with its fist inside the tank. The tank shuddered and warped inward as if it got cleaved with a gigantic axe. Out of the Tank Major's shoulder, a spent artillery shell ejected end-over-end in a backwards arc. It clanged to the ground forty feet away.

Boen saw the shoulder mechanism reload. Tank Major Janis pulled his fist away from the tank and walked over to the glass, just behind Lindo. Everyone watched in awe.

"This is our future, gentlemen. This is the eagle that carries the olive branch to all terrorists and enemies of the state. Wherever they are, wherever they hide, we can get them. And there isn't a damn thing they can do about it."

The crowd erupted into applause. Some of the men, hard men who had dealt with life and death on a grand scale for decades, cried. It was clear to them what Dr. Evan Lindo had created. It was clear to them what Dr. Evan Lindo was: a savior to the United States way of life. A savior for all of those who feared the end.

= = =

The presentation couldn't have gone better. Representatives from each military division congratulated Evan afterwards. They all wanted to discuss the Tank Major's effect on their current operations.

What they didn't know was that Ward Williams and Evan had come to an agreement before the presentation. Evan had brought him back to meet Tank Major Janis and to understand the technology.

Evan had learned six weeks before that Ward didn't like him, never had. Felt that he was a little fucking nerd who wanted to wear big boy pants. Probably guzzled WarDon's load. All good stuff to know. Evan didn't hold grudges. He let the King Sleeper massage those synapses to make Ward a bit more amenable. After a few weeks Ward thought his first impression of Evan was a bit harsh. A month later, he had called for advice.

While before Ward would have vehemently opposed what Evan wanted to control, now he was finishing Evan's sentences.

". . . as I designed and implemented the technology . . ." Evan said.

"It would only make sense that you were at the helm," Ward nodded enthusiastically. "Totally. There's been nothing like this before.

We've had weapons, we've had soldiers, but never this gray area." Ward cocked his head like he just had a whiz-bang of an idea. "General Boen should be a part of this. He could help train the soldiers and coordinate the missions."

Evan feigned skeptical. "You think?"

"Definitely," Ward said. Evan looked deep in thought. He rubbed his scruffy chin.

"You know Mr. President, that would be best. It would allow us to play to our strengths. I can focus on the technology and the overall health of the soldiers, and General Boen could focus on the operations, training, and integration with the other military branches."

"That's what I was thinking," Ward said. They were both nodding like pigeons in the park.

"It's perfect." Evan checked his watch. "Almost time. Thank you, sir."

"Glad I could help." Ward flashed his bleached choppers.

Evan had planted that suggestion in fuckface's head about a week ago. It would be odd to not have a high-ranking officer on board and General Boen, while an obstacle, was a lesser evil than some lower ranking military advisor who was climbing up the career ladder. And he was temporary and less adept with the technology. Maybe in a few months he'd die in his sleep.

= = =

General Boen waited while the various high ranking officers congratulated Evan and the place cleared out. Jan said goodbye and hobbled away shaking his head at what he had just seen: a movie come to life. Ward had pulled Boen aside after the demonstration and briefed him on his upcoming duties.

Evan shook the last General's hand and came over. "I need to pack Tank Major Janis up, shall we?"

He and Boen walked out of the hamster cage and across the destroyed landscape left in the colossus's wake. Boen stopped and looked at the Humvee wreckage. The truck was completely flattened. He had to step over shards of engine block.

"So he did this without the artillery discharge?"

"Correct. Electric motors have one hundred percent torque at one rpm and each major motor in his body has at least one thousand foot-pounds. Think two V-8's are swinging his thousand pound arm."

"Unreal, Evan. Truly."

They made it through the garage door. Tank Major Janis sat to their left on what looked like a huge gothic throne. Technicians scurried over him like spiders.

"We've had the mechanical technology to build a bionic for some time, but it was the Mindlink that made it truly possible," Evan said, attempting modesty.

"Science fiction has talked about this for a hundred years, but talk is cheap. You did it," Boen said. They were now in front of Janis. Seated, he somehow appeared even more hulking.

"How are you soldier?" Boen asked.

Janis crooked his head down to see them. "Doing fine, sir. Doing fine."

"How does it feel to be the most powerful man to ever walk the earth?"

"Just happy to be of use. I think Dr. Lindo could hit a switch and turn me off if he wanted to, so I'm not going to get too cocky," Janis winked. Evan mimed pressing a button.

Two technicians muscled off the artillery magazine from one of his shoulders. Another two on a hydraulic lift guided it onto their platform.

"General Boen will be heading the strategic aspects of the Tank Division," Evan said to Janis.

"Excellent, I've heard great things about you, sir. My team leader used to take direction from you."

"John Raimey, I know," Boen said.

The gothic metal chair hissed and clanked. The technicians up top gave thumbs up.

"Step back," Evan said to Boen.

"Excuse me," Janis said. He stood up. A truck designed to transport him reversed in. Even five feet away, Boen couldn't see Janis's face due to the girth of his chest. It was what awed children to their fathers.

Janis walked away and his body was surprisingly quiet. When he climbed into the rear of the truck's trailer, it buckled under the load but the grace in which the Tank Major got up and in was remarkable. It truly moved like a man.

"This is the coolest thing I've ever seen," Boen said. Evan smiled.

"How many are you planning to build?"

"This model? None. Janis is the prototype and already I've learned a great deal from him. He's ninety-five percent of what I want out of the battle chassis. Depleted uranium armor—as you well know—is the strongest armor we currently manufacture, but it does have vulnerabilities."

"Not many," Boen said. "Are you talking EFPs?"

Explosive Formed Penetrators were a type of bomb used by terrorists in the Middle East to breach tank hulls. They used a convex copper plate that on detonation became a molten slug moving at incredible speeds.

"See? Exactly. Right away you went to it. So would our enemies," he continued. "I'm working on an osmium and depleted-uranium alloy encased in a revolutionary ceramic."

"I've never heard of osmium."

"It's actually quite common. The rolling ball in ballpoint pens is osmium, but it doesn't play nice with others. And alone it's brittle. But the properties of this armor are astounding."

"It would stop an EFP?" Boen asked skeptically.

"An eight inch thick plate is equivalent to six feet of rolled homogenous armor," Evan replied. "How would you like to proceed?"

"Well, I see the Tank Major as intelligent support for a special forces unit. If they were breaching hostile buildings, the Tank Major could act as a cow catcher breaking through, with the team right behind using him as a smart shield, fanning out when they went in. We should start with about twenty guys. I'll pick them if you don't mind and we'll get training, learn the strengths and weaknesses, adapt from there."

"What about the press?" Evan asked. "Ward wants the world to know about this."

"There are terrorist acts every month nowadays. I say we make an example of one and let some footage leak out. That'll get everyone's attention just fine."

= = =

In his private cabin two train cars down from his creation, Evan dreamed. In it, an army of Tank Majors stretched into the distance, lumbering into a city. Columns of nuclear fire littered the landscape and a Tank Major turned to regard one as it rose, its pulsing mushroom cloud reflecting off his helmet. The Tank Major was unmoved. Unconcerned. He continued into the battlefield.

Evan dreamed of Beijing covered in the hottest fire; he pictured Britain with buildings crumbled to ash. His giants occupied both, fully exposed, peppered with mortars and missiles and lead, their armor ashen and beaten, but not broken. The enemy surrendering at their feet, heads cowered in submission.

He dreamed of a caravan of millions crying in each other's arms, dragging whatever they could with them as they evacuated their burning city, understanding that it was all over, that the U.S. had won. *More.* That Evan had won.

The world as mine.

He looked down on the cities from the clouds. He hovered over the destruction like he was omniscient and omnipresent. Like he was a god who no longer hid behind faith.

= = =

After the demonstration, Cynthia let Evan take the acclaim. She was the first to leave. Since Sabot's departure two weeks before, Evan had assigned her two bodyguards that worked in shifts: Edward Chao and Alan Kove. Chao was an asshole, but Kove had a sweetness to him. Kove led her through the doorway to the waiting car. He seemed genuinely concerned with his charge.

She didn't understand what had happened. The night Sabot vanished, she noticed his absence an hour afterward. She looked around the room for him, went out into the hall, and then assumed that he had left to handle some work minutia that he didn't want to burden her with.

When she got to the penthouse, the lights were off. "Sabot?" The dark room absorbed her voice and answered it with silence. She called him. Straight to voicemail. She called down to the front desk and the receptionist said she hadn't seen him that evening.

For two hours she waited, compulsively checking her phone and e-mail. She called again. Nothing. Maybe something happened to his mom. She called Linda, Sabot's mother, who lived in a house outside the city. She had visited it with Sabot a year before.

Linda answered the phone. "Cynthia," she said. "Unknown" on the phone pad was always her.

"Is everything okay?" Cynthia asked.

"Yes. Why?" Linda sounded concerned.

"I don't know where Sabot is," Cynthia said. "He isn't answering his phone. I thought, well, the worst. Maybe something had happened to you or Trina."

"When did you last speak to him?"

"Three hours ago," Cynthia replied. She heard Linda sigh with relief.

"Oh good. I spoke with him about an hour ago. He's coming over tomorrow. Are you guys okay?"

Cynthia didn't respond right away. She held the phone loosely in her hand. Tomorrow was Thursday. Nothing was wrong at home but he wasn't coming in to work. Her stomach ached.

"Cynthia?" she heard the tinny phone say.

"I don't know, Mrs. Sabot. Please have him call me."

He never did.

They pulled up to MindCorp. Cynthia turned to Kove. "I'm dropping you off."

"Ms. Revo, I'm supposed to be with you at all times," he replied.

"Those aren't my orders and I'm a private citizen."

Kove didn't move. He wasn't sure what to do.

"Alan, do I have to open the door for you? Call Evan if you want, but do it outside. I'm not asking."

Reluctantly he got out. Cynthia pressed a button near her seat.

"Take me to one-nineteen Pine," she said.

They idled outside of Linda Sabot's house. Cynthia was paralyzed. One half of her was mournfully sad, the other was furious at the way Sabot had discarded her without an explanation. After the years together, she deserved more.

Finally she got out and walked to the door. She pressed the doorbell and heard its echo inside. She listened for the low thump of footsteps approaching. After a minute, she stepped over into the bushes and peered into the house. It felt empty.

"You're messing up my mom's bushes," Sabot said from behind her. She turned and saw him. His shirt was soaked in a V from a long run. He was breathing heavy. She went over to him and punched him on the shoulder.

"What are you doing to me?" she asked. She felt the comfort of being around him, even now, just as old ex's still invade each other's space unknowingly. But she was confused. He didn't seem angry.

"I needed time to think," he said. He walked to the door and took out a key. He held the door open. "Let's talk inside."

She sat at the table and he poured both of them lemonade. The kitchen area had Midwestern touches. A corner shelf with porcelain figurines and antique knick-knacks near the floor. Flower print wallpaper that was accented with a white wood baseboard. It reminded Cynthia of her childhood home.

He gave her a glass and sat down across from her. He didn't speak right away. He took big gulps of the lemonade and looked at the outside patio.

"Please," she said.

He put his glass down and watched her the way he looked at her guests.

"Do you love me? Did that go away?" she asked.

"Of course I do," he said. "I just couldn't stay. I knew we'd talk sooner or later, but I needed time to gather myself. I don't want to be in rooms where decisions cost lives. When I met you, I thought those days were over. I had to use my military background, but a bodyguard was different than the military. It was defensive. I could rationalize that."

"What does that have to do with us?" Cynthia said. "If I don't help the military, someone else will. I thought I was doing the right thing, I thought you approved."

"You're playing God," he said.

Cynthia looked at him bewildered. "Giving someone CPR is playing God."

"You don't know what you're building, Cynthia. You have no idea. If these things get built, it doesn't matter if we're right or wrong, we can force our 'right.' And you're doing it with *him*."

"Evan isn't as bad as you think," Cynthia said.

Sabot made a face. "I know the 'Evans' of the world. They are small men with hidden agendas. They are the Dictator's kids who rape, rob, and kill because they can't be stopped. I've been in these waters far longer than you. And being smarter doesn't help. You can't guess what a snake will do when it doesn't know itself."

"Come back," Cynthia said weakly.

"I can't, babe. I love you, never think different, but I'm so disappointed. The life I thought we'd have, it's not going to happen. And I know the way I handled it was wrong, but you are pushing the world to war and you cannot rationalize your way out of it. 'Someone else will do it' isn't good enough, Cynthia. LET THEM."

"I just want you back, Sabot," Cynthia said.

"I'll come back if you stop working with Evan. If I can get back the woman that saved the world and still asked for my advice and comfort, I'm there."

"I can't now. We're under contract," she said. Her voice could barely be heard.

"We could go anywhere and no one could touch us," Sabot said. "You could walk away."

"I can't," Cynthia said. The truth was, Cynthia had not been challenged mentally in almost a decade and finally she had a project that was out of her scope and required her constant attention and innovation to succeed. She couldn't leave that. Without the intellectual stimulation, she thought, she might as well jump out the window.

Sabot stared at a spot on the table. "That day in the hospital, I saw the future. Cities were on fire, people were covered in soot. Some were holding loved ones that were dead or dying. And I knew that future was true, like God had planted it in my head. I had two options. One was to kill everyone the room. Five lives for a billion, that seemed fair."

Cynthia's eyes were wide with shock. Sabot was serious.

"If you hadn't been there," Sabot snapped his fingers. "It would have been an easy decision," he continued. "The other was to leave. Don't think I don't love you, it was the only thing that stopped me. And don't think I'm not here for you. If you change your mind, if you need help getting out, I'm the man. But I can't be around for this. Because next time, I'm not going to hesitate or waver. Innocent people will die from your invention, Cynthia. Next time, I'll make the right decision."

Cynthia walked out of the house stunned into silence. It took her three tries to open the car door. She didn't remember getting back to MindCorp, but she was on her couch. She cancelled all meetings and turned off all outside communication. She sat, huddled in the dark, neither eating or sleeping, searching her soul and wondering how the most loyal and caring man she had ever known had seen in her something so vile that for a moment, she meant more to the world dead than alive.

PART II

"Do not let spacious plans for a new world divert your energies from saving what is left of the old."

—Winston Churchill

CHAPTER 12
THREE MONTHS LATER.

Xan was unraveling. He looked down at his hands. They shook side to side like he was waving off a play. His eyelids twitched uncontrollably. He sat up in his bed. It looked like his office, down to the coffee maker, down to the red, jagged horizon to the west and the hilly fields to the north. It gave him a center. But it wasn't real. He had been online for almost four months, with his physical form nestled into a chair at their Core next to S-04, who—against all odds—was still alive and kicking.

He had meant to come out a month earlier but the physicians that monitored his body and mind suggested that he continue. It would take two weeks to bring Xan back to consciousness, like a deep-sea diver slowly rising to the surface to avoid the bends. And every minute was precious, more precious than his health, more precious than oil. There was too little time. Grain-by-grain it vanished into the trough of the hourglass; when the world would be won or lost.

His paranoia had been vetted. China's policies had continued to shift toward those that favored the U.S., and the countries that comprised the European Union had shifted even further. The politicians were being brainwashed. As a Sleeper, Xan shadowed the new Chinese President and his advisors without their knowledge. And this is where he found the anomaly. Of the five thousand micro-frequencies used by the Mindlink to send and receive data, three had been hijacked. They fed deep into the brain. The signals were staggered, the three frequencies combined to make a whole, but they didn't shove the message into memory. They let the brain connect the dots.

The messages weren't blatant. They were tailored suggestions to each individual based on their memories. "Your mother always dreamed of moving to America," was one message Xan deciphered. This was sent again and again, a thousands times a day, to the new President. Xan researched the President's mother and found that she had gone to college in the U.S. and she had always wanted to move there. Many times she would tell her son, now President, how wonderful it was. Another he deciphered: "United we can defeat the terrorists." This was being sent to the military advisor for the President. There were more, but Xan had seen enough. Time was too short to be overly curious.

As soon as he went under, Xan tagged the top military officials in the U.S. These tags monitored key words or spikes in activity and flagged them for Xan. Three months ago, every military official's online activity spiked at 2:00 p.m. U.S. Central Time. On the dot. Xan hacked into the files of a Jan Hedgegard, a Navy Admiral who, judging from recent photos, had died and never got the memo. His correspondence to subordinates was unencrypted. He spoke of a 'Metal giant.' Jan, in his old age, would fall asleep during the day, sometimes with his Mindlink on. Xan waited like a cat burglar. The Forced Autistic allowed him to easily hack through the security protocols set up for the Admiral and reach into his head. He found the visual memory. Xan saw the giant destroy a Humvee truck and punch through a cement block, rendering it to dust. The creature was beautiful. An engineering marvel. Tall and massive and shockingly graceful.

He watched a short man with glasses and a goatee field questions. The Generals applauded him. The giant walked up behind him. He was the man Xan had to know. He was the man three rows back.

Two days later he knew the chubby little man was Dr. Evan Lindo. A week later he had tagged the good doctor and all the staff around him.

Trends formed. A base in Virginia was important. Xan hacked into their employee database searching for low security personnel. He found a woman named Wendy Schaub who worked in the cafeteria. She delivered food to an atomic bomb shelter every morning. In that bunker she had seen "a man the size of a truck with a huge body and a small head," she wrote in her personal online journal, password protected with the name of her first dog and her birthdate.

He continued trolling lightly over the minds of the unsuspecting. A janitor cleaned the bunker. At one point a massive door "like those at a bank," was closing and inside he saw a "huge blue lava lamp bigger than a wall."

A Data Core.

Xan hacked into the energy grid that fed the base. Seventy percent of its power was diverted to the bunker. He hacked into the onsite hospital. Dr. Ian Wilkins was the neurologist. Wary of leaving a trail, Xan reluctantly hacked into his files. These weren't password protected with an old pet's name; he was now breaching true security protocols used by the United States. He could get flagged, even traced. But he had to know. It took Xan two seconds to read through two thousand files. One file did not list a name, address, or rank. But it did list sex: Male. And an age: twelve. The symptom: muscle atrophy, ligament and tendon shrinkage. Treatment: Passive physical therapy, stretching, and massage.

Passive. Not active. Not telling the dude in bed that he had to get off his ass and jog. Passive was for coma patients. Xan knew passive. A camera was pointed on his body, and as he processed this new information, he watched two therapists shake his arms out and stretch his fingers back and forth. A Sleeper was in that bunker. One that hadn't woken up in a long, long time.

A boy.

= = =

Xan made Mohammed uneasy. Even online, Xan was shaky and unsure. His eyes darted back and forth under heavy eyelids. He cracked his knuckles incessantly. His legs bounced on the stool, shaking the table. He looked like a meth head going through withdrawal.

They were in a sod walled pub built into a role-playing game. Around them orcs and wizards and knights mingled. Some screamed defiantly at others, grossly offended by a comment or jest directed their way. They would go outside to battle. Clans sat together discussing a quest they had just finished. It was odd seeing a barbarian with shoulders like bowling balls speak with the voice of a girl. It was even odder to hear an adult man recruit a kid to join an adventure.

"In order to gain sympathy, you have to incur sacrifice," Xan said. His right eye fluttered uncontrollably.

"You don't seem well," Mohammed said.

"I'm fine. I couldn't see more clearly."

Mohammed regarded his twitchy partner. "Why so many men?"

"You can spare eighty," Xan said. "Look."

Xan sent Mohammed images of the Tank Major demonstration.

"This is what they have now. We devised a way to neutralize it, but we need to see it in practice. What better coming out party for the Western Curse than standing on top of the U.S.'s greatest weapon?"

President Hu, Jintau's replacement, had died a week after he overturned a policy to open their oil reserve to the Coalition. He was found halfway off his Sleeper chair. A stroke. It was diagnosed as natural causes and Xan couldn't tell anyone different. If he had told them and they went online, then the King Sleeper (he'd learn what it was called) would know that HE knew. He checked his frequencies and they were clean. The Core he worked from was off the grid, virtually invisible. Rest in peace, Dr. Renki.

But it fueled his paranoia. He felt like he was the last sane man on earth. He heard voices all around him telling lies, whispering conspiracies. Was Mohammed compromised? Could he be? He was stupid enough to connect directly in. Xan was connected through another comatose husk in Norway. Was Mohammed real? Was this a trick?

The doctors told him he had to come out, that his mental health was at risk. He ordered soldiers to take them away. He forbade anyone on the base to link-in. All orders and decisions had to go through him, just in case, *somehow*, they had been influenced.

It was the boy, it had to be the boy. There was no other explanation and while Xan was one hundred percent certain it was true, he still didn't know how. HOW? How can this child do what he is doing? Combined with S-05 (S-04's heart stopped) Xan was as powerful as any other Sleeper in cyberspace and yet, to the King Sleeper, he was a gnat.

Xan had found enough schematics and anecdotal information for China to design its own Tank Major. The prototype was in its final stages. It wasn't as elegant, they didn't have refineries that could forge the hydraulshock mechanism, but it made up for it with size and firepower. It was fifteen feet tall with cannons mounted to its shoulders and a constricting attack that used its hydraulic-lined back to crush anything it got hold of. Like an American Tank Major.

It all meant nothing without the King Sleeper.

Xan pulled himself together. "I'm sorry. You've been patient and I know you've lost some followers because of this delay."

Mohammed and the Western Curse had done nothing since he had first met Xan.

"You do this and I'll get you a bomb. Fair?"

Mohammed leaned in. "Are you talking about what I think you're talking about?" he asked.

"Eight kilotons won't level a city, but the psychological damage would be immeasurable," Xan said. "In a highly populated area like New York, it'd kill millions."

Mohammed didn't move a muscle while he processed the trade.

"Eighty of my men, and the device you're providing will shut down the bionic?"

"And the necessary weapons to execute the job," Xan said. He looked directly into Mohammed's eyes. "And all the credit will be yours."

= = =

Evan had found a new drug.

The King Sleeper worked in eighteen-hour shifts. His missions consisted of three different tasks: gathering, destroying, and influencing. Depending on the breadth of each task, he sometimes did all at once.

Evan liked being Justin's father. That was a drug and by itself it seemed innocent. But the boy was abducted, his parents were killed at Lindo's order, he was twelve years old and he had been drugged unconscious for six months, and he, as the boy's father, was having him influence presidents and parliaments, and kill those who just wouldn't listen.

The Reverse Data Push. The ability of Justin's mindscape to expand rapidly and cause a target's mind to seize, stroke out, and die. The latest victim was President Hu after he vetoed the bill to share their oil with the Coalition.

The King Sleeper did this by planting a codec in a person's mind. That codec behaved like a latent malignant cell. It could be in there forever, never causing harm. Or with a simple data trigger, it could multiply by trillions, overloading neurons and synapses with junk information until the brain choked and fried.

So if being Justin's father was weed, for Evan, the Reverse Data Push was crack cocaine. Evan felt the guilt and the excitement all at once, like he was a kid watching porn with his parents just down the hall. But he couldn't stop himself. The King Sleeper was uploading this codec into the brain of every person online. Six billion people. The King Sleeper was ungodly powerful, but even then, he could only do seventy-five hundred people per minute. In two years, every man, woman, and child could live or die at Lindo's whim. Evan would be the sickled shadow in the corner of their eye.

The first five hundred people Evan implanted were his associates. General Boen was at the top of the list, as was the President, the Senators, top military brass, Cynthia and her scientists—and all of their families and loved ones. Anyone that could be an obstacle and anyone that they cared about who could be used as leverage. Evan knew that he couldn't have the entire Senate drop dead, that he'd need to use some restraint, but the very fact that he would *know* they had his little string of numbers in their head changed the game. He could be bold and brazen and demanding.

The boy asked him a question and Evan responded. Not as himself, but as Frank McWilliams, who had died in a shower and then burned with accelerant.

Evan was fine with it.

THE NORTHERN STAR: THE BEGINNING

CHAPTER 13

During the Great Migration, O'Hare International Airport was converted into a national train station. As Chicago grew out and rail became the de facto mode of transportation, O'Hare was the logical choice. It had pre-existing infrastructure that could easily be adapted and it had land. Fifteen years ago, fields surrounded it. Now it was skyscrapers.

Antoine Versad was a Frenchman. He had red hair, buzzed short, and a five o'clock shadow that had to be groomed once a day. He spent two years in the French army before getting kicked out for misconduct. The charges were dropped but there was nothing left for him in France. He came to the U.S. by boat hoping to change his fortune, and he had.

He felt the train slow down as they approached O'Hare from New York. He sat in the first class section of the train. Scattered throughout the other cars were eighty of his associates. Some looked like businessmen, some looked like hippies and students. They were white, black, Asian, Middle Eastern, Indian.

The common bond between them was the Western Curse and this mission. Strapped beneath each of their seats was a submachine gun with two hundred rounds of ammunition. In the cargo department they had twenty RPG's, fifty grenades, two M134 mini guns, and one hundred pounds of C-4 explosive.

The discipline and patience that Mohammed had instilled in the Western Curse had allowed his people to penetrate deep into the arteries of American society. The rail was going to be exploited today. Tomorrow it could be the shipyards or the power plants.

Antoine was in charge of this mission. The goal was to take over the station, gather as many hostages as possible, and kill one every five minutes until the giant came. Antoine had a very sophisticated computer with him. It created its own network that hacked into anything with wireless connectivity within fifty yards of it. A Chinese operative had passed it to Mohammed, who had passed it to Antoine.

"This computer is worth twenty million dollars," Mohammed had said when he handed it over. "Don't drop it."

Mohammed had told him that the hack would burrow into the giant and render him useless. The RPGs, the C-4, the miniguns, all of those could damage it, but the computer was what would disconnect the human from the machine. When that happened, Antoine would stroll up to the man buried in metal and shoot him in the head. They would broadcast it live throughout cyberspace. It was the Western Curse's coming out party and Antoine would be the star of the show.

From his window, Antoine watched O'Hare as they approached. He had done reconnaissance on it twice now. It was a huge structure, but they had enough manpower to take over its entrances and then collapse back into its heart and set up the defensive measures.

The train pulled into the terminal and its electric motors hummed down. His travel neighbor said goodbye and Antoine wished him a good time in Chicago. Antoine reached beneath his seat and pulled out a small plastic briefcase that had been attached underneath. Inside the case, like all the others, was an Uzi-Pro submachine gun. It was the size of a large handgun, but it fired nine millimeter at a rate of one thousand and fifty rounds per minute, and it had a fifty round magazine and three more spares.

He stood up with his two packages and no one blinked. He and the others shuffled out of the train and each team of four splintered off to their assigned exits.

It was 12:10. Perfect. At 12:30 the operation would begin.

= = =

"I was just about to call you," Evan said. He was watching the news report. Eighty to one hundred terrorists had completely shut down O'Hare train station and they had five hundred hostages. They called themselves the Western Curse and a red headed Frenchman ranted to an IP camera about what they stood for, blah, blah, blah and then shot a hostage execution style.

"This is the one," General Boen said. "I hope Janis squishes the Frenchy's head between his fingers. Can you believe this guy? He's already shot five hostages."

"He'll get his. I've cleared the rail from Virginia to O'Hare. The team is assembling and we should be outbound in thirty minutes," Evan said.

"Excellent. I'll be there in twenty." Boen had relocated outside the base to train the special forces unit attached to Janis. They settled on a team of six.

Evan rubbed his eyes. They were killing a hostage every five minutes. Even at two hundred and fifty miles per hour it would take them three hours to get there. Over sixty people would be dead. *Nothing I can do about it.*

They were shooting them in front of the camera. They put the hostage on their knees and told them to say their name, where they were from, and what they wanted to tell their loved ones. And then the French guy would say "the victims in the Middle East never had that courtesy," and he would shoot them in the head.

Evan decided he would extend that same courtesy to the Western Curse. Camera on, say what you want, until Janis crushes you down. And when he got to the Frenchmen, he'd do it slow, let him know that he was going to hell. That was the problem with countries facing these threats— they were too polite, too bound by the bizarre etiquette of war. Evan liked the Middle Eastern philosophy. *An eye for an eye.* Hell, double it up, do a twofer. *Two eyes for one. I betcha crime would stop then.* Evan walked out of his office and his security detail swept him toward the train.

= = =

Tank Major Janis had six assistants that worked in four-hour shifts due to the radioactive toxicity of his suit. They were all scientists and engineers. The assistants were needed because his movements were now an exponential equivalent to what they had been. He couldn't scratch his face, each fingertip was as big as his cheek and he would fracture his skull. He couldn't bathe, he couldn't change the contents of his nutrient pump or waste canister. He couldn't write or flip a page in a book. The assistants did this and after a while, the six of them melded into an extra pair of hands that worked around him, always keeping him comfortable.

He was on the train. Sue, the assistant on shift, scaled over him like he was a climbing wall. She oiled the gears in between the armor, she checked the hydraulshock chamber for any obstruction or loose fitting components, she shaved his face. The relationship between him and his assistants was like an evolution of nature, an Egyptian plover cleaning the teeth of a crocodile.

"How am I looking, Sue?" Janis asked. He saw her working on his left shoulder.

"Good, big sexy," she said. He dug Sue. She was a little Asian woman, mid-twenties, with brains and attitude.

"Eric, put out your hands, por favor," another technician, Jed, requested. He handled diagnostics of Janis's implant. Sue jumped off him and he raised his thousand pound arms in front of him.

"Wiggle'em," Jed said.

Each finger, the size of a man's arm, moved up and down like he was playing a piano.

Jed was checking for latency: Janis's brain commands, the implant's interpretation and conversion of these commands, and the battle chassis' accuracy of the conversion. Finger movement was the easiest movement to measure and the most difficult for the implant to interpret. Everything looked ducky.

"Excellent, Eric. We're running at less than a tenth of a second delay," Jed said. He turned to two soldiers nearby. "Load'em up."

Janis opened the chamber of each hydraulshock. The two men unlocked the armory on the opposite side of the train car. On the ground were two loaded hydraulshock magazines. Each housed six artillery rounds that, when Janis punched, generated over three and a half million foot-pounds of energy. The total weight of a loaded magazine was three hundred pounds. Together they grabbed the handles of one and lifted with their legs. They crab walked one to Eric's right side and the other to his left, breathing heavy from the exercise.

They climbed up Janis and knelt near his neck. Janis effortlessly lifted each artillery magazine to his shoulders. The men guided each onto rails mounted into his shoulders and locked them into place. Done, they jumped down and cleared away. With a CLACK! the hydraulshock chamber slammed shut and loaded one round into each arm.

"What's our ETA?" Janis asked. They had quarantined him from his six-soldier team due to the health risk. Thirty minutes before the train was to dock at O'Hare, they would meet up with General Boen for a final run through.

"We're forty-five out," Boen said over the comm.

Janis listened to music before missions. It calmed him. Sue cranked *Amnesiac,* a classic album by Radiohead. Janis closed his eyes and meditated, thinking about the upcoming battle, his movements, ways he could protect the team.

The train stopped one mile short. From the live video the Western Curse broadcasted on the web and the schematics of the building, the terrorists were on the gate-level floor at the center of Terminal 3.

General Boen routed their train to Terminal 1. This allowed them to arrive on the terrorists' blind side. The Western Curse had taken over Terminal 3 at 12:30 p.m. It was now 3:30 p.m and the sun was still out. For one mile, the Tank Major and the soldiers would be completely exposed either to sniper fire or the tell of their strategy.

"Good luck," Boen said.

Janis and his team ran through a tall field, cutting across unused tarmac that time and weather had broken up into a million-piece jigsaw puzzle.

Janis had trained with these soldiers for three months under the watchful eye of General Boen. The addition of a Tank Major to a small team posed both benefits and problems. The biggest problems were noise and weight. At its quietest, the Tank Major sounded like a gas-powered car at idle. At its loudest, when the engines were spun up for battle, the room would shake from the energy.

Tank Major Janis weighed four tons. This allowed him to cut through vehicles and walls like they were made out of paper, but it also reduced his applications. Not all floors could handle four tons spread out over two feet.

In tests, Janis would fall right through some floors when he tried to walk, let alone run. So it was quite possible that in battle, he would be left behind as his team went up stairs to face a combatant that had high offensive capabilities. Modern industrial buildings, like skyscrapers, could support his weight, but the elevators in them could not.

However, under the right circumstances, the benefits were astounding. Tank Major Janis was an active, intelligent, and offensive human shield. The soldiers were trained to 'stack up' behind Janis and allow him to take the brunt of the enemy's offense. This reduced the human infantry to a two hundred and seventy degree window of danger and it also allowed them to peel off discreetly at doors or behind other structures, completely hidden from the enemy's view.

The benefits outweighed the negatives a hundred fold. But just like all weapons, there was a time and a place to use it.

When they got within rifle range, the six soldiers got behind Janis. He became their shield. When they got underneath Terminal 1, two of the soldiers branched out ahead. They were fast and quiet, the scouts.

They got to a garage entrance of Terminal 1. This would get them into the service level of the building where luggage was sorted and the equipment was stored. Janis easily forced the gate open.

Once again, the six soldiers stacked behind him as they entered. Inside, the scouts moved ahead, calling clear through their closed circuit comm as they weaved between the conveyor belts and through the compressed air powered service vehicles.

"We're in Terminal 1," Janis said in his comm.

"Looking at the schematic," General Boen said. "You are at a service elevator. Past that are stairs that lead up to the main floor. Ignore those. Past that is a service tunnel that connects all of the terminals. It's used for VIPs. We have word that it hasn't been used since the conversion to rail. Sending the schematic."

Janis received the schematics wirelessly. He behaved as the team's data center. Within one hundred yards of his position, his team could download information into their comm sent to him by Command. The soldiers paused and reviewed the data in their viewfinder before moving on.

They passed the service elevator and stairs and found locked double doors. Janis pulled them open and the men stacked behind him. Below were stairs that disappeared into black.

"Activating night vision," Janis said. The inside of his helmet went from clear to a light green. A few visible steps into an abyss turned into a stairway that went down one hundred feet.

"We're going down. Expect a communication drop out, this thing is deep," Janis said.

"Roger," Boen replied.

Janis barely fit in the stairway. He squatted and hunched over, using his arms as braces against the wall. His feet were articulated, but even then, the stairs were tough. Under his weight the cement crumbled and the metal supports shuddered like a taut guitar string. The team stayed back until he had reached the bottom.

"I made it," Janis said.

The soldiers hurried down.

"The gate floor can hold you?" a scout named Estevan asked skeptically. Behind her it looked like a truck had tried to scratch its way through.

"So they say," Janis said. Estevan nodded. Good enough for her.

The hallway was long and straight, easily a half mile. There were no obvious ambush points, so they moved quickly. At midpoint, a hallway turned to their right and a sign said "Terminal 2." They continued on. At the end of the hallway was a set of stairs that led up to Terminal 3.

"Command, can you hear me?" Janis asked. He got nothing.

"I'll go up first," Janis said. He used all four limbs like a gorilla and crunched up the stairs. When he got to the top, Estevan came up with a camera wand. She put it under the door and looked around.

"We got three hostiles in front of us," she whispered. "I can't see behind. They know about this door and their guns are raised. They heard."

"Let's say hello," Janis replied. Estevan slipped back to the bottom of the stairs and got ready with the rest of the team.

= = =

David Hannah wasn't from the Middle East. He was from Berkeley, California. His parents were professors there. David grew up in a beautiful cottage overlooking the ocean that his mom had inherited from her father who had inherited it from *his* father, who had breached the shores of Normandy in World War II. While they ate dinner, as the sun sunk behind the endless sea, his parents would rant about the evils of their country. How corporations ran it. How the middle class was drying up. How we imposed our will on other nations. The irony was lost on them.

"The President is a puppet," his mother used to say over dinner. Tonight it was soy burgers and kale salad. "Corporations run the show, David. You might as well not even vote."

His father chortled at a comic in *The New Yorker*.

He legacied into Berkeley and there he was introduced to the Western Curse by his roommate and fellow political activist/anarchist.

"Who are they?" David asked while they ate a panini made with free-range chicken, gluten and pesticide free bread, and a slice of locally grown tomato.

"They're an organization that is against the Coalition's abuse of power. And they are *funded*, bro."

"Terrorist?" David asked. It sounded like an Islamic thing and those were everywhere. Nowadays if you closed your eyes and threw a rock, you'd hit some Islamic fundamentalist group.

"They don't care about your religion, where you're from, nothing like that. They just care that you believe in the message and want to do something about it." His roommate passed him the information he had printed out. David pushed the last of the sando into his mouth and licked his fingers clean of organic mayo. He flipped through the pages. "Huh. Looks like something worth checking out."

Now, he really wished he had skipped that meeting.

"Uh, Antoine?" David said into his walkie-talkie. Behind two large doors he heard a grindstone move up the stairs. The other soldiers looked at each other nervously and retreated. David didn't notice.

"Yes?" Antoine crackled over the radio.

"Something's down here," David said. The noise had stopped.

"Soldiers?" Antoine asked. David could hear the excitement in the man's voice. He wanted a battle.

"I don't know," David replied.

"Report back when you do." Antoine got off the channel.

David held an AK-47. Holstered was the Uzi-Pro. The other soldiers were gone. He looked around and saw them hiding behind the various machines and pillars in the room. He slowly walked up to the door.

"What are you doing?" a soldier hissed from behind a conveyor belt. David put his finger up to his mouth, telling him to shush.

Ten feet from the door, he learned what was behind it. The clatter of an accelerating rollercoaster vibrated through the room. A buzz filled the air. David didn't know it, but his hair stood on end.

WHAM! The doors flew off their hinges and for a second, David thought he was staring at a giant mechanical bull. It came out on all fours and then rose onto two legs. David could see a man, impossibly, looking at him from inside. It hissed and groaned, the whine originating from gigantic drive chains that spun in random orbit around its waist. They crackled with electricity.

David raised his gun to fire but it was too late. Janis grabbed him and pulled him into the spinning chains, eviscerating the Berkeley graduate like he had been dropped into a Cuisinart. The majority of David splattered against the wall to Janis's left. A thick, red, tapenade of skin, bone, and guts.

The terrorists opened fire on Janis. The bullets harmlessly flicked off his armor. Janis charged through the conveyor belt and stepped on one, smearing him across the linoleum.

Another terrorist launched a forty millimeter grenade from the underbarrel of his rifle but he was too close for it to arm. The grenade ricocheted off Janis with a twang and exploded against a wall, showering the room with shards of cement and dust. The terrorist switched over and opened fire with the AK, but it was pointless. Janis hammered him down, bursting him open like a ripe tomato.

Janis's squad rolled through the entrance and chased down the remaining terrorists. Most had fled when the mechanized god had risen before them. It was covered in Berkeley's blood. It looked born from it. A pagan sacrifice made in vain.

"We're a go. I repeat we are a go!" Janis said over the comm.

"Roger. You are a go," General Boen repeated.

"Go! Go!" he heard the other soldiers say. They were stacked behind him again. A set of stairs led up to the main floor. Janis spun up again and his body shook from the horsepower and torque that it took to give him strength and speed. He charged up the stairs.

= = =

Antoine heard the volley of gunshots over the radio and the wet gurgle of death. The giant was here. Antoine quickly hit the key command on the laptop. It began hunting for wireless protocols to hack. Three hundred yards down the hall he watched the giant rise from a stairwell.

It was big. Even far away, he could see the distinct armor: the solid chest plate, the carved armor that wrapped around the joints. The way slats in its thighs undulated with each foot impact, absorbing the weight. It was astounding. Pairs of little boots scampered behind it like a centipede. The infantry.

"One hundred yards," Antoine reminded his second lieutenant. He held the detonator. They had planted the charges. They wanted the soldiers close. They wanted the giant.

Antoine glanced at the computer. It had found a military wireless protocol. Antoine smiled as they approached. They expected him to be scared, but he knew what they didn't: the moves had already been made. The checkmate was just a formality.

= = =

They were using the hostages as human shields.

We should have predicted this, Janis thought. The soldiers behind him couldn't open fire. Even from here, Janis couldn't tell a terrorist from a hostage. In front of the crowd were sixty bodies piled like dirty laundry. One shot every five minutes with no demands, just as promised.

They wanted this, Janis thought. *They want to die.*

Janis stopped.

"Let the hostages go," Janis said. He voice was amplified.

No one answered. Janis could see that some of the people were crying and scared out of their minds. They were clearly held against their will. But others were drawn in, a sign of shock, but also calculation. They were at a stalemate.

"What do you want?" Janis asked. Some whimpered cries filled the air, but no demands. He turned off the loudspeaker.

"What should we do?" Janis asked Boen over the comm. General Boen watched the situation with a camera mounted inside Janis's helmet.

"At your eleven o'clock, one row back is a man with red hair and a beard. That man is Antoine. He's the one shooting the hostages. He is the only terrorist who we have a clear picture of. Hold . . ."

Janis could hear someone speak to General Boen. It was Lindo.

"Okay. We have confirmation that their video feed to the web has been cut," Boen said. "Proceed forward."

"What about the hostages?" Janis asked.

"Eric, they're gonna kill them anyway. They've made no formal demands and they've already shot sixty. You'll have to make the decision between hostiles and friendlies on the fly, but a Tank Major running into the crowd will disperse it. Over."

"Over," Janis said. Ignore the human shield. That was what he was just told. Before his hands thunder down, look into their eyes and decide good or bad. There would be mistakes.

The greater good.

We don't negotiate with terrorists.

Janis accelerated forward; inertia overcome with the instant torque of his electric motors. Beneath his feet the polished granite floor evaporated into dust, pluming around his feet like pollen.

Antoine choked when the giant charged. The four hundred hostages screamed in fear and scattered, ignoring the guns pointed at them. The human shield was supposed to stall the military. But instead, the giant closed in as if everyone was declared guilty.

"Blow it!" Antoine yelled to his second lieutenant. Nothing happened. He turned to see a fat woman scratching at the lieutenant's face; it was mutiny on a grand scale. The giant had turned an orderly hostage situation rabid. The room shook from his approaching footsteps. Antoine shot the fat woman in the stomach and followed up to the head. "Blow it!" he screamed. The second lieutenant hit the button.

Behind Janis the floor exploded upward and then tumbled thirty feet below. In front of him, the same thing happened, opening a fifty-foot chasm between him and the terrorists. They were stranded on an island. Janis could jump down unharmed, but the six behind him could not. Thirty feet was too far for them when the ground below was tons of ragged steel and stone, angled and sharp like pikes in a punji pit.

"We lost Mitch!" Janis heard over the comm. Whether Mitch was dead or alive wasn't the question. He had fallen below. It was now five soldiers and the giant completely exposed with no exit.

The wail of miniguns filled the air. A section of crowd exploded into meat, popping and pulsing as they slopped to the floor. A few fortunate souls crawled through the blood and gore to escape the hail of lead. Janis's armor sparked like flint on steel. They were trying to kill the soldiers huddled behind him. Janis heard Estevan scream as a round tore through her thigh. Janis crouched like a hockey goalie to block the bullets from getting through.

Janis could barely hear the comm. Lead drummed off his helmet and the miniguns screamed.

"THEY'RE FLANKING. WE CAN'T STAY UP HERE!" another soldier, Hostettler, yelled.

Janis saw the terrorists on each side run from support pillar to support pillar. They had assault rifles. He would live but his team, flesh and blood wrapped in Kevlar suits, would get overwhelmed. He saw twenty on both sides, covering and moving, basic military training. His team hunched against his tree sized legs and took aim, keeping their sights between the pillars the terrorists would have to cross.

Antoine watched from the cover of a men's bathroom as the giant hunched down to save his companions from the volley of lead. He saw his soldiers flanking, getting past the immovable man. He smiled. The computer had hacked into Janis and it was now uploading the software that Mohammed had promised would end this. From the progress bar, it was minutes away.

"Hit him with the RPGs," Antoine said into his walkie-talkie. Four soldiers magically appeared from behind pillars, thirty yards from Janis.

Janis saw the vapor trail of the RPGs before he registered what was happening. Four RPG's hit him simultaneously. They rocked him enough that he had to brace himself with an arm against the ground, but they caused no damage. *We have to get out of here.*

"Are any of them at our back?" Janis yelled.

"No. We're clear on our back." Hostettler fired on three terrorists perpendicular to the Tank Major.

"Eject! Hang on to your guns," Janis said. "We're ejecting!"

Ejecting was used to remove "soft soldiers" from situations of imminent death. It had been practiced three times. The first two, Janis had broken the test soldier's legs and caused a concussion for another. He had to nail it.

"Estevan, you're coming with me," Janis growled.

"Yes, sir."

He could hear weakness in her voice. The minigun shot rounds powerful enough to kill a grizzly. He hoped the round had grazed her but her voice told him otherwise.

Janis's upper body moved freely three hundred and sixty degrees from his lower body. This was to dissipate the energy of an unsuccessful hydraulshock attack. He spun around and grabbed Hostettler and Woods.

"Ready?" he asked. They nodded.

Throwing them was like a human throwing a cabbage patch doll. They were so light in comparison that he couldn't go by feel. He threw them low, trying to push them just over the chasm to the other side. Too high and they would fall and break. But a push throw transferred the energy into a roll. They made it over.

He grabbed Johnson and Bush and did the same. They all hit fifteen feet past the moat and tumbled another twenty. Each soldier rolled prone and immediately fired on incoming hostiles.

Estevan was as bad as Janis thought. The round had hit her below the knee and her shin was a bent twig, barely attached. A pool of blood beneath her dripped over the side.

"Hang on Estevan. Hang on," Janis said. He scooped her in his hands like he was holding a butterfly. Rounds rained on him, hitting his hands, his arms, his body. He felt another RPG hit his back to no affect. Syrupy blood dripped through his fingers.

"Hang on!"

Janis jumped down into the rocky debris and rolled to lessen the impact on Estevan. He heard her cry out. He stood up. The dust was thick, but he could see. Support pillars, ten feet in diameter were on each side of the hole. He moved quickly into the dark and put Estevan down.

"Stay alive," he said.

She nodded and tore at her clothing to make a tourniquet.

"Fuck them up," she said through her teeth.

= = =

Hostettler and Woods covered each other, backtracking and firing on the approaching terrorists. They had the left; Johnson and Bush took the right.

It was sticky. Hostettler had seen combat where splinters of stone flung through the air, dust obscured friendlies from hostiles, and the only thing you could hear was the ringing in your ears and the thud, thud, thud, of machine guns tearing at your position. This one was up there.

A terrorist—a young woman—came around a corner with an RPG, he shot her in the head and then shot the man behind her. More came. Johnson cried out, a round got him in the right shoulder. He switched the rifle to his good arm and shot from the hip as the other arm dangled at his side and the sleeve bloomed with red.

The ground coughed. That was how Hostettler would have described it. As if the earth hacked something free. He heard the echo of what they were trained to ignore, because the sound was so startling that the first time he heard it, he lost control of his bowels. He and the others dropped to the ground.

The comm earpieces had a low pass and high pass filter built in. These were designed to eliminate frequencies that could disorient them or cause permanent damage. The hydraulshock hit every frequency above and below what a human could hear. Five hertz to fifty thousand kilohertz. Their earpieces limited hearing response from twenty hertz to seventeen thousand kilohertz and rolled off anything above eighty-five decibels, hard limiting at one hundred decibels.

BAM!

A pack of terrorists to their left vanished in an avalanche of concrete, granite, and steel, that shifted fifty feet in less than a hundredth of a second.

BAM!

The dull roar in his earpiece. On Johnson and Bush's side, the ground was thrown onto the train tracks. Twenty terrorists vanished, blended into meaty clay by the tonnage of floor and structure that had been turned to rubble.

They were clear. They looked at each other, shell shocked.

"Janis, we are clear," Johnson said. "Thank you."

"Watch this," Janis replied.

Going away from them, the floor disappeared in a wave. Not from the hydraulshock, but from eight thousand pounds moving at twenty-five miles per hour snapping through each pillar as if they were brittle bones. The men at the miniguns couldn't react in time. The floor had become seismic, the energy led the charge like a sonic boom. They vanished in the wave of destruction, the floor churning and falling, plowed from below.

Antoine heard the mechanized monster beneath him and the screams of his comrades extinguished with a deep, thudding impact. The entrance of the bathroom hung at the edge of the abyss and he could see the giant's murky movement, a tarantula that had caught crickets in its burrow. He sprinted out the other side of the men's bathroom and ran away from the others that had stood to fight.

"I'm okay. I'm okay." But he didn't feel okay. He was shaking. He had seen the giant up close, he could picture it trudging forward, sniffing for him like a starving dog, smelling his cowardice.

"Shut up," he said to himself. He flipped open the computer that he was told would stop the beast. On its screen was a yellow smiley face and "file downloaded!"

But it hadn't worked.

What if it wasn't meant to work? What if it was for something completely beyond your pay grade?

Xan would have stood up and slow clapped at the revelation.

"I'm not expendable," Antoine said to himself.

"Get the FUCK UP," someone commanded.

Antoine turned into the gray muzzle of Mitch Ratny's SAW machine gun. When Mitch had fallen into the moat, he moved ahead two hundred yards to get behind the miniguns. His ankle was demolished, but he limped his way back up just in time to see this red headed pussy run away. He hoped Frenchy made a move.

= = =

All things considered, Tank Major Janis's first mission was a success. The female soldier—Lindo had no idea why a woman would want to do that kind of work—would lose her leg. That was the only military casualty. Including the sixty before they arrived, one hundred and twenty hostages died. Janis had killed thirty-five terrorists. The rest of the team killed twenty-five. O'Hare train station would need an extensive remodel.

The stench of the kill wafted through the train on the way back to Virginia. They hosed Janis down, but red pieces of meat continued to fall out of his gears and drop from his hands. The pressure sprayer took ninety percent of it away, but the other ten percent was like a splinter: it just had to work itself out.

They had the leader on the train. He was coming back to Virginia with them. At first, Antoine had been smug. "I want a lawyer," he'd demanded. Evan and the others laughed out loud. The man didn't get it. He was a ghost. Evan watched the resilience bleed from the man's eyes as the laughter continued like he had just told the world's best knock-knock joke.

Evan was now alone. He found the gentle sway of the bullet train soothing.

They didn't know what they were walking into. That was the problem with this mission. They got surprised. While Janis's open architecture allowed Command to upload or download information and pass this to the team, they had no real-time way of knowing what the enemy was doing. They didn't know position. They didn't know movement. Lindo and the others had gone in overconfident. They thought the Tank Major would cause the terrorists to fall to their knees and beg for mercy.

For his physical military inventions, Evan liked to sketch concepts freehand. He felt there was an art to it. In his lap was a pad of paper and on it was a flying disk. At its center was a turbine blade. Scrawled in the upper right hand corner was a description: "x-ray scope, infrared scope, HD camera, night vision scope."

Like the Tank Major, he could clearly see the design. He understood how it was powered and its purpose. He paused and looked at his drawing. He bit on the top of the pencil. And then he wrote "Hover-rover Concept" at the top.

It would be easy to implement. The majority of the technology needed was already built into the giant two train cars back.

= = =

The smell made Janis nauseous. It was like someone had shoved raw steak into his nostrils. Terry, the assistant on duty, was a fifty-year-old hippy with long gray hair, a walrus mustache, and a soft midsection. He was cleaning between Janis's armored plates and gears with a large hand brush and a power sprayer. The ground beneath them looked like a slaughterhouse.

Terry took a moment to throw up. He tried to move off Janis, but he couldn't jump down in time. Stringy green hurl splattered on Janis's left shoulder and rode down his arm.

"Sorry, Eric," Terry said. He pressure sprayed the hurl off.

"It actually made the room smell better," Janis said.

"How was it?" Terry asked. He worked Janis's fingers and the armor that protected his knuckles. They were matted with thirty different human meats.

"It was," Janis thought about it. It was so hard to describe. "It was like I was a kid and instead of playing with He-Man, I became him. You know how'd you have He-Man fight ten, twenty action figures? I used to make their castle out of Legos. And he'd just smash through it?"

Terry nodded.

"That's what it was like. It's a retarded way to explain it, but it was like I was He-Man. Like I was invincible," Janis said.

Terry turned off the sprayer for a second.

"I know I'm not supposed to ask, but what about all this?" Terry gestured to the pieces of people on the floor, slowly sliding toward the center drain.

"I used to have a hard time with it," Janis said. "But we got nine billion people on Earth. If you can't play nice in the sandbox, then you don't get to play."

Terry fired the sprayer back up.

"I'd like to see Estevan when we get back to base," Janis said.

"I'll put the request in to Dr. Lindo," Terry replied. He hoped the water wouldn't run out.

CHAPTER 14

Xan had been out of cyberspace for three weeks. It took two weeks for him to come up to full consciousness. Even with the electrodes and passive treatments, he needed a week of physical therapy to regain his strength. His first shower had felt like a re-birth. He had sex with a real woman. He ate a bacon double cheeseburger. And he waited for the Western Curse to hijack O'Hare train station.

From his office (*my real office*, he thought) he watched the same IP footage as the other three billion voyeurs when the Western Curse took over O'Hare. He waited for the giant. He wanted to see it in action. He had partial schematics and fragments of design taken from his months of hacking and trolling in cyberspace. While it was enough to build a prototype, it was not enough to truly understand how the engineering worked. They knew the American version had drive chains around its waist, but why? They knew the human body was suspended to avoid abrupt G-forces, but how? Guesses had to be made. He didn't have the technology to gather all he needed. He didn't have the King Sleeper.

His mouth hung open when he finally saw it. He believed its size, he understood its proportions, but he was amazed at the way it moved. It moved like a man, no reason to over describe it. It moved with the fluidity of a giant man. A perfect engineering accomplishment.

The video was cut before he saw its rampage, but he had enough footage for his engineering team to dissect and reverse engineer their prototype to a point of divergent similarity.

The mission to plant the program in the Tank Major was a success. The Tank Major was on a train currently moving toward Virginia at two hundred and forty-eight miles per hour. It left O'Hare National three hours before. He knew this because the program that was uploaded into Tank Major Janis's implant was pinging a GPS satellite high in the sky.

The program had many functions. The pinging was the simplest and least likely to be detected. For now, it was all he needed.

On a large monitor he watched a red dot from the GPS move across the U.S. map. Soon it would stop and twelve hours after that, he would initiate the next program. Hopefully within a week of that, then the final one.

A twelve soldier team was training for a very special mission, possibly the most important mission ever conceived. Xan would go, too.

It was good to get back in the field. He wouldn't lead the charge, he was too important, but he didn't mind wet work. It kept his mind fresh and aware of the real consequences of war, something that men in situation rooms forget when abstract dots represented platoons.

= = =

When Antoine demanded a lawyer and they laughed, he knew he was in a world of shit. The interrogators had beaten him so badly he had pissed himself. Now he was in a jail cell with his back against the wall, whimpering. He understood what it felt like to be on death row. The only difference was that Antoine's sentence could be short, it could be long, it could go on forever. No one knew where he was, no one was going to save him, and the men who had taken him were certain he had information they needed. A quick jolt of electricity would be welcome. A cocktail of poison in the vein, he would happily administer himself. No luck.

A boy stood outside his cell. Antoine hadn't noticed him before. He was lanky with dark hair that bordered pale, freckled skin. He watched Antoine without blinking.

"Who let you down here, kid?" Antoine asked. He sat against the wall opposite the bars. He smelled the toilet a few feet away. Over the rim he saw splattered hiccups of dried shit. He felt his urine soaked bottom sticking to his skin.

The boy turned his head like someone was speaking into his ear. For a second, Antoine thought he heard a whisper like a gasp of wind through a tree. It gave him chills. No one else was in the room, but *someone* was in the room. He knew it.

"What's going on?" Antoine stood up and walked to the bars. The boy did not move. He stood six inches away from Antoine, well within arms reach. Antoine looked up and down the hallway. There was no one else in the jail cells. He didn't notice this before, but there were no doors or stairs leading out.

"Hello?" Antoine screamed. He looked at the boy. Once again the boy had his head cocked like someone was speaking to him.

"Who are you talking to? What's going on?" Antoine said.

The boy's eyes went dark. Not dilated. They turned completely black, deeper than black. Antoine searched the hallway frantically and then retreated away from the boy. The boy rose into the air and floated as if he had been crucified. And then the room snapped like rubber. Antoine fell to the ground and when he looked up, a purple and white pulsing snake was growing from the boy's mouth. It slid between the bars toward Antoine. He ran to the back of the cell and scraped at the wall until his fingers bled. And when the amoeba snake attached to his head, he screamed in horror. But no one heard him, because he wasn't there.

Antoine had been drugged unconscious two minutes after he was put on the train. He was now five miles underground in Virginia, two hundred feet away from the King Sleeper who was now rummaging through his mind, learning everything about him, from his first kiss, to his greatest disappointment, even how he used to kill frogs for fun. The King Sleeper hunted down information on the Western Curse, liquefying Antoine's synapses as he went. *No reason to be gentle,* Justin's father had told him. This man was going to die anyway.

= = =

"Mohammed Jawal," Lindo said. He was in a virtual situation room with the President, General Boen, multiple military advisors, and an abnormally detached Cynthia Revo. He went through the material he had torn from Antoine, who was now a pile of ash that had been tossed into a field.

"I know him," General Boen said. He had met Mohammed years ago at the White House.

"Yes, many of you have shaken his hand. My intel didn't give me all of his motivations, but he is the head of the Western Curse."

Evan quickly read Mohammed's bio to the group and then he brought up a current photo on large screen. It was a jigsaw puzzle. His eyes were there, his mouth, his hair, but his forehead and the sides of his face were completely gone, just a low-resolution approximation of his skin tone.

"Why is the photo weird?" one of the advisors asked. Lindo ignored the question. It was "weird" because it had been pulled from Antoine's mind and people focus on certain parts of another person's face. Antoine hadn't really noticed Mohammed's forehead or cheeks. So it wasn't there.

"This is as up to date as we have. If we cross reference it with a previous picture." Lindo did so. It was a full body photo of Mohammed clean cut, standing next to a former President. "We have this."

The photo was perfect.

"This is our enemy," Lindo said.

"Where is he?" the President asked.

"Somewhere in New York. We're searching."

Online. That's all the King Sleeper is doing; looking for this motherfucker.

But Lindo kept that to himself. He still had full charge of the King Sleeper. He looked around the room. All of them had the digital worm buried somewhere in their brain, dormant unless Evan wanted it to wake. The folks in this room were on a need-to-know basis and, well, they weren't important enough.

= = =

Cynthia pulled the Mindlink off her head without saying goodbye. In the situation room, she just vanished. She curled up and sobbed. She couldn't do it anymore. Sabot was right and her ego had kept her blind to his revelation. She had been on anti-anxiety pills since she had confronted Sabot at his mother's home.

Afterwards she had searched her soul and instead of her conscience coming clean, it had morphed into a constant critic of her life.

"Loser," it whispered in her head when she woke up.

"What makes you so special?" her mirrored reflection would suddenly say.

She was losing it and she knew it, but a shrink was out of the question. At her office, she pressed her forehead against the window and peered down. One hundred and fifty stories. Her eyes traced left to where the glass met the frame.

One inch glass.

She pictured herself falling, her short hair violently pushed back, her cheeks rippling from the air resistance, the pedestrian's wide eyes as they scrambled out of the way as she shot toward them at one hundred and twenty-five miles per hour.

Too easy.

She shook her head and snapped back to reality. A depressed laugh escaped her.

"If there's a heaven, that wouldn't help me get in," she said. She felt the empty room. It was too big now. She was imprisoned by her riches. She knew what she had to do to get out of her funk.

"When you're depressed, clean out your closet," her grandma once told her when she had been down about a boy.

Keep moving. Be productive. But move in the right direction.

She pushed the bottle of pills off her desk and into the trash.

She hadn't walked alone in over a decade. It was night in a bitter January that greeted Chicago every New Year. It was ten below with wind chill, and she was wearing a sweater, pants, and light shoes. She didn't mind. It felt earned, a self-flagellation to absolve her past misdeeds. The cold cut into her, causing her to shiver and her hands to ache. It sobered her from her month long drugging and she felt her mortality.

She walked briskly, her head tucked down, her arms across her chest. He lived four miles away. If she made it, she would plead for her life back. If she didn't, she wouldn't have to.

Sabot woke to a knock on his door. He flailed until he got his bearings and then he hopped out of bed. He glanced at the clock: 3:43 a.m. He pulled a compact pistol from a nightstand and went to the door.

He didn't look through the peephole. He knew from a grim memory that if a person wanted you dead, they didn't need to get inside. Put the muzzle of the gun next to the peephole and wait for the light to go black. Boom.

He positioned himself to the side of the door and opened it quickly. Cynthia stood in front of him, shaking from the cold, the snow melting into her hair and rolling down her cheeks. He dropped the gun and pulled her inside.

"You're freezing, what's going on?" He pushed her toward the couch, grabbed a blanket and wrapped her in it. He quickly went to his bedroom and tore all the blankets off the bed. He came in and layered them on top.

"I," she started to say.

"One second." Sabot filled a kettle with water and put it on the electric range. He came back rubbing his hands together for warmth, she was that cold. She shivered violently. He sat next to her and warmed her with his body, running his arms up and down her back, trying to get the circulation going.

"I . . . m sor-ry. I sho—ldn't have co-me," she said.

"Shhh. It's cool. Let's get you warmed up and then I'll yell at you," Sabot said. She couldn't help but smile.

The tea helped. She sipped at it, letting it burn her mouth and tongue. Sabot leaned against a wall across from her.

"I can't do it anymore, Sabot," she said. "The Tank Major killed more than thirty people, more that weren't accounted for because they were collateral damage."

"Hostages," Sabot said. She nodded.

"Janis doesn't even know. They did DNA testing afterwards."

"The terrorists deserved it, Cynthia. They murdered innocent people," Sabot said.

"I'm not saying they didn't. They did. But saying it is different than seeing it." She shook her head, remembering.

"We have cameras mounted on the Tank Major. They send video and audio wirelessly to Command. You'd see a man raise his hands to block the Tank Major's punch. It'd be almost funny if I could get the look of those people out of my head as his fist came down."

She took a sip of her tea.

"I'll quit tomorrow, Sabot, if that will get you back. You're right, I thought the Mindlink and all the good it's done overshadowed this stuff. But I'm like a doctor that cured someone's cancer only to give them AIDS," Cynthia said. "I'll be remembered, I know that, it's inevitable, but I want to be remembered for good, for truly being good, not just brilliant."

"You're not going to like what I'm going to say," Sabot said. Without the light in his eyes, she would have thought he was rejecting her again, forever. She waited with one eyebrow raised. "You can't leave."

She slapped her hand down on the couch. "Sabot! Quit being a moving target! What the hell do you want?" she said. But she felt good, she felt like they were back.

"Evan—" Sabot began.

"Is frightening," she finished.

"No shit. I'm a great judge of character. Remember that," he said. "He has your technology. He can build these things until he runs out of metal."

"Yes."

"At this point, it exists with or without you. That ship has sailed. If you hadn't given it to him this would be a different conversation, but it's done. But right now, MindCorp supplies the implants and the software."

"Yes?" Cynthia said. Sabot was surprised she hadn't gotten it yet. He didn't know she had been stoned for a month.

"You can control it," Sabot explained. "Not completely, not in the open, but if things go awry. I don't trust Lindo, I haven't trusted anyone less in my life. But we need to be around him."

"We?" she said.

"Yes, we," Sabot said.

"We're the checks and balances," Cynthia said slowly. The fog evaporated from her mind and she understood what Sabot had spoon fed her: no nation could oppose the U.S. while MindCorp was partnered with them. But MindCorp was more than an equal partner. And instead of being a sheep, it had to be a wolf.

"How long have you been thinking about this?" Cynthia asked. She was impressed with Sabot's insight.

"When I opened the door and you were there," he said. "I would love for us to sit on a beach for the rest of our lives, get too tan, too drunk and age poorly. But you're going to be remembered until the end of civilization, Cynthia. The time is now. This is your legacy. It's not about the invention or the power. It's about vigilance."

He let that settle in. "If I'm wrong about Evan, great. We won't have to do a thing. But we need to plan for the worst and now, while he needs you, is the time."

Sabot watched Cynthia as her amazing mind spun into high gear. She focused and the path of MindCorp, the U.S., and the world spun together in front of her like fabric from a loom. Each thread was a pathway and the consequence of each had to be known. There would be untold death if the U.S. went astray. She understood that. If she had to intervene, she would be committing treason and sentenced to death. She understood that too.

The debate could no longer be about nations and borders, it had to be about people and the greater good. Lindo couldn't be allowed to win. His interests were not the world's. It was as simple as that. Cynthia understood that all Lindo saw were flames and himself floating above them. She had to make sure that remained only in his dreams.

= = =

The next day, Evan got a call from Kove.

"Sabot's back," Kove said. "Cynthia says our services are no longer needed."

"Hmm," Evan said. "Okay. Report to the Derik Building."

"Yes, sir." Kove hung up.

Sabot and Cynthia had made amends. Evan thought about it for a moment and then pushed it aside. He was testing a new technique. Before, he would connect in as Justin's father and guide him, but he wasn't in control. He wanted to *feel* that power instead of just standing next to it. He wanted to ride the lightning. But Justin was too aware.

Evan acquired ten death row inmates who were now unconscious, shaved bald and strapped to Sleeper chairs around him. His hands were tacky from their blood. He had worked on them all night, installing contact patches into their skulls. The next step was to perform Forced Autism on them. And then he could test his hypothesis.

He looked up from the last inmate and caught his reflection in the shine of his surgical tools. His face fragmented across them like a horror filled kaleidoscope. His smile bent around the tray, leaping from blade to blade and he thought what he was seeing was prophetic: it would work.

The big idea was close. Unnecessary, premature right now, but this was the first step. Why be one when you could be ten? Or a hundred? Or a billion?

Why just be one?

He forgot about Sabot and Cynthia and what that could mean, and got lost in his own mind. It was the only place he cared for now.

CHAPTER 15

Raimey fought the darkness for four months before it finally won. He felt sorry for himself. He couldn't turn over. He was tired of sitting in his own filth. The sponge baths and diaper changes eroded his ego. But watching his beautiful wife slowly break down was what took him.

There was no way to avoid it. She was one of the strongest women Raimey had ever known, but in the six months after the bombing, she had aged a decade. Deep frown lines were visible even while she slept. Streaks of gray threaded through her once jet black hair. And purple moons outlined the base of her eyes.

She was the breadwinner, mother, and wife. And that was all superseded by her nursing duties. He remembered the sex they had when he first came back, the way she had rode him. That passion lasted for a month before the toil of a hundred diaper changes, a spilled catheter ruining a rug, the neighbor's relentless pity; when all of that dug at her will like a thousand pick axes, chop, chop, chop.

General Boen had kept in touch but even though Raimey had grown desperate enough to beg, Boen had nothing for him.

"In time, John. Just not right now. Is the government coming through?" Boen asked. They were but it wasn't enough. Tiffany had cut hours to take care of him.

For John, the world was in a constant eclipse. He would catch himself staring at the wall for lengths on end, not even bothering to turn on the TV. He could feel himself shit his pants, the crackle and pop of his fart and the warm pile spreading out inside his diaper. He would try to hold his pee, but if Tiffany was gone too long, he would sit in it, smell it.

She had been getting sick a lot lately and they both knew it was from the stress.

"Babe, you need a break from this," Raimey said. Tiffany tried to ignore what he was saying. Vanessa had left the dinner table and it was just the two of them. Tiffany started cleaning up.

"Hon! Please," he said. She turned to him. He remembered when her eyes would bathe him with warmth, when the good times of their life were like embers, keeping the love aglow. She had doll eyes now. Not out of hate, but out of exhaustion. The marathon was longer than she had thought. "Sit down. We need to talk."

She did. She rested her head in her hands. "I'm fine, John," she said.

"No, you're not and we're not," he said. He swallowed. "I'm an anchor babe, and I'm dragging both of you down."

For a second, he thought she was going to slap him.

"You. Are. Not. Don't think that! I love you!" she said.

"I love you too, but that has nothing to do with it. I'm wearing you out. I'm not saying let me drive out into the cold and don't look for me, I'm just saying you and Vanessa need to take a break from this. Go somewhere without me. We can hire a nurse or something."

She didn't want to say it was a good idea, but he was right. She nodded in quiet resignation. "I just need to catch up on sleep. I've had this cold. I should probably go to the doctor," she said quietly. "We could go to Florida, maybe. That's an easy train ride."

She put her hand out to him. "I don't like leaving you. I feel like I'm abandoning you." Her bottom lip quivered and she began to cry. "I'm just so tired."

John wished he could put an arm around her and bring her to his chest and massage her head while she cried it all out, but the days of simple support had passed. So many things he had taken for granted, and so many things he thought were their future, gone like ghosts.

= = =

She had bought the tickets, hired the nurse, and seen the doctor. Raimey and Tiffany fought over the length of time, but Raimey insisted two weeks. She finally agreed. Tiffany needed it, and she needed to sleep until noon a few days in a row and feel sand between her toes.

The VA recommended the nurse. Nikki Johnson was a pleasant woman in her fifties. She was built out of different sized circles: round cheeks, round stomach, round calves and hands.

Tiffany and Vanessa were packed up and their suitcases were at the front door. Raimey wheeled over to them.

"I'll walk you to the subway," he said. Already he could see a change in Tiffany. Her head was up higher like the yoke of life had loosened.

It was late January and Chicago winters sucked. John was wrapped in three thick blankets but his mouth had to be exposed to move the joystick. The cold made his teeth hurt.

Vanessa suffered because of this too, he thought. He watched her pull her suitcase—pink and too small— inappropriate for a ten-year-old getting her dad's height and her mom's good looks. *She has already outgrown childhood and I'm the catalyst.* She no longer bounded along like she was skipping from one thing to the next. She moved with the thoughtlessness of an adult.

They reached the subway station three blocks from their house. For a second, it felt like he was saying goodbye forever. Then Vanessa hugged him.

"I love you, Dad. We'll call." She kissed him on the cheek.

"I love you, too," he said. She ran up the stairs with her bag.

"Don't go too far!" Tiffany called after her. She turned to John. "This will be good," she said. "Are you sure you're going to be okay?"

"Nikki seems nice. I can really let it go now," he said. "Tacos, chili, sauerkraut, anything I want."

Tiffany laughed. "Yeah, yeah."

Their eyes locked, connecting their souls. We think we know our future, that our plans are just process, but tell that to God.

"We should go as a family next time," Tiffany said.

"You rest up, have a Mai Tai. Let's start fresh when you get back. I think I'm going to get a job," Raimey said. Tiffany raised an eyebrow. "Online," he explained. "I tested well on the Mindlink and almost all military and police training is virtual now. I could do a lot of things."

"I hear it's good for other things too," she said and winked. She gave him a long kiss. "Thank you," she said.

"Have fun. Get a massage, lay by the pool."

He spun around and headed home knowing he had done the right thing. He felt better about what the future had in store.

= = =

It had been two weeks since O'Hare, and Janis wasn't feeling well. He couldn't pin it down. The first week he felt fine. They reviewed the footage of the attack, they discussed mistakes, and they drilled new techniques. The engineers pulled him apart to analyze wear and tear from the hydraulshocks. They repainted his armor. The soldiers came into his room dressed in lead aprons to shoot the shit. It was good.

But around a week in, he started to hear things in the night. His room was in the bunker a mile down from the surface. It was a cavern fifty feet by fifty feet cut into rock. The only furniture in it was his maintenance chair. It was a massive slab of metal that he locked into while he slept or when they maintenanced his brain and implant to merge him whole.

He first heard dripping water. If it had sounded far away, it wouldn't have bothered him, but it sounded like the water was dripping *on* him. He stood up and searched for the leak. The bunker was carved out of bedrock; water found its way in occasionally. He couldn't zero in on the leak and he couldn't sleep with that sound.

The next day someone down the hall wouldn't stop laughing and they had lungs the size of a zeppelin. They never paused for a breath.

"What's that guy laughing about?" Janis said, frustrated. It had been going on for hours. A technician was doing his daily diagnostic routine.

"Who's laughing?" the technician asked quizzically.

Janis gestured, careful to keep his hand away from the man. "The guy! He's been laughing all day, he won't stop."

The technician nodded and finished the diagnostic. Five minutes after he left, two shrinks came down. By then the laughter had stopped. After twenty minutes of probing questions, they went away satisfied. His diagnostic was clean. He was sane.

And then the headaches kicked in. Big ones. No light pressure at the temples, these were railroad spikes through the skull. Doctors drew blood, checked his vitals, and inspected the implant. Everything was fine. They asked if he had a history of headaches, he said no. They gave him a migraine medication and a sleeping aid.

He woke up the next day feeling a little better. Now the headache felt like a bad hangover. Everything he heard had an origin. And Estevan was here to see him. She wore the mandatory lead vest draped over her wheelchair. They couldn't save her leg. They talked about her physical therapy. She noticed he was closing his eyes hard and grimacing.

"What's wrong?" she asked.

"The headache's coming back," he said. His vision blurred, and for a moment, it bloomed with orange burst. And then the pain ramped full force. He reached for his head.

"STOP ERIC!" Estevan yelled.

He opened his eyes. His fingers were inches from his face.

-This isn't real you know-

"What?" Janis asked.

"What?" Estevan replied, confused.

"Didn't you just say something?"

She shook her head. "I'll get a doctor."

-You died at the UN-

"What are you talking about?" Janis said to Estevan. He looked pained. He stood up and paced back and forth never taking his eyes off her. His glare frightened her and she cautiously wheeled herself toward the door.

-It's time now-

"I didn't say anything, Eric. What's going on?" She spoke like she was talking him down from a ledge.

-We are taking you where you belong-

His vision bloomed again. It was orange and red. For a second a bony chatter echoed through his skull.

"You're not saying that? You don't hear that?" he pleaded to her. He searched the ceiling for speakers. Janis shook his head back and forth like a horse shooing a fly.

"I'll grab a doctor." She was already halfway out the door.

"Yeah. Okay." He breathed heavily. Sweat covered his face.

She left for help. But when she turned the corner and looked at him through the safety glass, her eyes glowed like coals and her smile was so wide it halved her head.

Janis was unaware of what he did next when he walked over to his chair, sat down, and fell asleep.

= = =

Xan planned the drop time twenty-four hours after the third and final stage of the program went into effect. He and his team were now two hours away, flying at ninety thousand feet in an aircraft that was built for a time when fuel was assumed. He and the twelve soldiers wore suits designed for high altitude jumps. While the entrance was grand, they would be leaving on foot.

The second stage of the program gave them the complete layout of the military base and the bunker where they kept the King Sleeper. They had used both Tank Major Janis's cameras and then the wireless transmitter built into him to hack the security cameras and access computers on the network.

Each of them carried a submachine gun, a pistol, a knife, and a brick of plastique for door breaches, but none of them expected to take the guns off safety.

Xan closed his eyes and pictured what the base would look like at this very moment. He wondered when they jumped if they would see the flames from space. It was possible.

= = =

Janis woke up in hell. His room was on fire, and ghastly creatures had stormed in. Their mouths were stretched long and filled with molten ash. Their eyes glowed like coals and spilled with blood. The demons chattered like snapping bones and their bodies moved in and out of focus, in and out of frame, like they were being projected from another dimension. The room itself boiled and the air shimmered like thermals down a long, hot highway.

Three surrounded him. Janis jumped off the table and fell to the ground. The three demons swarmed him and he screamed in fear and confusion and rolled over two of them like he was playing steamroller at a slumber party.

The other demon ran to a door engulfed in flames, impossibly so, impossible that the door could still be there with the intensity at which it burned. The demon tried to get out but Janis ran over and slammed it down with an open hand like he was squashing a fly.

He moved away from the door. The fire rolled off it and raced across the ceiling. He ran over and grabbed his helmet. He didn't have hydraulshocks, but he'd have to make do.

Did I die? The voice had said so.

Did I deserve this? he wondered. Did he deserve Hell? He had killed many in battle but it had been for country. Did that admonish his acts? In God's eyes did that justify what he had done? Was he good, was he bad? He thought he was good, he felt he had done good.

"But here I am, in Hell," he said. He cackled, sweat beaded on his face and rolled down in sheets. He ran through the door. Demons were all around him, some running toward him, most running away. Two wore white lab coats. Funny. Others wore dark black, others wore camouflage.

Tank Major Janis ran through them all, hunting them down, ignoring their gunfire. But he couldn't ignore their howling faces, the bone chatter from their mouths and the constant blood pouring from their eye sockets.

If he was going to Hell, so be it. If they were going to drag him into the depths, let them try. But if sins made the monster, he wanted to be king.

= = =

Xan was two minutes from the drop. His body thrummed with anticipation. The world around him felt more intense, more crisp.

"Sir, you need to see this," the pilot said in their helmet.

"Put it up on the screen," Xan replied. A flat screen lit up the front of their compartment. The belly of the plane was loaded with telescopic surveillance cameras. Below them was a warzone.

A thick black cloud covered the area, crackling with a lightning storm of orange as gas mains, ammunition stockpiles, and fuel depots exploded.

"Holy shit," one of his soldiers said. "Is it that powerful?"

Xan nodded. He touched a device on his shoulder that looked like a hockey puck. It blinked.

"The Wi-Fi scrambler is more important than your gun. Protect it at all costs. If it breaks, he will see you."

Each of them had the device attached to their shoulder. It sent out an individual IP address. When Tank Major Janis received the address, it would vector the vicinity of the transmission and blur his vision to it, blinding him to the location. Without it, they would be demons, just like the rest. With it, at the very most, they would be an eye protein floating past his vision.

They had an extra scrambler for their prize, the King Sleeper. Their transport, parked one mile away, had a more powerful version just in case the giant wandered past the border of trees and found the truck parked at their pre-chosen exit point.

A red light blinked above them and the screen switched to a thirty second count down.

"Opening the bay," the pilot said in that detached pilot way.

Xan and the others turned on their oxygen and gripped the handholds near their seats. The bay door opened and the atmosphere around them became so hostile that without their jumpsuits, their blood would boil.

"Go! Go! Go!"

One after another, the team dove out of the plane and into the quiet of space. Xan was the last to go. There was no oxygen at this altitude and in his field of view he could see the entire earth and the black it floated in. A GPS tracker in his visor pinpointed their destination. Right now, they were slightly over the Atlantic Ocean. With the spin of the earth, by the time they landed, they would be one mile from the base.

Xan felt like he wasn't moving. He rolled over. The plane was already a silver dot streaking across space. He realized that while the plane was getting the hell out of there, it wasn't going up any higher. *He* was falling.

He and his team descended at six hundred miles per hour. There was no flap in their suit, no push from air, no sensation other than sight as the earth got closer.

Xan began to feel resistance as they entered the thin atmosphere. They were dropping until eight thousand feet, where the parachute would automatically deploy. His team was in a halo formation. They didn't need any strays.

The wind noise rose to a whipping roar around his helmet. It would be another eight minutes before they deployed their chutes.

"Check," Xan said. They had broken into the atmosphere.

"Check," each soldier said around him, indicating they were fine.

The moon was nearly full and that gave Xan and his team enough light to see the white plumes of clouds approaching. They looked solid, and before impact, Xan closed his eyes for a moment, the old brain ignoring the new brain's knowledge that it was water vapor. It took just a few seconds to get to the other side and then they were looking at earth, their GPS coordinate now directly below them, but completely covered in black.

Their chutes deployed and each person felt the rip of deceleration as their parachutes grabbed at the air.

Xan couldn't see land. Instead he saw a clearer vision of what they saw on the plane. It looked like they were floating into a volcano. A ruptured gas main was a geyser, spewing a half-mile ribbon of flame and smoke into the air.

"Stay on course," Xan said. They had no visual on their DZ, but the GPS showed them the way. They entered the toxic black ceiling.

The noxious cloud broke two hundred feet from the ground. In its place was an oily haze. They landed one mile west of the base, detached their chutes and gathered in the cover of forest. They shrugged off their spent oxygen tanks.

"Turn the map on," Xan said. The air was so thick it felt like he was breathing through a straw. The GPS map on their helmet visors zoomed in to a detailed map of their surroundings. It showed them in relation to their destination and each soldier in relation to each other. It pointed them directly to the King Sleeper.

"Avoid engaging the enemy. They should never know we're here," Xan said. The soldiers nodded.

"You understand the priority," Xan said. The team had been briefed: if any of them got shot and couldn't keep up, they would be euthanized. If they were trapped with the King Sleeper, they must kill the boy and then themselves.

Their silence was agreement.

"For China," Xan said. They moved through the forest toward the base. Even from a mile away, they could hear anguished screams.

= = =

Glass was in the bunker, navigating through the gigantic round air ducts that were laced throughout the facility. When Janis went berserk, Glass quickly grabbed a submachine gun and night vision goggles. Within a fifty-foot radius around him, Janis was death. But not above. He had no projectile weaponry. Glass registered this and scurried up into the ventilation system like a rat.

The vents were dark and now the hallways were as well: Janis had destroyed the power grid. Glass flicked on the night vision goggles. The vents were large enough for Glass to move hunched over. They were thick enough that he didn't worry about falling through. He moved quickly and quietly and with intent.

His mission wasn't survival. It was to protect the King Sleeper. From above, Glass had watched Janis's rampage. Nearly everyone was dead, horribly so. But the King Sleeper had to survive.

He got to the King Sleeper's chamber. The Data Core was dark and so was the rest of the room. The King Sleeper was still there. His little body squirmed in his shackles like a newborn waking up from a long nap. Without being linked in, the King Sleeper would wake. The world he inhabited had disappeared.

Glass was at least eight stories above the floor. He looked for a place where he could exit the vent and climb down. He saw a vent near the Data Core.

He worked his way through the duct over to it and quietly popped open the vent, and pulled it in. He looked down. *Fuck,* he thought. This was a one-way trip. Once he dropped down, there was no way to get back up. He couldn't sling the boy over his shoulder and climb eighty feet up the Core. He would either have to hide with the boy or hope that Janis leaves the area. Neither were great options. Janis had night vision, he could see just as clearly as Glass could now. And apparently everything he saw pissed him off.

Glass gripped the edge of the opening and leaned outside with his legs coiled. After a silent three count, he jumped to the closest scaffolding. He made it. He pulled himself in and worked his way toward a large bracket that held the huge glass tube in place. He bellied up to the Core and shuffled his way around it as if he was on the window ledge of a skyscraper. On the opposite side was a large coolant pump. It was ten feet down and a good jump away. He lunged for it and when he hit, its thin metal case shattered the silence. He froze. In the distance he heard someone plead for their life. The room shuddered from Janis's answer.

Faster.

He hopped down as deft as a gymnast. The boy was nearly awake. Glass began unhooking him from the Data Crusher.

= = =

Xan and his team moved quickly through the base, heading directly for the bunker located on the northeast side. Xan was in awe. The Tank Major had only been in the hallucinogenic stage of the program for three hours and already the majority of the base was in ruins. It looked like the giant had quickly gone for the utilities—power and gas. The exploded gas main was like a sliver of the sun that had been brought to earth. The team tried to stay in the shadows, but the main wouldn't allow it. The fire followed their every step as if it were aware of their motives.

Remains of people were scattered throughout their footpath. Like shit at a dog park, Xan would avoid the leftovers of a hand just to step into a large intestine ejected from a crushed carcass. Xan had counted fifty dead, but that was just in front of him. All around, in his periphery he saw the ragged remains of soldiers and staff.

The Tank Major had found hydraulshocks. Two of the buildings looked like they had been shelled from above, the telltale sign of this weapon, from the reports Xan had recovered. A Humvee with a mounted turret was torn in half and hammered down into scrap. The hydraulshock, just like a bomb, created a shockwave from its lightning fast movement and the shifting of mass through the air. Soldiers grinned up at Xan with their faces completely peeled off from the wind shear.

They saw the bunker. Blast doors designed to withstand an indirect nuclear strike were torn off their hinges.

Xan saw no one alive but he felt their presence. They were in hiding. Up in trees, underneath rubble, cowering under the force of nature that was unleashed, that they thought they could control.

His team made it to the bunker doors without incident. The dark gaping hole dared them to come in and they took the dare without blinking. It was their mission. The elevator lift was working, but it would take too long and be too conspicuous. They took the stairs down into the unknown.

"No guns, unless absolutely necessary. He will see and register live fire," Xan whispered into his comm.

The GPS switched to map mode and used Wi-Fi access points to determine their location. When Xan got to the bottom, he immediately turned right and they headed directly toward the King Sleeper's quarters, a half a mile away.

The bunker was a simple layout, but gigantic in its scope. The hallway was over one hundred feet tall and nearly twice as wide. The rooms that jutted off this artery were massive too, some approaching the size of airport hangars. In all of them were bodies. Some vibrated with last gasps of cellular life. Some open and closed their hands. None made a sound.

Xan had a hard stomach, but even then, he almost gagged when he saw a woman whose upper and lower body had been hyphenated with her organs.

He tore her in half.

They heard the giant and all of them became statues. It sounded like a diesel hammer rhythmically driving a pile into the ground. He was walking.

Xan saw his silhouette as he crossed the hallway three hundred yards ahead. He was big. Reading his size and specs was different than seeing him in motion. He hoped the scramblers worked or they would see heaven or hell quickly.

"Keep moving. Stay against the walls and out of his path," Xan whispered. They continued toward the King Sleeper's lair.

They were ten yards from where they had last seen the giant when he came out of the room. He looked directly at them. Through the face shield smeared with black tar—Xan's night vision's interpretation of blood—Xan could see the lost look of the insane. Janis looked tormented and confused, as logic and reason were raped by his senses.

He stared directly at Xan and his team. Thirty feet away, four steps for this giant, and he squinted at them like he saw a girl he recognized from grade school. Xan knew what he saw: a deeper black. Xan could hear his team breathing over their comm.

It'll work. He's too far gone. If he understood, we'd be in danger, but he blew past reason a long time ago.

The giant didn't move. He just looked at them.

"You win. I can't take it anymore," the giant said.

Was he speaking to them?

"Someone kill me. Someone take me away from here," he pleaded. He turned down the hall toward their destination. And then suddenly he howled in rage and ran toward the King Sleeper.

= = =

Glass heard Janis scream and then he felt him charge like a bull. He pulled Justin off the crucifix, the mounted interface of the Data Crusher. The boy groaned. The harnesses didn't take long to remove from the boy's body, but the face shield took delicate hands and time. It was the fiber optic mount into the boy's brain. Glass pulled the boy down and into his arms. The room shook from Janis's approaching doom.

Glass spotted a back section of the Data Crusher that would be difficult for Janis to get to. It had girders and cement, things Janis could hammer down, but even then, there was a maze of thick supports that would give Glass time. Maybe, if Janis tried to get to the back of the Core, Glass would have a chance to escape.

He bolted with the child, ducking underneath the supports that anchored the base of the Core. He weaved between them with the boy in his arms, carefully protecting his head. The boy could lose a leg, lose an arm, but his brain was priceless, irreplaceable. Glass treated it like an egg, sacrificing his own body as he dove onto his back and shimmied deeper behind the Data Core, away from the crazed giant.

Janis ran directly through the Data Core. Fifty tons of ten-inch thick hard treated, non-conductive glass shattered and crashed to the ground. For Janis, it broke around him, drenching him in a hail of razor sharp plates. He moved forward as if the sky wasn't falling, as if the billion-dollar structure collapsing onto him was nothing more than rain. His eyes were wide as he watched Glass continue to worm away from him.

The shattered Data Core became a million falling knives. Even deep into the foxhole, Glass rolled over so his back protected Justin. The sheer tonnage crashed all around him. He felt both of his legs and lower back get pierced. He heard the crack of the ground beneath him and understood that at least one of the pieces had penetrated all the way through.

Glass breathed deeply and took the pain. Even now, he thought clearly. His heart rate was even, his adrenaline in check. He heard the equipment behind him get tossed aside and torn apart. He understood the giant wouldn't relent until it absolutely couldn't get closer. Glass rolled over onto his back and shoulder-walked deeper, holding the squirming boy to his chest. Glass's right leg didn't work. His left leg was fine. When he rolled over, he felt glass push deeper into his back, a fiery pain, and then the clear dagger broke off against the ground.

He could go no further. He was buried underneath the Data Crusher to a point that no one—had they not known Glass was there—would have been able to spot him. But the giant continued forward, pulling industrial equipment out like weeds. His murderous eyes never leaving theirs.

Glass pinned Justin between him and the wall and turned the boy's head so he knew he could breathe. He pulled out his submachine gun. He might as well have pulled out a straw and spitballs.

So this is it. He thought he was going to live longer. He checked the thirty round magazine on the MP5 and pulled back the bolt to make sure it was loaded. He had another magazine in his vest pocket.

The giant ripped apart metal beams that could hold up a skyscraper and then he was there. Glass had them against a cooling vent recessed five feet into the wall. The giant got on all fours, dominating Glass's field of view, as if he was searching under a couch.

He raked his hands into the opening, but Glass tucked his legs under his body. And then his body jolted and he started to get dragged out. Glass realized his right leg was tucked and out of harm, but his lame left still hung out. He reached for it and tried to break it free, but it was pinned between the floor and the giant's hydraulic fingers. The giant howled and scraped its fingers against the ground, dragging Glass out underneath them.

Glass had no choice. The giant's fingers crushed into his pelvis and shattered it instantly. Glass pushed with his good leg and got a foot reprieve. The giant had his knee. Glass turned the MP5's muzzle into his own thigh, careful to make sure that it was pointed through the thick. And then he fired.

Glass emptied the magazine, destroying his femur and shattering the leg, turning a two-inch swath into ground meat. The giant pulled and Glass—through all the pain—watched the leg tear away like it had been held to his body with string cheese. He felt the last of the skin stretch off like taffy. His leg vanished under the giant's hand and both disappeared from view.

He took the shoulder strap off the gun and tied it around the remains of his thigh. He screamed—something he never did—when he pulled it tight. Already, he had lost a liter of blood. But the boy was alive. Maybe only a few more minutes, but he was still alive.

= = =

Xan couldn't believe what unfolded in front of him. The giant had broken through the Data Core pursuing a man carrying an unconscious boy who must have been the King Sleeper. Xan had known the King Sleeper was young, but just like seeing the Tank Major, the abstract knowledge was vastly different than witnessing it first hand. The child, limp in the man's arms, caused his heart to sink.

Xan and his team had spread across the perimeter of the room after a third of the Data Core crashed to the ground. It was everywhere. Xan could feel himself breathing in glass dust and he and the others covered their mouth and nose the best they could. Their mission was in jeopardy.

"Give me your C4 charges," Xan said. The others moved to him quickly and handed over small bricks wrapped in a tan paper. "Get the boy at all costs. Meet at the rendezvous."

Xan had to work quickly. He put a detonator into the first brick of C4 and after a deep breath ran through the shattered field of glass zigzagging toward the back of the titan.

= = =

Glass was weak and barely conscious. Janis continued to scream and howl at them. His hands shot in and snapped like alligator jaws, but he couldn't get closer. Janis retreated for a moment, and through his night vision, Glass saw a small man approaching the Tank Major. He had a package in his hand. *Bomb.* The man placed it beneath the giant's feet and sprinted toward the exit. Glass turned his face against the wall.

= = =

Xan hit the trigger. The C4 blast was just enough to knock Janis forward. He fell to one knee and rolled back to his feet, frantically looking around him. The field of shattered glass was now gone. The blast turned the enormous shards into razored bullets as they exploded outward against the wall. Two of Xan's soldiers were mutilated and died instantly. The other ten were still alive, some with penetration wounds, but stable.

The giant forgot about the two howling demons burrowed into the crevice and he searched the perimeter of the room. He saw a demon staring at him from a corner. He ran at it.

Xan watched as the giant tucked his shoulder down and ran at one of his soldiers. The soldier tried to get out of the way, but it was no use. Without slowing down, the giant slammed through the soldier into the wall. The soldier splashed to the sides in a bloody puddle.

His scrambler broke.

Xan stood at the mouth of the tunnel. He put another brick of C4 down. The giant walked back toward the two demons buried in the electronics. Xan turned off his scrambler.

"I am the one who brought you here!" he yelled.

The Tank Major turned and Xan ran, knowing full well that Janis saw him. That now his eyes were coals and his mouth was stretched and deformed, and every movement gave off a shivering bone chatter that drove the giant nuts. He felt him give chase.

When the giant gave chase and ran over the C4 Xan had dropped at the front of the room, Xan popped the trigger. The explosion sent the

giant careening into the wall. Janis ground into it, but his legs kept
pumping and he used the wall like a training wheel.

Xan dropped another C4 brick—he had four more—and continued
to sprint toward the exit up to earth.

= = =

Glass saw nine soldiers appear out of the dark. Their faces were
covered, but he knew: Chinese. *Brilliant execution.* They moved in toward
him and he didn't fight. He sat in a pool of his own blood and his leg
continued to contribute like a leaky pipe. One of the soldiers pointed a
submachine gun at him. Two others worked their way in to the vent
pocket.

They pushed Glass over and he was too weak to stop them. He felt
the boy get pulled past him. He watched the boy, covered in his blood,
get dragged out of the recess.

Then they were gone. Glass pulled on his tourniquet one more time
to try and stop the flow and closed his eyes.

= = =

Xan couldn't continue the pace. His lungs were on fire and his legs
were rubber. He was out of C4. It had knocked the giant off course and
confused him, but it also infuriated the Tank Major beyond belief.

"We have the boy," one of the soldiers said in his comm. *Good.*
Ahead, Xan saw the stairway that bordered the lift to the surface. He
could feel the giant on his back. If he could just make it. He reached up
and powered on the scrambler.

Janis was fifteen feet away from the demon when it flickered in and
out of his vision. The demons couldn't teleport. He had seen none of
that in this battle. But this one was different; it had put up a fight. It
vanished and in one final salvo Janis detonated toward its last location.

Xan was twenty feet ahead of the hydraulshock impact. While the
explosion was contained in the Tank Major's shoulder, the concussive
blast still threw Xan forward. His eardrums ruptured and the blood
vessels burst in his eyes. His head snapped back, cracking vertebrae, and
the rubble from the wall pummeled him, spinning his body like a rag
doll, breaking his bones like toothpicks. He crumbled to the ground,
unable to function. He fought to stay conscious.

The giant looked his way, but not at him. It walked around him,
searching through the mountain of debris it had created by punching the

ten-foot thick reinforced concrete wall. The giant's foot crunched down inches from his face. But by the grace of God, his scrambler had not broken. The giant walked past Xan to the other side of the bunker and chased another poor demon hiding in the dark.

Xan's team approached him. They had the boy. Against his orders two of the men picked him up. He quieted down. He wanted to live. He wanted to see this boy take the U.S. down. The irony of it would be too much. The weapons they had so willfully used for their salvation would be their demise. Two weapons that should have never been created in the first place. In a rational world, in a *good* world, the demented mind that came up with these should have been rejected, cast out into the dark. The mind that created these gods of destruction should have been imprisoned with the key lost forever.

But the man was alive and well, with a nation behind him. And that couldn't stand.

CHAPTER 16

Cynthia threw up strings of acid and spit. She tried to pull away from the toilet, but her stomach collapsed onto itself and forced her forward as her body tried to expel from her mouth what she had heard with her ears.

A boy. It was a boy.

A moment ago, Evan had called an emergency meeting. He and Earl were heading to Chicago from D.C. on the fastest train they had. Cynthia had heard about the base in Virginia, but she didn't understand the real crisis until Evan had confessed over the phone.

"I found the anomaly," he had said quietly.

"What are you talking about?" In context to the attack on the base, she didn't make the connection.

"The anomaly. The source that caused your Colossal Core to be shut down."

"You said it was a re-route, DeKalb was a prank," she had replied.

"It wasn't."

Cynthia was furious. "What have you kept from me?! I won't lift a finger, do you understand? I will shut down everything right now if you don't tell me."

He told her. And she retched.

Now, finally, her stomach surrendered and she sat down next to the toilet and wiped her mouth with a towel. The cool tile felt good on her legs and she gathered herself.

The King Sleeper. Evan had found the anomaly and kept it from me. And it was a child. He had been using him for months for his own purposes.

Sabot walked into the bathroom with a glass of water. "They'll be at the Derik Building in an hour. We should head out," he said.

She loved that man. Never again would she let anything obscure that fact. Anyone else—she included—would have come in and said, "I told you so," whether with words or a look. But not him. He handed her the glass and rubbed her back and didn't say a thing.

= = =

Nikki was washing Raimey when someone pounded on the front door. She perched him up and went down to see what the ruckus was about. Raimey heard the murmur of a man and even though it was unintelligible, the tone was cold and firm.

"You can't just come in! John! John! Men are coming up!" Nikki yelled.

He could hear the footsteps on the stairs and then the bathroom door opened and two men he had never seen before walked in. They turned away when they saw him in the tub. The water was clear.

"Sir, I'm Alan Kove and this is Edward Chao. We have been sent here by General Earl Boen, Dr. Evan Lindo, and at the request of the President of the United States."

Nikki came in and pushed them aside to get to the tub. Alan looked at Raimey, saying with his eyes that she couldn't be here for the discussion.

"Nikki, it's fine," Raimey said. She grabbed a towel.

"Nikki," Raimey said firmly. She stopped. "Please leave us for a few minutes. I'm fine." Nikki looked at him, then the other men. She folded the towel, put it back on the rack, and left.

"What's going on?" Raimey asked.

"General Boen and Dr. Lindo are on their way from D.C. They are meeting with Cynthia Revo, the founder of MindCorp, at the Derik Building," Kove said.

"Alan, you couldn't be explaining this any slower. What the fuck is going on?" Raimey asked impatiently.

"We're not one hundred percent sure, sir," Chao chimed in. He looked like he would put his hand in fire to light a cigarette. "General Boen wants us to bring you to the Derik Building for debriefing."

"What the fuck can I do?" Raimey asked. His crippled nakedness in the tub emphasized the point.

"We don't know. But General Boen was very clear that he was *ordering* you to come with us," Alan said.

Raimey was a soldier, broken or not. And while he was confused by the sudden urgency after all this time begging for the military to throw him a bone, an order was an order.

"Nikki! I need to get toweled off!" Raimey turned to the men. "Unless you're gonna buy me dinner, can I get a little privacy?"

An hour later they pulled up to the Derik Building. They wheeled him directly into a large conference room. General Boen, Dr. Evan Lindo, and Cynthia Revo were present. Cynthia's bodyguard stood in the corner. They looked grim.

"John," General Boen said.

"What the hell am I doing here, Earl?" he asked.

Boen chuckled softly. Sadly. "You wanted back in. Remember how I told you to be careful what you wish for?"

Raimey nodded.

"This is it."

On a large screen, Evan Lindo and General Boen briefed Raimey on what had happened. The test he and Janis had undergone was to become a super soldier. For some unknown reason, Janis had gone insane and destroyed a military base. Almost all persons on the base were assumed dead. There was no communication in or out, no way to surveil with satellites because of the smoke, and no way to know if the King Sleeper—something Raimey didn't quite understand—was alive or dead. It had been six hours since the base had gone dark.

"You're telling me that Eric was strong enough to destroy a military base?" Raimey said. "How is that possible?"

"He is unlike anything you can imagine. All the comics you read as a kid, he's the real version," Lindo said quietly. He was still in shock. "You'll be better. We've improved the technology already. And the armor design of your battle chassis will be talked about in history . . ."

Raimey interrupted. "Stop. I haven't agreed to anything. I don't even know what you're really asking!"

"John, I'm asking you to become a Tank Major, infiltrate the base, and kill your best friend," General Boen said.

"That's a lot to ask, Earl," Raimey said. "So I'm a Tank Major, do I just come out of it after the mission?"

"It's permanent. Your spine is fused to the battle chassis because of the g-loads that occur while in the suit. There's no other way," Evan said.

"So, what? I just buy a bigger house? Come on! Would my family have to live on base?" Raimey said. He was incredulous at what they were asking. The live satellite feed behind them showed thick tendrils of smoke and pockets of fire. The images flipped through different light spectrums and he saw neon green bodies scattered around like toy soldiers.

"No. The suit is highly radioactive. You wouldn't be able to be with them. You'd be a weapon, John. The most powerful man in the history of the world. For your safety and theirs, they wouldn't be able to be around you," Dr. Lindo said.

"No way," Raimey said. He turned to General Boen. "What were you thinking, Earl? Do you really think I'd leave my family for this? Bomb the fucking place."

"WE CAN'T!" Boen said. "Not with the King Sleeper. I know what I'm asking, John."

"I don't think you do. After all of this, you get to go back to your ranch," Raimey said.

"Your wife has cancer," Evan said. The room went quiet. John's face crumbled with emotions, blindsided by the non sequitur.

"What are you talking about?" Raimey said. He looked sick.

"She went to the doctor a week ago. They did blood work. Abnormal proteins were found that indicate pancreatic cancer cells," Evan said.

"No, you're not serious. You're fucking with me. You motherfucker, how cruel are you?" Raimey said. He turned to General Boen, but Boen's head was down.

"Earl? Earl?!" Raimey said.

"I spoke with the doctor to confirm, John," the General said. He couldn't look into his eyes. "It's true. They have to do more tests to know the stage, but it's true."

"People beat it," Dr. Lindo said. "But the military insurance doesn't cover all treatment options."

John was silent. His head hung like it was broken.

"John, we know you're signing your life away. That's why Evan used Eric. But we have it from the President that your wife will get the best treatment, regardless of cost. They will have a military pension for the rest of their lives. And your daughter can go to any school from now through college and it will be paid in full by the United States government out of respect for your sacrifice," General Boen said.

"How much for the pension?" Raimey asked weakly.

"Triple what you are currently receiving," Boen replied.

John let out a defeated laugh. "You really know how to put someone in a corner." He looked up at all of them. "Lucky for you all the bad shit in my life, huh?"

No one replied. They all stared at their feet.

"How long do I have to decide?" Raimey asked.

"Now, John. We have to know the status of the King Sleeper," General Boen said. "You have no idea how important this is. I'm so sorry it has to be this way. You know I love you, Tiffany, and Vanessa."

"I know, Earl. I'm sorry for getting angry at you. You're a good man." Tears rolled down John's face. "They'll be taken care of for life?"

Dr. Lindo nodded.

"She'll get the best care, regardless of the cost?"

General Boen looked him in the eye. "The best that money can buy."

"Oh, God. *God.* Please. Fine. Fine. Take me away, do what you have to, but take care of my family."

Doctors and technicians burst into the room and took Raimey out of his chair. He was put on a gurney and wheeled out.

Boen glared at Evan and pointed to the surveillance monitor. There were hundreds of bodies on the screen. "This is your fault, Evan. Keeping the boy a SECRET?! The blood's on your hands."

Boen didn't wait for a response. He ran after Raimey.

A surgery that should take two weeks was going to be done overnight. A training period that normally would take one month would be done on the train. Raimey headed into the unknown with General Boen at his side. The General cursed God as they wheeled this broken, proud soldier away from his family, away from any semblance of a normal life.

After the doors closed, Cynthia stood up to leave.

"Where are you going? I need you to help," Evan said. Cynthia spun around and slapped him. He reeled back and put a hand to his face. He glanced between her and Sabot, who had quietly moved away from the wall.

"Ok, I deserved that," he said. He wiggled his jaw. "But these things still need to get done."

"A boy," Cynthia said.

"Yes," Evan replied.

"A boy!" she screamed and went after him again. Sabot intervened.

"I didn't make him!" Evan said. His upper lip trembled. "What would you do if you were me? Huh? You say to yourself you'd leave him be, but no way. Not you. Look at the way you protect your inventions. If you died, half the shit wouldn't work because it's gotta be yours."

"You reverse engineered a Data Core," she accused.

"Yes, I did! And I'd do it again! You want the common good all on your terms like you're some pious judge and jury. Well guess what? God didn't anoint you to divvy out crumbs how you see fit. You're a part of the problem."

They calmed down.

"What do you need?" she finally said.

"We need to know what happened to Janis and we need to make sure it doesn't happen to Raimey," Evan replied.

"Okay," she said. "I'll have it by tomorrow." She and Sabot left Evan alone in the room.

= = =

When Cynthia got back to MindCorp she immediately had a military Sleeper send her all implant maintenance records of Tank Major Janis. A Tank Major technician used a maintenance computer daily to analyze the interaction between the brain, the software implant, and the battle chassis. Its most fundamental purpose was to monitor the latency of physical commands and return sensory input. If the analysis came back within spec, the technician had done their job and as far as they were concerned, the Tank Major was functioning properly. It was no different than a patient going in for a routine medical exam. If everything checked out, the doctor would say the patient was healthy, not dive deeper to see if they had cancer.

If Janis had gone insane—and all signs pointed to yes—then Cynthia was betting dollars to donuts the software implant was the root. A part of her wondered if she was to blame, if she had omitted some crucial bit of code that allowed the brain and the implant to co-exist peacefully. She tossed that notion aside. If the code was corrupt, someone nefarious had found a way in and done a little tinkering. It was the only possibility. She lay back in her chair and closed her eyes. Code scrolled up in front of her filling her mind and senses. She started at day one. On day ninety-three she found a deviation. A line of instruction, miniscule in the sea of programming code, was sending a GPS ping in a timed interval. She checked the date. It was the day the Western Curse took over O'Hare.

Someone HAD gotten in. Lines upon millions of lines scrolled past her as she floated in front of it. It felt like her own thoughts, but bracketed and returned and terse in the programming language that was as native to her as English. One week after the GPS pinging code, she found a more complicated subset. It turned the battle chassis's cameras on. She found pages of code that hacked into the base's Wi-Fi network and its on-site servers. Another command uploaded information. She couldn't tell what had been uploaded off-site, it wasn't saved to memory, but she could tell that it *had* been sent. *Espionage.*

She rang up Evan.

"Yes?" His voice was shaky. She pictured him huddled in the corner of a dark room. Good.

"I've found a rogue, stepped series of code that was inserted into Janis's implant," she said. "He was compromised."

"How?" Lindo asked. He was instantly more composed. "O'Hare!" he said with a flash of insight.

"Yep. The first deviation came the day of that mission," she said.

"How long will it take for you to understand exactly what happened?" Evan asked.

"It came easier than I expected. Two hours," she said.

"Boen and I will come to MindCorp." He hung up.

Two hours later, Cynthia outlined to General Boen and Lindo the subtle progression to Eric Janis's insanity.

"This was a complicated and very well executed act of war," Cynthia said. "Janis was hacked and the code was uploaded during the battle at O'Hare."

"It was the Western Curse?" Boen said in disbelief. Cynthia and Evan exchanged doubtful looks.

"I think that group is a pawn to some other interest," Cynthia offered. "To hack into the Tank Major itself is a *huge* technological hurdle. To do so and then plant a program so sophisticated that it inserts itself into the firmware code of the Mindlink without causing any malfunction other than the ones they desired." She shook her head. "There's just no way. I don't care how well funded the terrorist group is." She continued. "They used a three stage code. The first stage was GPS tracking. Very simple and useful. Tank Major Janis was pinging GPS satellites, indicating his location."

Code scrolled down a large screen. Evan read it like a child reads *The Cat in the Hat.* Boen's eyes got tired and he focused on Cynthia.

"The second stage used the cameras built into Janis for surveillance. It uploaded the data to the Internet."

"You've got to be kidding me," Lindo said shaking his head.

"The third stage was what did Janis in. It caused the Tank Major to experience a deep sleep and then the program—Evan, do you see this?" She outlined some code on the screen. "When he was asleep, it uploaded and installed the rest of the program for the third stage."

"To drive him insane," Lindo said. The beauty of the Mindlink was used against Janis.

Cynthia nodded. "It's hard to say exactly how it functioned, but there is an uncompressed audio file that activates whenever he detects movement."

Cynthia cued the track. It sounded like monstrous teeth chattering in the cold. Everyone squirmed from the unpleasantness of the noise. Cynthia turned it off.

"There's also specific code to cause vision to bloom, and certain color spectrums are altered, especially white."

Cynthia was done.

"This is good detective work, but how does this help us right now?" General Boen asked. It was a question, not an argument. Lindo snapped away from his thoughts and turned to Cynthia.

"Raimey needs to be a closed system," he said.

"I've already begun modifying the implant program," she replied. She had predicted the necessary changes. "I've eliminated all wireless functionality and I'm building a closed system maintenance program. Tank Major Raimey will be unhackable and completely autonomous."

= = =

The anesthesia took Raimey into a deep, dark dream. He stood on a cliff, looking down into a valley. Small explosions rippled across it. The muzzle flash of ten thousand weapons cracked and popped like fireworks. Two masses converged on each other. A major battle was at its climax.

He looked down on them unconcerned. The war below held his interest, but he felt no fear. He knew they could do him no harm. Over the massive battlefield, an oily gray cloud spun like a cyclone. It stretched for the horizon, but a crescent slash of a red sun escaped its cover and cast the battlefield in long, deep shadows.

He was a metal titan down on the battlefield, charging the enemy. There were other giants running alongside him and he recognized them all: they were dead friends and soldiers, men and women he had seen get rippled with gunfire or blown to pieces by an IED. And they had not healed. They were encased in giant mechanized bodies, but their faces were red and raw, eyes out, jaws hanging and though they were running toward an unknown enemy ahead, they all looked to him with a hunger, like he had an answer they desperately needed to hear.

"How many are we going to kill today?" Janis said to his left. Raimey turned and Janis was there, wearing the battle chassis, just like the others. Raimey didn't know the intricacies of the chassis and so his subconscious didn't either. Instead the large frames of the Tank Majors consisted of an absence of light. A visualized form of void and nothingness.

"I'm coming for you," Raimey said as they charged forward, unconcerned with the threat downfield, more interested in talking amongst each other, death dealers understanding that what lay at their feet at the end of the battle was meant to die. If not, wouldn't God have intervened?

Janis smiled, but his jaw split in half right down the middle. Each side fell wide, like two limp flower petals. His tongue was an eel emerging from coral.

"You're going to end me," Janis said. He shouldn't have been able to talk, but tell that to the dream. His split jaw slapped down against the top of his metal chest. Droplets of drool gleamed on the dark frame, reflecting the bloody sun.

"I have no choice," Raimey said. The dead around him, all giants, echoed his words. "They had no choice." That's what they wanted to hear. *They had no choice.*

Janis laughed. It was syrupy. He was choking on his own tongue. "You can't say that now. When you were young and in the ghetto, that'd pass. But not now."

"But what about Tiffany and Vanessa? You loved them, too. I'm doing this for them! They can go on to be something. They can go on to live again!" Raimey said.

Janis gave Raimey a look like he just didn't get it.

"Who do you think we came here to kill, John?" he said.

Janis turned back toward their enemies and Raimey followed suit. In front of him were mothers and fathers, children and grandparents. They were huddled in groups. They were the families of the dead soldiers that Raimey ran with. Each giant was here to kill what was left of their legacy: their children's hopes and dreams, who prayed for their safe return. A parent's mortal wish for their children to live long, happy, healthy lives; to never see their gravestone. A wife or husband's desire to get back their soul mate, who loved them at their worst and their best; a whole, halved, that could never grow back.

Raimey recognized Janis's ex-wife, who only left after years of therapy. Janis hid behind humor. It was the callus that allowed him to go into battle never knowing if he would come out. She looked up at Janis and held out a flower. He greeted her by crushing her down, first with a scissor punch from his massive fist and then with his feet, jumping on her like she was a trampoline. His other family members did nothing. Each of them held out a flower, or a picture, or their arms for a hug.

Raimey turned to the rest of the Tank Majors as they rolled through their families in an orgy of death. The dark black shapes of the dead Tank Majors were covered in rivulets of blood, thick with tissue. Children were matted into the ground like tufts of grass. Grandparents were torn in half, their entrails stretched like an accordion. And all of the giants screamed in unison that they were doing what they had to do. That they did it for *them*. All the while, tearing the ones they loved to pieces.

Raimey knew what was ahead of him. He turned and saw Tiffany and Vanessa ten yards away, his long strides covering the distance in four steps. They knelt on the ground in each other's arms. Tiffany had no hair. Vanessa looked older and tired.

"We just want you back," they said.

Raimey raised his hand up in the air, eclipsing them from the dusk that would not die.

"I'm doing this for you," he said.

And then his arm swung down.

= = =

Raimey's eyes shot open. He tried to move. He heard a whirling and a deep vibration hurt his teeth.

"Whoa!" someone said. Raimey couldn't see anyone above him. For

219

the second time this year, he stared at the sickly white of fluorescent lights. He tried to move his hands and legs—he could feel them—but they felt nailed to the ground.

"Let me up," Raimey said, still disoriented by his dream. The last image echoed in his head, the shadow of his fist about to kill all that he loved. "Let me up!" Again, something sounded like a chainsaw revving.

"Shut him down! Shut the diagnostics down!" It was Evan Lindo. The whirling sound spun down and suddenly he couldn't feel anything. Evan came into view.

"John, you just woke up from surgery. We need to put you back under." Evan looked at someone out of John's view, clearly pissed off. "You're not supposed to be up yet. We need to keep you anesthetized because of the pain. Do you understand?"

"Tiffany, Vanessa," Raimey said.

"They're in Florida. General Boen has sent soldiers to inform them of what has happened."

"Alive?" Raimey asked. He felt the drugs hit and Evan began to float down a shrinking tunnel.

"Yes, John. They're alive. Calm down. Go to sleep. You'll be up soo—"

That was the last Raimey heard as he drifted into a state just north of coma, a place mercifully without dreams.

= = =

General Boen had observed the multiple procedures that turned his friend into a weapon. Throughout the process he had slept in the waiting room like a worried husband.

The last of the surgeries was done. Raimey's vertebrae had been fused to rigid bars that ran the length of his shortened spine. He had been mounted into the gelatinous suspension chamber that was itself mounted on shock absorbing rails in the battle chassis.

General Boen sat on a locker room bench while Evan cleaned up after the final surgery.

"How the hell is he going to be operational tomorrow?" Boen asked. The procedure was identical to what had been done to Janis, only accelerated. "The spinal fusion won't even be set then."

"Do you have another option?" Evan said through the shower curtain. Boen could see his feet and the slight tinge of pink from

Raimey's blood.

"Don't be a smartass," Boen replied. At seventy he could still break this twerp. "I've only been cooperative, haven't I? It's a valid question."

Evan came out with a towel around his waist.

"I'm on edge, sorry," Evan said. He took another towel and dried his hair. "We'll probably have to go in after the mission and repair the damage. He'll be on a drug cocktail that will numb the pain, but still keep him aware. It's basically morphine and crank."

"Hmm," Boen grunted. He didn't like this. He had known Raimey too long to treat him like a guinea pig.

"Janis could kill him," Boen said. Evan laughed. He walked into a changing room.

"Not likely, even with John doped up. John's battle chassis is light years ahead of Janis's."

"How can that be?" Boen said.

"A lot of times, the biggest technological leaps happen at the beginning. After that it just becomes refinement." Evan came out dressed in a clean set of scrubs. "I learn quickly, General Boen. John will be perfect, maybe too much so."

= = =

Raimey's eyes rolled open and the first thing he registered wasn't sight or sound, but pain. It felt like metal stakes had been pulled out of a fire and skewered down the length of his back. Uncontrollable tears rolled down his face.

"Pain," he groaned. He was groggy, uncertain of his surroundings. He was seated, perpendicular to the floor in a gigantic chair. Men and women in white coats moved around him.

"You have to ignore the pain, John. This is as much relief as we can give you. We need to keep you aware." It was Evan. He came into view beneath Raimey and his giant chair. Evan looked off to his side, but this time Raimey could track what Dr. Lindo was checking. Four technicians monitored giant flat screens above a wall of workstations. On one monitor a wire-framed brain spun on its y-axis. A cursor chased small points that were blinking. Another showed hundreds of different waveforms—brain waves. It looked like a computerized lie detector. Another showed John's vitals.

"Turn him on," Evan said. "John, we don't have time to get into great detail. The software implant—what the monitor with the brain on it shows—is booting up. When it does, I want you to think about stillness. Picture your hands and feet at rest. You are sitting on a chair, nothing more."

John felt the implant. It was like someone was pulling on the back of his skull.

"I feel something," Raimey said.

"Think stillness," Evan said.

"It's up," someone said to their side.

"How do you feel John?" Evan asked.

"I feel . . . whole." And he did. After the injuries, he felt phantom limb in all of his joints, like an itch that couldn't be scratched. He would forget that he had no arms and reach for something, only to be quickly reminded that he was an invalid. But now he felt whole. No tingle, no vague extension of his body that was nothing but air. He wiggled his fingers. He heard metal-on-metal clacking.

"John, slow up. Wait for my instructions," Evan said.

"It worked, didn't it?" Raimey said. He studied the giant chair he was sitting in. It wasn't a chair. It was *him*. He wiggled his left hand again and, to his left, a gigantic hand moved perfectly. He looked at his right hand and it did the same.

"I want to stand up," Raimey said.

"John, we really need to get through the diagnostics," Evan said firmly. Raimey suddenly felt a side-to-side sway of the room.

"We're on our way," Raimey said.

"Yes. We'll be there in three hours. We need to upload software into the implant before we release you from the maintenance chair. We have a lot to go through."

John calmed down. The sadness and longing to see his family was pushed back under the weight of what was ahead of him. He could feel his hands. He could feel his feet. And it wasn't in his dreams or a memory or his severed nerves firing for no damn reason. It was real.

He listened to Evan and followed his every instruction. In his focus, the pain got pushed into the background. He felt alive. He felt purpose.

He hated this mission. He hated the primary objective. But he loved that he was on a mission and that, as silly and simplistic as it sounded, he was special. He would curse fate and God later. But not now. Wiggle the fingers. Lift the leg. Open the bolt of the hydraulshock.

I'm a soldier, he thought to himself. The voice behind it was strong.

He saw a bent reflection of himself in the stainless steel armory doors. He looked like a massive armored Viking sitting on his throne.

This was always my fate.

For now and ever more.

= = =

The train had stopped five miles from the base to avoid contact with Janis. Ten minutes before, two men loaded the hydraulshock artillery rounds into his shoulders. They spun the helmet down onto his head. The five-inch bulletproof glass was shaped like a skull.

His implant was stripped of all of Janis's wireless functionality. He couldn't upload or download data to Command. He couldn't overlay maps to his position. He couldn't laser guide smart missiles or send GPS coordinates for mortal fire. Various attachments that Evan planned for future Tank Majors wouldn't work with him. His comm was a glorified walkie-talkie. The only access to his implant was through two feet of the depleted uranium/osmium armor. But he no longer needed the maintenance chair. He would never have to connect into a computer for the rest of his life. He was the deconstructed version of Lindo's dream.

"Is the pain bearable? We've pulled back the dosage," Evan said. He was climbing over Raimey, double-checking that everything was in place, properly oiled and functioning. This was too quick a turnaround. It made him uneasy.

"It's fine," Raimey said. It wasn't. It was so horrible that his body shivered in sweat, but it was what it was.

"When you get out, run around and get a feel for the battle chassis. Hydraulshock a tree. We need you to understand what your body can do," Lindo said.

"What are the limitations?" Raimey asked.

"Not many that matter for this. Just remember that the battle chassis can take a lot more abuse than you can. Stay out of heavy fires, you can suffocate. Stay out of water, you'll sink like a rock and drown."

"Can I jump?" Raimey asked.

"A little bit, but not really. Not of any usefulness."

"Speed?"

"Twenty-five miles per hour. You will get there quickly. It'll just feel like running."

"What can Eric do that will hurt me?"

"The hydraulshock is the only thing. If he's out, hit him and be done with it. We need to know the status of the King Sleeper. Your armor is three times as dense, you're bigger all around, and you're more powerful. Aside from the personal nature, this shouldn't be difficult."

John's chair let out a hydraulic whoosh and Evan stepped out of the way.

"John, can you hear me over the comm?" It was General Boen.

"Yes, sir," Raimey said. It was good to hear his voice.

"We have a GPS transmitter attached to the battle chassis. From that, we can guide you to and out of the base. Clear?"

"Clear, sir," Raimey replied.

"Alright, let's get going. The five mile distance will hopefully give you time to acclimate a bit to this new . . . situation," Boen said.

Raimey stood up. The train was tall, the internal room was larger than a semi truck trailer, but his head almost touched the top. For a second it made him dizzy, like he had stood up too quickly. Out of instinct he put his arms out to brace himself.

"Hold on, John," Evan said. He held a two-way radio to his mouth. "Take it easy."

John steadied.

"Trust the balance of the chassis. The gyroscopes are processing one million calculations per second. You're not going to fall. Turn to face the door and look straight out as far as you can see."

The door on the side of the train car slid open. Raimey was greeted by pine trees and a blanket of stars.

"Look ahead, not down at your feet, and step out," Evan said.

John looked to the horizon and stepped out of the train, trying to not think about it. He felt his foot press into the soil and when half of his weight left the train, the car rose six inches. Suddenly Raimey started to tilt forward.

"Trust the balance!" Lindo said. Raimey looked like the leaning tower of Pisa. "John!"

It was too late. Raimey overcompensated and fell forward down the embankment of the hill. When he hit the ground, he felt some pain, but the suspension that floated his body within the suit took the brunt.

Without thinking he put his arms down and pushed himself up onto his knees. He turned and looked at the train fifty feet up the hill.

"Whoever parked this damn thing on a hill is fired," Raimey said.

Both Evan and Boen laughed.

"Trust the—"

"I know, I know. Trust the battle chassis to balance," Raimey said. He went to stand, this time not gingerly like he had brittle bones. His body stood up unconcerned with the steepness of the hill. Simple as that.

He climbed back up to the entrance of the train and looked in. Even though his feet were four feet below the train tracks, he still looked down on Evan. His shoulders were the width of the entrance.

"You good?" Evan said.

In the helmet, he saw Raimey nod.

"Find the King Sleeper," Evan said.

"I'm going to try and save him," Raimey said. He was talking about Janis.

Evan shook his head. "It's too late, John."

"I can't just kill him. Not without trying."

"General Boen," Evan said.

Boen's voice crackled over the comm. "I get it, John. But just from infrared, we have a body count over two thousand. The mission is to find the King Sleeper."

"I can't just kill him. If he was driven crazy, it isn't right. He's the best guy I know."

He pushed off the train without asking permission.

"Alright, Earl. Where the hell am I going?" he asked.

= = =

The train was west of the base. Raimey walked around the front of the train to head toward it. When he passed the engine, he saw the conductors at the controls. They gave him a salute and he gave one back, dinging too hard against his helmet, still getting a feel for his new body.

It felt like he was in a giant baby bjorn. He rocked back and forth with each step, enough to slightly jar his vision. He felt lumbering. He was. Sensors built inside his feet fed him the feeling of pressure. He couldn't feel heat or pain through his limbs, but he did recognize when his ankle bent inward or outward to compensate for a variant on the ground.

"I'm going to jog," Raimey said into his comm. Interestingly, when he picked up speed the ride got smoother and he could feel his body floating. His vision was no longer jarred, but instead, it felt like he was riding a wave as he rose and fell by six inches or so, compensating for the increased forces of the battle chassis around him.

"It leveled out, didn't it?" Lindo said.

"Yep," Raimey replied.

"The suspension system doesn't completely compensate for walking. But if you run or start moving aggressively, it monitors the movement and counteracts it. The harder you go, the smoother it will feel."

"Cool," Raimey said. He was breathing hard and it came over the comm.

"Calm down, John," General Boen said.

Lindo cut in. "You're breathing faster because you're jogging and the old brain believes that you're exerting effort. It's a natural response, but obviously pointless. Try to regulate your breathing. Your body has gone through a tremendous amount of trauma in the last twenty-four hours."

"Okay," Raimey said and forced his breathing to slow down.

"Find a large tree and punch it. Hydraulshock when you get a feel for the range," Evan said.

"What about Janis?" Raimey said. He was told the hydraulshock was extremely loud.

"I'd rather he's aware of you and you know how to use it than otherwise. He's probably in the bunker," Lindo said.

Raimey saw a massive tree ahead of him. He covered distance so quickly, it was crazy. It felt like he was riding on the shoulders of a kangaroo. He shadowboxed to get a feel for the range and speed of the punches. He was fast. Not blindingly so, but as fast as a heavyweight boxer, with ten thousand times more power. He stood within range of the tree and threw a left hook. The pair of drive chains around his waist, each link as tall and thick as a man's head, spun counter to the other and his upper body swung into the punch. His eight hundred pound fist hammered through the tree like a wrecking ball. The trunk was four feet in diameter and his hand exploded through it as if it were rotten. The tree collapsed down to the base and then with a groan, fell onto its side, taking two smaller trees with it.

"We heard that," Lindo said.

"Holy shit," Raimey said under his breath.

"An eye opener, huh?" Boen said.

"I threw a short left hook and my hand went right through the tree," Raimey said. He brought his hand near his visor and looked for damage.

"My hand's fine," Raimey said.

"John, your hand can punch through tanks without any operational damage. The density of a tree is like punching packing foam."

Raimey opened and closed his gigantic hand, turning it knuckle to palm in marvel. He raised it up and slammed it to the ground. He felt his body bounce from the counter movement of his suspension. He slammed the right fist down and the other again, like a gorilla displaying dominance.

Raimey began to understand.

He found a tree twice as thick as the one he so easily punched through. He cocked his left arm back and through a mental checklist, readied the hydraulshock to fire.

He started the movement.

WHA-WHAM!

His vision blurred from the acceleration as the jelly in his eyes pushed back, altering the light as it hit the lens. The sound leveled off in his helmet but his body shook like a space shuttle on re-entry. He felt heat and out of his left eye he saw a sharp crack of orange light.

He was disoriented. Shards of wood fell around him in splintered hail. He looked for the tree. Most of it had vaporized. Sixty feet of it had exploded and the rest of the tree had been thrown forty yards. The top of the tree was in front of John, like it had slipped feet first on ice. The earth was raw around him. The branches of the surrounding pines were broken and bent away from him.

"I fired the hydraulshock," Raimey said.

"We know."

The train had rocked back and forth from the concussive blast.

"Is everything fine?" Lindo asked.

"Yeah, I just can't believe it," Raimey said. He didn't understand the power he had unleashed. For this tree it was complete overkill. Raimey could deliver five million foot-pounds of energy through his fist, one and a half million more than Janis. Evan learned quickly and he pumped all that knowledge into the body Raimey was now saddled with.

"Be amazed later, John. Get going," Boen said.

"Yes, sir. I'm moving toward the base," Raimey replied.

General Boen watched the GPS dot move toward the base at an even twenty-five miles per hour.

= = =

Janis woke in the corner of a bunker supply room. At first he didn't remember when he had fallen asleep and then it came back. He had chosen that corner because there weren't any flames and none of the demons chased him there. He was exhausted. Maybe it was over. He started to turn and he immediately sensed flickering orange in his peripheral vision. He retreated to the corner, sobbing.

He closed his eyes hard, hoping that when he opened them, what he had been a part of was a dream inside of a dream, a hallucination in the desert from a thirst deprived man.

It was no use. He could feel the heat build around him. He knew the flames were licking at the walls. He didn't hear the bone on bone chatter of the demons but he knew it was just because he was in the corner, hiding, like a bruised boy waiting for his next beating.

He had run rampant for over three days. He had no food or drink in that time. On base, they didn't keep his nutrient pump full. He felt the pain of hunger and his face was gaunt from dehydration. His teeth felt like fur and he rubbed his tongue along them.

I'm insane, he thought to himself. He tried to turn from the corner again but he saw the heat and below, just in view, the glowing eyes of a demon he had killed. Even dead, their big grins chattered, *ca-ca-ca-ca-ca-ca-ca-ca-ca-ca-ca-ca.* Endless.

Do the insane know they are? another voice asked. Eric didn't think so.

"Then I'm damned," he said aloud.

I will live in this purgatory forever.

Early into the massacre the fleeing soldiers and staff opened the blast doors to escape Janis's onslaught. He ascended out of the massive hollow and laid waste to the surrounding buildings and anything that got in his way. But the bunker was his sanctuary and after he silenced the chattering of bones, he slithered into its bowels like a snake full on prey.

The few soldiers remaining ran up and activated the doors to close.

Halfway down, Janis heard the warning blat of the siren as the massive doors slowly came together. *They're trying to trap me!* He flew up the stairs. The closing gap was too narrow for him to squeeze through. He hydraulshocked them from the inside. He hit them again and again and again until the hinge of one broke from the wall. They closed cockeyed. With all his hydraulshocks, save one, he hammered through. But the doors were designed for The Bomb. And while his hands were nearly indestructible, they had met their match and now they were a mangled wreck.

He heard the sound of a hydraulshock roll into the bunker. The lift tunnel acted like an ear canal, amplifying the blast.

It'll be John, he somehow knew. *No, impossible. John wasn't dead. Maybe he's come to save me?* They had been in deep together, in battles where bullets whizzed by their faces like mosquitos. And they had made it out alive, watching each other's six, not letting ANYTHING break their perimeter. But not this, no way. Raimey was an angel, but he didn't know this place.

Then it's the Devil.

Good. Better in fact. If it were Raimey, Eric wouldn't know what to do. He didn't know the way out and Raimey would be too stubborn to leave without him. They would protect each other while the demons surrounded them and take wave after wave until the ground was churned with dirt and blood and their feet slipped from the batter of it and the demons finally overtook them, finally tore in deep enough to still their heart and then they would be stuck in this world forever.

Better if it was the Devil.

Because I am strong.

The Devil has never faced anything like me.

And I have courage.

Others would look down in fear, but I will look down on HIM, so he knows that two angels had fallen, not just one.

And I have no fear.

I lost that long ago. If I kill the Devil, than all of this will be mine, and maybe, just maybe, it can be made into something better.

Eric Janis, the first Tank Major, turned from the corner, a weary look in his eyes. He stepped over and around the cake of murdered demons. Their mouths chattered in applause for him standing up to their master. Or they cheered for their master, who had finally come to avenge their brutal end.

= = =

Twenty years ago Raimey had trained at this base. But everything he remembered was gone. In its place were rubble, fire, thick toxic smoke, and the smell of the dead.

"The southwest corner of the base is destroyed," Raimey said.

"Roger that. The bunker is at the center of the base," General Boen said. "If you see anyone alive, let us know, but don't divert from the mission."

Raimey slowed to walking speed. He didn't know what he was looking for. Visibility was fine, the black smoke hung above him in a ceiling. The buildings were trash heaps.

"*Help*," he heard someone say. It was a stage whisper, the sound of a dying man.

"Got a survivor somewhere in the mess hall," Raimey said.

"Got it, we have a team moving toward you. They will not go into the base until that area is clear of the threat," Boen said. "Keep that in mind, John. I know Eric is a friend, but there are people there that need us."

"I know," Raimey said.

Raimey weaved through the wreckage toward the center of the base. Two Humvees were rolled onto their sides, the bodies of men crushed in and around them. A small subway train used as a feeder into the larger rails was toppled off the tracks. A fountain of electrical sparks crackled and arced against the cars.

More bodies. Bodies everywhere. Spent rifle casing around some, useless against giants. Raimey heard moans from another building and called it in. He saw the bunker. The massive doors, taller than a bus is long and wide enough for four, were torn outward.

Janis emerged from its darkness. Raimey began to cry.

"You're on fire," Janis said to Raimey. They were fifty yards from each other. Raimey didn't recognize him. His face was thin and weak, like a cancer was winning.

"Have you come to kill me?" Janis asked. Raimey wasn't sure what to do. The question seemed directed at him, but he was staring past

Raimey.

"I don't want to. Eric, it's me. It's John," Raimey said.

Janis laughed, but it was the laugh found in asylums: a sad, hollow, cackle.

"Yeah. You're John." Janis walked completely out of the tunnel and circled Raimey. "You'd use him against me, wouldn't you?" Janis hissed. The Devil had come in a suit like his. It was black and bigger. Flames rode its arms and shoulders. Inside the helmet, Eric saw the Devil stare back at him with hot coal eyes and the stretched, chattering grin. The Devil came prepared for war.

"Eric, you're sick. You have to stop. You have to see what you've done," Raimey said. Janis stepped on the dead as he circled, cracking their already broken bones without taking his eyes away from Raimey.

"They were demons, they had to die," Janis said. "Don't turn this on me. You brought me here."

"Eric, they'll make me kill you," Raimey pleaded. "Get face down on the ground, trust me. We can figure this out. It's not your fault."

"Not my fault," Janis said slowly. "Not my fault. I wake up here, all I've done is my duty. I know it's not my fault! But it was a mistake to bring me here. You think you're the only fallen angel!" Janis screamed. "I've fallen, too!"

Janis sprinted at Raimey and raised his fists.

Please forgive me, Raimey thought. He pulled back and waited for his old friend, long gone, to get in range. Raimey braced himself for the hydraulshock.

WHA-WHAM!

He felt the acceleration. Going through his friend was like going through a hologram. Suddenly, he stood fifteen feet past where he had last been. He heard pieces of metal hitting the ground around him. Janis's battle chassis had exploded into thirty chunks and they were falling back to earth. Five million foot-pounds hit Janis in the chest, cracking through his two-foot armor like it was an eggshell and scrambling everything underneath.

John turned to his fallen friend. A section of the torso just beneath the helmet was still intact. Raimey ran to it and knelt down.

Janis stared at him with wide eyes. His mouth quivered. Somehow he was still alive. He looked at Raimey, his eyes suddenly sane. The

Mindlink had shorted out.

"I'm better now," he said. His face shook in death throes. "Thank you, John."

Inside the metal head, the real one exhaled for the last time.

"I'm so sorry, Eric. I'm so sorry. We were supposed to do this together," Raimey said. The tears hit the inside of his face shield and pooled into the center, bending his best friend's open mouth into a joker smile.

Raimey sobbed and stayed by his friend while the teams came in to retrieve the dead. The King Sleeper was missing. Raimey heard it over the comm. He didn't care. He sat by his friend and thought of nothing but Eric Janis's life. They had grown up together, they had laughed together, they had shared family pains together, and now they had died together. One heart kept beating on, that's all.

= = =

After four hours, they finally got Raimey back to the train. He stood in front of his seat.

"I want to see my family," Raimey said.

"John, we talked about this. It's dangerous. You're radioactive and the emotional trauma . . ." Lindo started.

"Save it. I just killed my best friend. And you need me more than I need you. I'm fine dying. I wish I would. I need to see them. I need them to know how much I love them. I'm not doing anything until I do," Raimey said.

"I'll set it up, John," General Boen said over the comm.

"You promise, Earl?" Raimey said.

"With everything I have," Boen said.

John stared at Evan in a way that made Evan step back. And then Raimey sat down and felt his body lock into the chair. He was so tired and he was in pain and he was mourning. All he wanted was to feel Vanessa's hand against his skin.

Wish in one hand, shit in the other, and see which one fills up first.

John hated that saying. But he knew the answer.

CHAPTER 17

Xan barely survived. When the giant approximated his location and fired the hydraulshock, the backsplash of debris crushed his body. Eight compound fractures splintered through his skin and an artery ruptured. He almost bled out on the way to the transport. When they got him to the vehicle, a soldier reached into the open wound and found the artery. It had retreated deep inside his thigh. They clamped it off and he was in and out of consciousness the rest of the trip. He felt the truck bouncing onto a dirt road. He heard the plane on takeoff.

He woke up in the infirmary at his base with tubes snaked up every hole. Doctors and nurses worked and spoke in the room, but Xan was confused, he couldn't hear them. Finally a doctor noticed he was awake and wrote on a notepad: "Your eardrums are ruptured."

Xan tried to speak but he chewed on his breathing tube. The doctors discussed in silence and then pulled it out.

"I'm deaf?" Xan said too loud. The doctor nodded yes. "Where's the boy?"

Minutes later, Xan's head scientist on the project came into the room.

"We have the boy under the same drug cocktail the Americans used," Dr. Kim said. "We understand the dosages and frequency. The boy is in a lucid coma."

All of this was dictated on a screen for Xan. His deafness was frustrating, but he didn't have time to feel self-pity.

"We found a command log built into the boy's mind," Dr. Kim said. "It was implanted there as a checklist, a 'to do' list. We're going through that now to understand all that he's done, and more importantly, what he's capable of doing. He's told us some, but he's confused. He asks for his father."

"He's conscious?" Xan asked.

"He can be communicated with, yes," Dr. Kim replied, his words quickly appearing on the screen.

"Can I speak to him?"

"We don't know if that's safe. He's contained in a construct that he thinks is real," Dr. Kim replied. "He has no idea what he's done. He just thinks he's sick."

"You cannot command him to do complex tasks right now,

correct?" Xan replied.

Dr. Kim nodded.

"If we can't use him like they did, what's the point?" Xan said. "I'll go in. This is my project, you have my contingency instructions as approved by our President."

An armored caravan took Xan to the secretly built Colossal Core. Xan began the build after his first contact with Harold Renki. It had taken over two years and while there was still more to be done, the Data Core functioned properly. Even then, Xan had seen what lay ahead. He had pictured rows upon rows of Chinese Sleepers around the massive Core protecting their online infrastructure. They were the soldiers of the new world.

The temporary Core Xan had used with the Forced Autistic was built in a hangar. This was built properly underground. It was deep in Beijing, intentionally among the hundreds of millions of people, buried underneath the innocent so that any retaliation would be weighed and measured. The U.S. would not go to war. If the situation were reversed, neither would China. They would compromise. The threat of the King Sleeper's immense power would drive the world sane. Xan didn't want war. He wanted a reset button so the world would have a future.

Xan saw the Colossal Core alive for the first time when the elevator down revealed its glowing, pulsing brilliance. For a moment he felt no pain, the silence was a gift, as he basked in the glow of China's salvation. He was wheeled over to the boy. Justin was mounted into the crucifix, with the metal shield covering his face and the large blue fiber optic tubes coursing data directly into his brain.

To the right of the boy was the massive Data Core. It stretched to the ceiling. Behind the crucifix and the boy was the Data Crusher, where the boy was fed the relevant raw data from the Core and where the boy could manipulate that data in return. The Data Crusher was a massive hard drive that spun at fifty thousand rotations per minute. It was an engineering feat more impressive because the hard drive plates were ten feet in diameter. The whole system weighed eight tons. Two tons consisted of a concrete base designed to keep the Crusher from rocking itself off the foundation like an unbalanced washing machine.

Data was laid on the plates and manipulated real time, only to be pulled off a thousandth of a microsecond later and fed back into the fiber optic core. The process was transparent to anyone in the world.

When they wheeled Xan to the boy, he felt the powerful thrum of the Data Crusher. They raised his chair and put the Mindlink on him.

"Are you ready sir?" Dr. Kim asked. There was no monitor, but Xan knew what he said.

"Do it," Xan replied. He felt the pull of the Mindlink and then the room around him disappeared.

= = =

Xan floated in black.

"Dad?" a boy asked. By his voice, he was nearby.

"No, I'm not your dad," Xan said. In cyberspace he could hear. He didn't realize how much he already missed it.

"Who are you?"

"They call me Xan."

"Is that your name?"

"No. My birth name is Caro Shin."

"Why do you go by Xan?"

"Shin is Korean and I live in China. Status is important here. Xan was the name I used since I was a boy. Why is it so dark?"

"I don't know." The boy was scared. "It went black some time ago. Are you a doctor?"

"I'm a scientist," Xan said.

"I'm still in my coma?"

"Dr. Kim can you hear me?" Xan asked.

"Yes, we're here," Dr. Kim replied out of the ether.

"Build a construct; make it pleasant," Xan said.

The sun broke on the horizon and rose quickly over distant hills, each one covered in luscious green. A river glistened ahead of Xan, the flowing water and serene surroundings an ideal of the real thing. The boy was to his right, twenty feet away.

"Your name is Justin, isn't it?" Xan asked. The boy nodded, uncertain.

"I'll leave if you want me to, but we need to talk," Xan said. "Would you walk with me to the river? Have you ever seen one?"

Xan walked toward the river. He could hear the rustle of the trees, the chirping of birds, the pleasant white noise of the water flowing away. The boy kept his distance as they walked to the river front.

Xan sat down, cross-legged. He found a smooth stone and chucked it into the river to hear it splash. He let out a long sigh.

The boy stood.

"I wouldn't trust me either. I wouldn't trust anyone, anymore," Xan said. "How long have you been here?"

"Two days. The doctor and my dad said I was close to being healthy, that my brain was responding to the treatment." The boy's face crumbled. "It's not true is it? Are you going to tell me I'm not getting better?"

"Worse. But I need you to listen and be tough. Can you do that?" Xan asked.

"Yes."

"Do you remember when you first got online and flew to the moon? You don't know it, but what you did wasn't supposed to happen. The program was specifically restricted from doing that. YOU made that happen. You re-programmed the program."

"I just flew."

"Your conscious mind, yes. But not your subconscious. Do you know what your subconscious is?"

The boy nodded.

"For whatever reason, Justin, it allows you to do amazing things online. You are the only person to ever hack into a MindCorp Data Core. It was considered impossible. Teams of Sleepers have tried and the general consensus was that the Cores were unhackable. You shook down a Colossal Core in two minutes. And the military noticed and they found you. You are the most powerful Sleeper in the world."

"I hit my head riding an ATV," Justin said. Xan shook his head sympathetically.

"No, you didn't. That memory was put in your head just like this river. Justin. You have been unconscious for over six months in a medically induced coma. And you've been used by the United States as a weapon."

"I don't understand," Justin said. His right hand slapped against his thigh. Xan had read about this nervous tic.

"You don't have to right now. I'm a high up official for the Chinese military. We took you from a military base in the U.S. because they had you manipulating our economy and other nasty things. Evil things."

"I don't understand what's going on," Justin said again. He was a genius, but he was twelve and he felt like everything in his head was a lie.

"I'm going to bring you out of this medically induced state. You are going to wake up in a military base with a bunch of people that look like me. Are you ready for that?"

"How do I know it's real?" Justin asked. He looked lost.

"Take a rock near you and cut yourself, and then decide it should heal," Xan said. Justin looked at him reluctantly. Finally he took a rock and scrapped it across his forearm. A line of blood budded on his skin.

"Think it healed," Xan said and Justin did. The small cut vanished.

"When you wake up and do that trick, think all you want, but that won't happen." Xan stood up.

"Why are you helping me?" Justin asked.

"Because I can't make you do the things I want you to do," Xan said. "You need to know the truth and then you can decide. You are a weapon, Justin, a unique and masterful work of God and your life will never be normal. Either by your choice, or by force, your fate in this world has already been sealed. I know it's a heavy thing to hear, you're a boy, but it is what it is."

"You're leaving?" Justin said.

"Yes. You'll see me very soon. The real me." Xan glanced at the sky. "Adjust the construct for real time."

"Yes, sir," the ether said.

"It will take ten hours to pull you out completely; the drugs are heavy sedatives with unique properties," Xan said. "The time you feel now will be real. When this all starts to get blurry, just close your eyes and try to sleep."

"Xan, are you a good guy?" Justin asked.

"You're smart, Justin. I read that. China would think so. The U.S. would want me dead. I have hurt people for what I see as the greater good," Xan said. "Is that a good enough answer?"

"I guess so."

"Take this time to process what I told you," Xan said and then he disappeared.

= = =

Xan woke up to silence. Dr. Kim was visibly angry and pulled a monitor over to Xan's bedside.

"You destroyed the false construct! We could have used that," Dr. Kim wrote.

Xan gestured with his good arm for Dr. Kim to come closer. When he did, Xan grabbed him with surprising strength and almost pulled him onto the bed. Xan's eyes always looked the same.

"The construct was broken. This is the only way to get the boy's trust. Never scream at me. Understand?"

Dr. Kim bowed repeatedly in subservience. Xan released him. His instincts told him he had done the right thing. The boy's government had murdered his parents, taken him against his will, and used him under the auspice of a gross, inhumane lie. Children are children because they lack reason. They are children because they cannot control their emotions—anger the worst of all. Xan would only have to tell the boy the truth. No lies, no coercion, just hook up the Goliath and let him avenge his family against a David that had run out of stones.

Xan closed his eyes and pictured the slow rolling river, and tried to feel its calm.

= = =

The sedative the U.S. had used and China had replicated was a predictable drug and it was ten hours on the nose when the boy opened his eyes and awoke to the world. When he started to fidget, Xan had him disconnected and moved to his quarters. The boy opened his eyes and saw the man he had spoken to by the river.

"Hi, Xan," Justin said. He rubbed his eyes.

"I'm deaf, Justin," Xan replied.

Justin looked at him surprised and then he saw a screen on Xan's wheelchair. On it was "Hi, Xan."

"It takes what you say and puts it on the screen," Xan said.

"Cool."

"When you're ready, I'll show you rest of the base. We can even get a breath of fresh air. There's a lot I have to tell you."

Justin blinked his eyes a few times extra wide and looked down at his forearm. No cut.

"You can try it if you want, but this is real. I don't choose to be deaf with no leg and a gimp arm," Xan said. For emphasis, with his good arm he picked up the other and let it flop back to his lap.

"Where are my parents?" Justin asked. It was inevitable.

"Rest a little bit, get your bearings and when you're ready I'll tell you everything." Xan left the room.

Two hours later he and Xan were being pushed through the throng of Beijing's crowds. A discrete perimeter of soldiers kept a cushion of space around them. Earlier, Justin had tried to stand up but his legs were too weak and he almost toppled over.

"I want to walk," Justin said when Xan came in to check on him. He had found Justin on the floor.

"Then walk." Xan waited patiently as Justin struggled, but he finally stood up. His legs shook like a newborn colt's.

Justin grimaced. "It hurts."

"Yes," Xan said. "It's the atrophy. You're young. You'll recover quickly."

The city was alive. They wheeled through a busy market that hadn't changed in two hundred years. Justin stared at the skinned ducks hanging by their feet and the poor caged crickets in full witness of their brethren skewered on sticks and smoking over a fire.

"This is China?" Justin said.

"Yes."

Justin slapped his face, trying to wake up. He had withdrawn into the wheelchair.

"That won't help," Xan said. He turned his wheelchair toward him. "Do you believe this is real?"

Justin knew it was real. Online his body felt light, his mind as open as the sky. In the real world, a fat man sat on his chest and everything was loud and distracting and scary. The marketplace was his nightmare. Around him swarms of people went about their lives, bartering, selling, laughing, yelling. They glanced warily at Xan and his plainclothes soldiers. Justin saw mothers usher children in the opposite direction. The smells that filled the air were pleasant and foreign. He nodded.

"I will only tell you the truth. I have told lies before, but that won't get me what I want," Xan said. "But the truth hurts."

"My parents," Justin said. It was clear. They would never let someone take him. Tears spilled out.

"Your parents are dead. I don't know the details, but it was the U.S. military, so the only comforting thing I can offer is that it was quick."

"The blonde man. The long haired blonde man." Justin rocked back and forth, hugging himself. He looked up at Xan. "A man came to our door from the military, he spoke with my dad. He spoke to me and I told him about the plane ride to the moon."

"I don't know, Justin. I don't have that answer," Xan replied.

"His name was Mike Glass. That was his name." Justin heaved and gasped, the analytical side of his brain overcome by his emotions.

Xan remained quiet. The bustle of the market continued uninterrupted by this revelation.

"That is the hardest thing I have to tell you, Justin. When you're ready, I'll tell you the rest."

Back at the base Xan told Justin how the U.S. had used him while under the false construct of a coma. How the King Sleeper had influenced nations and persuaded policy changes favorable to the United States. How he was manipulated to hack into unsuspecting minds and even kill. Xan pulled no punches and the boy grew to trust Xan quickly. He had eyes that Justin took to be kind, not knowing that they never changed.

A week later the boy went online of his own free will. After tests, he built his own construct, a place in cyberspace where he was comfortable. It was his farm. He built his parents and they were exact in their likeness. In a distant field he even had a combine moving row-to-row, knowing that Margarito and Fernando were at the wheel.

Xan visited the farm and met his parents.

"This is your home?" Xan said to Justin.

"Yep. It's not fancy but I liked it," Justin said. His parents walked by him and his eyes saddened. But he liked what he had done. It was better than a funeral or a tombstone. It was a living memorial, a constant reminder of what he had lost, but also of what he once had had.

"It's beautiful, Justin. As peaceful as the river," Xan said. They both watched his parents go into the house. "I will ask you to do things and show you the way. I'll explain why. And you can decide. Deal?"

"I don't want to kill anyone," Justin said. His lip trembled. He understood that he had that power, but murder wasn't in him.

"I'll never ask that, Justin. I'm not looking to end the world. I just want to bring it back into balance."

"What first?" Justin rose a foot off the ground. He closed his eyes and the air shimmered around him as the fabric of time began to tear.

"I want you to map out the U.S. banking system and their credit unions."

"That sounds boring," Justin replied.

"Finance is a nation's blood, Justin."

The air around Justin rippled. Outside the construct in cyberspace, his mindscape unfurled like the top of a parachute. It was a green fog infinitely growing.

"You should probably step back."

Xan did one better and disappeared back to the real. He had the first of multiple surgeries scheduled for this afternoon. He looked at his limp arm. *Amputation.* He raised his right arm and inspected his hand. He opened and closed it. He pressed it against the cold rail of his wheelchair. He pressed his palm against the sharp edge of a table. *Never again.* The Shin battle chassis had passed its final prototyping. The military was manufacturing one per day and they were ramping up more factories. The entire government had gone off-line. They were receiving psychiatric evaluations to determine what affect the King Sleeper had had on them. And they were furious. They had been raped and they wanted war.

"You don't have to do this," a female voice said. He couldn't hear her, but he saw the words fill the screen. Xan had told the scientists on the battle chassis project how he wanted to proceed.

"So they send you to convince me otherwise," he said. He turned to an attractive woman in her thirties. "How's your morning?"

Xinting was a top scientist at the Colossal Core. He had recruited her when she was sixteen. In another reality, Xan thought, they could have been more than just colleagues. Her knowledge was commandeered to develop the implant for the Shin battle chassis.

"We have plenty of soldiers that willfully volunteered."

"Are you worried for me?" Xan teased. He knew she saw him as an elder, but he couldn't help it.

"Yes," she said matter-of-factly. "You're too important to be the test subject. You found the King Sleeper, you created all of this and without you we wouldn't have had a chance. We need you."

Xan changed the subject. "How is he doing, in your opinion?"

Justin had grown attached to Xinting. When Xan saw this bond, he encouraged it. The boy needed a sanctuary. A person he could confide in that wasn't in a uniform or white coat. She joked with him. She played with him. Justin loved puzzles. HUGE puzzles. They even had a game where the pieces of three would be mixed together. He solved them quickly. The boy cried in her arms when he talked about his mom and dad. One night, under heavy guard, Xan let Justin go to the home Xinting shared with her parents. This freedom had made Justin more amenable. Dr. Kim, who had fiercely disagreed when Xan had removed the construct, apologized daily.

"He doesn't have Asperger's," Xinting said. "In the U.S. file he was diagnosed with it, but he only has the symptoms. His brain is just different." She went back to the old subject. "You are risking your life, Xan. We don't know everything yet."

"I've always heard that Chinese women are subservient, but I've never met one," Xan mused. "If I can ask our young soldiers to give up their able bodies for China, then I can give up my lame one and lead them. It's fitting, Xinting, don't you see? I've always been in the shadows and after this I can never hide again. There are too many shadow men. Too many puppeteers. It's time we turn on the light and watch the cockroaches scatter. Including me. We need an honest world."

"Will this give us one?"

"As long as the overpowering influence doesn't subvert its own intentions. This is the closest we will ever be."

= = =

Xan's surgeries would take weeks to complete. He had provided Xinting a list. She showed it to Justin before he linked in.

He looked it over. "No one will get hurt?" he asked. There were over two hundred tasks. His right hand tapped his thigh.

"Xan has respected your wishes," she said. "He wants your gift to cause our countries to unite. It may not seem so, but his plan is for peace. We need each other, Justin. We need to be united in this new world."

"Will you come with me to the farm?" he asked. She recognized that he was about to cry.

She knelt down eye-to-eye. "What is it?"

"My parents don't have anything more to say." His lip trembled. "They sound like me."

Xinting's heart broke. She hugged him.

"Of course, Justin. Of course. I'm honored to."

She ordered technicians to install a Sleeper chair next to the crucifix.

At the farm, she met his parents. She pet his dogs. She waved to Fernando and Margarito as they passed by in giant red combines. Dr. Lindo had adjusted the construct so that time stood still as the days spun into months. Justin did the opposite. An hour in cyberspace was one minute in the real world.

"I don't belong out there," Justin explained. "This is where I'm me."

"You're beautiful in either place."

Justin smiled.

In his front yard, Justin rose into the air. The Colossal Core thumped with his power. He began:

—Mirror Data Node 2 in New York and Data Node 1 in Chicago. Hijack Cores. Hack respective stock exchanges. Back up stock prices. Replace all stocks with randomly generated share prices.—

They laughed at dinner. His was a big belly laugh. They ate spaghetti and meatballs.

—Shut down all electric grids to U.S. military bases around the world.—

He showed her how to shoot his rifle.

—Disconnect all communication systems for U.S. military bases around the world.—

They walked through the fields. Justin told her about things he learned from his dad. She spoke about her childhood friends.

—Disconnect U.S. military radar surveillance on the Eastern Seaboard. Hack ballistic missile silos and disconnect all overriding protocols. Target Washington, D.C. Initiate test launch sequence.—

Xinting cried discussing her inability to bear a child.

—Hack into credit unions. Back up credit records. Erase all credit records.—

Xinting noticed that Justin's parents weren't around any longer.

—Hack the Washington, D.C. power grid. Shut down all power to government buildings.—

Winter came. Overnight Justin created a huge hill with a ski lift. They went sledding the entire day.

—Crash Data Node 12 in Washington, D.C.—

He was teary eyed all-day and combative. When she finally got him to speak, he told her he was horrible to his mom when she was alive and

"I can't take it back."

—Crash Data Node 3 in Los Angeles.—

She had told Justin a few weeks before that she had never celebrated Christmas. Christmas morning, she walked down to a beautifully decorated tree. The dogs sat in front of it, wagging their tails. Underneath it were a pile of gifts. Justin was making breakfast.

"But I don't have anything for you!" she said.

"You're my gift," he said and hugged her.

—Hack into CIA and copy files of all current covert operatives. Contact operatives and tell them they've been compromised. Twenty-four hours later post list with attached government files to all message boards and news outlet.—

They sat near a creek. Spring had arrived. "Would you be my step mom?" he asked.

—Hack into . . . —

She loved this child as if he was her own.

CHAPTER 18

Evan was in his office at the White House. The lights were out. He was disconnected from the Mindlink. He was sulking.

It was no secret. The Chinese had the King Sleeper. They had found Mike Glass clinging to life but conscious enough to point at three Chinese soldiers that had died at the hands of Tank Major Janis. One had been crushed into a meat rug. The other two were rippled with glass shards. One week later, the U.S. economy was in shambles, Washington, D.C. had been cast into the Dark Ages, and the military was on life support. *Fucking Panama could invade us.*

And that was what they *saw*. The problem and beauty of the King Sleeper was that it was difficult to know when he was being used. Who knows what else he was doing . . . maybe all the politicians in Washington would vote that our new national anthem was "Freebird." As stupid as it sounded, it could be done.

Evan rarely drank, but now was as good of a time as any. Next to him was the same bottle of scotch that WarDon had drunk before he decided to punt. Half the bottle was left; it was old, very old. It had been in WarDon's effects, meant for his family. Evan had plucked it out without a stutter in his step. He thought it was funny to have the bottle. He thought, one day, he'd toast to his fallen comrade. Without him, none of this would have been possible.

"What's wrong with me?" Evan asked the room. The black curtains let some light in and the two windows stared at him with cataract eyes. He pushed himself deeper into the corner to avoid their gaze.

He felt like a boy. Like when he was a boy. Always close, but never quite number one. He was never an athlete, it wasn't about that. He thought athletics, on the whole, were a retarded waste of time.

His dad was a physicist, his mom a shrink. They had always instilled in him a sense of expectation, but never of love. His parents didn't love each other after all; their marriage just made sense. His dad used to bang the babysitter. Evan remembered that. He was young, it was a memory built with fuzz from lack of understanding, but the hug he gave Kim, the sixteen-year-old next door neighbor, wasn't done the right way.

His mom lived at her practice. Dinner was quiet and tight lipped. Conversations were always about work. Evan remembered telling them that he had a girlfriend—Tara—when he was ten.

"I love her!" he exclaimed. They had been together for one week. She was a third grader and pretty. She wore a side ponytail that he dug.

"You don't know what love is, honey," his mom said dismissively before she slipped a piece of pork chop into her mouth. The conversation turned back to themselves.

A child is forced to see the world through their parent's filter and the predilections and values that color it. Evan only got their attention when he excelled academically because that was all they knew and how they assessed worth, and so he did that.

He began college at the age of fifteen and he still felt stupid because he had a classmate who was fourteen. He got doctorates in medicine and mechanical engineering—which his parents approved of—but his doctorate in cyberphysics confused them.

"What are you going to do with *that*?" his dad asked. They didn't pay for it and he had reached an age where he wondered why the fuck they cared.

Luckily, they died. His father loved to smoke his pipe late at night while he read. He fell asleep with it. It was peaceful. The fire ate up his dad. *Closed casket for pops.* But at the funeral, his mom looked like she was sleeping.

He was already wired the way he was, but at least he didn't have to hear their fucking nagging and backhanded praise anymore.

"I know what's wrong with me," Evan giggled. "I just want to make them proud."

He took a swig directly from the bottle. It tasted of caramel and fire.

He stood up and paced the dark room. He wouldn't be beaten. No. But even if he found the King Sleeper online, it would be impossible to find its tail. It had one, but to find it, you'd have to penetrate its immense mindscape. If it knew you were in it, it could kill you.

Evan went to his desk and hit the speaker.

"Yes?" the receptionist asked.

"Get me Cynthia," Evan said.

"Cynthia Revo?"

"Who the fuck do you think?" He spat.

A slight pause. "Hold." She went away.

Evan paced the room.

"Evan?" It was Cynthia. He shot over to the phone.

"We can't trace the King Sleeper's tail because of the mindscape, it'll chew up anyone who tries," he said. "How else could we find him?"

"Are you drunk?"

Evan looked at the bottle in his hand. Most of it was gone now. "Definitely."

"The Western Curse," Cynthia said. It took Lindo a minute to even recall who they were. The fucking terrorists at O'Hare.

"Why do you say that?"

"They used AK47's, RPG's—old weapons, and yet they happened to have state-of-the-art miniguns and a computer that could hack into the Tank Major and upload a virus. They're a contradiction and that contradiction indicates a partnership with funds." She continued. "Do you remember Harold Renki?"

"Yes, your scientist who was murdered," Evan replied. "What's the connection between him and the Western Curse?"

"None. But there is one degree of separation."

"China?" Evan said.

"Specifically a man named Xan," Cynthia said. Her research on Harold Renki had proven fruitful. While he had been squeaky clean online, Sabot had found detailed information in a hidden safe at his estate and multiple online aliases.

"I've heard the name," Evan said.

"He's the Chinese version of you, Evan," Cynthia said. He could hear the scorn over the phone.

"Can you find him?" Evan asked.

"No. There's no trace of him anywhere online."

"Mohammed Jawal, that's what the little French fucker told us," Evan said. The nightmare with Janis and the King Sleeper clouded over his initial desire to hunt this guy down and skull fuck him. "Thank you, Cynthia." It was genuine, rare.

"Sober up, Evan," she replied and was gone.

= = =

Cynthia hung up the phone. Sabot stood next to her with his hand on her shoulder.

"His ears must have been ringing. Why just me?" General Boen asked. He sat across the desk at her private request.

"Do you trust Evan?" she asked.

Boen crossed his legs and straightened his suit. "Not as far as I can throw him." He was still furious at Evan for keeping the King Sleeper secret.

"I have information that I, as a private entity, do not have to share with you. With this information and a properly executed strategy, it will lead you to the King Sleeper. Evan wants war. It doesn't have to end that way."

"I hope you're right," Boen said. "What do you want?"

"Evan's out, that's all."

"I can't keep him out forever."

"Not forever, just for this. You can throw me under the bus afterwards, I don't care. But I trust you Earl. The King Sleeper isn't good for you and he isn't good for me."

Boen wiggled his jaw while he weighed his options. *Fuck Evan,* Boen thought. *The little prick only keeps secrets.*

"Deal," Boen said.

Cynthia told him what she knew and the strategy they formed together was intricate, yet executable, and beautiful in its trickery. Basically, why Boen liked his job.

= = =

Mohammed Jawal got a message from Xan in the Western Curse shareware to meet. Per their established protocol, Mohammed responded by inserting into the code the time and place.

= = =

Six hours after his meeting with Cynthia, General Boen was at JFK airport walking into an airplane hanger where they had transported John. While most of JFK's runways had returned to nature, the government kept three operational. The mission would start in one hour. But there was another issue to attend to. And Earl kept his promises.

"They're here," General Boen said. Raimey began to stand.

"Hold on a second," Boen said. "We almost had to force Tiffany to come here. When I sent soldiers to Florida, it was bad, John. I think you understand the hurt they're feeling. They're both confused. I explained the best I could, but you know, they don't want to hear it from me."

"Does Tiffany have cancer?" Raimey asked.

"Yes. She initially refused treatment, but she's going now. It's far along, but the doctors are hopeful."

"So she understands why I did this," Raimey said.

"Yes, but no," Boen replied. "You're this now." Earl gestured at his giant frame. "But you're still John Raimey. Be that today, the best you can, because you might not see them again."

Raimey looked at Earl with sorrowful eyes.

"I'm sorry, John. But it's the best advice I can give you. Come with me." Raimey stood up and followed him out the large hangar door. "You have one hour and then we have to go."

= = =

The prep for the mission had already begun. A stealth bomber had been pulled into an adjoining hanger. A team of mechanics worked under its belly, modifying the bomb bay to handle Raimey as a payload, and to create a livable space for the small insertion team that was coming with him.

Inside, they disassembled the plane's current bomb delivery system and removed it piece-by-piece through the bay doors. Sparks cascaded down and countless voices yelled "careful" throughout the entire process.

Boen guided Raimey across the hangar and past staring eyes to the opposite end where a tall curtain cordoned off the area behind it. Boen stopped short.

"Tiffany is in there. Make this count."

Raimey nodded and Earl pulled the curtain aside. Raimey stepped through. Tiffany sat in the middle of the room. She wore the light lead apron that everyone around him wore. Her eyes were red rimmed and wet. When she saw him, she withered and fell to her knees.

He walked over to her and knelt down, worry across his face, aching in his chest. He reached a hand out and quickly retracted. He could offer no comfort.

"I had no choice, Tiffany," he said softly. She continued to heave, her head turned downward, her body cast in the darkness of his giant shadow.

"Tiffany. Please. *Please*. I didn't know what to do. They told me about the cancer," he said.

She turned up to him, still huddled over like she was waiting for a blow. Her lost expression was the same as he had seen in his dream. Terrified disbelief. A horrible lie vetted true.

"General Boen, Dr. Lindo, *the President*, they promised you would get the best treatment and that you both would be taken care of, forever," Raimey said. She was still looking at the body before her, the giant metal shape that housed her husband, but her eyes would snatch a glance at his face and his face was his. Everything behind armor except his eyes that pleaded for her to accept him or at least speak. He was crouched over close enough to touch, his head two feet from hers, looking into her eyes.

She reached out slowly. Her hand first rested on the giant chest armor, gripping the top of it like a rail. Over it she could see his neck and the very top of his chest. She reached up to his head and he crouched lower to aid her. She put the palm of her hand on his cheek and then ran it over his face as if she were blind and this was their first meeting. He closed his eyes and took it all in. He remembered what General Boen had said: this touch, this interaction, this memory, could be the last he ever knew of the woman before him. His heart burst from the thought of it, but he willed himself into the moment, because no future moment is truly known.

"You should have waited," she said, her voice barely a breath. "We could have made this decision together. WE are supposed to make these decisions together!"

Her hand dropped to her side. She turned away from him and looked out into the hangar, her eyes distant and unfocused. "You were going to apply for an online job, remember? There you'd be fine, able-bodied."

"You're sick."

"We would've had a chance!" Tiffany yelled. "We would have been together! Dammit, John. What did you do? We can't take this back. *There is no going back!*"

"They needed me, Tiffany. What I'm doing could save the world."

"We needed you, too. They would have found someone else."

John had nothing to comfort her. He loved her more than he loved himself. He cared for her and Vanessa enough to let the world burn ten times over, let the innocent die, just so they could live. He knew this. In some small way, his new form was that incarnation.

"I love you so much, Tiffany," Raimey said. She finally looked at him again. He was knelt before her like a knight bowing to his princess.

"I love you, too. I just thought we had more time," she said. She stood up and went to him. She kissed him on the lips and looked into his eyes. She kissed him again and then put her face against his, cheek-to-cheek.

"Vanessa can't see you like this," Tiffany said.

"But she's here!" Raimey pleaded.

"What would a ten-year-old girl take from this? *I* can't process this! Look at you! You're a weapon! How can you comfort her? How can you—"

"Tiffany, please don't go. This might be it. Where I'm going, I may not come back. I need to be around you. I need to see her. I know I'm asking too much, but please. Be angry with me later. Hate me later! For now, let's be us," Raimey said.

She stopped, her hand on the curtain's edge. Her head tilted down.

"I don't hate you. I love you so much I want to die. But I'm so mad. I feel so betrayed. I know you did this with good intentions, deep down I know. But us, John! Us! We are a family. We should be fighting together. You crippled, my cancer, our daughter growing up. Those are our fights!"

"How could I fight, Tiffany! How could I?! I was nothing! I'm not smart, I'm not funny, I don't have any money. All I had is gone!" Raimey howled. "I caused the cancer, I know I did. You never had a moment to breathe when I came back from the hospital. You never had a moment to think ONCE about yourself. I don't want you two to fight. I don't want you two to struggle. I want you two to have a life that will allow you to wake up and decide what you want to do that day. Not wake up and know that your day will be long and hard and it's all MY FAULT!"

Raimey's voice echoed throughout the hanger. He wheezed from the effort, from vocalizing his fears and his dead dreams. Of his struggle to do what's right, coupled with the knowledge that his arms and legs weren't enough for Uncle Sam. His life and family had to get thrown onto the altar too.

Tiffany was quiet.

"You didn't cause the cancer," she finally said.

"Please let me see her, Tiff," Raimey asked.

She was quiet again.

"She won't understand," Tiffany said. "Earl?"

251

"Yes?" Boen was on the other side of the curtain.

"Could you escort me to get Vanessa?"

"Of course."

Tiffany turned to John and looked up into his large, watery eyes.

"You can speak with her through the curtain. It'll be better this way. I want her to remember her dad as a man. This is too much."

Raimey nodded. She was right.

"Thank you, Tiffany," Raimey said.

"I already miss you, John," she said, a sad smile on her face, reminiscing of their time, knowing, as he stood in front of her, that all the good memories had passed.

She blew him a kiss and ducked through the curtain. Raimey waited. His heart beat like a drum. He finally heard his daughter's voice as they crossed the room.

"She's here," Tiffany said through the curtain.

John told his daughter all the things that a child should hear. How she was special, how she changed his life. He told her about his childhood and his parents and how, while they loved him, they showed it in hard ways and how he promised to be a better dad and better husband when he was an adult. He told her about when he first laid eyes on her, about how beautiful Tiffany was, and when she held Vanessa for the first time, that memory seared in his mind. He told her about the first time she spoke and the one time she called someone an "asshole" when she was three and how he and Tiffany laughed till they fell while they tried to tell her it was wrong. He told her everything until it was hard to breathe and the pain became unbearable. Because that one-inch curtain between them may as well have been a vast sea. Because Tiffany was right. Vanessa couldn't see him like this. The memories he had of her would be tainted by this encounter. The memory of her face, contorted into a scream when she saw that her dad had become the boogeyman.

They left. John sat down. Earl walked in and John waved him away. He felt nothing. But nothing had feeling. It was dull and numb and filled his entire body with a sadness so great, it felt like every cell was crying. He would never recover from this. There was no way to.

"It's time, John," Boen said.

CHAPTER 19

Mohammed walked through a replica of a space station found in *2001: Space Odyssey*. He had seen the movie many times and the exacting detail of the replica impressed him: the bleach white hallways, the CRT screens for phone calls, the red lounge chairs. Hipsters dressed from various eras were scattered about. Earth and the stars swapped places again and again outside panoramic windows.

He saw the man that he knew would be Xan. He was small and Asian and he had sad eyes. Mohammed walked up to him. Xan didn't turn. He watched the rolling stars intently.

"That was quite the trick you pulled on me at O'Hare," Mohammed said. "If I hadn't gotten so much in return . . ." He trailed off but the tone was threatening.

"I wouldn't disconnect if I were you," Xan said with a woman's voice.

Mohammed immediately understood he had been ambushed. "Why?"

"If you do, you will die. Right now, the U.S. military, with another Tank Major, has surrounded your safe house. We work with them now. If I tell them you've disconnected without hearing what I have to say, they will come in and they will kill every last one of you." Not Xan paused. "Do you know who I am?"

"Cynthia Revo." He looked around the room as if that gave any measure of his true danger.

"I found your shareware program floating in my space," she said. "It took a while. Clever."

"Thank you."

"You're an educated man, Mohammed. In many ways I empathize with you. But I know, fundamentally, we'll always be on opposite sides. Neither philosophy is very good at compromise."

Mohammed listened.

"I don't care about you. Right now, neither does the U.S. military. We need you to contact Xan."

"Am I negotiating a plea deal?" Mohammed asked, disbelieving.

"No. This deal guarantees that you live one more day. You do this and Xan responds, we leave you alone for twenty-four hours. I suggest you use that time wisely and disappear."

"How can I trust your word when history shows me all the ones that have been broken?"

"I'm not here for a philosophical debate. Today, right this moment, there are bigger fish to fry than you. This deal has a quick expiration. Sometimes you just got to roll the dice."

= = =

Cynthia snapped awake.

"How did it go?" Sabot asked.

She smiled. "Mohammed will post the message in ten hours. He said it takes up to two for Xan to respond."

"Perfect."

There were no military teams around Mohammed's safe house. A Tank Major didn't hide in the shadows. For Earl and Cynthia's plan to work, timing and luck were everything. But for Mohammed, the decision was simple. If the creator of a new universe hacked in and tricked you to meet her, and then she showed up as an exact duplicate of your funder, and then she told you that they knew your location and that you could choose to either die now or get a momentary reprieve for one small betrayal, no matter what cards she may be holding—it could be a pair of twos—you don't call that bluff and push everything in.

= = =

While Xan used a live host to throw off his digital tail when he met with Mohammed, when he communicated with the shareware for the hundredth of a second it took to confirm location, he used no such precaution. Eleven hours after Cynthia had threatened Mohammed, Xan had replied. Cynthia grabbed the digital tail and quickly traced it back. It originated at an undocumented location in the middle of Beijing. She analyzed the data input and output of the surrounding area and like an x-ray—with fiber optic lines as the bones—she knew that a hidden Colossal Core wore one square mile of that region as a hat.

She contacted Earl and sent him the image file. She transposed the blue cords of data activity with a map of the region. The data paths circled the center like water down a drain.

"That's a very populated area," Boen said, concerned.

"No," Cynthia replied. "It's the *most* populated area. And it's the market hub for that section of the city."

"Shit balls," Boen said.

"Shit balls, indeed."

"I've ordered a satellite pass, hopefully that'll add to what you've sent me. We need to know where to get in."

"An x-ray pulse should show that," Cynthia said. "You can hide a Colossal Core from peeping eyes by throwing some shacks on it, but it's still a million tons of concrete and steel. Whatever's over it is superficial."

"Roger that," Boen said. "You ever think about joining the military?"

She heard the smile in his voice.

"There's no money in it, Earl," she replied.

= = =

John and the insertion team knew how quadruplets felt. They were crammed into the B-2's modified bomb bay. Thirty minutes after he had seen his wife and heard his child, he was airborne. They were eleven hours into a thirteen-hour flight to Beijing. Three of the six soldiers that Eric Janis had trained with: Hostettler, Johnson, and Ratny, were on board. Ratny had been on leave when Janis went berserk. Hostettler and Johnson had been in a hospital recovering from gunshot wounds. There was no more room.

They were in a pressurized drop container that had a guidance system like a smart bomb. The toilet was a bucket epoxied to the floor. A small wireless monitor showed their progress. For the last hour, Hostettler had been fidgeting.

"I have to go," Hostettler said.

"Noooo," they all groaned, including John.

"Which one?" Ratny asked, optimistically.

"Not the one you're hoping for." Hostettler's stomach gurgled in agreement. "When it gets down to it, probably both."

"I could have been a pharmacist," Johnson said, immediately unhappy with his life decisions.

John and the team didn't have time to train together but they all bonded while Hostettler faced them, ass on a bucket, and crapped his brains out. The ventilation system was ill-equipped.

CHAPTER 20

The surgery requirements for the Shin battle chassis were much less intrusive than the American version. It was arms and legs; everything else remained. Because of the size of the Shin battle chassis—it was fifteen feet tall—they had some latitude on the soldier compartment. This allowed them to quickly prepare soldiers for the program.

Just like the American version, Xan's spine was fused with a connecting rod into the chassis. Unlike the American version, which assessed g-load and compensated with thousands of points of data, the suspension device for the Chinese version was mechanical. Xan was mounted into the chassis with gas shocks that allowed up to two feet of up-and-down movement and a foot side-to-side. It was crude, but they would evolve the platform over time.

Because Xan had a fully articulated spine, the doctors used a Botox derivative to paralyze the muscles in Xan's back so that he wouldn't fight against the spinally fused suspension bracket in the heat of battle. Xan was both numb and tender, depending on the section of his truncated form. His limbs haunted him, even with the implant.

"We're troubleshooting the software, we'll figure it out," Xinting said.

"It works, Xinting," Xan said. "We built a Tank Major in two months. It took the Americans years of physical development and all of the resources that MindCorp could offer."

"But you're in pain," Xinting replied. "The American version doesn't have this ghosting."

"Ramp up production. It can be fixed later."

The government's trust in Xan had become so complete, that his orders were law. Once Xan had come to and they knew the software—however flawed—worked with the body, they had immediately culled four more soldiers. Two Chinese Tank Majors were now on base.

Amidst all of this, Xan had reluctantly agreed to meet Mohammed. At this point, he wasn't sure the benefit, but Xan believe in managing his resources. He no longer laid down to link-in. He sat in a throne built into his new quarters at the base of the Colossal Core. His hearing was back. He heard the whirl of server fans and the *chunk-chunk-chunk* of the King Sleeper dismantling the U.S.'s digital infrastructure.

On Tank Major Xan's back were two sheets of armor that

connected to his metal spine like an insect's wings. Underneath those were huge hydraulics that anchored to the three foot wide, depleted uranium spine. The black casement and nickel piston of the hydraulics looked like exposed ribs. They connected to jointed parts of his body that controlled his arms and legs and chest armor. Combined, they also allowed an intense constriction. A wedge, like a thick ax head, was built down the front of Tank Xan's chest. If he grabbed another Tank Major and pulled it in, the compressing hydraulics would cleave it against the wedge, puncturing through it like the carapace of a crab. A grenade launcher was mounted on one shoulder, on the other was a cannon modified from their fighter jets.

Unlike the American version, all of Xan's movement was powered with hydraulics. Decompression pumps were paired with each hydraulic piston to allow him to move quickly, but the faster he moved, the less powerful he became because of torque bleed.

Xan left his message in the Western Curse shareware and walked out to the floor. Two of the Tank Majors were based topside in false shops. The other two had been sent out for military demonstrations, not unlike what Xan had witnessed through Jan Hedgegard when he had probed his mind.

Xinting lay next to Justin in a Sleeper chair. She was semi-conscious. Justin had requested her presence when he was online, it soothed him and he could multi-task: re-route supply chains in the U.S. to increase the chance of famine. Play cards. Stop freight rail and shut off their cooling systems. Go-kart race. Bring down a credit union and its backup servers. Watch old action movies. Time was layered in cyberspace, just like thoughts. Especially for him.

"How is he holding up?" Xan asked Xinting.

"He's fine. But we should take him offline soon," Xinting replied distantly. "He's been on for five hours."

"Very good. Have him finish up. Thank you, Xinting," Xan said.

The U.S. had used the King Sleeper for subterfuge. They were looking at long-term political influence and gain. Xan was using Justin as a hammer. He wanted to force the truce. Everything Xan destroyed could be re-built. The systems and files smashed and erased could be restored quickly by the King Sleeper. Xan had Justin push the U.S. back to the Dark Ages to reveal the world's perilous balance between order and chaos. This was a warning, a call for level heads and competent leaders, and no more of the men three rows back, including Xan. Xan watched as Xinting began to power down the Data Crusher to pull the little boy out of his crucified shackles. The white flag wavering across the battlefield should have already happened. But nothing from the U.S. This bothered Xan greatly. The air force was on high alert, Xan had warned the interim President of a possible military incursion. Silence wasn't a sign of submission. It was a sign of planning, plotting. It was a sign of war.

= = =

"You're lucky you're made of metal," Ratny said. "My body is stiff as hell."

"I'll massage it if you like." Raimey offered his massive crushing hand.

"Funny."

They all wore darting eyes and nervous smiles. Five minutes before, the small monitor inside their now-agreed-upon-prison lit up and General Boen wished them luck. There would be no comm. There would be no backup, just an evac point at the bay twenty miles east. A fishing vessel would take them to an Ohio-class submarine waiting quietly offshore. Capture the King Sleeper, get him to the sub, or neutralize him.

"God bless you, and get home safe," Earl had said. The picture froze.

"Two minutes out, gentlemen," the pilot said. Inside the drop container a red light blinked off and on and they heard the whine of the bomb bay doors opening beneath them. The three soldiers strapped themselves into harnesses connected to the sidewall. A minute later, they felt themselves tumble into space. Smart bomb technology guided them to their location.

Their only window to the outside world was an altimeter. Ratny was closest to it and he called out their altitude as they descended.

"Sixty-five thousand feet."

"Fifty thousand feet."

"Thirty-five thousand feet."

"How won't they see us?" Johnson said. They were tumbling directly into Beijing.

"They'll get a visual, but no radar. It's stealth," Ratny said. "Twenty-

258

five thousand feet."

Hostettler puked and wiped with his sleeve. "Hope the parachute works."

"It's some NASA shit. It's a late stage with boosters," Johnson said. "It doesn't open until three thousand feet."

"Fifteen thousand feet."

"I'll bust us out of here. You guys have the GPS in your headpieces, right?" Raimey asked. They nodded. "Good. Tell me coordinates, I'll launch the hover-rovers and send them ahead. Stay safe. I need eyes. Send me at'em, guide me like a missile."

"We'll get you there," Hostettler said. "I'm sorry about Eric, he was a good guy. No mercy today. These were the guys that did it."

"Oorah," they said in unison.

"We'll keep behind you or to the alleys. Call out if you're going to unload a hydraulshock," Johnson said. "We'll support you the best we can, but we need to make it to the Core."

"Five thousand feet."

A moment later the parachute slammed them into their seats. They rechecked their weapons. Raimey's body began to vibrate as his waist chains spun up.

= = =

Tank Major Li saw the object drop from the sky. He thought it was a meteor until the parachute deployed. He called it in and ran to greet it. He wanted to try his new body. The crowd scattered away from him as he burst out of the false store. A dozen soldiers followed him in a truck.

All market activity stopped. Customers and shopkeepers stepped out to watch the strange, wedge shaped object as, even with the parachute deployed, it came in too fast directly at the market. One hundred thousand people watched it descend. On its back were wings and they adjusted the descent, finally turning the wedge parallel to the ground. A thousand feet above the crowded, silenced market, rocket boosters erupted to slow it down and the crowd screamed in panic and ran in all directions. Li and the soldiers were less than a quarter mile away and the crowd felt trapped, a mechanized giant on one end and what could be a bomb or an alien spacecraft on the other. They were a school of fish avoiding predators, darting and surging to get out of the way.

The stealth ship landed and the parachute—as big as a hot air balloon—lazily followed.

"Do not approach the crate," Xan said in Li's ear. That order echoed to the soldier transport. "Reinforcements are behind you."

Li ignored the order. He felt invincible. They had run parallel assessments of the Tank Major the Americans had built to their own and, in almost all cases, the Chinese one was superior.

The object looked too small to house a Tank Major. The truck drove to the opposite side and trained its .50 caliber machine gun on it. The soldiers got out and formed a wide perimeter. Against the orders barked over the truck's megaphone, civilians filtered back into the alleys at what they perceived as a safe distance to see what was going on. They stared in awe at their mechanized soldier.

The foreign object hummed with building energy. Li trudged forward to within ten yards. He aimed the grenade launcher and cannon on it. He mentally adjusted his hydraulic system for speed, sacrificing power. In this mode he was fast, and in training they would treat their arms like maces, carrying the energy, curving back, using the momentum as it built with rotation. He could adjust the power on the fly.

The panels of the crate shook violently. Static electricity danced across it and the curious crowd became less curious and retreated. Li walked forward just as the crate exploded outward and a giant unfurled from its cocoon. Its body was matte black, almost rubberized. It wasn't as bulked down with armor. And unlike the Tank Major they had studied to emulate, it was nearly Li's size and equally wide. It locked its eyes on him and charged. Li shelled it with his weapons.

"Hit the deck," Raimey yelled to his team. They sprawled.

The Chinese Tank Major tried to veer out of the way. Raimey scissored his right fist down onto its shoulder and reared back his left to hydraulshock.

WHA-WHAM!

Li exploded across the marketplace, two hundred pound pieces blasting through shops and carts, clearing the area around them in rough swaths. Raimey didn't wait; he felt the pecking of bullets against his back. He turned and charged the truck. He conserved the hydraulshocks and ran through it, collapsing its roof and tearing it in half.

Prone, Hostettler, Ratny, and Johnson fired on the Chinese soldiers who stood like mannequins while the giant demolished what they had thought was invincible. They collapsed from headshots and chest shots before they even raised a rifle.

PUNG! Two hover-rovers erupted off Raimey's back and spun into the air. They arced forward, gaining elevation as they went. Raimey—and only Raimey—now had eyes. The Tank Major/hover-rover system was completely closed and unhackable. He had HD, UV, infrared, and night vision. They gave off no heat or radar signature. Already, they were dots in the air. They looked like a kid's lost balloon.

"GO! GO! GO!" Ratny screamed. The three soldiers jumped up and sprinted through the crowd to a nearby alley. They would use Raimey as a distraction while they worked their way to the Core using the corrugated alleyways as cover.

The hover-rovers showed reinforcements vectoring in. Hundreds of troops and armored vehicles. Soldiers on roofs carrying long tubes. No more giants. A tornado siren erupted from his body, a courtesy to civilians, and equally, a warning of what was coming: a chance to retreat or surrender.

"I'm coming," Raimey said. His momentum built quickly as he charged as the crow flies toward the Colossal Core.

"We're a half mile away," Ratny said, panting. They had two-way radios attached to their helmets. Raimey had a speaker version jury rigged to the inside of his. "Still no soldie—we're taking fire! Fire ahead of you!"

Raimey heard the sharp echo of assault rifles ahead and to the right of the main road. He flew a hover-rover toward that location and found the hostile group. He had adjusted quickly to the multiple sight lines. It had become as natural as breathing and it gave him a monumental advantage.

"Hole up. I'm coming," Raimey said and he veered toward the sound.

Twenty Chinese soldiers were stationed on top of a roof camouflaged to look residential. Potted plants decorated the ledge, old dresses and shirts fluttered on a clothesline. Training rote in Johnson's mind saved him from a bullet. He sensed movement above him and immediately took cover. Where he had just stood freckled and twanged with lead. Ratny and Hostettler took cover and called it in.

They heard Raimey coming. It sounded like an industrial accident at a steel mill. Suddenly the bottom half of the building with the soldiers turned to smoke.

WHA-WHAM!

The hydraulshock report shot past the team and even with their earplugs, they cupped their ears in pain. Shacks around them toppled over and the five-story structure fell away like it was built with cards.

"Clear," Raimey said. They heard the deep impact of his feet and the metallic frenzy of the drive chains fading as he continued toward the Core. The team altered their course around the new rubble, ignoring the screams of the few soldiers that somehow survived, and sprinted to catch up.

= = =

Xan watched the small team and the new Tank Major approach on a surveillance monitor. This Tank Major was much different than the first. It was larger and it looked less encumbered with armor. It was much quicker. It had dismantled Li in less than a second and Xan watched through violently shaking surveillance cameras as the perimeter outpost evaporated in demolition.

"What should we do?!" a technician asked. They saw what was coming. Xan watched as the Tank Major ran ahead of the team and bulldozed through buildings like they were paper. They were moving fast to avoid reinforcements. They knew where the Core was.

A tank blocked the road and his other Tank Major flanked the American. Xan watched the tank recoil as it fired the 120mm cannon. He watched as the American sprinted away from Xan's Tank Major through buildings. They crumbled behind him and his Tank Major followed.

He's luring you. No.

The tank tried to maneuver, but the surrounding buildings crowded it in. Suddenly the giant was on top of it, hammering down with huge fists.

It moves too fast.

It jumped off and the cameras shook violently again. When they settled, the tank was engulfed in flame and twisted out. *Hydraulshock.* The Chinese Tank Major fled. Xan wasn't sure he wouldn't have done the same.

"Leave," Xan said. He turned to the entire team. "There's nothing for you to do here now."

On his order, the technicians scrambled away, afraid for their lives.

The boy was still in the crucifix. It took an hour for the Data Crusher to spin down and when it did, the boy could safely regain consciousness. For a moment, Xan thought Xinting had abandoned Justin, but then she appeared from the hallway that led to Justin's room. She had two bags in her hand.

"Xinting," he raised his voice to be heard over the *thwap-thwap-thwap* of the Core.

The base rattled from an explosion above them. *The hydraulshock.* They were already here.

She ran to Justin. The Data Crusher wound down. It would still be dangerous to unhook him. Xan looked at the bags. They had to have been pre-packed. One was for her, the other for the boy.

"You need to slow them down, Xan. I need at least ten more minutes." She looked up at the noise. A distant chatter of gunfire found its way down.

"You knew," he said, unaccusing.

"In my training, at one point Cynthia Revo had tried to recruit me," she replied. Cynthia had found her again, ten hours before and told her what was going to happen.

Xan stepped forward. "She can't have him." Xinting moved in front of Justin with her hands up. Gunfire rattled overhead.

"She doesn't want *anyone* to have him. She said she never wants him to connect in again. She sent me money to take him away. It's enough to live on forever. She doesn't care where I go, her only condition was that he can never go online."

"We can't rebuild what we've taken away without him," Xan said. Xan didn't want to leave the world wounded. Without the King Sleeper, the seeds of economic collapse he had planted would continue to grow. The banks and credit unions would be castrated bulls unable to proliferate.

Another burst of gunfire came from above as the infiltration team pushed forward. Twenty stories up, Raimey was working his way to the Data Core with his team playing peek-a-boo behind him with firearms.

"It'll have to sort out on its own," Xinting said. "Cynthia told me that the U.S. mission is to either retrieve the King Sleeper or kill him."

"You're not defecting?" Xan asked.

Xinting shook her head violently. "No. I love China. I don't want to leave, but I think I have no choice. No Xan, I just want this poor boy to live."

Xan looked down at Justin. His little frame rustled around in the rack, beginning to awake.

"I want that too," Xan said. The U.S. couldn't have him and he wouldn't let the boy die. It was settled. "Please tell Justin I said goodbye."

"I will. Thank you, Xan."

Xan and Xinting looked at each other for a moment. They could have been more.

"I'll get you ten minutes," he said and ascended up the walkway to meet his guests.

= = =

Raimey hydraulshocked the entrance and they quickly infiltrated, using Raimey as the battering ram. For a normal team, the resistance from the Chinese soldiers would have been overwhelming, but with John, they may as well have been firing blanks. Ratny and the others hid behind Raimey as he progressed through the base. The quarters were tight, the top three floors—only one of which was actually on the surface, just like a MindCorp Node—were office space.

They finally found a bank vault-like door with a hand scanner.

"Get back," Raimey said.

WHA-WHAM!

The vault door didn't have time for its metal molecules to bend. It shattered inward like a sheet of ice. The team stacked up, went through, and was met with a torrent of gunfire from all sides. From behind John, the team heard the metallic thoomp of underbarrel grenades exploding against him. They felt the flecks of bullet fragments redirected off Raimey's impenetrable shell.

"We got to get back!" Johnson yelled. Raimey walked backwards slowly, keeping them shielded. When they had retreated past the vault door, Raimey charged back in. They heard the effortless destruction as Raimey tore through the defenses, the gurgled screams cut short, the grenades detonated to no effect. Two minutes later, "clear." They came in guns up, but they could have run in with toy windmills, there was nothing to shoot.

Bright blue radiated the area. A cyclical blat filled the room. The team stacked up behind Raimey and followed him to a walkway that surrounded the Colossal Core.

"Holy shit," Johnson said. None of them had ever seen anything like this. The Core looked suspended in mid-air. Only when they squinted through the piercing blue light could they see the shadowed support lattice that connected it to the surrounding walls. Its base was two hundred feet below. The Core cast the cavernous space in deep shadow.

Gunfire hit Raimey. Ahead, four Chinese soldiers retreated to another alcove built along the path. Ratny and the others returned suppressive fire while they moved forward. The Chinese rolled a flash bang out. It bleached Raimey's vision momentarily, but the open space and the intense blue light from the Core minimized its effect. Raimey caught the tail end of their retreat as they used the metal buttresses along the walls for cover.

"They retreated again," Raimey said. The others grunted assent. The walkway curved around the Core, gently corkscrewing down. The *thwap-thwap-thwap* was deafening. The energy in the air, tangible. Little white electrical arcs jumped across Raimey's armor.

They whittled away at the Chinese soldiers. Finally, almost halfway down, Ratny found the thigh of the last one and, as he limped away, followed up with headshot.

"That's all of 'em," Hostettler said. They moved faster. Closer to the ground, they could now see a woman. She was reaching up for something above her. Their view was partially blocked by the massive blue tube and a metal structure that resembled a cross.

"Stop!" Johnson yelled. The woman worked faster. He fired a warning shot past her. She flinched and pinned herself closer to the thick cross. As the team rotated around the Core they saw what she was working on: the King Sleeper.

Johnson fired again, intentionally wide. She dropped to the ground and then quickly resumed.

"Go!" Raimey yelled. The three soldiers sprinted ahead of Raimey. The walkway was too narrow for him to move fast and the platform vibrated from his weight.

Twenty feet ahead was another large support buttress. Ratny,

Hostettler, and Johnson reached it and suddenly they were thrown out toward the Core.

They screamed as they fell one hundred feet. They crashed into tall server bays and pin wheeled into the ground, instantly dead.

Raimey ran to see what had happened when a Tank Major stepped out from the shadow and tried to push him over the ledge.

It sounded like two cars colliding. On instinct, Raimey ducked low like he was avoiding a tackle as Xan wrapped his arms around him. He had no room to hydraulshock and he was positioned sideways to the massive Chinese Tank Major, unable to turn under its incredible grip. Raimey dug his legs in and pushed back, but Xan was too powerful. The hydraulics hissed while they extended, wearing down the resistance of Raimey's hip mounted electric motors.

Raimey could hear the other man scream with rage. Raimey's outside foot lost traction and suddenly he was at the ledge where the other soldiers had fallen to their deaths. He could see their sprawled bodies below.

Without warning, Raimey let himself drop to the platform. The Chinese Tank Major's power suddenly met no resistance and, for a second, Xan teetered over Raimey, unbalanced. Raimey exploded upward, flipping the giant off his back and over the side. Xan grabbed Raimey's leg and pulled him down with him.

They clawed at each other as they fell. At the bottom, they crashed into the sea of servers that exploded out in shards and sparks. The cooling system for the CPU's ruptured and freezing air covered the floor in fog.

Xinting worked frantically, Justin was almost out. She fumbled at the locking clips that held him in place. Two tries for each and she pulled him down. She worked on the interface that attached to his head, that allowed the data of the world access to his mind, and he, to its secrets.

Raimey was punch drunk. He tasted blood. A warning in his head told him that a right leg suspension unit was broken. But he was alive. He heard a death rattle behind him. He was laying on the other giant. Suddenly, its arms came up and wrapped around his upper body in a hug. And then he heard what sounded like a trash compactor. The sound thickened and Raimey's head cleared when he saw his chest armor buckle. He was being crushed.

Xan had him. The Chinese design didn't have the suspension system like the American Tank Major, and the fall had ruptured his organs. But while the blood filled his lungs, he still had time. He wrapped his arms around the American and initiated the constriction.

Raimey's arms were pinned to his sides. He tried to struggle free, but he couldn't move. He watched as the ceramic coat of his chest armor shed under the increasing hydraulic vise. He heard a loud pop from his back. Again he tried to struggle, but the Chinese Tank Major was too big. Raimey's momentum, kicking and rocking couldn't overcome the eight-ton anchor that held him tight.

"No one should have the boy," he heard the man behind him wheeze. He sounded terminal. Raimey didn't know what he was talking about. "No one should have the boy," the man killing him said again.

Like a submarine that hit crush depth, Raimey's chest armor suddenly caved and he felt intense pain as if his lungs were too full of air. It was the opposite. His human body was being crushed.

Raimey quit struggling. He was glad he had gotten to see Tiffany and speak to his daughter. The goodbye was warranted; this was the end. And maybe that was a blessing. Every second without them, he felt pain. It was one thing to have lost a loved one, but Raimey had forced a false imprisonment. He had taken their combined life and pulled the thread. It was he and them now. When he died today, he would be remembered fondly, hopefully. If he lived, no matter the reason why he did what he did, there would always be an empty place at the table. He would always be the dad that didn't come back home.

The hydraulshock slides.

Raimey didn't understand, the suggestion came out of nowhere. The voice was distant, but familiar, echoed down a long hallway. He didn't take investigate further. He leaned his head against the back of his helmet and started to close his eyes.

THE HYDRAULSHOCK SLIDES!

It was his daughter, Vanessa's, voice screaming for him to fight. For him to think his way out.

John was aimed the wrong way. But the slides on each shoulder that reduced the felt recoil and reloaded the hydraulshock rounds, were not. Because of the Chinese Tank Major's width they were aimed right at his shoulders.

John fired two rounds at once. His arms boomed and rattled, his legs kicked from the incredible force of the hydraulic fluid shooting through his body. The depleted uranium-osmium alloy slides, the strongest armor ever devised, crunched into Xan's shoulder joints. Raimey fired again. And again. The slides bit through deeper and deeper until the shoulder joints cracked like clay. Raimey felt Xan's bear hug give and he struggled up to his feet.

He faced his enemy. The man was going toward the light.

"We need to reset," Xan gasped. "No one can have the boy. We have to save the new world. We have to be united." He smiled. It was filled with blood. "We'll kill ourselves. No more shadows. We'll kill ourselves."

The man died.

Raimey walked through the fog and found the woman kneeling over the King Sleeper. A strange mask covered his face. His body was gaunt and thin. She looked up at him, pleading. One of her ears bled from the hydraulshock blasts.

"Do not do this!" she said.

"Shut up," Raimey said. "Give him to me."

She unlatched the Mindlink interface and pulled it off the King Sleeper's head. It was Vanessa. She was unconscious, almost completely naked. Quarter sized electrodes wrapped around her shaved head.

And then it was a boy. A young, skinny child. A past memory flickered in his head. He had seen this boy. He had met him. *The attack on MindCorp*. He had gotten his father and the boy a car ride home.

"What is this?" Raimey asked. "Where is the King Sleeper?"

"You don't know?" she said, her eyes narrow. "You came all this way and they didn't tell you?"

"He can't be a boy," Raimey said. Boen hadn't said a word. Why? Was he afraid he wouldn't go? Did the other soldiers know? Or did they think it didn't matter, that he would do his duty regardless?

"His name is Justin McWilliams and he's twelve years old. He was raised in DeKalb, Illinois by Frank and Charlene McWilliams, and they were murdered in cold blood by your military because of his gift."

The boy woke. His eyes fluttered open and he saw a bionic, like Xan, standing over him. It opened and closed its hands as if it wasn't sure what to do.

268

"What happened?" The boy looked around. The Core had flickered black; the room was filled with a bone chilling fog. He didn't see Xan sprawled out in the decimated server bay.

"There was an explosion. This man is helping us get out of here," Xinting said. "We're leaving so you'll never have to do this again."

"Really?!" Relief washed over the boy's face. He hugged Xinting. "I'm so tired of doing bad things. I just want to rest."

She looked to Raimey as she stood up, cradling the boy. "No country should have him," Xinting said. The same as the Chinese Tank Major. "Why are we so cruel to one another?"

Raimey said nothing, but he knew why. *Because without the weak, how would we know we're strong?*

The boy was buried in the woman's arms, sobbing. Just a young, scared boy. *How dare we.*

"Go," Raimey said. "Before I change my mind, go."

Raimey walked toward one of the giant buttresses against the wall.

"What are you going to do?" she asked.

"I'm going to tear this down," he said. "He's dead, you understand? He died here, today."

"I understand." Xinting hesitated and then bowed. She and Justin ran out of the room.

By his count, he had three hydraulshocks left. There were four support buttresses that surrounded the open Core. *Evaporating three should do.* To reinforce a lie worth telling, he reared back on the first, and while the world fell around him, he felt at peace for what he had done for that little boy. He fired again.

He pictured Vanessa, lying there in Justin's place, and he shuddered at the thought of what he would do if his little girl had been taken from him.

I would go to the ends of the earth for you, my dear. I would hunt down everyone involved and everyone that knew, and I would tear them apart far after they confessed and pled for mercy. Because what mercy did they give you? I would never stop until you were avenged, because you are more important than my heart and my life. In you is my soul.

He reared back and fired. The earth trembled in the wake of his will.

EPILOGUE

John Raimey was exchanged back to the U.S. quietly. China apologized for the rogue actions of Xan Shin, a military advisor who, in the wake of the sequential deaths of their Presidents, had grossly abused the lack of oversight for his own personal vendetta against the United States. The U.S. graciously accepted their apology and in a separate conversation, agreed to share their data on the Tank Major, if China in turn would share theirs. Both countries would work together in the face of the true threat: Mohammed Jawal and the Western Curse. The two new Presidents even shook hands for a photo shoot.

In joint statements broadcast around the world, China and the U.S. outlined in fine detail how the Western Curse—the same organization that terrorized and killed over one hundred hostages in the O'Hare Hijacking—had executed advanced cyber terrorism on both the Chinese and U.S. government's economic systems. Both countries would stop at nothing to apprehend these cyber terrorists. After a week of turmoil in the financial markets, things settled down. Especially when MindCorp jumped in. Some stocks even went up.

"She's a cunt," Evan said. General Boen was in his office. "She thinks she owns the world. She thinks that SHE'S the government. It's getting out of control, Earl. Do you know that MindCorp bailed out the credit companies? They had enough cash on hand to provide five hundred billion dollars. Half of that, *they gave away*. The other half is for whenever they can get paid back, dollar for dollar. Said it was half her fault, she had gotten lax on security." Evan shook his head, frustrated, unbelieving; don't people see? "I feel like I'm the only sane person in the world."

The King Sleeper is dead. Evan had been furious at General Boen when he had finally got news of the mission. Boen had explained that Cynthia Revo would have it no other way. Earl stressed that while *he* trusted him, Cynthia did not. She felt betrayed by Evan for keeping the anomaly— that had hurt her business and that she had sought *him* to find—a secret.

Earl kept silent and let Evan vent. He and Cynthia had come to an understanding. They had formed a common bond. Earl listened to the man, who was backed by the President, backed by the Senate, backed by the House, and loved by the military, as he expunged on the way things ought to be. Finally Evan ran out of breath. The room was quiet.

"I don't like where this is going," Evan said, shaking his fat head. "I don't like this one bit."

You and me both, brother.

ABOUT THE AUTHOR

Mike Gullickson writes Science Fiction and Fantasy Novels. He lives in Manhattan Beach, California with his wife, two children, and dog—Oliver—who is nice most of the time.

To learn more about Mike's upcoming work or to connect with him online, please visit him at www.mikegullickson.com, or follow him on Twitter: @mikegullickson

OUT NOW!

THE NORTHERN STAR: CIVIL WAR
THE NORTHERN STAR: THE END